Dear Dad,
 I thought you might enjoy reading about the Prime Minister of Samoa!

Love,
Biden

PĀLEMIA

PĀLEMIA

Prime Minister
Tuila'epa Sa'ilele Malielegaoi
of Samoa

A MEMOIR

with Peter Swain

Victoria University Press

VICTORIA UNIVERSITY PRESS
Victoria University of Wellington
PO Box 600 Wellington
vup.victoria.ac.nz

Copyright © Tuila'epa Sa'ilele Malielegaoi & Peter Swain, 2017
First published 2017

ISBN 978-1-77656-105-6

This book is copyright. Apart from
any fair dealing for the purpose of private study,
research, criticism or review, as permitted under the
Copyright Act, no part may be reproduced by any
process without the permission of
the publishers

A catalogue record is available at the National Library of New Zealand

Typeset in Untitled Serif and Untitled Sans by Klim Type Foundry,
with titles in Churchward Samoa Bold

Printed by Printlink, Wellington

Contents

	List of Illustrations	6
	Foreword *Tuila'epa Sa'ilele Malielegaoi*	9
	Map of Samoa	12
	Preface	13
Prologue:	Political Leadership in Samoa	17
Chapter 1:	Assassination in Apia	25
Chapter 2:	The Boy from Lepā	32
Chapter 3:	O le Ala i le Pule le Tautua – The Road to Leadership	54
Chapter 4:	Member of Parliament for Lepā – The Long Apprenticeship	80
Chapter 5:	Pālemia – Prime Minister of Samoa	162
Chapter 6:	Tuila'epa's Premiership	237
Epilogue:	The Future	261
Appendix:	Tuila'epa Sa'ilele Malielegaoi's Parliamentary Career and Matai Titles	265
	Glossary	270
	Abbreviations	271
	References	277
	Index	282

List of Illustrations

Malielegaoi Veni and Leasunia Lupesoli'ai, Tuila'epa's parents.
Form 1A, 1958, Marist Brothers' Primary School.
Lepā village.
St Paul's College Second Fifteen, 1964.
St Paul's College 6A, 1964.
Newman Hall boarders at the 1965 Students' Ball.
Forestry gang after a day's work pruning pine trees near Putaruru.
Graduation from the University of Auckland, Master's in Commerce, 1969.
Gillian Meredith at her 21st birthday.
Tuila'epa and family in Brussels, June 1979.
'A balanced family, four girls and four boys.'
Tuila'epa and Gillian with their eight children, their spouses, and twelve grandchildren.
Tuila'epa inspecting the status of the fuel pipeline that lies at the bottom of the harbour entrance.
Tuila'epa practising archery for the South Pacific Games, 2007.
Tuila'epa receiving his silver medal for archery, South Pacific Games, 2007.
Tuila'epa practising shooting for the South Pacific Games, 2007.
Tuila'epa still playing cricket. Fifty years and over team, 2016.
Palemene O Samoa, 1979–1981, Tuila'epa's first Parliament.
Palemene O Samoa, 1982–1984.
Cabinet 1988. A decade of political stability begins.
Cabinet 2011–2016. A new dress code suitable for the tropical climate.
Cabinet, 2016–2021.
Tuila'epa at the Cabinet table watched over by his predecessors.
Tuila'epa, first official portrait as Prime Minister, 1998.

Tuila'epa attending the ACP Council of Ministers with Pule Lameko MP and African and Caribbean colleagues, 1980.

Meeting of the Tokyo Trade Fair, 1985.

Ministers of Finance of the Commonwealth, Jamaica, 1989.

Meeting the Chancellor of Germany, Gerhard Schroder, December 2003.

Prime Minister Tuila'epa addressing the United Nations General Assembly, New York, 2016.

Meeting the Secretary-General of the United Nations, Ban Ki-moon, New York.

Tuila'epa addressing the ACP Summit.

Meeting President Xi Jinping of China, Fiji, 2014.

Meeting Prime Minister Junichiro Koizumi of Japan.

Palm 7 Meeting of Pacific Islands Forum Leaders with PM Shinzo Abe of Japan, 2015.

Tuila'epa arriving at the ACP Leaders Meeting in Port Moresby.

Meeting Prime Minister Modi of India, New Delhi, 2015.

Meeting Pope Francis, December 2015.

Tuila'epa delivering the Plenary Address to the United Nations Conference on Small Islands Developing States, September 2014, Samoa.

Saofa'i for Ban Ki-moon, Secretary-General of the United Nations.

Inaugural Meeting of Polynesian Leaders Group, November 2011, Apia.

Tuila'epa recognised as Grand Chief of PNG with Acting Governor-General Hon. Theodore Zurenoc and Kiribati President Anote Tong.

President Obama and Prime Minister Tuila'epa and their First Ladies, Michelle and Gillian.

Pacific Islands Forum Meeting, 2015, Papua New Guinea.

Prime Minister John Key and Tuila'epa watching Manu Samoa play the All Blacks, Apia Park, 8 July 2014.

Inspecting the Samoan Rugby High Performance Unit with the Chinese Ambassador, Vincent Fepulea'i, and Matafeo George Latu.

'Switch sides' protesters outside Parliament Buildings.

Facing the 'switch sides' protesters with a smile and a laugh as they sing Happy Birthday to Tuila'epa, 14 April 2009.

Facing the 'switch sides' protesters.

Protest leader Toleafoa shakes hands with Tuila'epa.

Forum for India–Pacific Islands Cooperation, Fiji, 19 November 2014.

Fiamē Mataʻafa Faumauinā Mulinuʻu II Building, Apia. The Cabinet Room is in the rooftop *fale*.

Faleolo International Airport terminal.

Lalomanu following the tsunami.

Tuilaʻepa participating in a public discussion on cancer prevention.

Tuilaʻepa and Gillian on his maiden visit to Tokelau. The police patrol boat was donated by Australia to patrol Samoa's economic zone.

A Royal Samoan *ʻAva* Ceremony to welcome cast and crew of *Survivor*. Two series were filmed in Samoa.

Tuilaʻepa with Miss Pacific 2016 contestants.

Tuilaʻepa receiving the flag at the funeral of Leota Ituʻau ʻAle.

Tuilaʻepa with Joseph Parker, WBO Heavy Weight Boxing Champion.

Honorary doctorate, Victoria University of Wellington, 2015.

All photographs are from the collections of the authors or the government of Samoa

Office of the Prime Minister
Apia, Samoa

Early in 2015, Dr Peter Swain paid me a courtesy visit at my office. In the course of our conversation he casually mentioned that it would be very useful for posterity if some of my experiences during my long years as leader of our government were recorded in a memoir. I had also been thinking along the same lines, but these are the kinds of activities that are more often undertaken when one has retired. However, by then the memory has often become blurred and much is therefore lost. It is also unusual to write one's memoir when many actors involved are still very much active. I knew that the retelling of past events could open up old wounds.

But history is history. Things must be told exactly as they occurred, otherwise the underlying lesson is hidden and buried.

Peter Swain's casual, thought-provoking comments lingered on in my mind, and we agreed to start on the project of compiling a memoir. Over the last year Dr Swain has made several visits to Apia to conduct interviews at my office, in between appointments; at my home at Ululoloa, after hours; and in my hotel rooms, when I was transiting Auckland during my brief visits to New Zealand for official government business. I am indebted to Peter for his capacity to capture much of the detail of our long conversations, for stimulating my recollections of past events and for compiling this memoir.

In the 2016 general election, the Human Rights Protection Party (HRPP) won 47 out of our 50 parliamentary seats, a record achievement, with the opposition party being demolished in the process. We were given an overwhelming mandate by the people to execute our policies over the next five years. I face a huge challenge as leader of the HRPP and leader of government to deliver on the promises set out in our 2016 General Election Manifesto, a process we have faithfully followed since the HRPP won its first election in 1982 and in eight successive general elections. My undivided attention is called upon to govern Samoa, and I therefore have no spare time personally to write a memoir for posterity.

This simple political story focusses on issues of great political significance that have a bearing on the development and progress of the long-term vision of the HRPP, and especially on what government must do to raise the well-being and standard of living of our people.

The HRPP leadership recognised, right from the beginning, that good financial, monetary and economic management, and balanced social development also promote good politics, from the point of view not only of our people but also in the eyes of our donor partners who greatly value the proper use of their development assistance.

Whilst the narrative focusses on the leadership and power struggles throughout the period of the HRPP's custodianship, the party's ascent to power can also be seen as an accident of history. Party politics was regarded as divisive long before the HRPP came to power. The single event that changed the political landscape in Samoa was the three months' strike by public servants over the refusal by the government of Prime Minister Tupuola Efi to compromise on the Public Service Association's (PSA's) request for an overdue salary increase in 1981. The high-handed manner in which government handled this very sensitive issue, including the mass dismissal of all those who went on strike, on top of the many economic hardships suffered by the public in general, led to its demise. The general election that took place less than ten months after the strike could not have been expected to return a government that was so unpopular. The HRPP became the natural alternative choice under these circumstances.

The opportunity given to the HRPP leadership was immediately used to rebuild an economy that was in complete ruin when we took over. Measures were put in place straight away, with the help of the international community, to restabilise the economy and revive the private sector – the engine of growth. The recovery was rapid, distinct and noticeable. And from that time onwards, the HRPP became known as a 'Party of Doers' and the 'Party of the People'. Actions speak louder than words. Subsequent HRPP governments have worked hard to sustain this legacy.

I want to pay a special tribute to our first two Prime Ministers, the Honourable Va'ai Kolone and the Honourable Tofilau 'Eti Alesana, for their leadership of the HRPP from its beginning to where it is today and for their personal and political vision. I learnt much about the unique science of Samoan-style politics from these two leaders. I also learnt from the Honourable Tupuola Efi who, in September 1970, was the newly appointed

Minister of Public Works in the government of Tupua Tamasese Lealofi IV when I was the new Acting Deputy Director of Public Works. He advised me to talk to as many people as possible and to learn from them. Little did I know that twelve years later he and I would be in opposing political camps and yet we were both products of the same Marist Catholic education system.

I must also pay tribute to our HRPP caucus, Cabinet Members and supporters who have worked with me during these 34 years of governing. Nothing could have been achieved politically without their backing and their hard efforts to achieve our common goals.

Special acknowledgement is also in order for all the CEOs of ministries and corporations and the rest of the public service for their in-depth advice, know-how and technical inputs into the implementation of numerous projects carried out by successive HRPP governments. While administrations come and go, the public service remains as the permanent arm of government to carry out its policies.

What is told here, in connection with the successes of the development efforts of the HRPP, reflects also the collective contributions of everyone to whom I have referred. It is my hope that this memoir will be a useful guide to all aspiring politicians in the future, telling as it does the political path the HRPP has travelled, and providing a model of democratic government that shows how we tackled problems and stayed on course as we did during those 34 long years and beyond. Party politics in Samoa has finally put to rest the age-old 'born to rule' myth of the past.

Tuila'epa Sa'ilele Malielegaoi
Prime Minister of the Independent State of Samoa

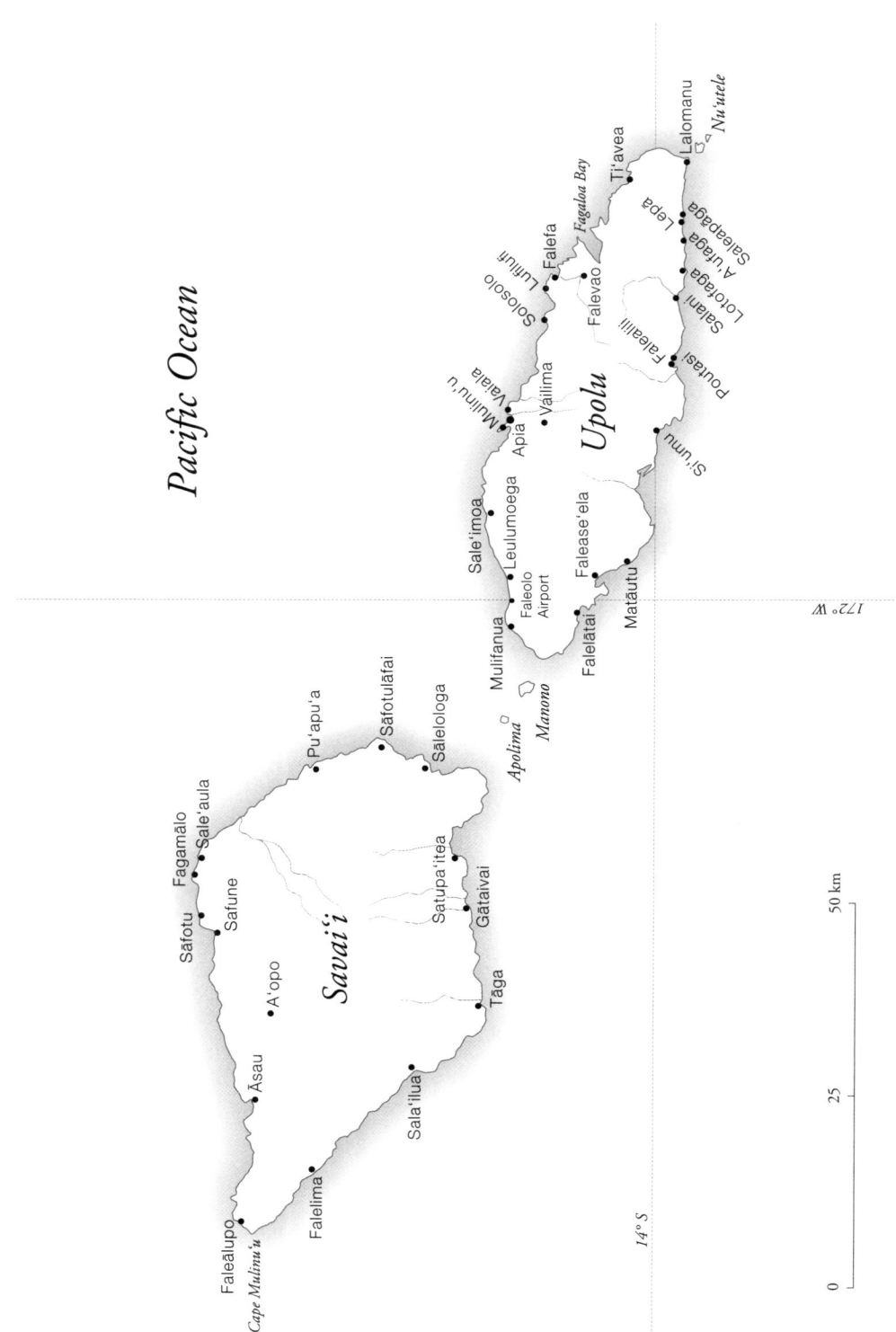

Preface

I first met Tuila'epa Sa'ilele Malielegaoi in the early 1990s. My wife, Luamanuvao Winnie Laban, and I were coordinating the South Pacific Consumer Protection Programme working across fourteen Pacific Island nations. One particular problem we encountered was the lack of laws to protect consumers and the Pacific environment where marketplaces were rapidly deregulating. Alongside consumer advocacy and education programmes, we drafted a model consumer protection law which we encouraged Pacific Island nations to adapt and enact. A number of countries had passed the law, but Samoa was slow to do so and the draft law had been bogged down in the Ministry of Trade, Commerce and Industry. It was my task to move things along.

I had been given three pieces of advice about getting things done in Samoa: first, 'use your family networks'; second, 'it's who you know, not what you know that counts'; and, third, 'go to the top'. So I spoke with our Aunty Fei, who was personal secretary to the Minister of Finance and Trade, Commerce and Industry, to see if she could arrange a meeting with the Minister. The next day I had a one-on-one meeting with Tuila'epa.

Aunty Fei showed me into the Minister's office. I was greeted by a gruff 'Hello' as Tuila'epa looked up from a stack of official papers. 'What do you want?' I stated my case and passed across a copy of the draft legislation. 'Hold on.' Tuila'epa read my paper, asked a couple of questions and then dialled a number on his phone. *'Falani, sau!'* (Frank, come.) Within a few minutes the chief executive of the Ministry of Trade, Commerce and Industry, Tuala Falani Chan Tung, was in his Minister's office taking orders to move the legislation along. Three months later the law was enacted.

From my first encounter with Tuila'epa, I learnt that he was a man of action rather than words, a man who knew how to make things happen in Samoa. I later came to understand that, whilst he was modernising and deregulating Samoa's economy, Tuila'epa was also concerned that people could suffer from the excesses of a free market economy and he was keen to advance policies and practices that were good for all Samoans and for the environment.

Over the following years I met Tuila'epa many times and followed his career with interest. I observed him managing difficult events and complex issues that were impacting on the people of Samoa. Tsunami, cyclones, economic crises, regional political upheavals, local political dramas and many other challenges were faced and managed with calm assurance. His steady leadership stood out in an unstable region during uncertain times.

There have been few political biographies of Pacific Island leaders, and there is little written about the thoughts and experiences of the first generation of prime ministers and presidents who led their nations from colonial times to independence. This gap has now been partially filled by books like *The Pacific Way*, Ratu Sir Kamisese Mara's memoir; *New Flags Flying*, interviews of early Pacific Island leaders, recorded and edited by Ian Johnstone and Michael Powles; and *Men of Mana*, portraits of Ratu Sir Kamisese Mara, Va'ai Kolone and Sir Robert Rex, by Kathleen Hancock. However, the literature on Pacific Island political leadership remains sparse.

The second generation of Pacific Island political leaders has faced many complex issues as the post-independence honeymoon glow faded and the realities of leading small island nations with limited resources, in a globalising world and during difficult times, set in. Prime Minister Tuila'epa Sa'ilele Malielegaoi is the standout leader of his generation and his story has many resonances beyond Samoa.

In 2012 Samoa celebrated 50 years of independence, and Victoria University of Wellington (VUW) honoured Tuila'epa Sa'ilele Malielegaoi with the award of a Doctorate in Laws *honoris causa*. The citation noted: 'He has presided over the most politically and economically stable and successful small democratic country in the Pacific. He is, quite simply, the most successful, the most eminent, and the most popular democratically elected politician in the Pacific.'

I have been privileged to spend many hours with Tuila'epa recording his memories, thoughts and observations about both his personal life story as well as his time as Member of Parliament, Prime Minister and regional leader. His detailed recall of dates, people, events, conversations and dialogue is remarkable. Tuila'epa has often been the target of criticism by journalists and academics from Samoa and elsewhere. As Prime Minister, Tuila'epa has not always been in a position to speak out and balance the public account. He wanted this book to be in the form of a memoir, based on his recollection of important events in his life, career and premiership, with background information that reflects the complexities and challenges faced in the governance of a Pacific Island nation. A memoir is an historical account or biography written from personal knowledge. This memoir aims to capture the voice, document the life and place in context a record of the most significant Samoan political leader of this generation.

Preface

Acknowledgements

Mālō le Soifua Lau Afioga i le Pālemia, Tuila'epa Sa'ilele Malielegaoi, *Fa'afetai tele lava*. Thank you for your generosity, openness, patience and participation in this project. Thank you for trusting me to tell your story. *Fa'afetai fo'i Gillian ma le 'āiga.*

Fa'afetai lava Pua'aelo Lene (Sipiki) and Siigavaa Saili-Sio (Sii) from the Prime Minister's Office for your support in organising my interviews; finding, retyping and sending me documents; and maintaining communications with your busy boss. *Fa'afetai fo'i* Vaovasamanaia Filo (Lapi) for your contributions. For assistance to access and permission to use photographs *fa'afetai tele lava* Papali'i Sonja Hunter, CEO, and Rosa Peniamina, IT and Graphics Design Officer, Samoa Tourism Authority, and Mamea Seupule, Editor, and Arnold Loia, Senior Layout Artist, Savali Newspaper, Ministry of Prime Minister and Cabinet. *Fa'afetai lava* Wilber and Andrea Stewart for your kind assistance with transport and logistics in Samoa. *Fa'afetai i le 'āiga potopoto i Samoa ma Niu Sila.*

I have drawn on the research and writing on Samoa's political history by Leasiolagi Dr Malama Meleisea and Fui Leapai Tu'u Ilaoa Professor Asofou So'o. Their work has been invaluable to this project. *Fa'afetai tele lava.*

My thanks to Fergus Barrowman, publisher, for his encouragement; to the team at Victoria University Press for their efficiency and editorial support; to Ginny Sullivan for her meticulous copy-editing and indexing; and to Holly Hunter for proofreading.

Half a lifetime ago Luamanuvao Winnie Laban took me to Samoa and has been my constant companion on our Pacific journeys. This book grew out of her insistence that we must listen to and record the stories of our Pacific Island leaders. *Mālō O si a'u lava avā fa'apelepele. Fa'afetai tele lava.*

While Tuila'epa's words form a substantial part of this narrative, the responsibility for the text is mine alone, including any errors, oversights or omissions.

Peter Swain
April 2017

Prologue:
Political Leadership in Samoa

The government of Samoa is run from the Fiamē Mata'afa Faumuinā Mulinu'u II Building on Beach Road in the centre of Apia. Senior government Ministers' offices are on the fifth floor of the office block and the Cabinet Room is adjacent to the Prime Minister's office. Cabinet Ministers sit on padded heavy wooden chairs around a large table. At the Cabinet table, presided over by the Prime Minister, important issues of the day are discussed, policies debated and decisions made. Here political leadership is exercised and careers rise and fall.

Looking down on the Cabinet table are six large photographs: five former Prime Ministers and the incumbent – history witnessing today's decision-makers. To grasp the pressures and burdens on the current Prime Minister, Tuila'epa Sa'ilele Malielegaoi, we need to consider a little history.[1]

The line-up of photographs on the wall of the Cabinet Room does not illustrate a simple chronology. Political succession in Samoa has often been contested. The caption below each photograph lists the dates when the subject was prime minister. Leaders have come and gone, and come, and gone again. Most of Samoa's prime ministers have served several terms. It takes some concentration, and knowledge of the political history of Samoa and the *Fa'asamoa*,[2] to unravel the labyrinthine order of over five decades of leadership.

The first Prime Minister was Fiamē Mata'afa Faumuinā Mulinu'u II. Mata'afa was chosen by the Legislative Assembly in 1959 in preparation for independence in 1962. He was elected Prime Minister unopposed after the 1964 and 1967 general elections. Mata'afa's prestigious *matai* titles, his status as *tama-a-'āiga* and his patrician leadership style, based on traditional Samoan concepts and cultural values, contributed to his lengthy leadership during the early stages of Samoa's political development.

---

1 This prologue has drawn on a number of sources, principally *Democracy and Custom in Samoa* by Professor Asofou So'o, 2008, and *Samoa's Journey 1962–2012* edited by M. Meleisea et al., 2012.
2 A Glossary of Samoan Terms starts on page 269.

In the lead-up to independence, there had been lengthy discussions on how to solve the problem of establishing a modern democracy, whilst at the same time preserving elements of Samoa's traditional leadership. Traditional cultural leadership in Samoa is exercised through a complex, hierarchical system of chiefly titles, *matai*, based on villages and districts.[3] Four ancient *pāpā* titles – Tui Ātua , Tui A'ana, Gato'aitele and Tamasoali'i – are reflected in the *tama-a-'āiga*: Malietoa, Tupua Tamasese, Mata'afa and Tuimaleali'ifano, who are accorded joint paramount rank in modern Samoa.[4]

The tension between the needs of a modern world and the imperatives of custom and tradition, the *Fa'asamoa*, is a recurring theme in the narrative of Samoa's political history and leadership. Accommodations have been made to seek a balance to achieve stable government in this emerging democracy.

Constitutional conventions in 1954 and 1960 and a United Nations-sponsored referendum were conducted in the lead-up to independence.[5] These exercises in national self-determination resulted in a Constitution that describes Samoa, in its Preamble,[6] as 'an Independent State based on Christian principles and Samoan custom and tradition'.

The solution, in the case of establishing post-independence political institutions, was the development of a Westminster style of Parliament leavened by *Fa'asamoa*, that comprises a Head of State (*O le Ao o le Malo*), who assents to Bills before they become law, and the Legislative Assembly, which formulates and passes Bills. A Council of Deputies (*Sui O Le Fono a Sui Tofia*) to act for the Head of State in his absence was also established. Until 1991, when universal suffrage was introduced, only *matai* could vote and become Members of Parliament (MPs), apart from two Individual Voters' seats to provide representation and a voice for non-*matai*. The Individual Voters' seats were abolished in 2014. Today, there is universal suffrage and it is still only *matai* who may become MPs. Samoa is governed by a Parliament of Chiefs.

At independence, the problem of what to do about *tama-a-'āiga* was finessed by appointing the paramount chiefs Malietoa Tanumafili II and Tupua Tamasese Mea'ole joint Head of State, Tuimaleali'ifano Suatipatipa to the Council of Deputies and Fiamē Mata'afa Faumuinā Mulinu'u II Prime Minister. These

---

3   For a comprehensive description of Samoan chieftainship, hierarchy and indigenous institutions, see Davidson, 1967; Gilson, 1970; Kramer, 1994a and 1994b; Meleisea, 1995; and So'o, 2008.
4   Control of these titles is vested in groups of *tulafale*, orator chiefs, representing confederations of districts: *Tumua* on Upolu; and *Pule* on Savai'i, Manono and the Tuamasaga district in Upolu.
5   See Malo O Samoa, 1960.
6   It is significant that this statement appears in the Preamble but not in the Articles of the Constitution. Whereas the Preamble provides guidance, the Articles have legal effect.

appointments allowed for cultural concerns and sensitivities to be satisfied by filling the leading roles in the new democracy with customary leaders.

This elegant solution would provide political stability in Samoa during the first critical decades after independence and build a solid foundation for the stability and continuity that has been the aim of Samoan governance. But it also created tensions.

Under Mata'afa's leadership, consensus politics was the order of the day. The Prime Minister chose his eight Ministers. Often he chose his critics and channelled their energies into their portfolios. There was no formal opposition party; those who were not Ministers became the 'opposition'. This was the consensus politics of personality and persuasion. In a small country that was trying to find its own way in the first years of independence, and where everyone knew each other's strengths, weaknesses and family connections, these arrangements appeared to work for a while, but not for long.

The development of political parties would wait until the 1980s. In the meantime, Mata'afa's leadership was initially unchallenged. However, it was later contested and, after three terms as Prime Minister, there was a change of leader.

Tupua Tamasese Lealofi IV was elected Prime Minister after the 1970 general election in a close contest with Mata'afa and the young Tupuola Tufuga Taisi Efi.[7] Tupua Tamasese Lealofi IV had succeeded to the paramount family title after the death of the joint Head of State, Tupua Tamasese Mea'ole,[8] and continued the leadership of Parliament by *tama-a-'āiga*. Younger leaders, often university educated overseas, were starting to emerge, challenge the old guard of village-trained, customary leaders, and question the view that leadership was the prerogative of *tama-a-'āiga*. But change was slow.

Mata'afa was returned as Prime Minister after the 1973 general election and held the role until his sudden death on 20 May 1975. The Head of State, Malietoa Tanumafili II, appointed Tupua Tamasese Lealofi IV to replace Mata'afa. This arrangement had some critics[9] but held, until the 1976 general election, due to deep respect for the *tama-a-'āiga*.

Tupuola Tufuga Taisi Efi became Prime Minister in 1976 in a contest against

---

7   Later known as Tupua Tamasese, and also as Tui Ātua Tupua Tamaese.
8   Tupua Tamasese Mea'ole was the brother of Tupua Tamasese Lealofi IV and father of Tupuola Tufuga Taisi Efi.
9   Extra-constitutional appointments of a prime minister by the Head of State occurred on three occasions and caused considerable political tension and anxiety until constitutional amendments clarified the role of the Head of State, and Parliamentary Standing Orders established that the prime minister was to be the party leader commanding a majority in the House.

his uncle, the sitting premier Tupua Tamasese Lealofi IV, and retained the role with a reduced majority after the 1979 general election. He was a progressive politician with a liberalising agenda and the first non-*tama-a-'āiga* titleholder to become Prime Minister. (Later, he would accede to the Tui Ātua Tupua Tamasese title and become *tama-a-'āiga*.) In his rush to wrestle the prime minister's position from Tupua Tamasese Lealofi IV, Tupuola Efi unknowingly set the precedent for future non-*tama-a-'āiga* titleholders to take over after him. The gentlemanly consensus politics of the post-independence period was ending, power politics had started and turbulent times were ahead.

Va'ai Kolone had contested the leadership with Tupuola in 1979 and was defeated by one vote. Kolone was amongst the founders of the Human Rights Protection Party, together with Tofilau 'Eti Alesana, other former and existing MPs and senior public servants who had been dismissed by Tupuola's government through Commissions of Enquiry, including Unasa Lavea Schmidt, Police Commissioner; Patū Afa Hunter, Director of Lands and Survey; Dr Vermeulen, Chief of the Division of Public Health; Matatumua Maimoana, Head of Nursing; and Toalepai Toeolesulusulu Siueva, Director of the Samoa Ports Authority.

Dr Vermeulen took a court case against the government. After lengthy proceedings, Justice Mahon's Judgment in the Supreme Court of Western Samoa, on 2 May 1985, ruled that Dr Vermeulen's allegations of malice and abuse of public office had been proved. Substantial damages and costs were awarded to the plaintiff.[10]

In the meantime, the apparent violation of the human rights of the public servants dismissed by Tupuola's government and the high-handed way the young Prime Minister had used his public office were the catalysts that led to the formation of the first political party in Samoa and the reason also for its name: the Human Rights Protection Party.

Va'ai Kolone, a respected senior *matai* and successful businessman from Savai'i, was elected leader of the HRPP, and Tofilau 'Eti Alesana, also from Savai'i, his deputy. Party politics was beginning.

In the early 1980s Samoa was facing major crises, both economic and constitutional. Rising prices of imported goods and declining agricultural productivity and commodity prices led to inflation running at around 38 percent. The Public Service Association sought a 30 percent pay increase for public servants, counter offers were made and rejected, and industrial strike action was taken.[11] Demonstrators petitioned Parliament, the economy ground

---

10 See Mahon, 1985.
11 For more on the PSA strike, see Meleisea and Schoeffel (1983: 105–8), and Snell (1992: 69–84).

to a halt, people took sides and the country was divided. The strike dragged on for three months. Samoa was financially insolvent, and social instability grew.

Eventually public servants returned to work, following a court order overturning a decision by the government to dismiss all public servants who were on strike. Ironically, the gains in salary secured by public servants came from a committee set up by the government but chaired by opposition deputy leader, Tofilau 'Eti Alesana. The government had run out of ideas and the HRPP politicians provided the answers. The strike was over but the residue of bitterness that the strike had generated lasted for some years and led to a change of government.

Meanwhile, a Supreme Court appeal against the Electoral Act of 1963 had led to a constitutional challenge against aspects of *matai* suffrage. The appeal was upheld by the Chief Justice, R.J.B. St John, an Australian jurist, but revoked by three judges from New Zealand who concluded that 'These . . . are questions, not of law, but of social and political policy . . . [that] . . . are to be decided by parliament, not by the courts.' A subsequent vote in Parliament for universal suffrage was narrowly defeated.

Uncertainty over the immigration status of Samoan migrants to New Zealand had led to the decision of the Privy Council in 1982 that Samoans and their children born before 1948 were New Zealand citizens. The fear that 100,000 Samoans would choose to move to New Zealand led the Muldoon government to establish a protocol, agreed to by Samoa under pressure from New Zealand, that removed this right but allowed Samoans to apply for citizenship under a 'quota system' of 1,100 Samoans per annum, provided they had a guaranteed job in New Zealand. The 'quota' has rarely been achieved.

These crises, and discontent over Tupuola Tufuga Taisi Efi's handling of the disruptive Public Service Association strike, added impetus to a challenge for leadership and changes to the way politics was transacted in Samoa.

In the April 1982 general election Va'ai Kolone narrowly defeated Tupuola Efi. His prime ministership was short lived. An election petition in September 1982 was upheld in the Supreme Court and Va'ai Kolone's government was removed from office. Less than 24 hours after the court ruling was made, the Head of State hastily appointed the recently defeated Tupuola Efi Prime Minister and asked him to form a government. An electoral petition that voided the result of the Salega constituency led to a by-election that returned an HRPP supporter, which upset the delicate balance of power in the Parliament. Another by-election on the second Saturday of October 1982 resulted in the election of the HRPP candidate. On 21 December the government's Budget was rejected by a vote of 23 to 21, ending Tupuola's three-month third term as Prime Minister and opening the way for Tofilau 'Eti Alesana, now leader of the HRPP, to be elected premier on 30 December 1982. Samoa had four prime ministers in one year.

Tofilau reappointed all of Va'ai's former Cabinet Ministers to his new Cabinet and added Tuila'epa Sa'ilele Malielegaoi as a new member.

The HRPP won a landslide victory in the 1985 general election, gaining a two-thirds majority, but Tofilau's prime ministership was not secure. Va'ai Kolone returned to Parliament through a by-election in 1983 and made unsuccessful moves to get his old job back. Some HRPP Members, who were unhappy that they had not been appointed to Tofilau's Cabinet, formed a faction under Va'ai Kolone's leadership and joined Tupuola's opposition party. They planned to introduce a no-confidence motion to defeat the government's Budget when Parliament was due to meet in June.

A filibuster stalled the inevitable. Finally, in December 1985, Tofilau's term ended when his 1986 Budget was defeated and he subsequently resigned. The Head of State did not take Tofilau's advice to dissolve Parliament and call new elections. Instead, he asked Va'ai Kolone to lead a coalition government for the rest of the parliamentary term.

The 1988 general election pitted a Va'ai Kolone-led coalition against the HRPP led by Tofilau. It was a close-run thing, with political manoeuvres from all parties and defections from both sides. Tofilau had the numbers and set about forming a government. The defeated coalition united under Tui Ātua Tupua Tamasese (formerly Tupuola Efi) who established the Samoa National Development Party (SNDP) with Va'ai as his deputy leader. For the first time Samoa had two political parties, one in government, the other in opposition. Party politics had truly arrived and Samoa entered into a period of greater political stability.

Tofilau introduced a legally binding pledge of allegiance for prospective HRPP MPs to strengthen and consolidate the party and avoid the divisions and defections that had split past administrations. Parliamentary Under-Secretary and committee chair positions were established to reward loyal MPs, feed the ambitions of new MPs and strengthen the government caucus. Three other developments – accelerating the improvement to roads, extending electricity coverage throughout the country and a national referendum on universal suffrage –consolidated support for the HRPP and led to victory in the 1991 general election.

The 27 seats won by the HRPP in 1991 were supplemented by independent MPs and defectors from the SNDP. Tofilau 'Eti Alesana won the prime ministership with 31 seats, which he later strengthened to a two-thirds majority with the support of MPs crossing the floor, enabling the passing of two Bills to amend the Constitution and a law change. The first amendment added two more parliamentary seats, increasing the number to 49. The second amendment increased Cabinet posts from eight to twelve Ministers.[12] The law change increased the parliamentary term from three to five years. The HRPP party apparatus was further strengthened by the election of a deputy party leader, Tuila'epa Sa'ilele Malielegaoi, then Minister of Finance and Deputy Prime Minister.

Tofilau 'Eti Alesana had led Samoa through a turbulent period and then set about putting in place reforms, and a succession plan, that would lead to a long period of political stability under stable leadership. He convincingly won the 1996 general election and continued to consolidate his legacy until his health failed in office in 1998, shortly before his death. On 23 November 1998 Tuila'epa Sa'ilele Malielegaoi became Prime Minister of Samoa. Tuila'epa subsequently won the 2001, 2006, 2011 and 2016 general elections to become Samoa's longest-serving Prime Minister.

As Tuila'epa chairs Cabinet meetings, the portraits of his five prime-ministerial predecessors look over his shoulder. The weight of history bears down on all leaders. In Samoa the burden of history is personal, real and very close.

---

12 With twelve Ministers and twelve Under-Secretaries, plus the Prime Minister, the government had 25 votes and a majority in the 49-member Parliament.

CHAPTER 1

Assassination in Apia

Was the bullet that killed Samoan Cabinet Minister Luagalau Levaula Kamu on the night of Friday 16 July 1999 intended for the new Prime Minister of Samoa?

That is a question that Tuila'epa Sa'ilele Malielegaoi has often thought about.

Nine months into his premiership Tuila'epa was facing a number of challenges. At home, times were tough, people were worried, there was political unrest, changes were underway and the future was uncertain. In the Pacific region, civil conflict had broken out in the Solomon Islands, Fiji was facing political uncertainties that would lead to another coup, and commentators talked of an 'arc of instability' causing unrest across the region. The economies of the Pacific Islands were in trouble and the global economy was also weak. Aid to developing nations was drying up, and climate change and natural disasters were threatening the Pacific. There was plenty to occupy a new Prime Minister. And now there was a political assassination.

Not all the senior Members of the Human Rights Protection Party had been happy with the appointment of the brash young Minister of Finance, Tuila'epa Sa'ilele Malielegaoi, to succeed the popular, but elderly and failing, Prime Minister Tofilau 'Eti Alesana in late 1998. Samoa had become used to the stability of Tofilau's decade-long premiership, but change was underway.

Tuila'epa, who had a Master's degree in Commerce and had worked as an economic expert at the African, Caribbean and Pacific (ACP) General Secretariat in Brussels, had returned to Samoa at the request of the Minister of Finance and the Financial Secretary to head the Treasury. Instead, he entered politics. As a reformist Prime Minister, Tuila'epa was working to modernise the economy, open up Samoa to foreign investment and trade, and increase commercial activity. The old system of politics, based on patronage and village loyalties, was seen as an obstacle to modernisation and economic liberalisation.

Tuila'epa had initiated market reforms including the lowering of business taxes, privatising public assets, the removal of trade barriers, and reforming the public service to increase transparency and accountability. New Ministers, like Luagalau, were helping to drive the agenda for change and were replacing aging or non-performing Ministers. A generational change was taking place in Samoan politics.

When Tuila'epa took over as leader he reappointed all the Ministers in Tofilau's Cabinet to their old portfolios, except for Leafa Vitale. The Electrical Power Corporation (EPC) was taken away from Leafa and given to Luagalau so that Leafa, who had been a very active Minister of Public Works, could concentrate on reforming the Postal and Telecommunications Ministry.

Further changes were made when Tuila'epa shifted the Ministry of Women, Community and Social Development from To'i Aukuso to Leafa, who was relieved of the Postal and Telecommunications Ministry. Gafa Elisaia was made its head to expedite the reforms, but he also failed so Tuila'epa took over the Ministry and the reforms were subsequently driven through.

At a party caucus meeting in April 1999, Tuila'epa proposed dismissing Aukuso and Leafa from the party altogether as their activities were causing animosity against the HRPP, and division and ill-feeling within the party. The discussion gave an opportunity for Members to speak out against these two and support Tuila'epa's leadership. However, several older Members favoured forgiveness, after Aukuso and Leafa denied any wrongdoing, and they were pardoned.

Tuila'epa's supporters, including Luagalau and Tuala Sale Tagaloa, Minister of Lands, Survey and Environment, were on the rise and the old guard was in retreat. The battle for the political future of Samoa had largely been fought out quietly behind the scenes, but it would soon dramatically break out in a shocking, public tragedy.

Friday 16 July 1999 was to be a grand occasion, a night of celebration and fund-raising. A ceremony to mark the twentieth anniversary of the establishment of the HRPP, Samoa's dominant political party, was underway at the Centenary Hall at St Joseph's College in Alafua. Luagalau and Tuala were the joint masters of ceremony for the evening and all the HRPP notables were present.

Luagalau's task was to introduce Tuila'epa, the Prime Minister and leader of the HRPP, who would then welcome the guests and launch the celebration. The officiating Ministers and the Prime Minister all wore matching formal white *lāvalava* and suit jackets. In the darkened venue one could easily have been mistaken for another.

Behind the open brickwork wall of the Centenary Hall near the stage and hidden by decorative *tapa* mats was 34-year-old Eletise Vitale,[1] son of embattled Minister Leafa Vitale. He was armed with an M16 rifle.

What happened next was a series of events that would leave one man dead,

---

1   Eletise is sometimes referred to as Alatise.

three men jailed for murder, a country in crisis and the Pacific region in shock.

Shortly after 8 p.m., after introducing the Prime Minister, Luagalau walked to the back of the stage. He was shot point blank through the heart and collapsed.

Moments before, to a standing ovation, Tuila'epa had arrived at the microphone to deliver his speech. He heard a noise that he thought was a burst of static on the sound system. Tuila'epa delivered a short speech and left the stage. He then noticed a commotion behind the stage.

Bleeding and fatally wounded, Luagalau Levaula Kamu was rushed to the national hospital, where he died 30 minutes later.

Leafa Vitale, who along with other Ministers had accompanied Luagalau to the hospital, informed Tuila'epa that Luagalau had died.

*

The assassination of Luagalau Levaula Kamu was to become a defining test of Tuila'epa's leadership.

He recalls:

I looked at my Ministers. They all looked sad, including Leafa. I spoke to them: 'Tomorrow is Saturday, we will meet tomorrow. A Cabinet meeting at 10 o'clock.'

We met at 10 the next day. I summoned the police to give us the details of their investigation. I asked them to watch the airport and also the wharf for any suspicious-looking characters for departures and also incoming visitors.

That was Saturday. We buried Luagalau on Thursday afternoon.

On Thursday evening the police released the details about a suspect for the first time. A man had been sighted by boys sitting outside the hall. They described a man wearing army fatigues, carrying a red duffle bag and wearing a red cap. In the bag he was carrying a rifle. This man had been sitting outside the hall, by the car-parking spots, where two or three boys from the area were joking with him. All these details were shown on TV to the public on Thursday evening.

Tuila'epa said that he was the first to know who shot Luagalau.

The next day I came into the office in the morning. I was working away, when at 5 minutes past 8 I was told by my secretary there was a young man outside who wanted to talk with me. So I sent for him.

He said, 'I saw the programme on TV last night and, looking at the duffle bag demonstration and the army uniform and the cap, I immediately knew who it was. It was my relative, the son of Leafa.'

I said, 'How did you know?'

He told me, 'I was standing by the Nazareth church not far from my house, and Luagalau's was not far away. It was about 4.30 or 5 o'clock. All us youngsters were congregating about the Nazareth church field at Ululoloa trying to get enough people to play volleyball that evening. Then I saw my relative walking and he was walking straight towards me. I said to him, "Look, look, come and play for our team." He was wearing sunglasses and he walked straight past as if he did not know me. I suspected that he was high on marijuana. And he was walking towards Luagalau's house.'

That was Friday at 5 o'clock, and by 8 o'clock Luagalau was dead.

[The young man] said, 'I have to be very careful. This guy plays with guns. My life will be in danger if he knows I've revealed the details to you.'

Tuila'epa told him not to worry. He called the Police Commissioner, who came and took over the investigation.

In the interviews with the police that followed, the informant insisted that he would talk freely if his wife and two children were secure. The New Zealand High Commissioner, Mac Price, was contacted, and in less than 48 hours visas were obtained, travel arrangements made and the family was flown to New Zealand for their safety.

Eletise Vitale was quickly captured and jailed. He was charged, pleaded guilty and was convicted of the murder of Luagalau Levaula Kamu. Vitale was the hit-man, but there were others who supported him: he had not acted alone.

At Eletise Vitale's trial, the Attorney-General, Brenda Heather-Latu, said that another man had been hired for the assassination but To'i Aukuso and Leafa Vitale, who were frustrated by the reluctance of their first choice to do the job, turned to the younger Vitale.

Based on Eletise Vitale's testimony, the former Ministers were arrested, tried and convicted for plotting the assassination of Luagalau Levaula Kamu.[2]

Eletise Vitale had testified that in June 1999 he was picked up from his father's plantation at Vaovai, Falealili, where he worked as a labourer, and taken to his father's office in a government building. To'i Aukuso and his father Leafa

---

2 In April 2000 Leafa Vitale and To'i Aukuso were convicted of murder and received the mandatory sentence of death by hanging. Their sentences were commuted by the Head of State to life imprisonment. To'i Aukuso died while serving his prison sentence. Leafa Vitale was parolled in 2010 for health reasons, and his son Eletise was parolled later that year. On 6 August 2012 Leafa Vitale was pardoned, along with other prisoners, in an amnesty to celebrate Samoa's fiftieth anniversary of independence.

Vitale were in the office. Eletise Vitale said that his father then explained to him that the Prime Minister, the Minister of Lands, Survey and Environment, and Luagalau wanted to take everything away from them. Eletise Vitale said he was promised money or a new house if he successfully carried out the job, and that his father and Aukuso ordered him to carry out the killing.

In the Samoan world, loyalty to 'āiga, family, is paramount. Samoan identity is bound by lands and titles, who you are and your place of belonging. When these are under threat, emotion and family loyalty may overrule rational thought. Young Samoan men are trained to serve their chiefs and elders, and are taught that the orders of their elders must be obeyed without question. Eletise Vitale was primed to defend the honour of his family, to strike without question at those who threatened his father's and family's future.

*

Fifteen years after the assassination, Tuila'epa reflected on the events that led up to the tragedy and the motivations of those involved.

When Tofilau resigned on 23 November 1998, and I took over the post, it meant I had to select my own Cabinet. Because I needed to make sure that the government would run smoothly and that I was not landed with any problems, I decided to reappoint all the Ministers to their own posts, except one.

I decided to take away the Electrical Power Corporation from Leafa. I wanted him to focus on telecommunications because I was keen on pushing our ICT (Information and Communications Technology). I had seen some of the very strong push for reforming ICT as the backbone of the future development of education and telemedicine. It would also help us with tourism development. Leafa had been appointed as Minister of Telecommunications by Tofilau in 1996, and, strangely, he had taken over the EPC which was normally a corporation coming under the Public Works Department.

With the appointments complete, the ministerial oaths taken and my position as Prime Minister secure, I thought everything was fine. The swearing-in ceremony started at 2 p.m. and finished at 3 and I went to my office and was home about 6 p.m.

Leafa turned up at my house. He came and said: 'I have come to see you. I would dearly love to have the EPC back. There are many things you do not know. The retired Prime Minister did not have confidence in Luagalau. Tofilau did not trust him because he and his partner had been operating the copra mill for several years and the reports on the operation are that they have not paid a single cent for the rent or power. So Tui, I was told by Tofilau that he would not allow Luagalau to be Minister of Public Works and Minister of the EPC because there would be a conflict of interests.'

This was news to me. I told him I'd think about it.

The following day I summoned my first Cabinet meeting as Prime Minister and I told my Cabinet, in general terms, that 'some of you may not be happy with my decisions, and at any rate I have not made a major reshuffle, except one or two ministries and corporations. I want you to know that my decision yesterday stands.'

Leafa immediately said, 'That depends, Mr Prime Minister, on whether it is accepted.'

I looked at Leafa and said, 'Leafa, you know what to do if you don't want it.' Meaning resign. His challenge made me think, why is he angry? He should be happy that he was appointed and continued in his appointment as a Minister.

Several days later I got a note from Luagalau, the new Minister for the EPC, drawing my attention to the existence of a reported contract for tree cutting that was operated by Leafa and To'i Aukuso. The contract was for a quarter of a million Tala, every year. Luagalau said that he had asked for reports and was informed that there was no such cutting by the contractors. In fact, the trees were being cut by the employees of the EPC, and the Minister and the other MP were just taking the money and no work was being done.

I did think subsequently that none of that would have happened if the CEO was not also colluding. The same CEO was subsequently charged on another illegal transaction, convicted and jailed.

When I was asked by Luagalau what to do about the tree-cutting contract at the EPC, I said, 'Terminate the contract. That's corruption. We should never allow that.' Immediately it was slashed. Two days later I got a letter from To'i telling me that the contract had been rudely terminated by the new Minister and could I please help to have their project reinstated. I just filed the note and ignored the request altogether. That was just a few weeks before the Minister was killed.

What I heard afterwards from the [police] report was that I was originally targeted.

*

We may never know if the bullet that killed Luagalau Levaula Kamu was intended for the Prime Minister. But we do know from Eletise's testimony that the assassin's actions were fuelled by the conspirators with the idea that Luagalau, the Prime Minister, and indeed Tuala Sale Tagaloa, Minister of Lands, Survey and Environment, were the architects of the political demise of Leafa Vitale and his close ally To'i Aukuso. All three were their enemies. Were all three targets? They were all on the stage that fateful night. They were all of a similar build and wore identical clothing. Did the assassin panic after the first shot? Was the next shot for the Prime Minister? We will never know.

What we do know is that Tuila'epa Sa'ilele Malielegaoi was the voice of reason at that time of crisis. He pulled his Cabinet together and addressed the nation, appealing for calm in a televised address shortly after the shooting by saying: 'These are the kind[s] of days that test our wisdom and also test our confidence and patience. Samoa was not easily startled like a fish in shallow water . . . [B]ecause of our Christian foundation we stand firm.'

When asked if he was afraid that he had been targeted, that his life may have been at risk, Tuila'epa said that from time to time his personal security had been threatened by 'nutters', but he was convinced that his destiny was already written.

Tuila'epa is a man of faith who believes that our stories are all written in the 'Book of Life', and though we cannot know what our end will be, it is already determined. He says, 'So why worry? Make the most of the time you have and do the best you can with your allotted time.'

This certainty of purpose has helped guide Tuila'epa through many difficult times as Prime Minister, and has been a feature of his leadership. Tuila'epa's faith, sense of direction and leadership were built on the foundations of his childhood in the village of Lepā. We now go back to the 1940s to see how a village boy from Lepā started on his path to leadership.

CHAPTER 2

The Boy from Lepā

The Prime Minister of Samoa has a long name, Tuila'epa Sa'ilele Malielegaoi, and is also the bearer of seven other *matai* titles: Fatialofa, 'Auelua, Lupesoli'ai, Neioti, 'Ai'ono, Galumalemana and Lolofietele,[1] as well as the title Grand Chief of Papua New Guinea.[2] As a boy, he was simply known as Sa'ilele.

Young Sa'ilele Malielegaoi was raised in a large, extended family in the village of Lepā. Life was simple. The *Fa'asamoa* provided the structure and processes for family and village life.

In this chapter, often through his own words, we follow Sa'ilele's journey from his early village life in Lepā, through his primary and secondary education in Apia, to his undergraduate and postgraduate studies in Auckland, New Zealand. To understand the attitudes, behaviour and values of the man who became Prime Minister, we need to develop an understanding of the history of the nation of Samoa, the culture and complexities of the *Fa'asamoa*, and the village life that was central to shaping the life of the boy from Lepā.

Lepā and the Fa'asamoa

The village of Lepā is on the south coast of Upolu in the district of Ātua.[3] It is one of the most distant villages on Upolu from the capital of Samoa, Apia. In the 1940s and 1950s, when Tuila'epa was a boy, it was very difficult to travel to town. The buses to and from Apia only went as far as Falefa on the north coast and Falealili on the south coast. The journey from Lepā, some 30 kilometres, had to be made on foot, over Le Mafa Pass to Falefa, or along the 25-kilometre stretch of coast to Falealili.

The *Fa'asamoa* is literally the Samoan way of doing things and refers to traditional practices, customary behaviour, and mutual assistance in the village context and beyond. The *Fa'asamoa* is both a social structure, organising the

---

1 See page 267 for a list of Tuila'epa's *matai* titles, their locations and connections. The Tuila'epa title qualifies him to sit in the Lepā village *fono* and to stand as a candidate for Parliament.
2 The Grand Chief of Papua New Guinea was conferred, for services to the Pacific region, during the Pacific Islands Forum Meeting in Port Moresby in 2015.
3 Refer to map, p. 12.

shape of the community, and a set of cultural processes and protocols that determine the pattern of village activities.[4]

The village *nu'u* is the main unit of social organisation in Samoa. Each village is governed by a *fono,* the council of *matai* that consists of the heads of extended families, or *'āiga*. The village is organised within age, gender and cultural boundaries.

The word '*matai*' derives from *mata i ai,* meaning being set apart or consecrated. Chiefly titles are bestowed on individuals chosen by the elders of the family at a *saofa'i*, a titling ceremony. Potential *matai* must have the requisite genealogy to qualify, but, importantly, must also have served their families well and have demonstrated leadership of and wisdom in village and family affairs.

There are two kinds of *matai* titles: *ali'i* and *tulafale*. *Ali'i*, also known as sitting chiefs, derive their authority from sacred origins and aristocratic lineages. *Tulafale* are the talking chiefs or orators, custodians of the genealogy of the *'āiga* who act as the voice of their *ali'i* at ceremonial occasions.[5]

In a Samoan village, untitled men (*taule'ale'a*) and women (*tama'ita'i*) belong to two groupings. The young men belong to the *'aumāga, o le malosi o le nu'u*, the strength of the village, undertaking all the manual work required in the village such as fishing, cultivating the plantation, preparing the *umu* (stone oven) and serving the *fono*. All the girls and young women of the *nu'u* belong to the *aualuma*, the honour of the village. Traditionally the *aualuma* undertake 'women's work', such as weaving mats, preparing food and other activities. The proverb '*O le teine o le 'I'oimata o lona tuagane*' (a girl is the pupil of her brother's eye) refers to the closeness of the relationship between brother and sister. The young women and men of the village, whatever their blood relationship, are as brothers and sisters.

The children of the village are raised by, and are part of, the extended family. While mothers and fathers have primary responsibility, older sisters and brothers care for younger children, as do aunties and uncles and all the adults in the village. From an early age children will be assigned tasks, such as sweeping up leaves and helping with domestic activities. They serve their elders at mealtimes and quickly learn their place in the village hierarchy. Children are prized by a rural village community and treated with affection and tolerance, but they are not the centre of attention, as is often seen in child-centred, urban, nuclear families.

Along with the *fono matai*, the *'aumāga* and the *aualuma* is a fourth group:

4   Refer to the References for a range of standard texts on the *Fa'asamoa*. Some of the descriptions of the *Fa'asamoa* in this chapter were drawn from Swain, 1999 and 2014.
5   For a comprehensive description of Samoan chieftainship, the *fa'amatai* and the traditional Samoan hierarchy, see Davidson, 1967; Gilson, 1970; Kramer, 1994a and 1994b; Meleisea, 1995; and So'o, 2007.

the *Komiti a Faletua ma Tausi*, the Women's Committee, which consists of the wives of the *matai*. Samoans traditionally marry outside their village, and a married woman must move to live in her husband's village. The *Komiti a Faletua ma Tausi* is *in*, but not *of*, the village. This is a fine but important distinction because wives of *matai* have no formal say in matters relating to lands and titles in their husband's village. But they have a large say in their village of origin where their brothers may be *matai*. Influence in Samoa follows bloodlines.

A fifth important organisation in each village is the church. Villages tend to be identified as aligned to one of five main Christian denominations: Congregational Christian Church of Samoa (EFKS), Catholic, Methodist, Church of the Latter Day Saints and the Assemblies of God.

Christianity is symbolised in the village by the large church, *fale sa*, and the grand *fale o le faife'au*, the pastor's house, which is often the largest and only two-storeyed residence in a village. The church buildings demonstrate the wealth and power of the church and the pride of the village in their Christian devotion. The church minister, *faife'au*, or priest, *patele*, like the *faletua ma tausi,* is in the village but not of the village, and the pastor or priest does not have a say in the village affairs of the *fono*.

The village *fono*, *'aumāga*, *aualuma* and *Komiti a Faletua ma Tausi* all have parallel church responsibilities. Status in the church hierarchy mirrors village status and groupings: church elders are invariably senior *matai*, and the *Mafutaga a Tina* (Church Women's Fellowship) is largely comprised of the *Komiti a Faletua ma Tausi*.

Prior to the introduction of Christianity, *'āiga* had household gods, *aitu*, and the *ali'i* had spiritual as well as chiefly duties. Tagaloa, the creator of the Samoan cosmology, was referred to as an *atua*, the title now given to the Christian god introduced in the 1830s. The linkages between the traditional organisation of a Samoan village and the church today are very close. Spirituality pervades all village activities, and prayer and church are part of everyday life: they are not reserved for Sundays. But spiritual and village governance matters are dealt with in separate fora. Everything and everybody has an assigned role and place of belonging in a Samoan village community.

It was within the structure of the *Fa'asamoa*, in the village community of Lepā and in the embrace of his *'āiga*, that young Sa'ilele Malielegaoi spent his first five years. During those years, while he was immersed in the *Fa'asamoa*, his formal education began. Family, education, the church and the *Fa'asamoa* were the foundations on which Sa'ilele Malielegaoi's values, behaviour and attitude to life were built. In later years he reflected on his early education.

Sa'ilele was my *taule'ale'a* name. In fact, in Samoa if you are called Sa'ilele, that is your name. We never had any surnames in the past until the Europeans introduced the practice we now follow. You took the chiefly title of your father to be your surname. Malielegaoi was my father's chiefly name.

My first education was at our Sunday School under the guidance of our pastor from the London Missionary Society (LMS) church in my village. The LMS church changed its name to the Christian Congregational Church of Samoa in 1962 to herald its independence, following the example set by our political leaders as our country readied itself to become independent from foreign rule. My father was a deacon and treasurer for the church until he passed away in June 1987. His biological father, the Reverend Toese Petaia Muliaumasealii of Fasitoo Uta, was a missionary in Papua New Guinea. My family therefore was steeped in Protestant Christian traditions. The Sunday School taught me how to read and do very simple arithmetic – adding, subtracting, dividing and multiplying.

My first instruction at the Sunday School was the study of the seventeen letters of the Samoan alphabet and learning to read selected passages from the Bible to test our progress in correctly pronouncing combinations of letters. In this way we were quick to grasp the relationship between the boring and seemingly meaningless recitation of the Samoan alphabet and its application to the written word. This opened up a new world for me, a four-year-old, in that I realised suddenly that I could equally match the adults' skills in reading the Bible word for word and passage by passage during church on Sundays. It opened my small world quickly to a hunger for knowledge.

The custom of the Congregational Church was to bring in examiners each year for the examination of different grades in reading, handwriting and arithmetic. It was such an important event that the parents did not work that day. It was like a holiday. They all sat outside the church where their sons and daughters were undergoing their examinations. At the end of the examinations, the results were read out for all the village to hear. Those who came first would be given special prizes at a feast at the pastor's residence where the proud parents would lavishly contribute so that the whole village would be fed.

The young Sa'ilele was honoured this way, and still remembers how it felt.

It gives so much prestige to the child's mind. Education was an awakening. One's mind was awakened and you became hungry for more knowledge.

The Congregational Church practice of responsive reading of biblical verses was especially interesting for the precocious, competitive and increasingly successful young Sa'ilele.

When I was very young I would read the Bible, in the Congregational way of reading and responding, with the pastor reading one passage and the congregation reading the next passage, one after the other, alternately. The fact that I could read so fast made me proud. Proud that I could beat adults. I could pronounce the words as accurately as the adults in the *gagana Samoa* (Samoan language), and while I could understand some words, the big ones I did not understand. Especially when talking about ghosts, *fa'atuatua*.

At five years and six months I went to the government primary school in our village. Our class of five-year-olds, about 25 in all, was housed in a leaking thatched-roof *fale*. We sat on mats, resting on a floor of pebbles and crushed coral. Sometimes our teachers would take us out, under the shade of the breadfruit trees, for our classes. We enjoyed the fresh air and the clear blue sky above. Those of us who did well in the pastor's Sunday School also performed well in primer 1. The subjects taught were not very different from the syllabus at the pastor's Sunday School.

Reading had unexpected advantages. Reflecting on his childhood sex education, Tuila'epa recalled:

Once we came to understand how to read the Bible, we would always like to read the Old Testament stories. We would read about what King David did to women. We learnt about things that were not told to us by the pastor. But they were there, in the Bible. I always remember when Albert Wendt's book, *Sons for the Return Home*, was published. There was an article that came out in the paper. Some people were queuing to buy the book but others, particularly college students, were queuing up to buy the Bible. Jokingly, one of the news media people asked: 'What is the point? I see that you are not buying Mr Wendt's novel *Sons for the Return Home* that has just come out today. Why are you buying the Bible?'

And this fellow laughs and says, 'It's a great sex book for us these days.'

Common diseases at that time included yaws and skin worms, which were spread quickly by germs carried by flies. Those affected were kept under mosquito nets in the daytime. My mother told me that, as a toddler, I was covered with yaws and the mosquito net was necessary to keep the hungry flies out. The medical officers from Apia paid periodic visits to our school to treat yaws and skin worms. This was an embarrassment for the young boys who had to bare their bottoms for a complete visual check up. The uncircumcised amongst us were sorted out and the operation performed there on the spot, sometimes with the mothers standing by with stinging lashes of bound coconut leaves and twigs ready to convince their sons, with a forced smile of genuine motherly love, that being circumcised was proof of a son's courage and manliness and reason for a mother's pride.

Nowadays, children must have a good breakfast before going to school. Not in our time. It was typical for every house to have a hanger in the back part of the *fale* into which *taro*, bananas and *palusami*, leftovers from supper the previous evening, were stored in a food basket hung high up beyond the reach of prowling dogs, cats, pet pigs and other night-time scavengers. This food was a welcome treat for the rats that descended from their hideouts in the thatched roofs to self-serve in the pitch darkness of the night. In the morning, if you saw a big rat bite on a piece of *taro*, you bit it off, spat it out and the rest was your cold, ready-made breakfast eaten as you darted off to school. There were always ripe coconuts and paw-paws to balance these improvised meals. In the villages, access to any fruit, regardless of whose land it grew on, was the norm. Any fruit tree, therefore, belonged to every kid in the village.

Life in the village, during my childhood, was simple and possibly not much different from the way our ancestors had lived for millennia. A normal day started when the sun was already high in the sky. Two meals a day was the norm: one at around 11 in the morning and the second after evening prayers at night. At dusk, it was prayer time. The sound of hymns sung in harmony would burst out from every home. It was as if each family was trying to outdo the others in the beauty and volume of their music.

There was no need to work all day every day. Subsistence farming was the norm. There was no pressure to plant beyond family needs and sharing took care of any food shortages. Occasionally, a small trading vessel would call in from Apia to take away dried copra and to restock the village store.

Kirikiti (Samoan cricket), *velovelo* (spear throwing) and *tagāti'a* (darting a light stick along the ground) competitions were popular pastimes. There were night sports like *igāve'a* (hide and seek) and *togi-a-gogu* (*nonu* throwing at night) that the young adults in the village especially enjoyed. For hide and seek, participants were grouped into two parties (one hiding and the other seeking). Points were awarded for the most members who successfully made it to the goal (such as a sand mount) without being touched on the head. The losing team then 'shouted' the winning team by preparing a feast of *koko alaisa* (cocoa rice) or *kopai* (a sweetened soup of round flour balls) the following evening. Young men and women were mixed in each of the teams. This was an opportunity for a male to woo a female, who was inaccessible at any other time due to the watchful, protective eyes of her brothers. Occasionally, a young couple would disappear into the darkness of the night and elope to the safety of their relatives in a neighbouring village. They would return later as man and wife, sometimes much later with offspring, when anger had subsided and the recognition had sunken in that a valued new pair of strong hands was available to serve the wife's family.

A second night sport, which is rarely heard of today, is *togi-a-gogu* (throwing the *nonu* fruit). At night *nonu* fruit were thrown from a distance to where a crowd of young men and women were assembling in anticipation. There was a rush to pick up the fruit thrown in the darkness. The accidental landing of fruit on people's heads was not infrequent. The one who caught the fruit then dashed across to reach the sand-mount goal to score a point. The team with the lowest number of points would again bear the cost of a feast to be held the following evening. These traditional sports were popular because they provided occasions when young people were able to mix together socially.

Cricket was by far the most popular sport. Samoans had played *kirikiti* before they had ever heard of rugby. Just about every village had a concrete pitch to play on. Tournaments were regularly organised between villages. There are no upper limits to the number of players, although the two teams competing must have equal numbers. There is no age limit, and the smallest possible number in a team is two. Cricket was indeed the national sport because it was the only sport that every Samoan of any age knew how to play.

Shark-lassoing competitions, between my village of Lepā and Saleapāga, were an exciting community sport. Up to twenty young men in a long boat, *fautasi*, would sail out to sea with several live pigs to use as bait. Five miles out, in shark-infested waters in the deep ocean, pigs' blood would be spilled and pork pieces tied with sennit ropes woven from coconut fibres would be thrown out into the ocean then slowly pulled back to the boat. Sharks were drawn in to the side of the long boats, attracted by the odour of raw pig flesh and blood. As the shark tried to bite the bait as it was pulled in and up, a loop of rope would be quickly slid down over the shark's head and tightened. Simultaneously the shark was stunned with one strike of a solid piece of wood on its head. Strong hands would rapidly pull the tail end into the boat. Six or seven sharks brought in by the young men would feed the whole village for a week. During the days of plentiful shark fins and meat, the household *umu* were busy. Dense smoke would hover over the village every morning as hot stones from open ovens were used to heat and reheat shark meat and bake breadfruit and *taro* for the day's feast. Then there would be cricket, involving the whole community, for the rest of the day and the rest of the week.

Tuila'epa remembers that relations between men and women living in village communities during the 1950s were less complicated and freer than they are today.

I used to tell this story to demonstrate the dramatic changes in attitude. In my village there was a running stream, still running now, but very low. In the days before cars, the water was deep and the volume of water was fast. Our house was at the end of the village. There were two deep pools: a women's pool on the seaward side with a huge stone wall to slow down the quick flow of water, and adjoining that the men's pool. We started going to the pools to have our wash at 4 o'clock when the sun was still up high. The ladies all bathed naked and no one cared, because we saw them naked in the pool all the time when we passed by to get to our pool. One of the things that you had to be careful about was not to wet your *lāvalava*, the one you'd be wearing before the bath and after the bath. So what we did was to leave our *lāvalava* up on top and jump in and swim about naked just like our womenfolk. And no one complained to the pastor! He was the only one in the village with a private shower.

Parents

Sa'ilele's thirst for education came from his family.

My father, Malielegaoi Veni, was educated at the village school. These were government schools, primary at Lepā and Logologo Secondary, not far from Lepā. This was where he sat and passed the exam to go to Avele Agricultural College, a college set up by New Zealand not only for Samoa but for the other islands under the New Zealand administration: the Cook Islands, Niue and Tokelau. My father told me he was seventeen years old when he was notified that he was accepted at Avele College.

    He set out with his adoptive father, Lolofietele Sialavai, to accompany him to Avele. They walked, not taking the coastal route, but going through the mountains to the north coast. They reached Le Mafa Pass and stopped there to rest, drink some cool water and have some *taro* for lunch, looking down at the coastal villages of Falefa and Falevao.

Then, my father told me, he was suddenly overwhelmed with sadness about leaving his parents. He felt he would be neglecting them. He was carrying a heavy load of clothes and food, *taro*, and would not see his parents for the whole year he was away at school. After the meal, when they were just about to continue walking, he said, 'Dad, I've changed my mind.'

'What?'

'We will go back.'

'What do you mean?'

'I cannot leave you and Mum alone. I have to go back with you and take care of you.'

His dad tried hard to convince him that education would open up a whole new world and provide a better future for the whole family, but my father said, 'No. I will come back with you and take care of you.'

So my father was the only one of his three brothers who never went to formal education in town. He stayed home to serve, to *tautua*, the family.

In my father's time there was no regular transport to the market in Apia. There was no need to have a big plantation because if you had a big plantation you had nowhere to sell the surplus. It was too far to go to the city. So we planted just what we needed, not too much, just a little bit extra.

Later, during school holidays, Sa'ilele would work with his father on his plantation and assist in the subsistence agriculture of the village.

In the village, in the days when bananas were a major export earner, we had a small banana plantation[6] intermixed with *taro*. I was the main worker who helped my father. As my elder brother was not reliable, my father depended increasingly on me during the school holidays to regularly inspect our small plantation and spray the newly flowering buds of the new bunches of bananas with DDT in order to ensure that the buds were protected from insect pests. That was my major preoccupation in our plantation. But much of my time I spent spear fishing. It was a hobby that made me a provider of protein and vitamins for my family, spearing reef fish. All this contributed to my

---

6   The banana industry in Samoa reached a million cases exported by Samoa to New Zealand in 1960. Pests and diseases eventually destroyed this industry completely and now Samoa only produces bananas for the local market.

experience of taking care of our parents and our family. My job was to attend to this physical work for our family and then attend to my studies when the school term began.

My mother, Leasunia Lupesoli'ai, was born in the village of 'A'ufaga, which lies to the west of our village of Lepā. Saleapāga village lies to the east. These three villages of Lepā, 'A'ufaga and Saleapāga together comprise the Lepā Political District.

Leasunia Lupesoli'ai had four sisters. In Samoa, a family of all girls has low economic status. It meant the sisters had to do hard physical work on the plantation to survive. They also participated in spear fishing and other forms of reef fishing. Whenever they needed more help, other families were always ready to offer it. My mother's education was limited to the LMS pastor's Sunday School, just enough to learn how to read and write. The rest of her teenage years were spent caring for her sick mother.

I had never bothered to enquire how my parents came to decide to tie the knot, and why my father never bothered to venture out far for more challenging pastures beyond the village next door to seek and choose a wife. For whatever worldly attraction they saw in each other, their decision to make a lifetime companionship was to create my insurance policy for a future political career, which would set me on a path to serve my village, district and country over a long period of ten parliamentary terms and ten general elections. Why? For the very simple reason that the voters of my parents' villages, namely 'A'ufaga and Lepā out of the three-village constituency, would always consider my candidacy to be that of a 'son of the soil', a term that describes the offspring of a mother and father from the same constituency, and vote accordingly in support.

I dedicate this memoir to my parents.

Leaving Lepā

Sa'ilele vividly remembers the day that he spontaneously left his childhood behind and departed Lepā for Apia.

There was a big wedding held in my village back in the 1950s. The bridegroom was Mose Fruean, a newly ordained pastor of the Congregational Church, and the bride Matagitau was from my family. All of our extended family, and every distant relative, came for the wedding.

That is where I met my aunt, Tafale Tasi. I would never have met her if it wasn't for that wedding. She had a son, Semi, whose father was a United

States Marine who had come to Samoa in 1942. Semi drew my attention, being the only white relative amongst the many who gathered to attend the wedding. I felt a little tinge of jealousy that he was different from us. Though Semi was two years older than I, it did not stop me challenging him to a fist fight only a few feet from his mother. She did not hide her disappointment that her son was being roughed up by a half-naked brownie.

My aunt, whom I had not met before, said, 'Who the hell are you?'

'Sa'ilele,' I replied.

Sa'ilele happened to be the name of a pastor who died in 1945 who I later found out was her uncle. My parents named me Sa'ilele in the hope that I would follow in the late pastor's footsteps and become a preacher.

'Oh', she said. 'Who is your father?'

'My father is Malielegaoi.'

'Oh.'

She said Malielegaoi was her first cousin.

Then she said, 'That's nice, would you like to come with me to Apia?'

I said, 'OK, I'd like that.'

She said that we would be boarding the long boat very shortly.

I ran down to our house. It was three houses away. I had my little sister with me. I just came to the house and said to an elder sister of mine, 'Hold on to this little kid, tell our parents that I am going to town.'

The long boat, to carry the newlyweds to the nearest bus stop at Falealili some 25 kilometres away, was about to leave. So I grabbed myself a shirt – I was naked apart from a *lāvalava* – and returned straight away to the beach and jumped into the boat. This was at about 10 o'clock in the morning, I thought I'd be coming back in the evening. So I never said farewell to my parents. I just took off.

The great urge for me to go to Apia came from the numerous exaggerated stories from my older brother, Manoa, who accompanied my father on his rare visits to Apia. Manoa used to talk about the wonders of Apia: the big buildings, the many different cars shaped like oversized safes that moved on their own power without anyone pushing, and the sweetest, and yet the coldest, food item on Earth called *aisakulimi*. Ice cream was a hot dream for any child of our time in our backward community. We all wanted to have a chance to go to Apia and see all these wonderful things that we did not have in our village. These were the items that I wanted to see and taste before returning home that evening.

The boat went on and on, and on and on. It must have been hours before we finally reached our destination to catch a bus to Apia. The bus from

Falealili had a limit of 33 passengers. On this day, close to 50 passengers were carried, including those sitting on the roof and any space available. Not to mention pigs and baskets of *taro* at the rear of the bus. The route to Apia was through Leulumoega, crawling most of the way because there were too many passengers and there were so many potholes in the road. Nowadays, it takes one hour to drive the same route. It took up to five hours in 1950.

That was how I came to Apia to go to school. I stayed with my aunt, went to school and only returned to the village for school holidays.

We would come back by bus to Falealili and I would walk all the way to the village by the seashore route. In those days, before the advent of modern toilets, you had to sometimes revert to the inland route to avoid unwelcome deposits on the beach and to walk in the shade of the trees. Modern sanitation and tourism have changed ancient habits and now Samoa's beaches are very clean.

I always remember, when we passed through Salani, that we had to take the route by the shallow end of the stream by the sea. At high tide we would take our *lāvalava* off because we would get all wet as we swam across. That's why, when I became Prime Minister, I was determined to build the bridge that is now in place to make it easier to cross from one village to the next.

The Mystery of Sa'ilele's Date of Birth

The 'official' birth date of Sa'ilele Malielegaoi, the boy from Lepā who became Prime Minister, is 14 April 1945. But, as with many events in his long and interesting life, there is more than one story. The truth sometimes takes a long time to be revealed, as he recounts in the tale of his birth date.

I have just discovered my real birthday. When I was a boy in Lepā, birth dates were never serious affairs to note. So when I attended school my father gave the teacher a birth date that made me young enough to meet the entry requirements.

I thought that 14 April 1945 was my real birth date. In fact, I had a birth certificate to get a passport when I finally got a scholarship to go to New Zealand. I took my birth certificate with me to New Zealand and it was lost.

When my first passport expired in 1970, I had to renew it. I was told by the Immigration Department that I had to produce an official birth certificate. So I went to the Registry Office to get a birth certificate and they tried to find my name. My name is not in the record. There is no record of my birth. All my brothers and sisters were registered there, but my name was missing. That was a mystery.

I had my suspicions. Perhaps my father had changed my birth date to make me seem younger so that I would qualify to attend school. The question was: how could this happen? The answer was that a fellow in the Registry Office in those days was a relative of my father. So they must have cooked up the books and created an artificial birth certificate for me. The 14th of April 1945 was never my real birthday, and I had never wanted to celebrate it.

When all of Samoa's birth dates were computerised in 2000, they had to take my birth date from my visa, because my passport was now the only source document. I could not get a birth certificate from the Births and Registry Office because there was no record of my birth. This was the situation until September 2014, when I finally solved the mystery.

This is how it happened. The pastor from my village, the Reverend Suafa'i, was dying and I went to visit him. The date of my birth still had to be determined. I remembered that the Congregational Church had a tradition that the pastor must always keep a book to record important events in the village, including the dates of births and deaths, baptisms and dismissals from church activities for sinful conduct. The book may be over a hundred years old.

I asked the pastor, 'Do you have the records of the church?'

'Yes', he replied.

'How far back?'

'They go back to the 1900s.'

'Can I have a look?'

'OK, have a look. There is the book.'

So I picked up the old book and flicked the pages back to 1945 and my name was absent. In 1946 my name was absent. In 1947 my name was absent. In 1948 my name was absent. I went back to 1944 and my name was there, the 14th of February 1944. So that is my real birth date. The mystery was solved.

Will I rectify the record? I will defer to the wisdom of Pontius Pilate: 'What I have written, I have written.'

Schooldays in Apia

Education was not compulsory in Western Samoa when I was a child, and gaining entry to a good school in Apia was difficult for a boy from a distant village.

In the best government schools in Apia, under the New Zealand colonial policy, the authorities were very strict on two entry requirements. Firstly, if you were over five-and-a-half years old you could not be accepted into school. You were too old. Secondly, you had to have an English name. So we had situations where the children's mother was of European descent and the children would take her name rather than their father's.

These policies were both potential handicaps for Sa'ilele Malielegaoi. But he was not to be denied a formal education. Early in his life Sa'ilele found his way around bureaucratic barriers, something he would make an art of in later life. His father had clearly sorted out the birth-date barrier, and going to a Catholic school would beat the English name requirement of government schools.

When I came to the city to live with my aunty I did not enter the Marist Brothers' School straight away. It was the best private school at the time but a very difficult school to get into. First things first, I had to become a Catholic. Up to that time I was not a Catholic, and there was nothing to show that I was a Catholic. What you needed to have was a baptismal certificate. So I got to be baptised again in Apia in order to get the baptismal certificate, which became my passport to go to a Catholic school. I have been a committed Catholic ever since. The *Diary of Saint Maria Faustina* was a great influence on me and I have read her story of Divine Mercy many times.

The only Catholic school that would give me the opportunity to register was Father Felise's school, located right next to the Marists at Mulivai. I attended primer 1 in 1951 for a whole year and I was very strong in arithmetic: addition, subtraction, multiplication and division. In 1952 I was promoted to primer 2. All was going well but at the end of 1952 there was a scandal and the school closed.

During the 1952 census, when people were required to provide the names and parents of all family members, a woman at Togafuafua village had revealed that her two children were fathered by Father Felise, the priest. He was the greatest preacher of our time. He would celebrate the 7 o'clock mass at Mulivai every Sunday morning. The church was always full. He was such an orator, a brilliant speaker. Father Felise was well known for turning out good, well-educated people from his school. He was a popular priest. Suddenly the news came out. Father Felise disappeared, out of sight, and so the school had to be closed. That was in 1952 and everyone got transferred to Marist. I was sent back to primer 1.

I had always wanted to enter the famous Marist Brothers' School, but when I did I had to go back to primer 1. That felt like taking one step forward and three steps back. I had been in primer 1 at primary school at Lepā in 1950, primer 1 at Father Felise's primary in 1951 and now primer 1 at Marist in 1953. Four years at primer 1 level for a nine-year-old, given my real birth date. A kind of world record that no student would ever like to celebrate!

I had been in primer 1 at Marist Brothers' for several days when Brother Pafelio, who was in charge, decided that my reading and my arithmetic were quite advanced, so he promoted me to primer 2. That went on until two weeks from the end of the year. Then Brother Pafelio caught me napping when I should have been reading our only textbook, *Old Mother Hubbard*. Our routine included praying three times a day, reciting the times tables from two to twelve at the top of our voices, and reading *Old Mother Hubbard*. I was often bored, and slept in class when I could.

Brother Pafelio was very angry when he caught me cat-napping. He said to me, 'I should kick you out, why don't you read the book?'

To avoid the cane I said, 'Brother, I have read the whole book.'

'All of the book?'

'Yes. The whole book, many times.'

'Then do your tables.'

I said, 'I know all the tables. All the tables from two times to twelve times.'

'OK. Come, come, come . . .'

To my surprise, Brother Pafelio promoted me to primer 3 immediately, two weeks from the end-of-year exams.

I had been well trained by Father Felise. I sat the exams. When the results came out I heard my name called out, saying that I would be promoted directly from primer 3 and I would miss primer 4 and go straight to standard 1 the following year. Then I went step by step from 1954 onwards.

Sa'ilele completed his primary education at Marist Brothers' School in 1959. He then advanced to St Joseph's College for secondary education until 1963.

Life in Apia

I lived with my aunty's family at Saleufi in Apia all that time. Only at Christmas holidays would I be able to take the bus back home. It did not go all the way. Usually my father would come to Apia and accompany me from the bus stop at Falefa or Falealili and we would walk the rest of the distance to Lepā. We would walk through the hot afternoon. We would walk and walk and walk. We would feel thirsty, hungry and tired and then my father would say, 'Oh, let's invite ourselves in for a free meal.'

We would turn into a family of his choice.

My father would address the family starting with the typical salutation of Samoan oratory for that village and its prominent chiefs. This is the etiquette that sets the tone for the traditional introduction to establish the cultural ties between the host village and ours. Then he would state his title and refer to me, his son. My father would say, 'We are hungry and we have decided to rest for an hour.' (All I wanted to hear about was the food.)

Then the activities would begin. The chickens were killed, the firewood lit, the *taro* prepared, the coconut milk extracted and within an hour the feast of the finest in Samoan cuisine was laid out before us to partake of. This was Samoan hospitality at its best. After an exchange of words of gratitude, we would continue on our journey completely refreshed.

Today, customary Samoan hospitality lives on with a big, big difference. The firewood is replaced by the gas oven, the chickens replaced by the pot of noodles and the coconut drink by the cup of coffee from an electric jug.

While Sa'ilele grew up in a village, from the age of six he mostly lived in Apia. When the roads improved, he was able to have more contact with his family in Lepā.

Fortunately the roads joined up for the first time in 1957 and the lives of our village people began to change. Then I could go by bus to my village in the weekend.

Marist Brothers' was a great school. We came in the morning and lined up in troop formation at 8. We did not sing the national anthem, we sang *Save Regina* in Latin, which no one understood. It is the Catholic hymn to honour Mary, the mother of our Saviour. After that, the drum would start up to teach us how to march in an orderly manner, part of the Marist Brothers' technique of introducing discipline to our thought processes, and then you were marched off to your classes. What I always enjoyed was the break at 10.30.

In those days, playing marbles at break time was a great sport. I played marbles. I was the champion marble player, and I took all the marbles off the other players. In fact, marbles was the only competitive sport I played at Marist Brothers'. I would walk in, play and take the marbles from all the other players. At the end of the year I would take a suitcase of marbles that I had won home to my village and trade the marbles with the boys in the village for coconuts which I sold to pay my school fees. Marbles was the only sport in which I was considered the champion at primary school.

Life at Saleufi in town was never easy. Tafale Tasi worked as a cleaner for the government-owned Casino Hotel at Sogi, where the Tusitala Hotel is now situated. She earned very little each week to take care of our small family of three. I was perpetually hungry. It was not uncommon for most pupils in our time to go to school without breakfast. But for our small family we had one meal daily, at night. If it was just a banana, that was it. Sometimes, we would collect bananas for our evening meals that had been dropped from the broken banana cases ready for shipment at the wharf. This was a common experience for the residents of Saleufi village. Later, when the road to Lepā opened, we were able to get baskets of food from the village to last us the whole week.

There was one time when Aunty Tafale sold our house on the leasehold land at Saleufi. We became wanderers from family to family. Several families took turns to host us until Aunty Tafale decided to build again on our leasehold land, which was still vacant and available. The hosting families must have had enough, seeing us as an extra burden to carry in addition to supporting their own families.

Fortunately the Saleufi community was a close-knit, church-based fellowship under the leadership of a very strong committee of women, *O le Komiti a le Losa*. Aunty Tafale was amongst the leaders of this strong fellowship that produced a family spirit in which every household was looked upon as part of one family serving the Catholic Church through the Maria Imakulata Cathedral at Mulivai. Helping one another in need was quite normal.

In 1955, I decided to leave Aunty Tafale and stay at Saina village in the home of my father's twin sister, some eight kilometres from the Marist Brothers' School at Mulivai. My oldest sister, Manuae, was staying there while attending Pesega College, which was an added incentive to shift. I lived there for a whole year. Along with the other students, we would wake up at 5 every morning, then walk to Vaitele to try and catch the Vaitele plantation manager's truck to Apia. If we missed the truck, then a long, eight-kilometre walk followed. Returning after school was a killer, especially walking the long stretch from Taufusi to Vaigaga where there was absolutely no shade from the hot afternoon sun. When it rained, we were thoroughly drenched, books included. This experience was enough to convince me that hunger was the lesser evil, and before the end of the year I returned to Saleufi. Aunty Tafale welcomed me back.

Whilst staying in Saina village I was introduced, by my aunt Mrs Tina Faigaa, to the profession of street vending, selling strings of fish caught by her husband on Saturday afternoons. This required home visits through the villages of Toamua and Puipaa. When I still had fish to sell, I would backtrack and walk as far as Vailoa and Faleata. At other times I carried baskets of coconut shell coals to sell. The money we received was used to buy fatty Kiwi mutton flaps for our Sunday *to'ona'i*. Buying and selling were part of my outside-school-hours education. Despite all the criticisms levelled against those who are engaged in the same activities today, I tend to take a softer approach because I see myself in those same young people who are trying to do exactly what I used to do in my youth.

I began my secondary education in 1960 at St Joseph's, Lotopā. The school site was an eight-acre cocoa and coconut plantation sold to the Marist Brothers by a very devoted Catholic family. It was a new college and students were required to help with the clean-up for most of the 1960 school year. Every morning we would bring a bush knife for manual work that we did after school. It was a joy to have access to the coconuts, guavas, paw-paws and ripe cocoa for our morning breakfast and lunch. The fruit was freely available until every tree was cut down to make way for the college sports field.

The 1959 National Public Service Examinations results were published in the papers in January 1960, to our college's great embarrassment. Not one candidate from St Joseph's passed. The National Public Service Examinations Certificate was the highest qualification recognised by the education authorities. Students at lower fifth (form five) were qualified to sit. If they passed, it was enough to look for a job. Those who scored highly were sent to New Zealand on scholarships for School Certificate and beyond. I was picked to sit my Public Service Examination in 1961 with twenty others from form four and fifteen from the lower fifth form, to boost the numbers. I was the only one who passed from our college. Later another student from the lower fifth passed on a recount.

At St Joseph's College, Sa'ilele progressed rapidly through the secondary curriculum, excelling in mathematics and passing the School Certificate examinations in 1962, the year Western Samoa gained independence from the New Zealand colonial administration. Up to that time, the New Zealand Department of Education was in charge of Samoa's educational standards, policies, curricula and examinations.

In 1963 the first University Entrance (UE) Examination was officially sat here in Samoa. Prior to that you would get a scholarship to New Zealand if you passed School Certificate. Then in 1963 the government decided to have the first University Entrance class in Samoa, just the one sixth form of twelve students who had passed School Certificate from Samoa College, five from St Mary's and me from St Joseph's. A class of eighteen. To me it was a very sensible thing to do, especially when you have to make good use of the teachers available. But for the Brothers at St Joseph's and the Sisters at St Mary's this was an ideal opportunity to begin their own sixth forms. We would be the guinea pigs!

I kicked off the sixth form class at St Joseph's and the five girls started off the sixth form at St Mary's. Around about April the Brothers told me they could not continue with me alone in the class. There were just not enough teachers to devote all their time to me. So they told me I must enrol in the Correspondence School, in Wellington, New Zealand, and continue my sixth form studies that way by mail. The teachers would support me. The Sisters did the same for the girls at St Mary's. In June 1964 I was informed that my marks from written assignments showed that I could be a candidate to be accredited University Entrance. Then in November I got a letter to advise me that I had my University Entrance accredited. I did not have to sit the exams. About two weeks later I heard that one of the girls at St Mary's, Sister T. Adams, was also accredited UE. The remaining sixteen students in Samoa had to sit the University Entrance examinations and all of them failed.

I was awarded a government scholarship to go to St Paul's College in Auckland for my upper sixth year in preparation for enrolling at the University of Auckland.

Leaving Samoa

I remember distinctly when I left Samoa. It was the 9th of February 1964. I flew from Western Samoa to American Samoa. Our airport at Faleolo had a grass strip; the aeroplane was a DC-3. I spent a whole day in Pago Pago waiting to catch a TEAL flight to Nadi. I stopped there, waiting for the flight to New Zealand. The whole trip took two days. When I finally arrived at Whenuapai Airport in Auckland, it was 10 o'clock at night. The principal of St Paul's, Brother Urban, was waiting for me. He picked me up and took me to the school. I attended St Paul's College as a boarder.

What impressed me most about flying on my first trip to New Zealand was looking down on the clouds – the view was fantastic. The clouds appeared like a collection of kapok, the cotton-wool-like material that my mother used to fill our pillows. Not only that, the International Dateline changed the dates as soon as we crossed over, one hundred miles from the most western part of Savai'i. Those two memories registered in my mind. Years later, when as Prime Minister I decided to change the date line, my mind went back to that first time I crossed it. I suppose it is like a first-time experience with anything. You still remember the occasion well and the memories that stay fresh in your mind: experiencing the International Dateline with the differences of dates, flying into a cold climate, looking down on the kapok clouds. That was my memory of arrival in the land of the long white cloud.

When I entered St Paul's in 1964, the real objective was to get me prepared for university and to brush up my English at the same time. Because I had plenty of free time, I devoted a lot of it to playing sport: rugby in winter, cricket in summer and chess in the evenings. However, my speciality was athletics. I ran in the 100 metres and 200 metres, the hurdles, and the hop, step and jump. All these are related. If you are a speedster you are able to participate in these related events. The St Paul's College 4 × 100 metre relay team at the inter-college athletics competition consisted of three Samoans – Norman McDonald, A. Reid and myself – and a Pākehā, Ross Pownall.[7]

During my school holidays at St Paul's I stayed with my elder sister in Ponsonby. I easily found work at local factories making good money to supplement my scholarship allowance. By September I had saved £200. Around that time a letter from my father came to the letterbox at my sister's home. Looking for news from home, I read the letter. My father wrote complaining that my sister had never sent any money home since she had arrived in New Zealand. After reading the letter I ripped it up. I knew how hard my sister and her husband were working, and how tough things were for them. I also knew that they sent what savings they had to his parents. I did not want my father's request to put more pressure on their household budget and relationship so I wrote to my father and asked him not to make any further requests of my sister for money and enclosed all my savings. My father used that money to build and stock a small village store that took care of their financial needs for the rest of their lives. My habit of working during the holidays and saving continued during my time at university. When I returned to Samoa, I had saved $4,000. I used that money to buy a two-acre section of land at Ululoloa for cash. At that time it was well out of town; now it is a suburb. This is where we built our family home and where we still live today with my family.

The University of Auckland

In 1965 I enrolled in the University of Auckland for a Bachelor of Commerce degree. I was told that I must pass all my subjects in my first year at Auckland or else my scholarship would be terminated because I was the seventh Commerce student from Samoa and the Samoan economy would only need one graduate in Commerce. We had too many. Many of my colleagues' scholarships were

---

7   Ross Pownall became a New Zealand champion hurdler. He represented New Zealand at the 1974 Commonwealth Games in Christchurch and in 1978 at Edmonton, Canada.

terminated during my time because of the perception that Samoa did not really need that many graduates in Commerce. Today, hundreds of Samoans are graduates in Commerce and we are still granting more scholarships in this field because there is no end to the growth of business and commerce as Samoa's economy continues to grow. We need people with the necessary training to build our human resources.

In my first year at the University of Auckland, the rigid conditions attached to my scholarship hung over my head like a sharp sword on a very thin string, reminding me constantly of my fate should I fail a subject in my first year. The harsh conditions of my scholarship haunted me as the last thought before I closed my eyes to sleep and the first thought when I woke up every morning. After I passed all my subjects in my first year, I finally accepted that my UE accreditation at St Joseph's in Samoa and my attendance at the University of Auckland were really not flukes.

I was lucky enough to be able to live at Newman Hall, a boarding house run by the Dominican priests, along with twenty other Catholic students. Newman Hall was only a few minutes' walk from the main campus of the University of Auckland. University life was an opportunity for me to learn the ways of Pākehā Kiwis and I easily made friends with lots of them. In 1967, John Uden, who studied Commerce with me and stayed at Newman Hall, invited me to spend a whole Christmas holiday with him at his family home in Putaruru.

I enjoyed working on his family's farm and then later as a forestry worker pruning trees during the 1967 Christmas holidays to earn good pocket money. I also became very active in the University of Auckland Catholic Students' Association and sat on its executive committee as treasurer. The president was Brian Lythe and the secretary Mary Dreaver. They later married. Brian was an MA graduate in Politics and became the University of Auckland counsellor for overseas students. He became a very close friend. We used to study together throughout the weekdays. He was a very humble man and I named my eldest son after him. Many Samoan students received tremendous help from Brian over the years as they struggled through their initial years of study.

I graduated with a Bachelor of Commerce in 1968 and took a further year to complete a Master of Commerce in 1969. It is fate. What I studied in Commerce had a very wide application. When I finished we were the last of the old degree before the University of Auckland reformed the degrees and they became specialist. Under the old system, there was Commercial Law, Company Law, Economics, Economic History, Statistics and Accounting.

Accounting was my major but I took Economics to the second stage. Many of the macro and micro components of economics had already been covered. So I had a pretty good grounding.

I did Politics as a minor, as an extra to my degree. I decided just to attend Politics lectures and listen very intently. What I wrote in the examination is what I got from the lecturer's mouth with very little extra research, and I passed. In Politics we covered the history of politics, mainly the essence of the division of power between the executive, the Judiciary and the legislators, and how the checks and balances in this system can effectively stop any abuse of power by one branch of government. We used a case study of the American Constitution as the basis of the course. At that time, I never had an inkling that I would become a politician where the knowledge of the science of Politics I studied at the University of Auckland would serve me well.

I had a very good grounding in Commerce, Economics and Politics at the University of Auckland. A broad education, not a narrow specialism. With my tertiary education completed, I flew back to Samoa in December 1969 to start my public service career as an Investigating Officer in the Treasury Department.

The boy from Lepā was coming home.

CHAPTER 3

O le Ala i le Pule le Tautua – The Road to Leadership

Tuila'epa Sa'ilele Malielegaoi's road to political leadership had two distinct paths: the path of *Fa'asamoa* and *tautua*, which has led to chiefly leadership; and the path of the *palagi* world of education, employment and public service, which has led to management, governance and leadership. These two paths have run in parallel, twisted, turned and eventually merged into political leadership.

In this chapter we will follow both these paths to see how Tuila'epa became a successful and respected leader in both the Samoan world and the world at large, and to learn about Tuila'epa's wife and family. We start with his early working life in Samoa then overseas in New Zealand and Europe, look at the events that led up to Tuila'epa's decision to enter politics, and consider the influence of the *Fa'asamoa* on his leadership style.

Early Working Life

Tuila'epa's formal education ended with his graduation with a Master's degree in Commerce from the University of Auckland and his return to Samoa to take up a position in 1970 as an Investigating Officer with the Treasury Department in Apia. Within a year he was promoted to Deputy Director of the Economic Development Department, and in the next decade he rapidly moved through the grades to become number two at the Treasury.

Before we take up the story of Tuila'epa's working life, we will go on a brief detour as Tuila'epa tells us how he met his wife and started his family.

I returned from New Zealand at the end of my studies in December 1969, and started my working career at the Treasury in early 1970. I can recall vividly that my very first day at work was also the day that Samoa was struck by its first airline disaster. A plane crashed into the sea killing everyone on board.

I went to a memorial church service at Mulivai Cathedral and I saw for the first time a woman who attracted my attention. I saw her again at another church service later where I noticed she sang in the choir at the Sunday morning services. To get to know her better, I decided to join the choir and sat on the bench directly behind her. I found that her name was Gillian Meredith and she worked at the Bank of Samoa. It was the only bank in Samoa in 1970.

At that time, accommodation for returning students and their families was hard to find in Apia. The only government apartments were taken up by returning students. Private accommodation was even scarcer. But I was fortunate to find a vacant apartment in a two-storey building at Moto'otua. I moved into my apartment in April 1970.

My one hobby was playing my guitar. Since attending the University of Auckland I practised every day. When I had nothing to do, I played my guitar and sang. Unknown to me, the sound of the music from my guitar and my voice carried to the other apartment residents. We were all under one roof. It was a lucky coincidence that one of the apartments was occupied by Gillian, her father and two brothers! Gillian's mother had passed away when she was a child.

For me, Gillian's proximity in the same building was a godsend. I had gone to all that trouble of joining the choir to be as close as possible to this lady and yet the Good Lord above had other plans to bring us together that were far easier than any human mind could fathom.

Most nights of the week, at around 9, I played my guitar outside the building as a way to draw Gillian from her hideout. It worked! But I knew her father and brothers were discreetly spying from behind their curtains. The couples in the other apartments, I found out, were also enjoying listening in to our informal musical performances, free of charge. We provided lullabies to send them to sleep after a stressful day at work.

In October 1972, we decided to marry. Samoan traditional weddings can be outrageously costly for the relatives of the bride and groom, particularly when the extended families are all participating. Weddings become an occasion to show off a family's wealth, whether in fine mats and or in cash. Gillian and I decided we would not allow our wedding to be an unnecessary burden on our parents and relatives. Her relatives were very wealthy, and it would have been a great embarrassment to my family if they could not match the value of the fine mats presented by her family and relatives. Money is the traditional responsibility of the bridegroom's family. My family was able to produce the fine mats, but not the cash.

It was a great relief when I finally told Gillian's father, Oscar Meredith, that Gillian and I had decided to marry. He consented to the marriage. Since

I would not have any invitees apart my own father and mother, it was agreed that Oscar would also reciprocate. It was so easy and simple. And since we would marry the following week, I would spend all my time preparing and we would not meet again until the morning of the wedding vows. Thus, any thoughts of changing the arrangements would be discouraged.

I had received notification that I had been accepted by the World Bank Economic Development Institute to go to Washington for a management workshop that included other senior officials of the World Bank members. Samoa was about to be accepted as the newest member of the World Bank and it was considered appropriate to invite a Samoan official from the Ministry of Finance to attend. I was due to leave in early 1973, which provided an excellent reason to Gillian's family, and the priest, for our visa applications to the United States and our wedding plans to go through smoothly so that I could undertake my training and, of course, we could go on our honeymoon without a problem.

The celebration of the mass for the wedding vows was fixed for the Moamoa Catholic church inland from Apia, not the Mulivai Cathedral, as we wanted a quiet wedding without publicity. Father Leamy, who later became Bishop of the Cook Islands, officiated at our wedding ceremony. The altar boys at Moamoa improvised as a choir and witnessed our wedding alongside our parents.

Our small wedding feast for about fifteen of our relatives was held at the residence of Oscar Meredith's cousin, Sam Meredith, in Alafua.

We now have a balanced family of eight children: four boys and four girls. They have produced twenty grandchildren. Gillian and I, with several of our children, are active members of our Catholic church choir at Siusega. One of our daughters is our choir instructor and pianist. Church music remains a passion for both Gillian and I. It was where our family world began and where it will also surely end.

We read much about the lives of many outstanding men and the good things they do, but often little is known about the part played by their wives. Behind the life of every man there is a remarkable woman, the wife who labours hard to take care of the family responsibilities so that the husband is free to fulfil a mission carved out for both of them. Yet she suffers as the husband suffers. She delights in the successes that her husband also celebrates. In times of disaster, she comforts and offers counsel that the husband knows come straight from the heart. In any memoir of one's life, it is an inexcusable omission not to acknowledge and thank your lifetime companion, the one who was always there beside you, every hour of every day, to the very end.

During this narrative we will see glimpses of Tuila'epa's private life and family. They are central to his story and, along with his strong Christian faith, are the foundations on which he built his successful career in the public service and later in politics. We now return to the story of his early working life.

I became an Investigating Officer with the Treasury when I returned from my studies in New Zealand. I came back to Samoa as a young technocrat. I was the only one with a Master of Commerce at the time. Working in the Treasury placed me in a strategic role that was valuable learning for my future posts as Minister of Finance and Prime Minister. I got an overall view of the functioning of all the ministries. Treasury was at the heart of government, and I was now in the heart of things. I very quickly became involved in policy. It fell on the head of the department and me to prepare reports for Cabinet on all sorts of issues, every week. Very often when my boss was out or overseas, I took charge of the Ministry. I was also introduced to managing a heavy workload which prepared me for much greater workloads later on.

The new government came in just after I kicked off at Treasury. Tupuola Efi was the Director of Public Works and he soon asked the Financial Secretary to transfer me from Treasury to be Acting Deputy Director for Public Works. That job meant I was like a personal secretary to young Minister Efi. He used to send me on errands.

I remember when he sent me to Savai'i to check up on the construction of plantation access roads at Saleaula. He told me that there was great dispute in the Cabinet as to whether to continue with the project of building plantation access roads. The government would hand out 800 Tala to a village and let them go and build the access roads themselves. Minister Efi asked me to go and see the construction of these particular roads for myself, to check up on roads in three other locations and to report back on the condition of the roads with my recommendations.

When I visited one particular road at Safa'i village, I found that people were building this road using crowbars and spades. They just dug the earth and piled it up at the centre of the road. But because there was no rock foundation you only had to drive your car on it and it sank. I came back and gave my report saying that the programme was useless. While the government had good intentions, no village could be expected to build durable access roads with bare hands, spades and bush knives. My report produced quite a sensation in Cabinet. The project had been going for ten years and now this young fellow was saying it was a waste of money and recommending that Cabinet terminate it.

Tupuola Efi called me one morning and said, 'Because of your report, the Prime Minister and Cabinet are all going to look at Safa'i Road. To see if what you said is true.'

I said, 'I think it is a good thing. They need to know why I made my recommendation.'

They went, came back and Tupuola Efi told me a beautiful story.

The Ministers had asked their drivers to speed up their cars, and because they were in a hurry and because the state of the road was so bad, the cars bumped up and down. The Prime Minister, Tupua Tamasese Lealofi IV, in particular got his head banged against the car's roof. When they came back, the decision-making was very fast. 'Terminate the bloody policy. The report is factual.'

So they ended funding village labour for the construction of plantation access roads.

I signed in at the Treasury every morning but spent all my time with Public Works as Acting Deputy Director. I was really doing two jobs. It did not take me long to see that I could not rise to further heights in the Public Works Department unless I was a qualified engineer. So I decided to leave and go back to Treasury.

One year after I had worked in Treasury, the Director of Economic Development, Hans Kruse, asked me to become his Deputy Director and within four weeks he had advertised the job in such a way that nobody else was qualified for it.

The Economic Development Department had Professor Panoff, a Professor of Economics, to advise us on economic development. He had taken two years' sabbatical leave from his job in Canada, and the United Nations sent him to Samoa. The professor was privy to all the goings on in the United Nations Development Programme (UNDP).

In 1973 the United Nations decided to terminate the job of Alistair Hutchison, who was then Financial Secretary, the Head of the Treasury. It was becoming too expensive for the United Nations to pay his annual salary.

Professor Panoff told me one day that there was a controversy in government: 'You better be prepared. The government has been told by the UNDP that they will terminate the salary they are paying to Alistair Hutchison to force him to go, so the job can be given to a local. The argument put forward by the government is that no one in Samoa is qualified. When we mentioned you, your government said that you are not ready. Under pressure from the UNDP they will now advertise a new post of Deputy Financial Secretary, Deputy to Alistair Hutchison, that will allow you to go across to Treasury.'

Alistair Hutchison came and spoke to me later about the government plans. What he did not know was that I already knew about the plans from Professor Panoff.

I went across to the Ministry of Finance in November 1973. In 1974 I decided that I needed to spend time at the New Zealand Treasury to get more experience before I could head the Treasury. So I waited.

During those years in Treasury I became very involved in high-level policy-making. Not many had that opportunity. I also took part in negotiations with the Asian Development Bank (ADB), the International Monetary Fund (IMF) and the World Bank. This international experience proved very valuable in the later years. Treasury was at the centre directing the progress of government. I enjoyed being at the centre but my career was stalled.

The year 1974 passed and nothing happened; 1975 passed and nothing happened. In 1976 Tupuola Efi became Prime Minister and decided that the Head of State should go on a world tour, and I was chosen to accompany the Head of State.

When I was told by Alistair Hutchison about that decision, I said, 'No, Alistair, you should accompany the Head of State along with the Minister of Finance. I must go to New Zealand to fulfil the promise made to me by the government.'

He agreed. I spoke to the New Zealand High Commissioner in Apia and I got the thumbs up to go to the New Zealand Treasury in September 1976.

Working and Living in New Zealand

In 1976 things in New Zealand were not good for Pacific Islanders. Some were being hunted down using dogs and deported as 'over-stayers'. This was all new to me. One day I was abused by old white men on a bus. They called me a 'nigger', and said, 'You should go back to where you came from.' I tried to keep calm.

After spending two weeks in government flats in Wellington, I needed to look for accommodation for my family. One day I saw a very small advertisement in the paper and I went to see the house, which was also very small. To me it was very nice, just right for my wife and two children.

I rang up the agent the following morning and she said, 'Oh yes, it's OK. It's been on the market for quite some time now. Do you want to go and have a look?'

I said that I had had a look and I would take it. She asked, 'What is your name?'

I gave her my name and spelled it out.

Then she said to me, 'Hang on, I need to check out something.'

She came back to the phone and said, 'Sorry, the house has been taken up already.'

I said, 'OK, that's alright.'

So I went to look for some more flats.

Two days later the same advertisement appeared. I rang up the same lady and I asked, 'This house that you have. Has it been taken by anybody?'

'No, no, no, nobody has taken it.'

'Oh, I see. Is it still available?'

'Oh yes, yes. It is still available.'

I said, 'I'm interested in the house.'

'Have you seen it?'

'Yes, I have seen it from the outside.'

She said, 'What is your name?'

I knew that my name struck an unwelcome chord.

I said, 'Don't worry, I will be there exactly at 9 o'clock tomorrow.'

I came off the phone and said to Gillian, 'Quick, quick, get my suit and have it ready.' The next morning I wore my suit, my tie, my polished shoes and I grabbed my briefcase. Anybody who saw me would think I was a young executive in some big corporation. I also had an umbrella and I took that with me. I walked to the bank, withdrew NZ$500, and packed my briefcase up with $2 notes.

At exactly 9 o'clock I walked into the office of the agent. I put my umbrella down. The lady behind the desk was just staring at me. I had my hair combed and I was exceptionally neat. I put my briefcase on the table and removed lots of papers so as to present the right image. I took out my wallet, which was so thick, and counted out $360, making sure she didn't see the twos.

And I said, '$360. Is that all you need?'

'Oh. No, no.' She was just dumbfounded. 'I, I, I . . .'

I said, 'Where do I sign? Where is your receipt book?'

'Here.' I took out my pen and wrote the sum down and signed it.

I said, 'Deal? Thank you very much. Thank you.'

She just stared at me. I took the keys and walked out.

After I closed the door I put my briefcase down and I laughed and laughed and laughed. We had got ourselves a house finally!

I soon found that there was no programme arranged for me at the New Zealand Treasury. I was more like a problem when I came in each morning. There was absolutely no programme. It didn't take me long to realise that what I had been doing in Samoa was at a much higher level. I was advising my government and when I came to New Zealand it was nothing of that sort, just pure clerical work. It was a complete waste of time – six months of useless training in New Zealand.

Finally, I went to Foreign Affairs and asked for my ticket back home. All I'd had to do was to fulfil the requirement that I spend time at the New Zealand Treasury. And I'd done my six months of apprenticeship.

I came back to Samoa in February 1977. Gillian was due to deliver our third child and she wanted badly for it to have New Zealand citizenship. I said, 'No, I'll go nuts if I spend another day here. My job is pointless and I just cannot stand the racist comments that I get on the streets.'

I was one of the victims of the racism during the Dawn Raids time. When we went up to Auckland for Christmas, I was refused service at the dining coach on the train. All I wanted was orange juice for my kids. I was furious.

Although my wife was only a couple of months away from delivering a child who could have been a New Zealand citizen, I said, 'No, we're going back to Samoa.'

Back to the Treasury

I was back in the Ministry of Finance in 1977. Tupuola Efi was voted in as Prime Minister and I was invited to a government reception he was to attend. I took a colleague from the Ministry of Finance with me, an adviser from the IMF who was an Indian. He gave me guidance and quite a lot of good tips on how to be resolute in my decision-making; and he said that I should stand up and be counted, that I should never be timid when facing Europeans. This guy gave me quite a lot of insight into management practices. Because of our special relationship five years before, when I'd worked for him, I considered the new Prime Minister more than a friend.

Tupuola Efi had finished meeting all the people who had marched up to him, and was now standing there alone. I thought that this was my time to introduce my IMF adviser. I walked up and said, 'Prime Minister.' He looked at me.

I gestured towards my colleague. 'Can I introduce to you my friend?' He just turned his back and walked away and went and talked to the other VIPs. He completely ignored me! That was the beginning of my insight into the real character of this man. I was very embarrassed. This high official of the IMF just looked at me, shocked!

I said, 'I am sorry, my friend. Apparently we are ignored by the Prime

Minister, both you and me. I was wrong. I thought he was my friend.'

So we walked away and that was the first time that I had seen Tupuola Efi very clearly. I decided I would revise the way I would approach him in the future.

Now that I was back, I was looking forward to my promotion to head Treasury. By the end of 1977, nothing had happened. Midway through 1978, nothing had happened. I decided to resign from the public service.

Twelve months before I had put my name in for a job at the newly established African Caribbean and Pacific Secretariat in Brussels. I had been attending meetings with my Minister in Brussels so I knew that jobs were available.

I went to Alistair Hutchison and said to him, 'I recall our meeting in 1973 when you came and asked me to shift over from the Economic Development Department to the Treasury because you said you would resign the following year. Cabinet decided that I had to go to New Zealand and work in the Treasury to get some experience. I have done that and I have come back and the status quo still remains. It's either you or me! And I have decided to resign from government. I will give two weeks' notice.'

Alistair apologised to me. His actual words were: 'Oh Tui, I have come to love the place. I still remember my promise. But I have grown to love Samoa.'

Alistair was an exceptional workaholic and I marvelled at the way he worked. In fact I got a lot of good training from him. So really, I thought, I had better leave him to the job. He had been working his guts out in the service of our government and he had been a great asset to Samoa. I had great respect for Alistair. I had decided that I would resign and join the private sector. I was thinking of forming my own public office as a chartered accountant and public auditor. I even saw the head of Polynesian Airlines, an old friend of mine – we were both graduates of the University of Auckland – and I asked him to join me and he agreed on a business partnership.

Off to Belgium

Two days later, out of the blue, I had a job offer. The ACP Appointments Committee had met in Brussels and gone through their job applications. The chairman of the committee was a fellow I was with at the workshop of the Economic Development Institute of the World Bank in 1973 and we had done our fieldwork together in Seoul, South Korea. He saw my name amongst the applicants. To the surprise of all the Pacific ambassadors on the committee, he said, 'I want this man. We should engage him. He is good. I know him.'

So it was a complete surprise. Several days after I resigned from my post in Samoa, I got a cable from the ACP Secretariat offering me a job. Could I come to Brussels with my wife and my children? The answer was yes. So I had to see my accountant friend again and tell him that our proposed partnership was off and I was going to Belgium.

I was about to formally leave Treasury when Alistair said to me, 'You know, I think it would be better if you took leave without pay, in case you want to come back to government.' It was a great piece of advice.

Samoa is a small place. Whenever I appeared at meetings with the Prime Minister, Tupuola Efi, I came with Treasury's strong views. I often questioned decisions by the Prime Minister. When financial policies were under discussion, I put my observations forward on suggestions that did not sound right to me, and I became a marked man. Tupuola Efi believed that anybody who expressed an adverse opinion to his views was deliberately against him, his person, his government and his policies. He had that weakness, which became his downfall.

Tupuola Efi did not know that I had many, many friends in the service. He would confide in people, saying, 'You know that young upstart, Tuila'epa? I swear I will never make him head of the Treasury.'

So I knew all along that I would not make it to the top while Efi was Prime Minister. I had to look for another place for advancement.

When I departed for Brussells, I left a letter with the Public Service Commission letting them know that I wanted to go on extended leave without pay. But to me, I was leaving for good.

I left with my family, thinking that I would never go back. That was my intention. The work at the ACP Secretariat in Brussels was very interesting. It expanded my understanding of the economies of developing nations and I gained new knowledge, extended my skills and developed a wide range of international contacts. All these would prove valuable in later years.

In 1979, about December, I got a cable message in Brussels. It said that the Minister of Finance, the Honourable Vaovasamanaia Filipo, would like to see me if I could fly to Yugoslavia to attend a meeting of the World Bank and the IMF. The Minister would be there with Alistair Hutchison and they had something to talk to me about.

So I took leave and went to Yugoslavia to meet them.

They both informed me that the Samoan economy was in deep trouble and they needed me to come back to Treasury. Alistair would leave Treasury and I would take over the moment I arrived. Remember that I had heard this before. Once bitten, twice shy. I was alert. Alarm bells began to ring in my ears. So I told them the usual, 'OK, let me think about it.'

I went back to Samoa at the end of 1980. I had got a renewal of my contract already at the ACP for three years. In fact, because of my involvement in budgetary reforms, the head of the ACP had asked me to become Chief of Finance. This was a big promotion. But I had already made up my mind that I would accept the offer by the Minister to become Financial Secretary in Samoa. Besides, my parents had started to pester me that all my sisters were now in New Zealand and they needed my help. Gillian was also continually pestered by her father to return. So we decided that we would return to Samoa.

Return to Paradise?

I came back. The deal was that Alistair Hutchison would resign and I would head Treasury.

The moment I landed in Samoa and started work, Fatialofa Momoe, the MP for Lepā, died. People erroneously thought that I had come back especially for the funeral. Fatialofa was buried on 2 January 1981. I thought, now I have an insurance policy: if the Treasury deal does not go through, I will have to face Tupuola Efi in politics.

I waited for my promotion, knowing that the Prime Minister was not going to be supportive.

Mr Hutchison said to me, 'I have already resigned as discussed. Has the Minister spoken to you?'

I said, 'No.'

He said, 'Why don't you see him and persuade him to make the decision now?'

'Alistair', I said, 'I am a professional. If I become Financial Secretary, I want to become a Financial Secretary in my professional right. If I go and talk politics to him, that does not seem right to me. Let him, in his own good time, make a decision.'

That was January 1981. Besides, I began to raise questions in my own mind. Why delay? Was there a change of mind? Then in March the public servants went on strike.

Just prior to the strike the Minister had asked me to accompany him to a council meeting of the ACP to be held in Belgium. I had worked at the ACP as an expert in trade, commerce and transport, and I had numerous friends in Brussels. I went with him.

Part of my assignment, after the meeting of the ministers in Belgium, was to go to Luxembourg, where a meeting of the parliamentarians of the European Union and the ACP was to be held. So we went there. It was essential that I negotiate with a Mr Muller, who was in charge of STABEX, a stabilisation fund set up to help moderate the decline in exports of ACP countries. In Samoa we were so weak financially that we were virtually bankrupt. We badly needed an advance from the stabilisation fund.

In Samoa in those days all the imported meat we had was rubbish: like the bones of poultry, and chicken and turkey tails, as well as mutton flaps. The best parts had already been removed. These were the only kinds of things we could afford to import and that was what we were eating. The shop shelves were completely empty. For six months in 1981, Samoa ran out of cigarettes for the puffers! People at the Department of Public Works, the labourers, would come in the morning, sign in and loaf about for the whole of the day because there was nothing to do. There was absolutely no money available for public works. The government was borrowing heavily from the banks and was heavily in debt to the suppliers.

Tupuola Efi refused to believe that a government could go bankrupt. He refused to put in revenue measures. That was seen as being too dangerous for the upcoming election campaign. That was the situation when the public servants put in their requests for a salary increase, which the government rejected outright for the simple reason: there was no money in the budget. And the government was in no mood to raise taxes and Customs duties to fund any kind of salary increases. The real culprit was the outdated salaries review system in use. It took years to complete a regrading cycle, and by then there was pressure for another review.

When the protest occurred, Vaovasamanaia Filipo and I were in Luxembourg trying to negotiate the release of STABEX funds. We had a claim for €1.5 million in STABEX funds at that time. I had communicated with the Financial Secretary in Apia that all we needed to do was to get Muller to agree to a specific amount. Then Alistair could negotiate a loan with the European American Bank in New York. We were in such a bad state that even securing a US$600,000 loan was a problem. We negotiated and negotiated, and finally Mr Muller said, 'You will get a least €750,000, half of the 1.5 million.'

I took out a blank piece of paper, wrote on it and gave it to him. It said: 'I, Mr Muller, confirm that Samoa is entitled to a drawdown from the STABEX fund of €750,000 you claimed.'

Muller signed it.

I sent that confirmation by cable to Samoa and Alistair was able to get a

US$600,000 loan from the American-European Bank in New York to keep the economy going. The economy was so bad that even when we needed to remit US$20,000 to replenish our bank account in New York for our Embassy, it took about three weeks before we could find the US$20,000 equivalent.

Meanwhile the protest was on.

Alistair Hutchison sent us a message on the PSA protest which read, 'Honourable Minister, the strike is on. We think it will be temporary. The good news is nobody in the Treasury participated and it should end in the next few days.'

When we arrived back in Samoa, seven days later, Alistair said that he was flying to Australia on urgent business related to the strike. He took off. I then summoned the Assistant Financial Secretary, Afoa Kolone, to update me on the strike. The number of people who were participating in the strike was increasing. It went on for three months.

Afoa Kolone told me that the situation was out of hand. The government saw no need to negotiate. I went to see the Minister and I took Kolone with me as a witness. I knew then what I would do. I would leave Treasury in two days' time. In two days' time the nominations for Parliament would be closed. I needed to put my name in and terminate my engagement as a public servant.

When I saw the Minister I said, 'We have just got back from Brussels. We got a note that the strike could be finished by the time we got back.' Afoa told me that more and more public servants were joining in. I went on to say, 'The whole problem with the public service is money. The appropriate ministry that should handle it is us, here in Treasury. It has been handled by the Minister of the Public Service Commission. He knows nothing about finance. Why don't you shift the problem over so that it becomes my responsibility? I, and my officers, will study it and come up with a resolution. Perhaps offer a 2 percent, 3 percent or 5 percent rise? Make them happy to come back and serve the country.'

The Minister said to me, 'Tui, we will never do that. Cabinet has decided it will make the public servants crawl back on their tummies. You know a hungry Samoan will do that.'

I said, 'Well, I have said what I have to say. I have to leave now.'

O le Ala i le Pule le Tautua

Entering Politics

I left. That was Monday.

Tuesday and Wednesday passed. I summoned two of my colleagues from Lepā to come to my home.

I told them: 'Tomorrow, I will put my nomination in and terminate my employment. I will enter Parliament. I will become a politician.'

They were very happy.

Five minutes before 12, the time when nominations were due to close, I entered the gate. They then closed the gate and I paid my nomination fee. Then I went to my Minister's residence.

When I walked in, Vaovasamanaia was standing on the porch.

I said, 'We both had an excellent trip overseas, but I have to see you again.'

He replied, 'What is it?'

'I came here to say to you that today I have resigned from government. I will now contest the election in my constituency of Lepā.'

He was shocked into silence. He was standing there still holding my hand then he asked me one question: 'Did anyone from the HRPP push you?'

I said, 'No. For your information, I took Politics as an extra subject when I was doing my Master's degree at the University of Auckland. So my interest in politics predates the existence of the HRPP.'

He said, 'I am sorry, Tui. I have not fulfilled my promise to you. But you know, with so many problems I forgot about it. We had the strike.'

I knew in my own mind it was not he who had made the decision. It would have been the Prime Minister, Tupuola Efi. All the words he had said when he vowed and declared that he would never make me head of the Treasury were quite alive in my mind.[1]

Vaovasamanaia said to me, 'Can I suggest you withdraw your nomination and I will make you head of Treasury tomorrow?'

I laughed. 'Are you serious? You know, Vaovasa, that you are a professional, a lawyer, and I am a professional man too, an accountant. When a professional makes a very, very in-depth decision, there is no going back. I have crossed the river Rubicon.'

That is what I said: 'I have crossed the River Rubicon. There is no turning back.'

He replied, 'Rest assured, if you miss out in this election I will make you the head of the Treasury.'

---

1   At the time Tuila'epa was very frustrated at not achieving his ambition to head Treasury. Today, he sees it as a blessing because, if he had become head of Treasury in 1979 or earlier, he probably would not have run for Parliament in 1981 and had a political career.

Tupuola's contacts were very strong in my district. Tupuola decided to back another high talking chief against me, another Fatialofa, who was in Tupuola's pocket. In fact, in my district no Fatialofa had ever been defeated in a general election until I decided to challenge him, and I defeated that Fatialofa.

Lepā is my village. Saleapāga is in my constituency. But my mother comes from 'A'ufaga, where I now hold the title of Lupesoli'ai. All the villages met. I am talking about seven villages. We met and then they started giving speeches.

One chief said, 'Fatialofa will run.'

Then Saleapāga proposed, 'Our candidate is Sogimaletavai.'

Lolofie said, 'Our candidate will become the MP for our district.'

Everyone looked at him. He spoke with so much authority they were wondering who he was talking about.

Then he said, 'I want to make a special announcement that our son, Tuila'epa, who has been in the upper echelon of the Treasury and who has spent years in Belgium, has returned to run for Parliament in our district.'

There was absolute silence, absolute silence.

Then the chairman said, 'Fatialofa, 'Auelua, we had better defer the decision. There is one more chief who has not made it to this meeting, Faolotoi. Faolotoi needs to be here.'

That was Saturday, so they deferred the decision for the next meeting.

I was about to jump into my car and drive back to Apia when a little girl nudged me and said, "Auelua Tufi wants to talk to you.'

So I went to 'Auelua and asked, 'What do you want?'

He said to me, 'Are you serious?'

'Yes, I am serious.'

'And which party are you going to run for?'

'I am sympathetic to the HRPP, but I have to run as an independent to confuse the government. They have so many supporters with money, particularly the McKenzies, who are related to my family Fatialofa. They have been backing Fatialofa and I am sure that Prime Minister Tupuola Efi will pour out money to try and defeat me.'

He said, 'I am happy to learn that you will run for the HRPP.'

He told me that Fatialofa Alaifatu had been backed by Tupuola.

The late Fatialofa was my cousin. We are all related and Faolotoi is his older brother. The old man, 'Auelua Tufi, who knew everything, said, 'Last week Efi promoted Faolotoi to be head of the branch at the Samoa Trust Estates Corporation (STEC), dealing with timber. He did that to defeat you, and to provide support for Fatialofa Alaifatu.' He went on to say, 'I will get all our family to vote for you and tell Fatialofa not to run. This is the time for you, our young son who has been educated. It is not a comfortable position for us old men in the village to run for these kinds of posts.'

I was so happy. Then he told me that Fatialofa's son, who was a driver for the hospital, came with trucks and trucks of beer and had parties with our village young men. He was backing his father to back up Tupuola Efi.

'Auelua said, 'I am happy that you are going to oppose the government.'

He was a cousin of Tofilau 'Eti Alesana who was also in the HRPP.

So that was Saturday. Sunday, Monday.

I decided to pay a visit to my cousin Faolotoi Vaalele. Here in town.

I went to Faolotoi and asked him, 'Old man, why didn't you turn up at the meeting?'

He replied, 'Oh Tui, I forgot all about it. Why didn't you come and pick me up?'

I said, 'I did not want to interfere with your freedom of decision-making.'

'I forgot all about it. What happened at our district meeting?'

'Well, there are three candidates.'

'Who are they?'

'The first one is Fatialofa Alaifatu, backing the government. The second one comes from Saleapāga. The third one is a candidate from Lealetele, our village.'

'Who is that?'

'Me.'

There was silence for a long time.

After a considerable pause he said to me, 'You know, cousin, I thought that you would bide your time. This is only a stand-in to continue the term of my late brother. So another Fatialofa should continue until the end of December. When we come to the general election, it's your turn.'

I said, 'Sorry, Uncle, I have to run this time.'

There is that great saying in Samoa: 'If you defer, there can only be two events: either you will be whacked by oncoming rain, or you could be bashed up by the villagers for wrongdoing.'

'It's my time. Sorry.'

He remained silent. He never spoke to me again.

I said, 'I have to go now. Thank you.' I saw that he was in pain.

That was Monday. Tuesday, Wednesday. Thursday, a cousin of mine arrived from the village.

She said, 'I have just been at the hospital to visit Faolotoi.'

'What?'

'I went to see Faolotoi. Apparently he suffered some strange illness after you left on Monday. It must have been something you talked about.'

'You had better go and visit him again.'

'I will go tomorrow as I have an engagement tonight.'

At 7 o'clock the next morning I woke up. That was in the days when we had messages sent through the radio. I heard this bell ringing signalling a funeral message. It was very short. 'This is the message for our family in Lepā. Please prepare our *fale*. We are bringing the body of Faolotoi, who died last night.'

It was so strange that when I arrived home from Belgium, Fatialofa died. And when I decided to run for Parliament his elder brother died too. To me it seemed to be some kind of omen. To me it seemed that the way was clear for me to run and that there would be no opposition to my aspirations. It now seems to me to be a very stupid way of thinking, but two men did indeed die on my run for politics.

There were two candidates against me. My victory was a landslide. That indicated the great trust that my people had in me right throughout the village. The family of Tuila'epa is filled with people who have direct relatives in Saleapāga. It was inevitable that I would win.

The Path of the Fa'asamoa

Throughout his life Tuila'epa has travelled down the path of the *Fa'asamoa* from village child to high chief. Growing up in the village of Lepā, the child named Sa'ilele learned to serve the elders of his family, extended family and village community. As a *taule'ale'a*, an untitled man, Sa'ilele belonged to the *'aumāga* of Lepā and served the village *fono*. This path of service ultimately led to him receiving the chiefly titles of Tuila'epa, Fatialofa, 'Auelua, Lupesoli'ai, Neioti, Ai'ono, Galumalemana and Lolofietele.

Even though he has been based in Apia for much of his life, and has been successful in education and employment, Tuila'epa has always maintained his connections to the village communities that raised him. To this day, Tuila'epa maintains a house in Lepā and regularly participates in the village *fono*, contributing to family and village *fa'alavelave* (occasions such as funerals and weddings).

Samoan chiefly titles are not determined solely through inheritance and birth-right, as in the primogeniture of the British royal family. The maxim, *O le ala i le pule le tautua* (the way to authority is through service), guides the selection of Samoan leaders. Potential *matai* must have the requisite *gafa* (genealogy), but must also have served their families well and have demonstrated leadership and wisdom in village and family affairs. The young Sa'ilele continued to serve his family and village communities and, over time, this *tautua* was recognised by the bestowal of chiefly titles.

All Samoans claim a place of belonging, a place that gives them identity. *O Samoa ua taoto, ao se i'a mai moana, aua o le i'a a samoa ua uma ona 'aisa*, Samoa is like an ocean fish divided into sections, reads a well-known Samoan proverb, which refers to the custom of dividing up a fish for distribution and the ordering of the lands and titles of the Samoan Islands.

Samoa is made up of eleven *itūmālō* (political districts) that were established well before European arrival. Each district has its own constitutional foundation (*fa'avae*) based on the traditional order of title precedence found in each district's *fa'alupega* (record of traditional salutations). The capital village of each district administers and coordinates the affairs of the district and confers each district's paramount title. The *itūmālō* are further subdivided into 41 *faipule* districts.

Land and identity are closely intertwined in the Samoan world.

Matai titles are specific to villages and districts, and the bestowal of titles on local leaders establishes their identity and identifies the lands that are their responsibility, consolidating the reciprocal relationships that are central to the *Fa'asamoa*. The structure of Samoan society is set out in the *fa'alupega*, a list of *matai* titles and ceremonial greetings, recited from memory when chiefs meet. Formal greetings acknowledge the title, rank, village and connection between those present, linking them with their mutual ancestors. The *fa'alupega* has been committed to print but is still principally an oral record, held in the memories of *tulafale,* and subject to debate and disputation.

Samoan society is hierarchical and communal. In 1892 Robert Louis Stevenson observed: 'They [Samoans] are Christians, church goers, singers of hymns at family worship, hardy cricketers . . . We have passed the feudal system; they are not clear of the patriarchal. We are in the thick of the age of finance; they are in a period of communism. And this makes them hard to understand.' Over a century later Samoa has entered the modern age of finance and globalisation but it has continued to maintain its communal foundations.

The Samoan Constitution is a blend of the Westminster parliamentary system and elements of the *Fa'asamoa*. *Matai* suffrage was established at independence, with only *matai* able to stand for Parliament and vote. Today, universal suffrage is in place but only *matai* may stand for Parliament. Gaining a *matai* title, and fulfilling their cultural obligations, are essential prerequisites for aspiring politicians. As a consequence, Samoan politicians learn and hone their leadership skills in their village communities before seeking selection for candidacy and election to Parliament. MPs must remain actively connected with their communities and involved in traditional service to their village (*monotaga*) to ensure that their local vote is secure.[2]

Tuila'epa recalls the advice he was given by his father in 1975 when he was conferred with his first title.

There are two steps to the conferring of the title. First the drinking of the *'ava* that indicates the family has agreed. That comes after long hours of talking. As soon as they all agree, it may be two, three or four hours. In my case most of the talking had been done beforehand, so it only took one hour. It was done in Apia, not in my village. The first part is not the important part. The occasion was important because one of the older untitled men in the family wanted to be conferred with a title also. But the older members of my family said, 'No. It will only be one that day.' I was given the title Tuila'epa and the final rites were conferred about two weeks later at Lepā, where all the rites must be performed.

At the end of the *saofa'i*, when it was just me and my dad, Malielegaoi Veni, he said to me, 'Now that you are a *matai*, listen to me very carefully, son. You must learn the full elements that make a chief a chief. You should first of all learn to joke. Learn to joke and engage in humour, debate and exchange. If you are able to do that, you will become the most influential speaker in the house of the chiefs, because you will entertain. You will entertain the full council with stories, with things that will make them laugh and lighten up any situation, especially when many of the discussions the council will have will involve heated debate and there will often be disputes that cause arguments and bad relationships between chiefs. But if you have that art, if you develop that art of making up funny stories that will lighten the burden of differences and make people very happy, you can influence the way you want the debate to go. After that, for the second part, you learn how to deliver a suitable Samoan speech, Samoan style. The third part of being a Samoan chief is to know the genealogy, the *gafa*, between our village and other villages. In that way you have a weapon with you that you can use to silence any opposing speaker. Members of a family should never conduct their business with formal speaking. If you are able to establish the genealogy between two villages, you can also say, "When I come, you

---

2   In the 2016 general election, several aspiring MPs were prevented from running for office due to their failure to demonstrate *monotaga*, including one candidate who was attempting to run against Prime Minister Tuila'epa in Lepā.

receive me with open arms without speeches because you are part of my family and of my village." To prove the point, you provide the genealogy.'

That is why a Samoan *matai* is very likely to be very powerful speaker on Samoan issues. So when a *matai* is good at English, he can also become a very good speaker, a good orator. When a *matai* becomes a good orator, his knowledge of internal politics is very good. Which is why Samoans who go to New Zealand often want to stand for a seat in Parliament there.

Malielegaoi Veni reminded his son that humility is at the heart of the *Fa'asamoa* and passed on to him an old Samoan saying for guidance: *E le taua le tofi, ae taua le fa'amaoni* (It is not the status or the position that is important, it is your ability to work hard, do good and serve others). The lessons Tuila'epa's father gave his son over 40 years ago have stayed with him. Tuila'epa's use of humour, his marshalling of facts, his ability to deliver a coherent speech in the Samoan style and his humility, gained through *fa'amatai*, have underpinned his political career.

Throughout his long career, Tuila'epa has been very mindful of maintaining his political base by connecting and balancing the affairs of the state with the affairs of his village. Maintaining this balance has kept him grounded and connected to his community, and has ensured that his decision-making and leadership remain relevant to village life. It has also ensured that he is re-elected.

Tuila'epa Sa'ilele Malielegaoi has met with the Queen of England, had audiences with the Pope, talked over global affairs with the President of the United States of America, and addressed the United Nations General Assembly and Security Council, but at heart he remains a village *matai* from Lepā.

Tuila'epa's detailed knowledge of the *fa'alupega*, *fa'amatai* and the *Fa'asamoa*, in relation to Lepā and the district of Ātua, has been the foundation of his political career.

I always make fun when I talk about my profession. My political district comprises three villages: Lepā, 'A'ufaga and Saleapāga. [He sketches a map on paper for the benefit of his listener.] My father was born here (Lepā). My mother comes from here ('A'ufaga). I used to joke, I love my father for not seeking far and wide for a partner. By just popping over the border and grabbing my mother, it meant that my future in politics would be secure.

There were times in my earlier career when Saleapāga would put up a candidate. There would be two candidates from here (Lepā), me and one from here ('A'ufaga). Sometimes there would be only two candidates: me and someone from here (Saleapāga). I always carry two villages because of my mother. I am a *matai*, a high chief from 'A'ufaga. That is where my Lupesol'ai comes from. It is both an *ali'i* and *tulafale* title, called a *tulafale-ali'i*, which means that you are both a high chief and an orator at the same time.

Tuila'epa illustrates where the centre of his political strength resides.

The highest orator titles here [Lepā] are Fatialofa and 'Auelua. The Fatialofa and Tuila'epa titles come from Lepā. Tuila'epa is in Lepā.

Lepā itself is divided in three sub-villages: Vaigalu, Lepā proper and Lealetele. From this village [Lealetele] I hold the Tuila'epa title.

The Ai'ono title – that's another story. That's my grandfather. My grandfather comes from the Ai'ono family who married the daughter of Neioti. And the offspring were my father and his sister. So all the other titles belong to Lepā, but not the Ai'ono part, on my father's mother's side.

Lepā is where I hold the two high orator titles. Fatialofa was conferred on me in 2010, and 'Auelua conferred on me in December 2014. With these two titles it is very difficult for anyone to stand against me.

In 2016 Tuila'epa won the Lepā constituency for the tenth time and his election was uncontested.

Tuila'epa again uses a hand-drawn map to illustrate where the Neioti title fits into the political geography of the *Fa'asamoa*.

You see when I travelled to Apia I would come from Lepā. This would be the route I'd take . . . and continue onto Falealili and in those days catch the bus to Apia. Alternatively, I could cut inland and pass though Falevao to Falefa and catch the bus. As you can see, people who come from my village to Apia could come through here, or come through there. All along the way they have always made friends, and right now we have relatives here and here. And the only reason that they get intermarried is because they are on the routes of our travel to Apia and back. The Neioti title comes from Falevao.

The *fa'alupega* may set out the list of *matai* titles, village by village, district by district, but it does not contain details of the stories and history of titles. These are held in the memories of *tulafale*. Orators have the responsibility of holding the oral histories of their village lands and titles and passing them onto the next generation of orators. They also need to know the interconnections between their lands and titles and others' lands and titles. But human memory is not perfect and at times it may be selective. In the past, warfare could ensue when debates about lands and titles could not be resolved within or between 'āiga. Today, disputes may be referred to the Land and Titles Court for resolution. This frequently happens if the bestowal of *matai* titles is contested.

Tuila'epa tells the story of one such conflict related to his Neioti title. To understand how that conflict was resolved, he goes back over a thousand years to the origins of the name Neioti.

The story goes like this. There was a Leutele who was the King of Ātua. One day his nephew arrived from Eastern (later American) Samoa, Pago Pago, and he walked straight through the village when they were having a big meeting. Which was an offence.

The order was issued: 'Kill the fellow! He is being impudent.'
This young man yelled out to Leutele, 'You are my uncle.'
Leutele replied, 'Oh sorry, don't kill him.'
That's how the name of the title came about: *Nei oti*, don't kill him.
And then, when Leutele found out about Neioti, he said to him, 'Nephew, there is one weakness in my kingdom, and the weakness is the pass at Falevao. You will take these men and you will reside inland. Your duty is to protect that pass, it is the weakest point in my government. And when you want to see me, this *matai* shall be your messenger. His title is Malaga (meaning journey). I also have a Malaga; he is my messenger to you. Whatever you want, send Malaga over; whatever I want I will send my Malaga over to you.'

That ancient story was used to resolve a contemporary conflict. Tuila'epa continues.

There was another Leutele who died some years ago, Keli Tuatagaloa. Some years ago that Leutele tried to confer *matai* titles in Falevao. And I said no. So we ended up in the Land and Titles Court.

Leutele said, 'I am the *pule* (the authority) over all.'
I said, 'No, that *pule* is dedicated to the nephew Neioti. The holder of the Neioti title [currently Tuila'epa] is the authority.'
Several pieces of evidence emerged at that court hearing. Leutele's messenger was called Malaga; my messenger was called Malaga. His lady, who officially performed the *'ava*, was Sailau. And my *taupou*, the village woman performing this task, was Sailau. My designated residence was in Falefa, but he did not have a residence in Falevao. The residence in Falefa was conferred on me by Leutele a thousand years ago when this proclamation was

made. It is called Laeimau.

In the court Leutele was asked: 'If he is not your relative, then how come he has a messenger *matai* title called Malaga and you have a Malaga?'

'I don't know', he replied.

'What about the *taupou* Sailau? He also has a *taupou* of the same name.'

'I don't know.'

The third question, and this is very strange because no *matai* has a residence in another village, was 'He has a residence in the village Falefa, your village, do you know about it?'

'Yes, I know about it . . .'

'Doesn't that tell you that there is a relationship between you and him?'

'No, there is no relationship', Leutele replied.

The court went into recess and when the judge came back he said: 'Things just don't happen coincidentally like this: there is a reason. And the reason is that the title Neioti [which Tuila'epa holds] is related to the title of Leutele.'

Tuila'epa later commented:

In fact, Leutele and Neioti are closely related. Neioti is from Falevao, next to Falefa where Leutele is from. But Neioti has the *pule* for titles from Falevao. So I won the court case, and all the titles he created were dissolved.

That was the decision. He didn't like it but later on, because Keli worked with me many years ago, we still had a bond, a connection. When he died I went and made a traditional presentation.

Tuila'epa's stories about titles carry multiple meanings reflecting the historical knowledge and metaphorical rhetoric of a skilled Samoan orator chief. This story illustrates Tuila'epa's clarity about the necessity to reconcile and heal a relationship following conflict. Reconciliation is deeply ingrained into the *Fa'asamoa*, and throughout Tuila'epa's political career we can see many examples of when reconciliation was sought and given. Tuila'epa's deep knowledge of *fa'amatai*, immersion in *Fa'asamoa*, and command of the *fa'alupega* and *tautua* to his villages have been stepping stones to his success as a politician in Samoa and given him confidence in the *palagi* world.

O le Ala i le Pule le Tautua

The Path of the Fa'apalagi

Contrary to anthropological evidence, Samoan history contains no tradition of migration from some other place to the Samoan Islands. *Samoa* may literally be translated as the sacred (*sa*) centre (*moa*). Samoans say they come from Samoa. When the European explorers arrived the Samoans called them *papalagi* (sky bursters) because they had literally arrived from outer space. In the two hundred years of contact, Samoan society and the *Fa'asamoa* have been subject to the impact of whalers, traders, blackbirders, missionaries, colonial administrators, development experts, transnational corporations and many outside agencies. In spite of these influences, the *Fa'asamoa* remains strong. Perhaps one of the greatest strengths of the *Fa'asamoa* has been its ability to absorb outside influences without diluting its fundamental nature.

Whilst acknowledging changes and adaptations of the *Fa'asamoa*, in the same breath, Samoans will say that it is unchanging. The continuity and flexibility of the *Fa'asamoa* give it strength and longevity. The *Fa'asamoa* seamlessly links the children of Samoa today to Tagaloa in the past, providing them with meaning, a place of belonging and a map for the future.

The process of modernisation, which has driven much of the social and economic development in Samoa, has encouraged Samoans to embrace the new and reject the past. As the English historian A.N. Whitehead noted, 'The major advances in civilization are processes that all but wreck the societies in which they occur.'[3] Unlike many other nations, the traditional society in Samoa was not completely wrecked by the advance of civilisation. The *Fa'asamoa* provides an echo of what was, and a sign of what may be.

Rather than acting as Adam Smith's 'dead hand of tradition', the *Fa'asamoa* is a living culture, adapting to the modern world, enabling Samoan people to create their own meaning and development. The *Fa'asamoa* provides the people of Samoa with a structure and process that enables them to negotiate with the agents of development and make their own judgements about what developments are in their best interests.

All Samoans, living in the modern world, have a double inheritance and have to learn to negotiate the complexities and confusions, excitements and joys of living in two worlds.

Tuila'epa has successfully negotiated the world of the *Fa'asamoa* and has been honoured with a string of chiefly titles. He has also successfully negotiated the *fa'apalagi*, the European world, completing Bachelor's and Master's degrees in Commerce at the University of Auckland, working as

---

3 See Whitehead, 1927.

an expert in trade, transport and communications at the ACP Secretariat in Brussels, qualifying as a chartered accountant and a partner for Coopers and Lybrand, and holding senior financial management roles in the Samoan public service before embarking on his political career.

Tuila'epa Sa'ilele Malielegaoi was awarded a Doctorate in Laws, *honoris causa*, from Victoria University of Wellington in 2012 in recognition of his achievements in Samoa, the Pacific region and the world at large. The following extract from the citation summarises Dr Tuila'epa's achievements.

Tuila'epa has been Prime Minister of Samoa for fourteen years and has maintained his popular mandate through three elections. In this position he has presided over the most politically and economically stable and successful small democratic country in the Pacific. He is, quite simply, the most successful, the most eminent, and the most popular democratically elected politician in the Pacific.

He is notable for a number of initiatives, including his direct involvement in the shaping of Samoa's strategy to develop as a destination for tourists, his leadership in the liberalisation of the Samoan economy, promotion of the private sector, his instigation of Samoa's accession to the World Trade Organization. He has also provided personal leadership on promoting education as part of Samoa's development path (including the National University of Samoa, the Scientific Research Organisation of Samoa and the Oceania University of Medicine, all of which are located in Apia) and addressing Samoa's health problems and social and economic development.

In the Pacific region, Prime Minister Tuila'epa is recognised as a senior statesman. He has attracted a number of regional organisations to Samoa, and has been the leading advocate for regional approaches to a wide range of political, security, education and resource management issues.

2012 is the 50th anniversary of Samoan independence. Scholars and students from VUW have had a major hand in shaping Samoan independence, and VUW is now embarking on an important new generation of initiatives with Samoa that will ensure that our profile in Samoa is ahead of that of any other New Zealand university. We believe that it would be appropriate to mark the anniversary of Samoan independence, and the importance of that relationship to VUW, by awarding an honorary doctorate to Samoa's most outstanding contemporary politician and leader.[4]

Grounded in the *Fa'asamoa* and successful in the *fa'apalagi*, Tuila'epa Sa'ilele

4   See Victoria University of Wellington, 2012.

O le Ala i le Pule le Tautua

Malielegaoi entered Parliament in May 1981 as the MP for Lepā. Tuila'epa's seventeen-year political parliamentary apprenticeship, leading to his premiership, is the subject of the next chapter.

CHAPTER 4

Member of Parliament for Lepā – The Long Apprenticeship

Tuila'epa Sa'ilele Malielegaoi entered Parliament in May 1981 and was sworn in as the independent MP for Lepā, starting his parliamentary career in the final months of Tupuola Tufuga Taisi Efi's second administration. These were turbulent years. Samoa's economy had virtually collapsed, public servants were demoralised after being forced back to work following a failed three-month strike, Parliament was locked in a series struggles for power and little parliamentary business was completed. Furthermore, the constitutional weakness of *matai* suffrage, the poor administration of the government and the corrupting influence of informal political arrangements had been exposed.

When Tuila'epa entered Parliament, the political leadership of Samoa was still unresolved. In the first twenty months of Tuila'epa's political career there would be four prime ministers and four administrations. Tuila'epa witnessed first hand, and participated in, many of the critical events. While he was new to politics, he learnt quickly and stored away that learning which would serve him well when he became leader. These unsettled times had a deep influence in shaping Tuila'epa's central political objective of achieving political stability.

Tuila'epa served a seventeen-year apprenticeship in Parliament before he became Prime Minister, learning from the successes and failures of the first generation of Samoa's political leaders. Tuila'epa had an increasingly important role to play during his first years in Parliament. He became part of a strong leadership team alongside Tofilau 'Eti Alesana, instituting major reforms that were necessary to re-establish political stability and get the economy onto a secure footing. Tuila'epa believed strongly in the premise that good economic management policies and responsible financial stewardship are essential for establishing long-term political stability. He was also at the centre of the consolidation of Samoa's first political party, the HRPP, during Tofilau 'Eti Alesana's leadership. In his mind, the direction Samoa needed to head was clear but there were many storms, dangerous reefs and turbulent seas to navigate on the way.

Member of Parliament for Lepā

In this chapter, Tuila'epa remembers, reflects upon and recounts some of the key events that shaped his thinking, his political management skills and his political leadership. Part 1 covers the years from 1981 to 1988. Part 2 covers the decade of stable government from 1988 under Tofilau 'Eti Alesana's leadership until he stepped down in November 1998.

Part 1. The Turbulent Years 1981–1988

May 1981 to November 1981 – Tupuola Efi's Second Administration

Tuila'epa Sa'ilele Malielegaoi entered Parliament as the independent MP for Lepā, after winning a by-election.[1]

When Tuila'epa entered Parliament, Tupuola Tufuga Taisi Efi was Prime Minister and he was under challenge from Va'ai Kolone, leader of the recently established HRPP, an emerging force in Samoan politics.

In his first eight months in the House, as the newest MP, Tuila'epa delivered his maiden speech, observed the final months of Tupuola Efi's second administration and prepared for the general election in 1982.

At midday on 3 September 1981 the new MP rose to speak for the first time.[2]

'Mr Speaker,' Tuila'epa began, 'I rise with due respect to speak on the Financial Statement by the Minister of Finance and the Supplementary Appropriations Bill. Before going ahead, however, I would first of all ask Your Honour with due respect to allow extra time as this is my maiden speech.'[3]

The Speaker was reluctant to give extra time, but an intervention by Hon. Leota Leulua'iali'i Itu'au 'Ale, a friend from university days, led to Tuila'epa being accorded the 'extra time without further interruption'. The new Member had done his homework. He knew the Standing Orders, had the backup of senior MPs and stood his ground. He quickly got into discussing the details of Samoa's failing economy and potential ways to turn it around.

Tuila'epa's maiden speech was long on detail and short on rhetoric. His opening paragraph covered a wide range of subjects: the state of the

---

1 The dates when the various governments were in power and a brief account of key events have been used as headings to assist readers to follow the complex narrative of Samoan politics over these two turbulent decades. The writer has drawn extensively on Professor Asofou So'o's excellent 2008 book, *Democracy and Custom in Samoa* and his other scholarship to shape this chapter (see also So'o, 1992, 2006, 2007, 2009, 2012; and So'o et al., 2006).
2 See Malielegaoi, 1981.
3 Members have 30 minutes' speaking time for the general debate on the Budget. Maiden speeches are given extra time.

economy, the impact of the recent 'trouble between the government and its workers', the effect on foreign trade earnings, fluctuations in the US dollar, the price of petroleum, increasing import costs, the high cost of living in Samoa, the Suspensory Loan Scheme for Agriculture and legislation for increasing Customs duties to improve government revenue.

His second paragraph began, 'I have a few suggestions . . .'. The remainder of Tuila'epa's maiden speech identified a series of problems and put forward a range of measures designed to stabilise and strengthen the economy, mend government's relationship with the public service, improve agricultural production and exports, strengthen overseas markets, upgrade shipping and roads, prevent wastage, revamp hydro-electric power generation, reduce unemployment, and strengthen healthcare and education, including assistance to church schools. Tuila'epa also pleaded for a more 'democratic' media that would give air-time to differing views rather than only 'beaming out the government view point'.

Knowing that all politics are local, and that the folk who voted for him would be listening to the parliamentary broadcast on 2AP, Tuila'epa made special mention of the state of the road between Lotofaga and Aleipata, via Lepā, and the need for the construction of seawalls and tarsealing of the road 'because the dust menace is getting quite unbearable every day in our village'.

Tuila'epa continued, aware of his rural constituency's complaints and echoing their views about disparities in the spending of public money, 'the roads in Apia township are being resealed over and over again which means that we are spending far too much money in Apia [and] paying little or no attention at all to our plight in the rural areas. Even the back, bush areas of Apia are sealed; that tar would have been quite adequate to relieve the situation in the rural areas.'

Tuila'epa concluded his maiden speech with an enigmatic tale. 'There is a story once told about a sprite[4] which went on a journey. On the way it first came to a maiden in tears in one village. On being asked about her plight, she replied: "I am ill." In sympathy the sprite cured her ailment. Next he came upon a dejected athlete, crying hard on the roadside. On being asked why, he said: "I cry because I am not in the rugby team as I do not know how to play open rugby." On hearing this, the sprite felt great pity for the man, and he just broke down and cried.'

Thus began Tuila'epa's parliamentary speechmaking. The careful

---

4   Tuila'epa's maiden speech was in Samoan. He used the term 'O le Atua O le alofa', and the English translation of the Parliamentary Hansard quoted uses the term 'sprite'. Tuila'epa translates the term as a 'God of Love'.

and prudent management of finance and Samoa's economy, and their consequences on the quality of life of the people of Samoa, remain recurrent themes at the centre of Tuila'epa's political speeches, along with jokes and stories that have a message.

From the outset, Tuila'epa knew how politics operated in Samoa and what side he would support. He recalls: 'I came in as an independent. Tupuola Efi was Prime Minister, a seasoned politician and very charismatic. It was a tricky period. When I became an MP, Tupuola suspected that, as an independent Member, I would not back him up.'

Political parties, at that time, were very fragile organisations that attempted to hold together the shifting allegiances that had characterised Samoan politics. The formation of a government, following a general election, was a fraught process. Recently elected MPs were collected into 'camps', with fluctuating membership, as leaders attempted to mould them into a united caucus to build a stable majority to form a government.

Tuila'epa vividly remembers the power struggle between Tupuola Efi and Va'ai Kolone as they competed for MPs to join their respective parties:

I had been re-elected as an independent, but I joined up with the HRPP immediately after the general election in February 1982.

On the Monday following Saturday's general election, there were seven delegations from Tupuola's camp who came to me wanting me to support their side. On Monday night I went to the HRPP headquarters instead and offered myself to the HRPP. The Members were extremely happy, and they immediately elected me to become the secretary of the caucus. I know that they did not trust me completely. So they needed to tie me down to a position. I immediately accepted the post of secretary to convince the HRPP of my support. As a technocrat turned politician, I had principles to uphold: I was not a party-hopper as was typical of politicians at the time.

Tuila'epa joined the HRPP and accepted the job of secretary because he wanted the party to win. He wanted Va'ai Kolone to become Prime Minister because he believed that the country needed a change in leadership and knew Samoa was already deeply insolvent. But he recalls that the HRPP contained a number of Members about whom he had doubts.

I did not trust their integrity. So I came in to the HRPP with some trepidation. There were people I had to be very careful about.

In the first week after the general election some of the seven delegations who came to me said that Tupuola Efi wanted to see me. Tupuola Efi was then Custodian Prime Minister. In a few weeks Parliament would decide who would be Prime Minister. So I went to Tupuola's office to see what he wanted.

When I arrived, he looked at me as if he was completely puzzled as to why I had come.

I said to him, 'I have come because some of your delegations came to me and said that you wanted to see me. Here I am.'

Tupuola looked hard at me and said, 'We thank you very much for coming. You know, Tui, I don't promise Cabinet posts to my caucus Members.'

I said, 'Tupuola, I only came because your supporters who came to see me requested that I come, and you being the Prime Minister of Samoa, I did as I was asked. Quite obviously, this was a mistake and I apologise – good day.'

'Oh no, please stay', he said.

I sat back down to hear him out.

'You know, Tui', Tupuola went on, 'you have been a senior public servant for many years and you are an ideal candidate for Cabinet.'

I cut in and said, 'Tupuola, I am not interested in what you are saying. I have work to do. As you know, I am a partner at Coopers and Lybrand International. Sorry, I have to leave now.'

'Please, please', he said. 'Look, I heard that there is a great dispute in the HRPP camp.'

'I was invited to the HRPP meeting last night', I replied. 'There is no such commotion. In fact, a decision was made last night to send a delegation to collect one more Member from Vailoa, Savai'i, who is an independent. That will give the HRPP more MPs. So whatever you heard was wrong.'

'Can I invite you to one of our meetings since you are an independent and you have also attended the HRPP caucus meeting?' he said.

'Yes, I will come and listen.'

'Then I will invite you to our meeting on Thursday.'

'Thank you', I said, and left.

This was on Tuesday.

I was now secretary of the HRPP caucus. It was great fun as we worked to consolidate our MPs. The delegation that had gone to Savai'i to collect the Member from Vailoa to raise our numbers told us about their trip.

They went by plane, and one of Tupuola's Ministers from Savai'i was on the same flight. In their discussion on the plane, this Minister said that he was going to grab the Honourable Seumanufagai, the recently elected independent

MP, on the request of Tupuola, to come and support their party. In fact, this was the fellow whom the HRPP delegation was going to collect. They never let on to the Minister.

I remembered then that when I'd talked to Tupuola Efi about the floating independent MP from Savai'i, I saw Tupuola's eyes keep looking sideways as if he wanted to get rid of me.

The story was that this poor Minister had revealed his mission to the HRPP delegation during the fifteen-minute flight. When the plane landed, the Minister went to the marketplace to eat some pie, while the HRPP Members went straight to recruit the Honourable Seumanufagai, who immediately packed up his suitcase to leave with the HRPP delegation.

They were about to leave his house at Vailoa when the Minister arrived and said, 'Seumanufagai, what are you doing?'

'I am going with these guys to support the HRPP.'

'But the PM asked me to come and . . .'

Seumanufagai said, 'Sorry. I am a supporter of the HRPP.'

There were lots of strange things that were happening at that time.

On Thursday, Vaovasamanaia Filipo, my former Minister of Finance, arrived at my doorstep early in the morning before daybreak with his wife, Leaupepe Faimaala, all dressed in suits as if they were meeting a VIP.

He woke me up and said: 'This is Thursday, Tui. Our party's meeting will begin at Tupuola's residence at 12 o'clock. Tupuola said that he invited you and he said that you will come.'

I had given my word to Tupuola Efi and I had to honour my promise.

'Yes', I said. 'I am a member of the HRPP, but I will come.'

I turned up at 12 o'clock. Tupuola's supporters were playing billiards. I told the Honourable Vaovasa that I had to leave at 1 o'clock to pick up my daughters from school because they were young. At 5 minutes to 1 Tupuola summoned the meeting and addressed it. At the end of his welcoming address it was 2 minutes past 1, which was beyond my deadline.

As Tupuola was speaking, I looked around and noted the faces of the men who were present. Up to that time, if we were playing the numbers game, there were 29 MPs who supported the HRPP. That meant that Tupuola only had eighteen MPs so it was quite clear that the HRPP should win. But at Tupuola's meeting I saw all these HRPP Members who had attended the HRPP caucus the night before. I thought, 'Hell, the HRPP could lose.' I knew these Members, because the membership of the HRPP was published in the newspaper prior to the general election. They were now going to support Tupuola after the election. My name was not published but an article in the paper made it clear that I was an independent. I was the only successful independent elected at the 1982 general election.

The HRPP MPs sitting there in Tupuola's meeting included Patū Afa Hunter, who was one of the CEOs axed during Tupuola's first administration. Patū was now seen as wanting to be with the winning party and at this stage the picture was confusing.

At exactly 2 minutes past 1 I got up and requested the right to speak. Tupuola agreed.

I said, 'Thank you for inviting me to your party's meeting. When Vaovasa, over there, came to invite me this morning, I told him that at exactly 1 o'clock I would have to leave to go and pick up my children and it is already past 1. Before I go I would like to address those newcomers into Parliament. My appeal to you is do not rush. Take your time. Take a walkabout like an *'ofu lu'au*, the person who prepares our traditional delicacy, *lu'au*. You can never tell that you are the best *'ofu lu'au* if you don't walk around and sample the different *lu'au*. You need to walk around to see who is the best. I would ask you, especially those who are first-timers, not to make your decision now about who should be leader. Tomorrow you should go to the HRPP headquarters and listen to what they say. In that way you will be better placed to judge who will be the best leader. For me, I have not chosen yet. My decision will be made in six weeks from now when we assemble in Parliament. Tupuola, thank you very much. I have to leave now.'

Tupuola got up and said, 'I regret that Tuila'epa has to say these things. But nevertheless what he has said has been said and I hope you will be back.'

That was the first and the last time I was invited to Tupuola's camp. I knew then that I had to work very hard to help the HRPP to win.

Two nights later, at the HRPP meeting, I could not hold my patience any more about the manner in which our deliberations were being conducted. The three who were conducting the meeting were Va'ai, Tofilau and me, the young upstart. The Members of the party were very careful because it was so delicate to maintain the numbers. I was impatient, however, with the slow progress and with the long speeches of no substance that were delivered by the Members at our meetings. I wanted to get things moving.

Since I had joined the HRPP, our meetings began at 7 in the evening with a prayer and a meal. At 8 o'clock we started our meeting and we never finished until 4 in the morning. The 25 Members who were there all had to speak, and when they spoke they gave a traditional Samoan speech that could last as long as 30 minutes. With 25 people, it went on and on. I got increasingly fed up. Especially when I came home in the early hours of the morning and my wife reprimanded me, asking, 'What the hell are you doing?', I was getting increasingly impatient and irritable.

Finally, on the seventh day, I broke. I let them have it.

'Tofilau and Va'ai, I am sorry I have to say this. I came under my own steam and I can leave under my own steam. But I have to tell you, the way we conduct our meetings is so ridiculous and all I hear is rubbish. Why should we all speak? All we do in our speeches is praise the dignity of the heavens we come from. We are talking rubbish. If we are going to be the government, we should use our time better. One hour talking about policies, that is more important to me than the pile of garbage we are talking about every night. We should begin to think about governing, to talk about serious issues. As it is, we finish at 4 o'clock in the morning and I don't sleep properly. I am getting sick of it and if we proceed beyond 9 o'clock tonight I will tender my resignation.'

I was so mad that I let them have it.

We finished at 9 that evening. From then on our meetings were cut down to two or three hours talking about essential matters. I am impatient and I can't stand garbage. I want meetings that are effective and only touch the important matters.

I then found out why the old guys tended to talk a load of garbage. It was because they had absolutely no idea how to run a government. Most of them were either listening or dozing. I was coming in fresh with all kinds of ideas. I wanted to get on with business.

Several days later, a member of Tupuola's party called on me. It was Mano'o Lutena, an MP from Falelatai, who was related to me and was one of the HRPP candidates who changed loyalty after the 1982 general election. He thought I supported Tupuola and told me what had transpired in their discussions. He showed me Patū Afa's name on their party list. Alongside Patū Afa's name there was a note in Patū's hand which read, 'Mano'o – Give me another 24 hours to think.'

Tupuola had 24 to our 23 by daybreak. By the time night fell, we were 24 to 23 because of Patū. He attended our meetings at night and Tupuola's meetings in the daytime.

I decided to talk to Patū.

At 5 o'clock in the evening Va'ai's son, Papu Va'ai, and two other HRPP supporters came to see me. They said they had seen Patū Afa's wife and gathered that he was still attending Tupuola's meetings. They said the reason why Patū kept dithering was because he was still trying to find out where I stood. To him I held the key to victory. So when they went to Patū's wife, who knew Patū's inner thoughts, she said, 'Go and see Tuila'epa. He is the only person Patū trusts.' That was why they saw me and urged me to work on Patū.

That evening I decided to talk to Patū. We talked for two solid hours under the breadfruit tree near Va'ai Kolone's residence after our party meeting ended at 9 o'clock. Everybody was watching us as we talked in the dark and Patū was unaware that our secret meeting was never a secret. For two solid hours in the dark we talked.

I said to him, 'Patū, you have to make up your mind.'

And he asked me, 'You are not supporting the HRPP?'

'I have always supported the HRPP. You should gather that I did not accept the secretaryship of the caucus for nothing. I thought you would know better. The economy is bankrupt and you were the head of the Lands and Survey Department and you were axed from your position on grounds that were malicious.'

And he said to me, 'So you are now with the HRPP?'

'I have always been with HRPP. Ever since I got into politics.'

'Oh. Then in that case, tomorrow I will gather my village to present me formally.'

The following day Patū went and asked the Vaiala village youth group to escort him. About a hundred strong marching like soldiers, with Patū Afa in front like the Commander in Chief, they came with flags and beating drums to present Patū formally to the HRPP.

That was the day we won the election. Only the formality to confirm our victory remained.

April 1982 to August 1982 – Va'ai Kolone's First Administration

On 13 April, Parliament elected Va'ai Kolone as the new Prime Minister by a majority of 24 votes to Tupuola Efi's 23.

On the night before Va'ai named his Cabinet, he told our caucus that he was finding it hard to pick his Cabinet. He said, 'Please help me. I really don't know how to pick this Cabinet. You are all qualified.'

We encouraged him by saying, 'Do what you know is best.'

That's what everybody was saying: 'We will back you up in other ways.'

I said the same thing.

After he read out the names of those selected for Cabinet, some of the old MPs openly wept because they had not been elected. I, for my part, said that there are many ways to serve the government.

Va'ai told me he wanted me to be the CEO of the Samoa Trust Estates Corporation, which operates all reparation estates under coconut and cocoa plantations.

I said, 'Va'ai, I thought that it was our party principle that we should never politicise the control of the state corporations. It leads to mismanagement.'

I waited to see if he would take any notice of what I had said.

When he made his announcements later, he picked Sam Saili to be the new CEO of STEC. Obviously he heard what I said and decided not to give it to me. It did not matter, I was already busy enough at my new professional practice.

Va'ai was Prime Minister for five months. Then came August. He was heading to the 1982 Pacific Islands Forum (PIF) meeting to be held in Rotorua, New Zealand.

At that time there was a legal action pending, brought against Va'ai by the village of Asau. It was rumoured that Tupuola was behind the village of Asau's court case. Tupuola Efi bears the Tufuga title from Asau village, the district that he first represented when he entered Parliament in 1965.

Prior to Va'ai's departure for New Zealand, he brought the issue of the proposed protocol with New Zealand to our caucus. The protocol would squash the legislation that allowed every Samoan born before 1948 to be a New Zealand citizen. I was against Samoa becoming a party to the proposal. The protocol was political dynamite!

I argued, 'Let us tell the New Zealand government it is not our baby. If they decide to squash it, it is their own decision.'

I did not want Va'ai to be dragged in to being party to the squashing of the Privy Council decision by law. Let the New Zealanders do that under their own steam.

That was not to be the case. Va'ai went to New Zealand and succumbed to the pressure of Prime Minister Muldoon. He bent under pressure. When he came back to Samoa he feigned illness and gave Tofilau the job of organising a meeting of our caucus and relaying the decision. Tofilau was now acting leader of Cabinet and spoke on behalf of Va'ai, defending his actions.

I got so mad I fronted up the attack. I was literally shouting at Tofilau and he shouted back. The dispute led to the party caucus and senior Members proposing a vote of no confidence in Va'ai's Cabinet. When it was realised that the majority of the party supported me, the senior Members quickly asked for a reconciliation and so the dispute was resolved and we broke for dinner.

Tofilau was furious with me for putting Cabinet to shame. He got his plate full of food and then threw it against the wall, breaking it to pieces. He busted out of the building. He had to pass me to get to his car, and I think that he was completely blind with rage.

I got up and shook his hand and said, 'Tofilau, let us put an end to this.'

Tofilau shook my hand involuntarily and walked out.

Pule Tuiloma Lameko, who was sitting at the end of the long table, got up and repeated what I had said to Tofilau.

Tofilau said to Pule, 'Get out of the way or I will knock your bloody head off!'

He walked off, jumped into his car and drove away in anger.

The following day Tofilau went to Washington accompanied by Pule Lameko and the Deputy Financial Secretary, Afoa K. Va'ai, to attend the annual meeting of the World Bank. When he arrived back in Apia, at 4 o'clock on Friday the following week, the court decision on Va'ai Kolone was just about to come out. It resulted in the dismissal of Va'ai and the HRPP government. Seventeen hours later, the Head of State invited Tupuola Efi to take over the Prime Minister's job and form a government.

August 1982 to December 1982 – Tupuola Efi's Third Administration

The Head of State invited Tupuola Efi to form a government, after an electoral petition against Va'ai Kolone was upheld by the Supreme Court and his seat was declared void.

Tupuola Efi was re-appointed Prime Minister after the fall of Va'ai. This was a highly controversial action and the second time that the Head of State had made a decision to appoint a prime minister without going through the process of summoning Parliament to vote for the MP who commanded the confidence of the majority of the MPs.[5] The reason given by the Head of State at the time was that the prime minister must be appointed immediately to take charge and that to summon Parliament at short notice was not possible.

The controversy continued. Tuila'epa's view is that the Head of State should have waited for two reasons: first, the number of MPs in both parties was even at 22, and, second, by-elections for two vacant seats were due to take place in a few weeks. Professor Asofou So'o later wrote[6] that 'The HRPP

---

5   The first time was when Prime Minister Matā'afa died suddenly in 1975 and Tupua Tamasese Lealofi IV was appointed by Malietoa to succeed Matā'afa.

6   See So'o, 2008, p.105.

believed that the Head of State's appointment of Tupuola as Prime Minister was unconstitutional – because both parties at that time had 22 seats each in addition to the speaker, who was an HRPP Member – and that he was repeating his 1975 action when he had appointed Tamasese to succeed Matā'afa.' This controversial incident was seen by many as a mistake by the Head of State, but traditional respect for Malietoa, and muted public criticism, prevented any further legal action against his decision.

Tulia'epa recalls the action the HRPP MPs took to vent their displeasure at the Head of State's decision.

Tupuola's Cabinet was sworn in one week later. The HRPP boycotted the ceremony and not one of the HRPP MPs turned up. This was a big embarrassment for the Head of State and the government. It was the first time ever that the oath of a prime minister was snubbed. It also embarrassed Tupuola and strengthened the argument we made that the proceedings were wrong, illegal and unconstitutional. To us the action of the Head of State was influenced by his *tama-a-'āiga* connections. He had become embroiled in politics.

We embarrassed the Head of State and Tupuola by not turning up at Tupuola's oath-swearing ceremony because the Head of State had done something we considered wrong, illegal and unconstitutional.

Tupuola Efi appointed only six Ministers of his Cabinet, leaving two posts vacant: the powerful posts of Minister of Finance and Minister of Agriculture. With two by-elections to be held soon, the situation was quite precarious. His plan was to offer these two vital posts to HRPP MPs to secure his position. On the second Saturday of October 1982, just prior to the Children's White Sunday, the Vaimauga West by-election was held and the HRPP won the seat. At 5 a.m. on Monday, Tupuola Efi visited me at my home and offered me the post of Minister of Finance. I told him that I would give him my answer at 9 p.m. at his home. I visited him subsequently and politely declined his offer. I learnt later that he had offered the other ministerial post to Le Mamea Ropati, who also declined.

By this time we had already worked on a strategy for the demise of his government. Mano'o Lutena, of Falelatai and Samatau, became the Minister of Agriculture, and Aliimalemanu Sasa Tevita became the Minister of Finance. Mano'o's appointment angered To'i Aukuso, a devoted supporter of Tupuola Efi who considered himself more qualified for the Minister of Agriculture post, and he thus joined the HRPP. This was a major defection to the HRPP for a change!

The HRPP won the second by-election and we now had the parliamentary majority. All we needed next was a parliamentary session to vote the government out.

When Tupuola's main Budget for the financial year 1983 was tabled in December, it led to a vote of no confidence and the fall of his government.

The strategy to defeat the government was worked out by an informal strategy committee of three: Tofilau, Matatumua Maimoana and me, with the help of a legal adviser, Tony Pereira. We decided to raise the issue of Tupuola's appointment as Prime Minister by the Head of State under the provision of the Standing Orders that allows any Member to raise an item of importance for debate; and if by 11 o'clock the matter is not resolved, it can be deferred for further discussion after the Budget speech. This was only a ploy. The real killer was to be activated on the second reading of the Appropriations Bill, after which the Minister of Finance could then proceed to present his Budget speech.

This is indeed what happened. There was much heated discussion over the appropriateness of Tupuola's appointment, and then after a long debate the motion was put forward to defer consideration until after 11 o'clock, while we moved on to the first and second readings of the Appropriation Bill. The Speaker put the question for the first motion for the first reading and it was passed. The second question was then put forward for the second reading of the Appropriations Bill. Tupuola got up and walked out to go to the toilet.

When the vote was taken for the second reading of the Appropriations Bill, the Speaker said, 'The Ayes have it. And now I invite the Minister of Finance to present his Budget speech.'

As the Minister got up, Tofilau stood and interjected, 'Mr Speaker, Point of Order.'

The Speaker replied, 'What is your Point of Order?'

Tofilau said, 'You have judged that there are more Ayes than Noes. I heard differently. I would therefore like to call a division.'

The Speaker replied, 'You are not the Speaker. I am the Speaker and I am sitting here in a very high seat from which I alone can best hear the Noes and the Ayes, and in my judgement the Ayes had a louder voice. But, in case I am judged wrong, I will now call for a Division.' Then he pressed the bell. The bell started ringing to summon all the MPs into the chamber for the vote count.

I saw Tupuola rushing into the chamber and when he reached his seat, he did not even stop to sit down but addressed the Speaker immediately.

He said, 'Mister Speaker! Mister Speaker, please, please do not allow this vote to proceed. Remember the Samoan proverb: "It may be your day today; tomorrow is my turn." This vote of no confidence is unnecessary.'

The bell was still ringing.

The Speaker said, 'Honourable Tupuola Efi, do you consider this as a motion of no confidence?'

Tupuola said, 'Yes, Mr Speaker. A vote against the Budget is indeed a vote of no confidence.'

The Speaker said, 'OK. You confirm that if we take this vote, it is a vote of no confidence?'

'Yes, I do.'

Then the Speaker stopped the bells and continued, 'Honourable Tupuola, sit down. Let me deal with the question first and then I will address you. Those in favour, please stand up.'

The Clerk of the House called out the names, counted the votes and declared, 'Twenty-two.'

'Those against, stand up.'

The Clerk of the House called out the names, counted the votes and declared: 'Twenty-three.'

Then the Speaker ruled, 'The vote of no confidence is confirmed. As such, the government of Tupuola Efi has fallen.'

There was pandemonium. It took some time for all the MPs to understand what had just happened. Our strategy had worked.

We were always very careful to keep the details of what we were going to do to ourselves because in Samoa it is hard to keep anything secret. Our MPs sometimes talk under the influence of alcohol, and in a small community a secret cannot remain so for long. We had to keep it close to our chests. Only our strategy committee knew the details. The Constitution is very specific on issues of confidence. No vote of no confidence can be allowed in our Parliament unless the Prime Minister has specifically given approval. Tupuola seemed to be unaware of the significance of confirming the vote of no confidence. That is why the Speaker chose to ask twice. And twice, Tupuola, without knowing it, put his neck into the noose.

December 1982 to April 1985 – Tofilau 'Eti Alesana's First Administration

An electoral petition declared the general election result in Salega void. A by-election resulted in an HRPP candidate winning, which gave the HRPP a one-seat majority in Parliament. Earlier, the HRPP had also won the Vaimauga West by-election. On 21 December Tupuola's Budget was rejected by 23 to 22 votes and on 30 December Tofilau 'Eti Alesana was sworn in as Prime Minister.

Because of the previous high-handed actions of the Head of State when he appointed the Prime Minister directly without summoning Parliament, Malietoa was now facing a more difficult situation with Tofilau 'Eti, a non-*tama-a-'āiga*. He was undecided about what to do. We had to send in Tofilau to ask him not to take on the burden by himself; instead, we argued that the best way forward was to have a general election.

When Tofilau went to the Head of State to recommend dissolution, Tupuola was there. Tofilau sat down and Malietoa said, 'Sorry, Tupuola is here. He recommends that we form a government of national unity in which you, Tofilau, will be Deputy Prime Minister and all the Ministers will be from your party but Tupuola Efi will be Prime Minister.'

Tofilau had come to the Head of State to present the HRPP position, to dissolve the House and call fresh elections. When Tofilau rejected Tupuola's proposal and asked for dissolution, the Head of State asked Tofilau to form his government with Tupuola leading the opposition.

For the third time, the Head of State played a central role in choosing who would form the next government. The oath-taking ceremony was scheduled for the following day, 30 December.

I was disappointed because I preferred dissolution as demanded by our party caucus. I was so disillusioned by the outcome of Tofilau's meeting with the Head of State that I refused to attend Tofilau's swearing in as Prime Minister. Besides, I never believed that I would be chosen for a Cabinet post because the dispute between me, Tofilau and Cabinet three months earlier was still fresh in memory. When my name was called out as a Minister in this Cabinet on 30 December, I was not there to take the oath.

I turned up at the celebration luncheon at 1 o'clock. Tofilau directed that the new Cabinet would meet at 2 o'clock. I was the only one yet to be sworn in.

The argument all along by the Head of State was that it was never easy to summon the House at short notice. That is why he said he had to exercise his discretion once again in appointing the prime minister, which to me was just pure hogwash! I wanted to test the truth of the argument that we could not summon a full Parliament to assemble at short notice. When the new Cabinet met, the only question we discussed was my proposition of summoning Parliament on 31 December 1982 to confirm the Prime Minister's direct appointment by the Head of State under the Constitution, that is, to confirm the election of Tofilau 'Eti Alesana after his appointment by the Head of State.

In my uncompromising mind, the first step had to be that Parliament elected, followed by step two, that the Head of State appointed whoever the Parliament elected. It had happened the other way around, the appointment of the Prime Minister first and election by Parliament second. A case of the cart before the horse! Regardless of this, I wanted Parliament to give its OK.

The call went out repeatedly by radio on the evening of 30 December for Parliament to meet at 9 o'clock the next day. The only business was a motion that Parliament confirm the appointment by the Head of State of the new Prime Minister. All the 49 MPs attended. We quickly disposed of the only item on the agenda, and Parliament rose again for the New Year celebrations.

I was also sworn in as Minister on 31 December 1982 in Tofilau 'Eti Alesana's first administration, the day that we finally disposed of the lie that Parliament in Samoa could not be summoned at short notice. This major achievement provided food for thought for more reforms to come on the process of future appointments to the posts of Prime Minister, Head of State and Speaker of the House.

In February 1983 we resummoned Parliament to approve the new Budget and a host of new policies to restabilise the economy of Samoa. We had to devalue the currency substantially to boost agricultural production and export earnings and make substantive amendments to 24 pieces of legislation, many related to improving revenue collection. The intention was to raise sufficient revenue and to re-energise the economy. There had been excessive borrowing from the financial institutions and thus crowding out of private sector development. We had to increase tax temporarily as government moved to raise funds to remedy the deficit. And we had to deliver the Budget within a very brief time.

The 1983 Budget speech[7] was to be delivered by Tofilau. He held the

7   See Alesana, 1983.

Finance portfolio. As Associate Minister, I was responsible for the Budget preparations and statement. There was much to do in a very short time.

As part of the preparations, we had to amend our tariffs legislation considerably. This meant that several items of legislation had to be drafted.

When we came to drafting the measures to amend the 24 pieces of legislation, including income tax amendments, contrary to my understanding that there was no problem in capacity, the Attorney-General, Mr Garneau, a Queen's Counsel from Canada, stated before Cabinet that his office could not possibly complete the legislative amendments for Parliament's consideration within the two weeks required.

The Attorney-General said, 'Sir, we cannot amend the legislation, we do not have the staff to do it.'

'How long will it take you?'

'At least twelve months', he replied.

'We have to present this Budget to Parliament in two weeks' time. It must be done within two weeks.'

'Sorry, Sir, we cannot do it.'

I recommended to Cabinet that we would have to let it out to the private sector, because the Attorney-General's Office did not have the capacity to fulfil the task.

The first lawyer I subsequently called up was Drake. I did not tell him straight away what I wanted him to do. I asked Mr Drake about his law-drafting skills. He said that the only drafting skills he possessed were the kind he had as a student.

I rang up another lawyer and I was told that he was at the market.

'What is he doing at the market?'

'He has a fishing boat, he is supplementing his income by going out fishing.'

I eliminated him.

So I called up Patū Falefatu, the present Chief Justice, who was then in private practice. Patū went through the legislation to be amended and he too declined the project.

Finally, I rang the last lawyers in town, Trevor Stevenson and his associate, Semi Epati, who later emigrated to New Zealand and became the first Pacific Islander to be appointed a judge in New Zealand. Trevor came with Semi Epati to my office a few minutes later, each carrying some thick law books that they dropped on my desk before saying anxiously, 'Now Minister, show us the legislation.'

'Over there, on the table.' They looked at the documentation very briefly and said, 'Fine. In two weeks we will have everything done.'

'Take it.' They picked up the legislation and as they walked out, I asked why they had brought so many books with them.

'We thought you might be interested to see that we are the most hard-working lawyers and therefore the best lawyers in town.'

They met all the requirements. Everything was finished in two weeks. We got the Budget prepared and the 24 amended laws drafted.

And then the invoice for the work came – 100,000 Tala, which is probably worth half a million today. So I queried his bill.

Trevor Stevenson replied, 'You asked all the lawyers in town and they couldn't do it. Only the over-worked and under-paid could do it.'

I called Alistair Hutchison, the Financial Secretary, for his advice about paying the bill. He also felt it was too much but like me he was unable to negotiate it downward.

I went back to Stevenson and asked again for a discount. He first refused, but finally agreed. I thanked Stevenson for his tolerance and thoughtfulness in accepting a full settlement cheque from the government for 97,000 Tala. I had anticipated an uproar in the Budget debate over the 100,000 Tala in legal fees and decided I would counter-punch with the argument that the legal drafting fees were actually much less than the costs would have been through the Office of the Attorney-General. In addition, the office was not able to handle the workload and a partnership with the private sector was a good policy that was to be encouraged.

Several days later the story came out in the *Samoa Observer*: 'Corruption! A hundred thousand to a local lawyer. This is absolutely unwarranted.'

It blew up in Parliament. Tupuola Efi, as usual, tried to make a loud noise about it.

I said in Parliament, 'The only thing that one must remember is that when the Attorney-General's office confirmed that they could not do it, what could we do? Government policy is that we must seek the private sector. That's it. That's what we did. That bill, 100,000 Tala, is wrong. We never paid 100,000 Tala. That's all garbage.'

Then six months later I found out what had really happened. Trevor had contacted an old friend from Auckland who was an expert on law drafting and offered him a paid holiday, with spending money in addition, for a small job drafting some legislation for our Parliament. He stipulated that the job had to be completed within two weeks.

So this poor guy drafted all the laws on his holiday.

*

A major problem we inherited was that the country was virtually bankrupt. So not only did we have to improve government revenue, by increasing taxation and duties, but we also had to re-energise the economy through changing interest and lending rates, and making sure the government would never ever again depend on bank borrowing and thereby squeeze out the private sector. Government had to broaden its own revenue base. We started to deregulate the economy. We also had to set up a Central Bank to manage our monetary policies, whereas previously the management of our monetary policy was conducted by the Treasury.

We also decided to revise the process for the allocation of foreign exchange reserves. Up to that time, we used to allocate foreign exchange to all importers and dealers at the beginning of each financial year. We decided to terminate the rationing system and open up the market. But not before we secured prior clearance from the IMF. If anything went wrong, they would come in to bail us out. It was a calculated gamble and it paid off.

In the first year, 1983, our foreign reserves jumped from zero to 12 million Tala. In the second year they doubled from 12 to 24 million. They went up and up until now we fix foreign reserves at 300–400 million Tala. That level is the equivalent of five to six months' of imports and is considered reasonable to keep our trade flowing smoothly.

We made a lot of changes in the laws to rebalance and stimulate the economy. After we passed the 1983 Budget, I led a delegation of officials to Geneva and Brussels including Herman Kruse, the Director of Economic Development, and Afoa Kolone Va'ai and Ai'ono Mose Sua. We spent two weeks in roundtable meetings with officials from all the international financial institutions when we told them that everything was back on track in Samoa. I also met with all the ambassadors and high commissioners of our development partners with whom we had trade relations, to convince them that they would have to re-establish their full trust in the new administration and our management of Samoa's finances now we had managed to put in place changes that would restabilise our economy. It was a major diplomatic campaign and a big public relations exercise.

Tuila'epa's university education in Commerce and Politics, his training and experience gained during his years working in the Ministry of Finance, Treasury and at the ACP Secretariat in Brussels, and the relationships he had built with the IMF, the World Bank, the European Union and other international financial institutions, were invaluable in the achievement of these reforms.

Tofilau remained Minister of Finance until the Cabinet reshuffle in 1984. The reshuffle came about because of the delicate diplomatic situation in Indonesia. There was a conference held in Jakarta in late 1983 and the new Minister of Foreign Affairs, Lauofo Meredith, attended to represent Samoa. Before Lauofo went, Tofilau told him not to say anything about West Papua: 'West Papua is part and parcel of Indonesia and we should not become involved in "internal" affairs of their government.'

What Lauofo did not comprehend was that this was a potentially explosive issue, a minefield, and at the Jakarta meeting he spoke out against Indonesia's policy on West Papua. Of course, the Prime Minister was informed about Lauofo's comments.

Prime Minister Tofilau was very angry. In the middle of a heated debate in Parliament, Tofilau turned to me said very quietly, 'Tui, I want you to know that I'm going to reshuffle the Cabinet. I will take back the Ministry of Foreign Affairs for the simple reason that Lauofo disobeyed my directive. Please understand that I have to take away from you the Ministry of Postal and Telecommunications and responsibility for Civil Aviation and Economic Development and give these to Lauofo to avoid embarrassment. Foreign Affairs is a major ministry, I will take it back.'

'That's OK with me', I said. 'Whatever you have to do, I support you.'

That reshuffle was announced the next day and I was handed the full responsibility for the Finance portfolio.

We got the economy going from strength to strength between 1983 and 1985. A general election was scheduled for 22 February 1985.

We had begun to see some crevices in the solidarity of our party. We had people with their own personal agendas taking advantage of the impending elections who were also becoming more daring with their demands on the government. For instance, when the Bill for setting up the Central Bank was proposed in 1984, Tagaloa Pita wanted to provide in the legislation for politicians who were qualified to become Governor of the Central Bank. He was very, very disappointed that I didn't support him in Cabinet or in our caucus to become the Governor of the Central Bank.

'A politician and a Governor of the Central Bank at the same time?' I raised that question in caucus. 'Never in my lifetime have I seen this happen. A politician administering the Central Bank of a country! That is the first recipe for disaster.'

Tagaloa was not very happy with that and he started to line up opposition against the Prime Minister and me in Cabinet. He only came back to the party meetings six months before the general election in February 1985.

April 1985 to December 1985 – Tofilau 'Eti Alesana's Second Administration

Led by Tofilau 'Eti Alesana, the HRPP won a landslide victory with 31 seats against Tupuola Efi's Christian Democratic Party's (CDP) sixteen seats. Another seat was later added to the HRPP following an election petition, giving a two-thirds majority.

On the first day of our caucus meeting after the election, we had to decide on the election of the leader. The discussion was long. A lot of the speeches by older and newer Members were saying that we should take time to think. In other words, many of the speeches aimed to defer the decision of electing the leader.

Tuila'epa saw that there was danger in the making. He takes up the story.

I raised my hand and I told a story, an Arabian tale.
 A frog was hopping along towards the Nile River to travel to the other side. When the frog arrived there the Nile was in flood and so he decided to wait until the flooding receded. Meantime, a scorpion arrived on the riverbank also wanting to go to the other side.
 The scorpion said to the frog, 'What are you doing here?'
 The frog replied, 'I am waiting for the river to calm down before I cross. It is flooding and flowing very swiftly and I have to wait. What about you?'
 The scorpion replied, 'I also want to get to the other side. Can you please give me a lift across?'
 The frog said, 'No, I don't want to take you.'
 And the scorpion said, 'Why is that?'
 The frog said, 'You may sting me mid-river.'
 The scorpion laughed and said, 'I am not that much of a fool. If I sting you we will both die. I will be drowned.'
 The frog said, 'That makes sense.'
 A few hours later the flooding receded.
 The frog said to the scorpion, 'Let's go now, jump on.'
 So the scorpion jumped over and sat on the frog's head. In mid-stream the scorpion stung the frog on its head.
 The dying frog turned around and asked the drowning scorpion, 'What the hell did you do that for?'

And the scorpion said, 'Don't you know, we are in Arabia!'[8]

Then I said to those present, 'I smell something terrible. Why is it that we should defer a decision? We should decide today. There is a saying in Samoa: *O le malaga e faiaga a lē timuia e fasia*. A traveller delayed may either be caught by the rain or be bashed by a stranger! Let us decide, now.'

But the old Members appealed to defer for the next 24 hours. So we deferred it to the next day.

At 7 o'clock the next morning I woke up and was getting ready to go to the meeting when I got a phone call from our *failotu*, our pastor for the caucus, the Reverend Liki Crichton. My friend the blind pastor.

He said, 'I want to tell you something.'

'Yes?'

'There is a plot. I was visited last night by the president of the party and he told me there is a plot to defeat Tofilau at the caucus meeting this morning.'

The plot ran like this. The previous night the plotters had gone and asked Va'ai to allow three candidates to run for leadership of the HRPP, one of them subsequently becoming prime minister. They asked him to agree to support the three candidates: Va'ai, Tofilau and Sam Saili. The reason why Sam Saili, former Minister of Finance in 1973 during Mata'afa's time, was to be put up as a third candidate was to split the vote. There were people who wanted Va'ai to be leader again. There were others who didn't like Va'ai and didn't like Tofilau who would vote for Sam Saili. The whole idea was to cut the support from Tofilau, who the plotters thought was too powerful; they preferred Va'ai to become leader because they believed they could more easily manipulate him. To be successful they needed the backing of Va'ai Kolone.

However, the 'real' plan was, if Va'ai agreed, that the plotters would throw their support behind Sam Saili and defeat these two old-timers [Va'ai and Tofilau]. Sam Saili would emerge as leader.

Tuila'epa recalled that all Members of the caucus were approached during the night, except himself, Jack Netzler and, obviously, Tofilau.

The reason the two of us were not approached was that we were the only candidates whom Tofilau handpicked to be in his Cabinet, Jack during Va'ai's time and me during Tofilau's first administration. So of the eight Ministers,

---

8   The story of the scorpion and the frog has a number of endings. Tuila'epa's is unique. The traditional punch line from the scorpion is: 'It's my nature . . .'. The story has been credited to Æsop and others; see https://en.wikipedia.org/wiki/The_Scorpion_and_the_Frog

the only two who were really handpicked by Tofilau were Jack and me. Va'ai had selected the others. When Tofilau became Prime Minister, Cabinet loyalty was still with the old boss, Va'ai Kolone.

In the minds of these plotters, Jack and I could never be persuaded to vote against Tofilau. Knowing that the pastor was so close to me, the plotters went to ask him to convince me to support their plot.

My friend Liki Crichton said to me, 'What do you think?'

I said, 'Look, I cannot buy that sort of rubbish. Tofilau is the kind of leader I would support. He is a strong and good leader for Samoa. He has courage, foresight and vision, and has proven himself a capable leader since he took over. He is a statesman.'

The success of the plot was dependent on changing the system of electing the leader. The plotters wanted to do it by secret ballot. So far, we had always used the Samoan way of selection. And that is that every Member had to speak at the meeting, saying who they would choose as leader. The key to defeating the plot was to follow tradition. I said to the pastor, 'I will see that the election system is unchanged. That is the key to defeating the plot. I will speak up and reject a secret ballot.'

The Malae-o-Matagofie, the venue of the meeting, was crowded in anticipation. The meeting began at 9 o'clock. Many people must have heard about the plot and they anticipated that something exciting was going to happen. In Samoa, nothing can remain a secret for long.

The chairman was Tuigamala Anetipa Lam Sam, president of the HRPP and Sam Saili's brother. The first speaker, as expected, opted for a change of the system. The second speaker was Sam Saili's brother-in-law, the Minister of Public Works in Tofilau's caretaker Cabinet.

This fellow said, 'I am the Minister of Public Works. When you run for Parliament, you aspire to be an MP. When you come into government you aspire to be a Minister. When you get elected as a Cabinet Minister there is one more step to complete your ambition, the leadership of this party. I consider myself qualified for leadership. But, because I respect the older generation, I will control my own ego.' That was the end of his speech.

The next speaker was Sam Saili himself, who said, 'I have been a Minister and I consider myself qualified for leadership and I propose myself to be leader of this party.'

The next speaker was an old Member who talked about the need for Va'ai and Tofilau to sort things out and come to an agreement on who was to be leader.

During that speech, Tuila'epa said, he was 'blasting two gentlemen on his left and right, Fepulea'i Semi and Toeolesulusulu Siueva'.

Tuila'epa remarked to them, 'It is not yet time for Sam Saili to lead this party.'

Tuila'epa did not know at the time that these were two of the plotters who had been busy visiting MPs at night and promoting Sam Saili.

Tuila'epa was the fifth speaker. He raised his hand and said to the president, 'I want to propose that Tofilau be the leader of the party and Prime Minister. And I must thank all of you who decided against having the election yesterday because it gave me time to solicit the advice of the elders of my constituency. They told me, "There is nobody intelligent enough to lead the HRPP except Tofilau." I therefore move the motion that Tofilau be our next leader and Prime Minister.'

Tuila'epa recalls:

Immediately the president called me out of order: 'Sir, you are speaking out of order. We are talking without naming names, we are talking about the system we are going to use to elect the new leader.'

I quickly responded, 'Excuse me. Why did you allow your brother-in-law to name himself as befitting the qualification of leadership? Why didn't you rule him out of order? Is it because he is your brother-in-law?'

Later, Tuila'epa reflected on his angry outburst.

I thought back to my brashness, my lack of respect for these elders. That is why I came in as an independent in the first place. I wanted to speak without fear. No one would ever be able to say about me, 'The HRPP invested a lot to get him elected and see the way he behaves.' No one would be able to throw that sort of rubbish at me.

'I can tell you, Va'ai, that I am disappointed. I recall asking you about the status of the election petition against you following the 1982 general election and you told us, "Don't worry, my sons who are learned lawyers will be able to handle the case." First, you embarrassed this party in 1979 when your own brother refused to vote for you. Imagine, your own family would not support you. The HRPP worked hard to put you in as leader.'

I wanted to squash the plotters.

'Then in 1982, after we appointed you, the court dismissed you. It was the greatest embarrassment for our party to have our Prime Minister dismissed. And we all went down with you. It is very surprising that you should consider running for the leadership of this party once again. Tofilau brought honour to this party in the two years of his administration.' My voice was getting very loud.

'He was courageous. This is what we need. He was able to withstand the barrage of questions and animosity from the opposition. We must also consider the traditional balance of cultural leadership in Samoa. The leadership of the HRPP to this day has been vested in Savai'i MPs. If Tofilau's term is not renewed, it is the end for Savai'i. It is time for the *Tumua* to take over.' (*Tumua* refers to the seat of oratory of the paramount orators.)

Once I had mentioned *Tumua*, all the *Tumua* opened up their eyes. The plot was over. Speaker after speaker hammered the Savai'i versus Upolu, *Tumua* versus *Pule*, argument.

About 4 o'clock To'i Aukuso spoke up. To'i's Samoan was not good and the way he spoke, in a high-pitched voice, was very funny.

He said, 'Thank you very much. I think we should support Tofilau. Though I like Va'ai, Tofilau has done some good.'

He said, 'Va'ai, please, let poor Tofilau continue again as Prime Minister. I, and a few others, have been secretly plotting to overthrow Tofilau and in his place put in Va'ai. But our real intention was to make Sam Saili the leader. Gentlemen, please, have pity on poor old Tofilau. He guided us so well. We better give the poor old man another chance to lead the party again.'

There was laughter because the way he said it was very humorous.

Va'ai was embarrassed that the cat was now out of the bag. He had to take the floor. This was close to 6 p.m. and there were only about four more speakers left. He was forced to take the floor because of the embarrassing revelation of the plot by To'i.

'I want to take the floor now', Va'ai said. 'The only reason I was interested in the leadership was because I was unhappy with you, Tofilau. Several times you stated publicly that you would challenge anyone who wanted to remove you physically from your seat. That made me angry. You think you are the only one capable. Now that I have stated what I thought, I surrender. You take the leadership.'

That was the end.

Immediately Tofilau spoke.

'I thank everyone here for the honour you have given me.' Then he delivered one of the best speeches I ever heard. It was as if he was addressing the nation.

At the end we all clapped. We got in our cars and when we came out, the whole road, right up to the clock tower, was filled with people on both sides of the road. They all clapped and clapped. It was the first time I had seen this happen. People were looking at us and waving their hands. We found out later that Tofilau's victory speech had been broadcast live over Radio 2AP.

Tofilau had saved the day and was elected leader of the HRPP. But Va'ai was not yet finished.

Before our meeting had ended it was agreed that the two leaders would get together and discuss a suitable appointment for Va'ai Kolone. The meeting took place on Sunday. On Monday Tofilau reported to the caucus, saying, 'As you directed, we met. Va'ai's eldest son Papu Va'ai was there to witness our discussion. Va'ai said that many of the party wanted him to stand for the election of prime minister when Parliament meets.'

Tofilau said to us, 'I have asked Va'ai to bring the discussion of the leadership back to the party today. It is an embarrassment that I am leader and Va'ai proposes his name for the post of prime minister. If you appoint him leader he shall also be the only candidate for prime minister. I will defer to Va'ai', Tofilau concluded.

Two of our older Members appealed for a compromise. I was the third one to speak. Still maintaining my high note and loud voice I said, 'It is ridiculous that we should discuss this without giving Va'ai the opportunity to confirm. Va'ai, was the report presented by Tofilau correct?'

Va'ai said, 'Tui, it is correct.'

'Then I will ask the right to speak.'

Tofilau said, 'Proceed, Tuila'epa.'

I said, 'Never in my lifetime have I come across something that is so naïve. The race is run and the loser asks to re-run the race. The country already knows who our leader is. If they hear that we have changed our leader again, what will they think of us? This is not a party of kids. We are all of one mind to respect one another. My recommendation is that we uphold the decision that we made already, that Tofilau remains the leader and that Va'ai should wait his turn for an appropriate appointment at a later stage. I move that as a motion.'

The motion was put. It was passed and we finished the meeting.

On Wednesday the caucus was to meet at 6 o'clock in the evening. I turned up at 5.30. There were only five people present, including Tofilau.

He said to me, 'You came a little late.'

'What?'

'You missed Va'ai and his son Papu. They arrived a few minutes ago.

Papu kept the engine of his car running and Va'ai opened his door, got out, walked to us and said, "Can I shake your hand?" I put out my hand to shake his and he said, "This is a good bye. Thank you very much. This is a good bye. I am leaving you, and I am leaving the party. Thank you. Good bye."'

That was how we parted with the former leader of our party.[9]

Va'ai's departure from the HRPP laid the foundation for the split that ended Tofilau's second administration. But he was not the only defector or aspiring leader.

When we hotly debated the election of leader, we debated Samoan style. Le Tagaloa Pita got up and said, 'I am the *ao pāpā* of Savai'i', meaning he was the most prominent of the prominent chiefs of Savai'i. 'By right I have credentials that should make me leader of this party and yet nobody has recommended me.'

When Tagaloa delivered those words he was angry with all of us, which is why he had to take the floor to tell us his credentials. At the end of his speech he said, 'Since no one cares that I am the most prominent chief of Savai'i, I am wasting my time here. I am resigning from this party.'

'Ai'ono Dr Faanafi, the very first Samoan to have a PhD and who subsequently became head of the Education Ministry, was Tagaloa's wife and an MP from Fasitoo Uta. She also rose and said, 'Since my husband Tagaloa has left, I have to leave the HRPP.'

Tagaloa and Faanafi left eight days before Va'ai.

These defections of senior HRPP Members in the leadership struggle between Tofilau and Va'ai contributed to a vote of no confidence later in December 1985.

Tuila'epa reflected on the background to the coup.

I think that Tofilau was over-confident because of our two-thirds majority. In hindsight, Tofilau could have eliminated the rebellion and maintained his leadership.

First there was the defeat of Va'ai Kolone and his supporters. Then, only two out of the eight former Ministers were retained in the new Cabinet. And amongst the new Ministers were several who were infamous wheeler-dealers. After the selection of the new Cabinet, we did not have another

---

9   Tofilau decided to terminate the existing party leadership arrangements and ruled that in the future the leader of the party would also be president of the party and chair party meetings. Later, when Tuila'epa took over, his words came true. Tofilau was from *Pule*; the next leader, Tuila'epa, was from *Tumua*.

meeting of caucus for three months. Caucus meetings were excellent occasions for raising all these sorts of issues and disposing of them. It was educational for me.

Tofilau was slow in patching up injuries. I felt for him and I did not blame him at the time. The majority of two-thirds was a significant boost to his ego. But he overlooked the delicate issue of the feelings and pride of the Members who missed out on Cabinet appointments.

When the break finally occurred, it changed my whole attitude. Up to that time, I felt that if anybody was to leave our party it could only happen to people who are uneducated. It could never happen to people who had been on scholarships and who had the training and the help of Western education, those who looked positively at the value of the many good projects executed to raise the standard of living of our common people.

Tofilau's political management of the situation, his Cabinet choices and his lack of communication with the caucus contributed to the rebellion.

When I came into Cabinet I was the only new Minister. The rest were from Va'ai's Cabinet before and had been re-appointed. When I joined the Cabinet I brought with me the main value of a public servant, namely, to serve. I was essentially a public servant. I often forgot that I was now a Minister. When I worked in the Treasury I was always dealing with policies and many of these policies were aimed at spending the little money we had wisely. We saw what happened with the damage to the economy during Tupuola's reign. There were several occasions when I spoke in Cabinet not as a Minister but as a public servant telling off the Ministers in Cabinet. Now that I was Minister of Finance I saw there was wastage in Finance and reacted to any proposal that would waste money. There were times when I even pointedly challenged the Prime Minister on some of the decisions he made while I was away at overseas meetings.

One time there was the purchase of a boat that was very costly. I thought it would be a very bad investment because we first should have found out more about the boat and whether it was suitable for Samoa. All I gathered was that the Minister in Charge of Shipping had gone overseas, taken one look at the boat and decided on the spot to buy it. He asked the Cabinet to approve it without the essential prudential due diligence being done. An engineer should have inspected the ship to determine if it was a seagoing vessel that could ply the waters between Savai'i and Apia. True, it was fast, but was it suitable? I was very disappointed and I formally challenged the Prime Minister on my return from overseas. I said to him, 'It seems you are ignoring the fact that you have a Minister of Finance to advise on these complex financial issues. I do not know if the proper negotiations have taken place, or whether some "under the table" payments have been made.' I was looking straight across at the Minister, whom I could never trust. That same Minister had to be later kicked out of the party by Tofilau for numerous lapses.

Several times I initiated changes to Cabinet decisions that had been made in my absence. When I came back I challenged and challenged and challenged till the decisions were changed. Tofilau saw that what I said made a lot of sense but it created enemies within.

Tuila'epa was the first politician in Samoa who was a technocrat familiar with international finance. He came in from a strategic post at Treasury where he was involved in Budget preparations and policy-making. He had excellent academic qualifications and good grounding in Treasury and the ACP Secretariat. All these things added up to his bringing a fresh, analytic input into Cabinet discussions and decision-making. He was a pioneer.

Samoa was moving from the personality politics of the first generation towards party politics with established policies based on a more rational, evidence-based approach. However, many of the politicians still in Parliament were still wedded to the old ways and Tuila'epa's pioneering approaches were not always welcomed.

These debates in Cabinet were agonising and caused ill-feeling towards me from some of my colleagues. I always remembered the advice given to me by my friend from the IMF, Dr Pandit. He said, 'If you always follow the truth, if you speak out without fear and always retain honesty, rest assured, you will have many enemies. But those enemies will fear you and respect you.' This was something that I always remembered. I thought that was bloody good advice from my Indian adviser.

Dr Pandit also said to me, 'If you make bad decisions and thereby break the law, wherever you escape to, the law will always follow you.'

These kinds of useful safeguards were always present in my mind. I raised them in relation to a lot of decisions when I saw there were irregularities. Because I changed a number of decisions it made the plotters create a kind of useful diversion. 'Look, our Prime Minister listens to one Minister only. Whatever decision we made when Tuila'epa was not here, he comes back and tells the Prime Minister to change it.' They never looked at the reasons why.

In late April 1985 there was a meeting in the Maldives. I was to go there and then on to a trade show in Japan. Just before I was due to go, during a Cabinet meeting we received a devastating letter from Sefuiva Sione MP accusing the Prime Minister of favouritism.

He wrote, 'Tofilau, you have appointed Ministers who were thieves, who are corrupt', and he named three. Sefuiva was not using the kind of language you expect of an MP. It was the language of the gutter. He was reprimanding us. He wrote, 'Tofilau, I will take it up and I will never stop until all of you are kicked out of Cabinet.'

The letter was very hurtful to the Ministers who were named. Tofilau showed it to the Cabinet.

I did not know at that time that there was a movement to kick Tofilau, me and the rest of Cabinet out. But towards the end of the Cabinet meeting, I said to Tofilau, 'I have a suggestion to make. My delegation to the Maldives and Japan includes only the CEOs of Treasury and the Development Bank. Can I ask you to put in the name of the author of this letter?'

'Why?'

'I want to have a quiet talk to him.'

It was approved. We would leave two days later.

I went home and rang up Sefuiva.

'Is that you, Honourable Sefuiva?'

Sefuiva was a former senior officer at Customs and we'd a very close affiliation in our public service days. We were both former technocrats. As deputy of the Treasury there were many times when I had summoned Sefuiva up for the Budget preparation.

'Sefuiva, it's me.'

'Why are you ringing me?'

He knew I would have read his letter because Cabinet had met that Wednesday.

'I have decided to put you in my delegation for the Maldives and Japan. I want you to travel with me.'

'Oh, I see. So you are bribing me. Your Cabinet is bribing me.'

'I tell you what, you turn up at my office at 8 sharp tomorrow with your passport. Exactly at 8 or I will remove your name from my delegation.'

I put the phone down. He tried to call me. I did not answer. He rang me up again. I did not answer.

At 7.30 the next morning he turned up at the office, all smiles.

I said, 'You had good sense to come, because I was going to axe you if you did not turn up at 8 o'clock.'

'I know you too well. I knew you would cut me out if I didn't come in at

8. Who would not welcome the opportunity to travel to those distant places with you? But I have one question. Did you get a copy of my letter?'

'Your stupid letter was read out, and I tell you that if the Ministers you named find you, they will strangle you. Be at the airport tomorrow.'

He came to the airport and we laughed and played cards all the way to the Maldives.

'How could you write such a stupid letter?'

'I have to make the Prime Minister open up his eyes to those crooks,' he said.

By the time we came back we had established a very close relationship.

Two days after our return Sefuiva rang and came to see me.

He said, 'There is something you should know. There are a lot of people leaving the party.'

'What?'

'They rang me up and they are going to meet tonight to create a new party to evict Tofilau and you. That is why I have come to seek your advice.'

'You go and spy,' I said.

'Oh, very good,' he replied.

'You go and listen, and then come back and we'll talk then.'

Sefuiva Sione went and attended the meeting and recorded all the names. Then he came back and said, 'Our government is going to be kicked out. There is a very solid coalition with Tupuola Efi. All our Members at the meeting signed the promise. I did not. I told them I had to think about it very carefully.'

'Don't you worry.'

I informed Tofilau that fifteen of our party, including Va'ai Kolone, had formed a coalition with Tupuola Efi and his party of twelve. They aimed to move a no-confidence motion at the June parliamentary session when we considered the Supplementary Budget. Their coalition had 27 Members to our twenty, which included the Speaker, Nonumalo Sōfara.

As soon as the Supplementary Budget meeting was called to order, the Speaker delivered a long-winded speech, a very circuitous speech, a speech that dwelt on the importance of government stability. Finally he ended, 'Because I value a stable democracy, by the powers vested in me I now declare that Parliament stands adjourned'. The opposition was angry they could not launch their vote of no confidence and we survived.

This was only the Supplementary Estimate stage. All we needed to do was continue on with the main Budget. New proposals would be on hold. We had to wait and eventually the day of reckoning would have to come.

It came in the last week in December when we tabled the Budget. We were prepared and had the legal advice of the Attorney-General. It was clear that the Prime Minister would need to give his consent for a vote of no confidence to proceed. In the Commonwealth parliamentary democracies, when a prime minister recommends for Parliament to be dissolved, a head of state should automatically comply.

The Budget session of Parliament convened in December 1985. Tofilau got up and said, 'I want to advise the Parliament that no vote of no confidence can proceed without the Prime Minister's approval. And I do not intend to give my approval.'

But the Budget had to proceed. So we put the Budget up and it was rejected. The coalition did exactly to us what we had done to Tupuola Efi in 1982. Except now, it was a coalition of Va'ai, our former leader, with Tupuola Efi.

Immediately after the defeat of the Budget, I got up and spoke in my capacity as Minister of Finance, and said that now the proposed Supplementary Budget was defeated and the government had not fallen, we would run according to the provisions of Public Moneys Act. I sat down. Parliament closed.

The opposition MPs were very confused because they thought we would fall. We didn't.

After the parliamentary meeting, Tofilau went to see the Head of State with the recommendation for dissolution and the Head of State refused. Tofilau got so angry that he shouted at Malietoa. It was a shouting match. Tofilau was related to the Head of State. His salutation is 'Lau Afioga Tofilau, the ninth family of the Malietoa family'.

Tofilau was so irate because the Head of State was once more making an unconstitutional decision about who should form the next government in the same fashion that had occurred in 1975 and 1982. All along, Tofilau believed we would face a general election. But the Head of State would not dissolve Parliament and call a general election.

So we were in limbo.

Tofilau was in a bind because he was also required as a chief of the Malietoa family to protect the Malietoa title. Finally he summoned the caucus and said to us, 'We can take the Head of State to court, but where would that lead us? One of the elements of the *Fa'asamoa* is respect. I must respect the Head of State, even though the decision he made is wrong. There is a saying: *Fai aso le Ātua*, God will give us another chance. My proposal is that I will resign voluntarily. If you agree, I will summon a meeting of

Parliament next week. I will go before Parliament and I will resign.'

That's what happened.

Malietoa did not ask Tofilau to resign. He resigned and all of us resigned. That was not before Tofilau made his resignation speech.

Tofilau said to the Parliament, 'Today I have decided to resign. But before I resign I feel it is right that I address you directly, Va'ai. How many times have I been accused as the person responsible for this hated protocol that deprives our people of the right of citizenship in New Zealand following the Privy Council judgment? And I accepted all these accusations as if I was the one responsible. You were the one who went over to New Zealand and negotiated this protocol and I have remained silent, all these days, because I remained loyal to you. Va'ai, we used to eat together and put our hands together in the same cleaning bowl. You were like a brother to me. You were the first Prime Minister from our party. We put you in that position. And what have you done? What have you done? I can tell you. I always remember what the first Prime Minister, Mata'afa, said in one of his major speeches: "Whoever betrays this country, this government and its people, it is better for him to tie a stone around his neck and drop into the deep ocean. It would be better if he was never born." I have decided to resign today so that you can come here and sit here. May God bless this House.'

It was a striking speech and it was a dramatic moment. It was in fact one of the most honourable speeches I have ever heard.

While Tofilau lost his post as Prime Minister he won a moral victory that laid the foundation for the HRPP's return to government.

January 1986 to April 1988 – Va'ai Kolone's Coalition Administration

Tofilau's 1986 Budget was rejected by 27 votes to 19. Tofilau advised the Head of State to dissolve Parliament and call for a general election. That advice was rejected. Va'ai's faction that had left the HRPP formed a coalition government with Tupuola Efi's recently formed Christian Democratic Coalition Party.

Tuila'epa remembered that there was a funny twist to the formation of government.

It was the first Budget meeting by the coalition administration. I went to Pago Pago, American Samoa, and did not attend the first Budget meeting.

I couldn't get a seat on the plane to get back in time. I rang up Tofilau to apologise for my absence and asked him how the Budget debate had proceeded.

Tofilau laughed and said, 'I started the debate. I got up to speak. After I spoke, the Speaker invited Members to speak. After a brief wait for some 30 seconds, the Speaker ruled to close the debate and he then asked the government to respond. Since the government did not have much to respond to, the Speaker thereby adjourned the session for the general debate and said that the next day we would start on the general debate of the Budget, item by item.' Indeed, the Speaker wanted to terminate the debate early because there was a wedding in New Zealand the following week that he wanted to attend. We had decided to filibuster and prevent him from attending it.

Here was our Speaker, Nonumalo Sōfara, trying to play a trick on us. We wanted to make sure that the Speaker knew he was our Speaker and that he had to listen to what we had to say. We appointed him when we had a two-thirds majority and the government could not remove him.

The coalition government now had 27 MPs to our twenty. So with our twenty we set about making things extremely difficult for the Speaker and the government. In the Budget discussion item by item, Members are only allowed to speak for fifteen minutes on each item. But with our twenty Members, minus the Speaker, that was nineteen each with fifteen minutes, which gave us 285 minutes' speaking time, or over four-and-a-half hours for just one item. And each speaker had two chances to speak. That made it nine hours for each item in the Budget, and there were over twenty items, one for each Ministry. So we could spend a whole year debating the Budget.

We decided that we would do that, that we would filibuster.

It did not take long for the Speaker to realise what was happening. Being an outstanding orator himself, fully versed in all the tricks of Samoan oratory, he knew he had to humble himself and beg forgiveness for wanting to leave in time for that wedding in New Zealand. So the Speaker begged us to help him in his task, reminding all of us that he was put there by the HRPP.

We met at lunchtime to consider his appeal. On the afternoon that we resumed, Tofilau said, 'We have considered your appeal, Mr Speaker, and we propose that we will respect your wishes and allow one speaker only for each item from our party – one speaker only instead of nineteen, and he will speak for only fifteen minutes. This is our special consideration for you, remembering that you are our Speaker. On one condition: that Members of the government do likewise. The moment they break this agreement, I am sorry but we will go back to what we were doing.'

But there was another big problem. Seven of the coalition party MPs had been contacted by some business people from the United States saying that they had some nuclear waste they wanted to bring to Samoa and dump at Fagaloa Bay. These seven MPs expected to benefit financially from the project. After this plan was revealed, both leaders saw that this was a very dangerous venture, and they both turned it down. But the seven former HRPP MPs became very frustrated about this issue and spoke against their government. The coalition was starting to come apart.

I got up and spoke for fifteen minutes. I sat down and one by one the seven on the government side each spoke for fifteen minutes to embarrass their leaders. When it got to the next item, Tofilau got up and said to the Speaker, 'What can we do? Sorry, but our agreement is hereby breached and it is not our fault.'

We broke for fifteen minutes for a cup of tea. I went straight across to Mamea, who was now a Minister in the coalition government.

I said, 'Mamea. I am sorry.'

'Thank you very much, Tui. We had made good progress until these bastards destroyed the beautiful compromise that we had achieved.'

So we went on and on and on and on enjoying to the fullest our role as opposition. This was December, and we were still meeting at 12 o'clock on Christmas Eve. The Speaker finally said, 'It is now 12 o'clock. And it is Christmas Day. In honour of Christmas we will be in recess tomorrow but we will resume on the 26th. Let me conduct a Christmas prayer. I would ask you to first to sing this hymn.'

We all sang together like a choir. At the end of the singing he led us in prayer and we dispersed to celebrate Christmas 1986.

That was when our Parliament was at its best. Because we, in opposition, never let the government better us or rest peacefully.

One of the most controversial events that occurred in our final session in 1987 was the proposal by the coalition government of Va'ai and Tupuola to close down Avele College and turn it into the venue for the National University of Samoa (NUS).

Closing Avele College would close a long history of educational assistance in agriculture from New Zealand, from which many other Pacific Island nations had benefited, including Niue, the Cook Islands and Tokelau. Students come here to learn about improving agricultural practices and productivity. For us the proposal to close Avele was outrageous. It was a good time for us to embarrass the coalition government now that the general election was just around the corner in 1988.

I remember getting up in Parliament and giving a long speech on the history of Avele College. I said, 'I can never forget that college because in sports they excel, in entertaining and marching to Parliament grounds to celebrate our independence. Avele College stands out in their green uniform with yellow stripes on their *lāvalava*, their yellow shell garlands and the lively clap dance they perform that is unforgettable. These cultural arts are carried back by the overseas students to their island homes, which is a great way to share cultural experiences. Above all, Avele provides another opening for our children's education, and to close it narrows the educational opportunities of our own sons and daughters. You are telling us that you will close this college? This is outrageous.'

Because we voiced our opposition so clearly, the Members of the government realised that this could damage their chances in the election. Even the government's backbenchers decided to disassociate themselves from the proposed plan and spoke against the closure. We successfully turned the issue into a highly emotional exchange.

A motion was put not to close the college, supported by the government's backbenchers, and we defeated the government! It was a great political victory, and one that shook the coalition government. It was also very divisive. Avele College old boy, Vaʻai, voted for the closure of his old school, but Fepuleaʻi Semi, another old boy and coalition government MP, voted in favour of his old school remaining open.

A second issue that caused division and tension in the coalition was the 'highly sensitive cultural issue' around the conferring of the *tama-a-ʻāiga* title of Tui Ātua Tupua Tamasese on Tupuola Efi. [From now on we will refer to him as Tupua.] The title was bestowed on him on 11 December 1986 and there was a series of hearings of challenges in the Land and Titles Court before the title was confirmed on 29 August 1987. Coalition government MP opponents included Fepuleaʻi Semi and ʻAiʻono Fanaafi, both former HRPP MPs who had switched allegiances. HRPP opponents included Fiamē Nāomi Matāʻafa and Tofilau ʻEti Alesana.

The traditional residence of the Tui Ātua title is in Lufilufi village, and Tupua was subsequently under pressure to stand for the 1988 election in the Ānoāmaʻa East constituency where Lufilufi is located. The incumbent, Faʻamatuāinu Tala Mailei, stood down to make way for Tupua, and Iuli Sefo, an HRPP stalwart and high-ranking titleholder, 'eventually succumbed to traditional pressure to withdraw his nomination'.[10]

At this time traditional loyalties of the *Fa'asamoa* came head to head with party politics, creating tensions between and amongst family members, villages and political alliances. The negotiation of these tensions is a unique and constant part of political life in Samoa.

Of his brief time in opposition Tuila'epa reflected:

I always want to tell these stories because of the depth of the opposition we put in. It was always exciting and amusing to stab, sit down and watch as the government struggled to respond. Why? The live debates disclosed how well prepared the Members were in handling issues raised in our political exchanges. None of the oppositions since then have ever attained the excellence that the HRPP showed when we were on the opposition benches during 1986 and 1987.

Perhaps that is nostalgia? It was the last time Tuila'epa would serve as an opposition MP.

Formation of Government – February to April 1988

The election results of 26 February left the two main parties finely balanced.

The coalition had not elected a leader prior to the general election. Va'ai and Tupua had both been elected to their seats unopposed and both factions of the coalition waited to see who won the most seats and held the balance of power. Who was to be the 'kingmaker'? Who was to be the king? Would the HRPP's election night majority hold up?

Parliament was due to sit on 6 April. There would be a month of moves and counter-moves as prospective leaders struggled to form a parliamentary majority. The brutal equation in any parliamentary arithmetic is 50 percent + 1. In a Parliament of 47, 24 was the magic number.

Va'ai handed over the leadership of the coalition to Tupua. The lines had been drawn. The contest had begun. The three independents who won seats, Sagapolutele Sipaia, Misa Telefoni and Tupuola Siaosi Hunt, were actively courted by both sides.

Tuila'epa takes up the narrative.

We had 23, they had 23. One Member, Misa Telefoni Retzlaff of Falelatai, would decide the party that would win. Misa, however, disappeared to New

---

10 See So'o, 2008, p.113.

Zealand and deliberately made himself a rare commodity.

We went into our camp and had a church service after the election, earnestly praying each day for Divine Intervention. On Easter Sunday, Pastor Nomeneta, of Vaimea village EFKS, conducted the service for the party. This guy was a real performer: like one of these evangelical preachers with a world-wide parish, he accompanied his preaching with actions. To deliver his messages he would dance, weep, laugh or look serious whenever the message seemed to demand a particular mood. I was sitting at the back with a new MP. We were right at the back. He said to me, 'Do you believe that garbage? How can the pastor say that we will win and we only have 23? We are losing. Misa will go and support his cousin Tupua. Blood is thicker than water.'

I was laughing. This first-timer did not know that the pastor was also an expert politician who was telling us exactly what we wanted to hear.

We were doing the numbers game. Sagapolutele had come back to the HRPP, so it was 23 to us and 23 to Tupua. The floating candidate was yet to determine his move. That was Misa. We knew that Misa was Tupua's cousin and might not come to us. Was there another floater?

Tupua had represented the Āʻana Ālofi No. 2 constituency, as Tupuola Efi, for six terms – or eighteen years. After the conferring of the Tui Ātua Tupua title, Tupua surrendered his constituency and ran in Ānoāmaʻa Sasaʻe. He wanted to ensure that his old constituency continued to support him. There was a very strong candidate, Tanuvasa Livi, who had run several times before under the banner of the HRPP. I think Tupua knew that Tanuvasa would win. So he convinced the district to have a meeting and to summon Tanuvasa to make a vow that if he won Āʻana Ālofi No. 2 he would support Tupua in Parliament. Tanuvasa made the vow.

In the meantime, Misa had disappeared to New Zealand during the five weeks of intense politicking at home. Misa's whole district was pro-HRPP. The previous Member, the Honourable Lupematasila Faʻamalama, was an HRPP supporter. Moreover, the Falelatai elders always saw Tofilau as their own son, because going back in genealogy Tofilau had roots in Falelatai – a factor unknown to Misa. So the Falelatai leaders knew that Tofilau was their own son and they wanted their MPs to support the HRPP. This was the situation.

The Thursday after Easter Sunday, Parliament was to meet to select the government. We were still short by one seat to form a government. How could we win? We kept working to shore up our numbers.

I had exhausted my own efforts to convince Tupuola Hunt of Siumu district to honour his undertaking to run as an HRPP independent. Now that he had won his seat, Tupuola refrained from attending our caucus meetings. I finally met up with Tupuola Hunt at Tofilau's request.

'Why was I not the official candidate?' Tupuola asked.

I said, 'You knew very well our party's policies. You are a registered Member of the HRPP, and because the sitting Member is the official candidate, you had to run as our HRPP independent.'

He said, 'I hear that the HRPP, because of its policy, will only appoint candidates to Cabinet posts who have been there before.'

'Wrong', I replied. 'I entered for the first time and I was made a Minister.'

'OK. Leave me to think about it.'

'Remember. It has always been our agreement that you would run as an HRPP independent.'

'Leave me to think about it', he said again.

He disappeared for the next five weeks. Tupua had grabbed him and locked him up somewhere. He was not seen by our side again until the opening of Parliament. This was the situation with regard to Tupuola Hunt, four days before we were to select the prime minister.

Something happened that tilted the balance in our favour. The chiefs and orators of Leulumoega district (the Āʻana Ālofi No. 2 constituency) decided to kill a few pigs and make traditional presentations to the coalition on Easter Monday. Tanuvasa Livi was so excited, so happy that his constituency was coming to the coalition headquarters and he was proud.

The orator speaker got up and said, 'Today, it is a great honour for us to come and make formal presentations for the *tama-a-ʻāiga*, Honourable Tupua who has represented us in Parliament up to this time.'

Then they made the presentations.

Since Tanuvasa Livi was now Leulumoega district's representative in Parliament, any presentations should have been made via Tanuvasa Livi. Instead, Tanuvasa was completely ignored. The presentations were made directly to Tupua, their former representative in Parliament.

This embarrassing episode was later explained to Tuilaʻepa by Tanuvasa.

Tanuvasa said to me, 'You know, Tui, I was most embarrassed. I was the MP for the district and I was sitting right there, in front, expecting to be presented with the traditional honour of a *sua*. But a *sua* was presented to those on my left and to my right and I was completely ignored. I thought, So this is it. After I gave them the promise of my support, I was being treated like a pig that was fenced in. A nonentity. That was the end of it. So, full of embarrassment, I rang up my wife and told her, "Go and get that huge pig and make a presentation on my behalf to the coalition today. Then ask for my mats and suitcase and tell them you are taking them home to clean up."'

His wife said, 'Why are you doing this?'

Tanuvasa said, 'We are changing course. Tonight we will go and re-join my own party, the HRPP. If the district does not know how to respect me in the traditional manner, I too will refrain from honouring my commitment.'

While this was happening, Tuila'epa recalls, Misa returned from New Zealand and was summoned by the Falelatai district. The meeting was to decide which party Misa would support.

There are four prominent high chiefs in Falelatai. When they decide, that is it. Lupematasila Faamalama spoke after the *'ava* ceremony. Misa was there. It was full. Lupematasila Faamalama, the outgoing MP, said, 'I want Misa to go and support the HRPP.'

Then another high chief, an old man named Taefu spoke. 'I want Misa to go and support the HRPP.'

Another old prominent chief, Nanai, spoke up and said, 'I want Misa to go and support the HRPP.'

Three out of four; the decision was made.

But it was not over. Misa Faitala, the guy who made Misa Telefoni a chief, had yet to speak. Remember, Misa Telefoni had no blood connection to Falelatai. His Misa title was a gift for taking up a court case, a very difficult court case involving the whole district. Misa did it for nothing, free, *pro bono*. Out of gratitude, the chiefs, particularly Misa Faitala, conferred the Misa title. Misa Faitala was a supporter of the coalition.

Misa Faitala opened up and said, 'Before I speak, first of all I ask Misa Telefoni: Misa, what party do you prefer?'

Misa's response was, 'The HRPP has always been my party. I support it. The proof of that is that in 1983 they held a fund-raising party and I donated 4000 Tala and Tofilau is my personal friend. However, up to now Tofilau has not contacted me but the *tama-a-'āiga* [Tui Ātua Tupua] has spoken to me offering me a ministerial post in the Public Works Department in his Cabinet. Because our roads are in a terrible situation, naturally I should now support the *tama-a-'āiga*, Tupua, because with funding from Cabinet our roads will be built.'

Then Misa Faitala said, 'The reason I ask this question is that I wanted to know Misa's mind. This is what we ought to do, rather than deciding for him. But what can we do when the three of you have been visiting Tofilau and getting money from him? You have been bribed by the HRPP.'

Apparently Misa Faitala was sitting between Sila and Taefu. Sila had his umbrella and Taefu turned around at the same time and said, 'Shut your bloody mouth, we never went to Tofilau.'

Sila raised his umbrella and hit Misa Faitala's head. And the other old guy turned around and hit Misa with a fist. Which really did not do much damage, as they were old men.

The *'aumāga* ran over and stopped the fight. It was just stopped when a car took off. It was Misa Telefoni. He was frightened.

The usual Samoan custom of reconciliation then happened. Sila apologised. Taefu apologised. Misa Faitala accepted. They all agreed that Misa Telefoni should now give his support to the HRPP. Then they directed two chiefs to look for Misa Telefoni and tell him to send cars over to pick up the villagers to present him formally to the HRPP.

They arrived at Misa's place in the evening, between 6 and 7 and he was not there. When Misa finally met the envoy he said, 'Sorry, I cannot accept. I will have to go now to Tupua and offer my candidacy for his acceptance.' Immediately, Misa jumped into his car and sped over and formally entered Tupua's headquarters. They ordered beer and celebrated.

At the same time the HRPP was having a church service at Tofilau's residence at Moto'otua. I arrived after 7 and the service was already underway, so I went to Tofilau's *fale* next door. One of the supporters said, 'You are not taking the evening prayers?'

'Let them conduct the service. It would be an embarrassment for me to arrive late. They will tell me off.'

The other guy said, 'You are going in?'

'No, no.'

'You will miss the excitement.'

'What excitement?'

'Did you know about Tanuvasa?'

'What?'

'Tanuvasa is sitting right there.'

I got up and went in. I saw Tanuvasa. Then I remembered the prophetic words of the Reverend Pastor Nomeneta the day before when he said, 'If God is with us, who dares to oppose us?'

Tuila'epa reflected on the difference between the two events, the two parties and their values.

Tanuvasa entered our camp and we had a thanksgiving service. Misa entered the other camp at the same time and they had a beer-drinking service to celebrate.

At about 3 in the morning, I could not sleep with the excitement – we finally realised we had won. Three general election victories in a row!

Tanuvasa being a leader from his own district, a Christian and a deacon, said, 'I need to write a letter of resignation to Tupua and Va'ai.'

Two of our Members, Leafa Vitale and Leota Lu, offered to deliver it. At 3 a.m. they drove in a pickup truck to Tupua's camp and there were guards at the gate.

The guards said, 'OK, come in.'

They went in. Only a few were awake. Anetipa Lam Sam came to meet our two guys. He said to Leafa, 'How are you?'

'Great. Can you deliver this letter?'

'Can't you come in?'

'No, we have to leave.'

So they delivered the letter and left. Fifty yards away they parked their truck and walked back in the dark to see what was happening. Immediately all the lights went on. Anetipa had just read the letter and was shouting, 'Wake up, Wake up, we've lost! Tanuvasa has betrayed us!'

The following day Tofilau convened our caucus to appoint the Speaker of Parliament. We had the numbers now to form the government. Aeau Peni of Falealupo, a new MP, was chosen unanimously as our Speaker. Tofilau had just begun his congratulatory speech when we heard the high-pitched voice of an orator outside begging Tofilau to accept a request for Tanuvasa to accompany them back to their village for a very important meeting. It was so important that all the village chiefs had come specially to accompany Tanuvasa Livi. They said that the matter at hand could only be deliberated on by the Council of Chiefs at the traditional meeting *fale* at Nofoali'i. There were three buses all packed with young men to back up their request.

Our headquarters was surrounded by about two hundred guards all dressed in black *lāvalava* and shirtless. Each young man was carrying a long package wrapped in a coloured *lāvalava* – 12-gauge shotguns. The guards were all from Lauli'i village where Tofilau held the title of Maposua.

As I had suspected, Leulumoega had come to take Tanuvasa by force, but now that they saw our headquarters was well-guarded they changed tactics, sat down under the *'ulu* tree and decided to take the safe option of talking the problem out. We came out to meet them

Tofilau grabbed the *to'oto'o*, pushed it down into the earth and said, 'Chief Taimalie! King Galumalemana had three children by his wife Galuegapapā – namely, Taisi, Nofoasaefa and Puamemea. Tupua Tamasese Efi is the bearer of the Taisi title. I am the bearer of the Tuailemafua title, descendants of Puamemea. Must you uphold one and reject the other of the same blood? Why?'

Tofilau turned towards Tanuvasa and issued the order: 'Tanuvasa, these are your elders. Get up and speak!' It was a tense moment for us all. One wrong word spoken and it could be bloodshed. But before Tanuvasa could speak, Chief Alipia of Leulumoega rose, grabbed the orator's staff, and responded.

'Tofilau, you have spoken well and with wisdom. You are correct. You are indeed blood brothers with Taisi Tupua Efi. We did not therefore come to take Tanuvasa from you. Tanuvasa, you stay here. Support Tofilau. All we wanted was to seek clarification on the nature of the oath of allegiance you had given us. That's all. But you must now understand that Tofilau is no different from Tupua. The two are blood brothers. In short, stay here. Support Tofilau.'

Then Tanuvasa Livi stood up and spoke very briefly and to the point. 'Alipia and our district, I have no remorse. My only regret is that you have come to look for me like a runaway criminal. I thought you had come to visit your loving MP in the traditional manner and to make traditional presentations! I support Tofilau, who is none other than the brother of Tupua, and with those words I thank you for agreeing that I stay here.'

Then, another of our orators, Tuilagi Vavae, MP, under the instructions of Tofilau, delivered a long orator's speech which ended with the presentation of big fine mats, barrels of salted beef and cartons of canned fish.

Tuilagi's oratory was outshone by Alipia's choice of words, expressing their depth of gratitude at the turn of events and the gifts.

Alipia said, 'Thank you, Tofilau, for your kindness. Thank you very much. Thank you very much, Tofilau.'

Tofilau quietly said to me, 'Tui, listen very carefully. Mark my words, Alipia is an accomplished wheeler-dealer. Tupua sent them to come here to persuade Tanuvasa to go back and he does not expect them to come back empty-handed. When they go back with their *'ie toga* and *povi māsima* (salted beef), they will go straight home and never go back to Tupua. They will go back to Leulumoega and celebrate the occasion. What more can you get? Fine mats and food for the rest of the week. Great performance. Tupua will be kept waiting indefinitely.'

And they did exactly that.

Tofilau went to the Head of State to present our position. Our position was to dissolve the House. Tofilau came back and told us the Head of State said that Tupua had come with a proposal for a government of national unity, which Tofilau rejected. He restated his case for a dissolution. The Head of State then said, 'Tupua, I think it is fair now. Let Tofilau form up his government and you play the role of opposition.'

Two days later Parliament convened and Tofilau 'Eti Alesana and his new Cabinet were sworn in. As I drove out from Mulinu'u, I spotted three bus-loads of young men from Lauli'i parked on the seaward side of the Mulinu'u square. They were watching the flow of traffic that signalled the peaceful conclusion of the formation of government brought about by the two kingmakers: Misa Telefoni and Tanuvasa Livi.

Part 2. Stable Government – 1988–1998

April 1988 to December 1990 – Tofilau 'Eti Alesana's Third Administration

Election night results of the 26 February general election gave the HRPP 25 seats. Recounts reduced that number to 22. The outcome was finely balanced until defections from Tupua's coalition gave the HRPP a majority of 24 to 23 to form the government on 6 April.

The election of Tofilau 'Eti Alesana's third administration ended the most exciting, unstable and dramatic period in Samoa's modern political history. Tuila'epa had entered Parliament in May 1981 and, apart from the period of Tofilau's first administration (December 1982 to April 1985), much of his time in his first seven years as an MP had been occupied with the politics of survival rather than governance.

Tuila'epa recalls:

We had few debates in Parliament to discuss any important development issues. It was survival mode. Political manoeuvring. It was an excellent illustration of an unstable government that was more concerned with survival than anything to do with the governing or development of the country. We rarely met to talk sensibly about governing the country. All we were doing was manoeuvring, manoeuvring, manoeuvring to see who would take ultimate control of the government.

The next decade would be a contrast to the 'turbulent years'. Tofilau, with the support of Tuila'epa, would secure his leadership and develop a legacy of a long period of stable government enhanced by legal and political reforms, the consolidation of the political party system and an informal succession plan. Tuila'epa would put Samoa's finances on to a secure footing, modernising the economy, developing infrastructure and restructuring the public service. International relations would become an important aspect of Tuila'epa's growing portfolio of responsibilities as it was during this period when Tofilau's health started to decline. However, all would not be plain sailing. Two extreme weather events and protests would leave major scars on this decade.

Putting in place a new government was the first step. Tuila'epa takes up the story.

We assembled at Parliament and Tofilau was elected Prime Minister on 6 April 1988. He again appointed me as his Minister of Finance. Immediately after taking the oath in Parliament I was informed that, as the Samoan Minister of Finance, I was now the chair of the Board of Governors of the Asian Development Bank and that I had to leave in a few days for the annual Board of Governors' meeting in Manilla.

When I arrived, President Aquino was the new president, having recently taken over from Ferdinand Marcos. I was soon plunged into a very sensitive foreign relations problem that posed a potential embarrassment to both the president of the ADB and the new, democratically elected President Aquino of the Philippines.

It was also a problem that faced me as chairman of the Board of Governors. The People's Republic of China (PRC) had been admitted into the ADB the previous year, 1987. They should have attended the annual meeting but they refused to come because they wanted to see Taiwan kicked out first. Knowing that they couldn't do that, they decided, therefore, to boycott the meeting. But they decided to turn up in 1988 when I was the new chairman.

By tradition, the chairman of the Board of Directors hosts a welcome reception, preceding the opening of the formal meeting, to which the delegates of all the countries are invited. On this occasion, some 30 minutes into the party when everybody was happy, the protocol officer of the ADB came up to me and said, 'We have a problem.'

'What is the problem?'

'The delegates of the PRC have protested. They're very angry because the Taiwanese turned up wearing pins on which "The Republic of China" is printed in large letters.'

Part of the agreement for the membership of China stipulates that Taiwan must never use the words 'Republic of China' in any form to refer to their country, Taiwan. There is only one 'Republic of China' and the correct official label is 'The People's Republic of China'.

The protocol officer warned me that there could be big problems ahead.

What was I going to do? I had to think fast and find an immediate solution.

I said to the protocol officer, 'The meeting opens tomorrow at 10 o'clock. I badly need a rest. I will withdraw now, and you stay and say farewell to the guests on my behalf.'

Because of my absence I hoped the Chinese would have no chance to express their disappointment.

I was wrong: at exactly 12.30 a.m. the phone in my room rang. The phone kept on ringing and ringing. Then I knew the Chinese would not stop.

I answered the phone, 'This is the chairman of the ABD Board of Governors. What is it?'

'Sir. This is the Chinese delegation.'

'What do you want?'

'My minister wants to see you immediately.'

I said, 'I am sorry, I am in bed, it is bedtime.'

'Sir . . .'

'It's bedtime.'

I put the telephone down.

Again it rang and rang and rang. I lifted it up.

The caller shouted, 'My minister tells me that if you don't meet now we are going to make an ugly scene tomorrow. We are going to protest. We are going to boycott the opening and embarrass the government.'

'OK. I will see you at 7 o'clock sharp tomorrow morning. But not now.'

I hung up and immediately rang my twelve-man delegation.

'At 6 a.m. you all need to come here and we'll go for a walk. We will walk for a total of 45 minutes then come back, shower and dress formally. Be at my room at 7. We are going to meet the Chinese PRC delegation. You must also alert the Taiwanese that I want to see them at 8 o'clock.'

At 7 the following morning we met the PRC minister. She spoke in Chinese and was translated. She asked me to use my powers as chairman to be strict with the Taiwanese as they had committed breaches of the agreement with the ADB. She reminded me that as chairman I had the power to discipline the Taiwanese. I listened very carefully. When she finished I was silent for two minutes. She kept looking at me. I kept looking at her.

Then I said, 'Have you finished?'

'Yes, sir,' was the impatient response.

'Is this the only garbage that you woke me up at 1 o'clock in the morning for?'

'Yes, sir.' She started to go red in the face.

'If this chairmanship was occupied by an American or Russian, would you ring them up at 1 o'clock in the morning?'

She said nothing.

I said, 'You know, I am extremely disappointed that you, a governor, should think that you have the right to wake me up in the middle of the night to listen to your backyard dispute with Taiwan. It's your backyard dispute and you bring it here to this international organisation, this august body, where we talk no nonsense but matters of finance.'

My remarks were translated, and I could see her getting redder and redder all over.

I continued, 'You try to tell me how I should do my job as chairman as if I do not understand. You are presumptuous. You think I don't know how to run this organisation. I know exactly my role. My role begins to take effect from the moment I sit on the chair to conduct the proceedings. Outside of the meeting room I have no business to interfere with members' freedom. Maybe you have your own ways to conduct meetings? But it is not the way we do business in the ADB. I tell you again, I am disgusted by the way you have behaved. If you are a minister of state, then behave like one. This is my warning to you. Should you disrupt the meeting tomorrow I will throw you out of the meeting. Then I will summon a media conference and through the media I will speak directly to your bosses in Beijing. I will say, "Never, never again send stupid people like this to come and represent your country and embarrass your government." This is the end of our meeting.'

My remarks were translated. She got up and left. She was very red in the face.

At 8 o'clock the Taiwanese walked in. I said the same thing to them.

'You make a scene at the meeting and I will have the guards evict you from the room. Then I will summon a media conference and tell your people, your bosses, not to send foolish ministers to future meetings of the ADB.'

So they all left.

Two hours later I delivered the opening address. The Chinese never spoke up or caused any disruptions to the proceedings, nor did the Taiwanese. At the end of the meeting, the Chinese minister got up and she said, 'Chairman, president, members, I want to thank you all for agreeing that my country will host the ADB annual board meeting in Beijing next year. Now I invite my fellow colleagues from Taiwan to come. We will welcome you all to our country.'

After the formal meetings, the leaders of each delegation usually have a brief meeting with the president of the ADB to discuss any bilateral issues. After I met with the president, a Japanese national, he walked me to the door and out to the lift. Later the secretary of the ADB said to me, 'The president was so grateful for the manner you smoothed over the looming dispute between the two Chinese. The president has never before walked a governor to the lift. This is the first time. He has done it to show you his gratitude.'

I had wanted to tell him that walking is the best exercise for any president in office!

There is a postscript to this story.

In April 1989 I went to China for the ADB Board of Governors' meeting. It was interesting when I saw a newspaper article quoting the same Chinese woman minister who was now chairing the Beijing meeting. She said, 'I have to extend my gratitude to the ADB for agreeing that we host this meeting. I am very busy with the arrangements, but there is one person I would especially like to make mention of and I look forward to meeting him tomorrow. He is the outgoing chairman of the ADB Board, the Honourable Tuila'epa.' I saw her the following day on a courtesy call. She was all smiles and very friendly.

We passed Tiananmen Square every day to attend the plenary meetings of the Board. There were always people hovering around the great square. It was only in the evenings, when I turned on CNN in my hotel room, that I learnt that something was brewing. We did not see any disturbances. Those were the times when control was very tight, when government reforms on press freedom were beginning to take shape and reformers were pressing for more than the authorities were prepared to tolerate. It was when we dispersed, and I was in Hong Kong, that the news came out of the crackdown on the students' movement. Which was kind of strange because we were there and didn't see any apparent tension. The severity of the government's reaction received much publicity, attention and condemnation world-wide, and many official visits to Beijing were cancelled.

In late 1988, before the Tiananmen Square incident, Tofilau had arranged with the Chinese that he would pay a state visit to China. When all the other nations were boycotting China, Tofilau decided that he would proceed with the visit. The Australian, New Zealand and American diplomats tried hard to persuade him not to go. Tofilau kept telling them that he would go. He argued that what had transpired was an internal matter. So Tofilau displayed the independence of his decision-making and he went to China.

This came to be an historical state visit for China because Tofilau was the first head of a government to formally visit the country following the Tiananmen Square incident and to break the boycott. Because there were discussions on assistance from China to be held, I was required by the Prime Minister to accompany him. When we arrived, the government organised a full military guard of honour and a 21-gun salute to welcome Tofilau and our delegation. There were press releases about the Samoan Prime Minister's visit to China and how the Chinese government was most appreciative. In the meetings that followed, led by Premier Li Peng, we put it to the Chinese that we needed their help for a building for our central government offices. Many of our ministries were operating from offices scattered all over Apia. The Chinese responded positively and funds for the Fiamē Mataʻafa Faumuinā Mulinuʻu II Building were secured. This central government five-storey office building became the biggest building in Samoa and houses the offices of the Prime Minister and Cabinet and several ministries.

An event of great significance politically, which almost destroyed the cohesion of the HRPP, occurred in early April 1989 when Tofilau was struck by an angina attack and had to be rushed to New Zealand for treatment. I was in Auckland, on my way to Beijing for the ADB meeting. So I visited Tofilau in hospital. He said to me that he had just received a comforting cable from Sir Guy Powles, former Governor of pre-independence Samoa, and he'd told him, 'This is plain sailing.' He'd had the same multiple bypass operation. So Tofi felt a great comfort. I was happy to see him and I left for Beijing.

While Tuilaʻepa was out of the country, and Tofilau was having surgery and recuperating in New Zealand, a new set of plotters were at work in Samoa.

Two of our backbenchers became so convinced that the Prime Minister might not survive his ordeal that they began to create their own factions in preparation to challenge the leadership of the party. Professor Tuaopepe Wendt, former head of the agriculture campus of the University of the South Pacific (USP) at Alafua, who defeated the Honourable Mamea for the Lefaga and Faleaseela Constituency at the 1988 general election, was leader of one faction; the Honourable To'i Aukuso led the other faction.

Both To'i and Tuaopepe, together with other members of Parliament's Public Accounts Committee, were specially appointed by the Prime Minister on my advice to be watchdogs against any abuses perpetrated within any ministry of government or a semi-independent corporation. The Public Accounts Committee was the ideal training ground for new MPs to learn about the good governance principles of transparency and accountability. The committee's brief was to study reports and budgets and question the government on inappropriate spending. What happened, in hindsight, was that the committee members, instead of serving the party interest in promoting good governance, used their positions to nit pick and back stab the Prime Minister, and other Ministers in Cabinet, including me. They used the opportunities they got to advance their own political agendas.

There was a lot of internal plotting to take over the government should Tofilau die during surgery, and the Public Accounts Committee members of our HRPP were at the centre of the plot.

There was one occasion when the committee came to see me. At that time I was Acting Prime Minister, as Tofilau was overseas attending the Commonwealth Heads of Government Meeting (CHOGM). The committee members were concerned with the way we were approving tenders to construction companies that were well known to be anti-HRPP.

I said to them, 'Look, government policies stipulate that all public works must be tendered out. What matters is the competence of the tenderers and that the price of the job should be cost effective and competitive. The government must be professional and objective in its decision-making. We are guided by two criteria only, professionalism and competence.'

Their spokesman objected. 'We disagree with you. You must give jobs only to those companies that support the HRPP. These anti-HRPP companies will fill up their pockets with money from the jobs we give them and will become so rich they will use the moneys they get from us to defeat the HRPP Members at the next general election.'

I said, 'I'm sorry. I can't accept your logic. What would you do if by the end of our term we had done absolutely nothing, and we tell the constituencies that all these companies doing public works are working against us – the government and the party – and not for us? What do you think they are going to say? We put in Parliament people who are intelligent, not fools.'

They took exception to my response.

Professor Wendt said to me, 'Tui, you had better listen to us. We can really make things hard for you. We can easily throw stones at you when Parliament meets.'

I responded, 'Felix, I like that. You can come with sacks of stones into the House. But I will bring only one stone and with that one stone I can hit you all! So don't you threaten me.'

We didn't see these Members again at our caucus meetings for three months. At one meeting, the Prime Minister told us the reason those backbenchers did not show up was that I had been disrespectful to them during his absence when I was Acting Prime Minister.

Another major decision Cabinet made in 1988 was to ban the export of tropical timber logs. At one of our Cabinet meetings, the Prime Minister confided that he was intensely pro-environmental protection. He did not want any more logging done. Tofilau and I were always for the protection of the environment. This commonality of interest led to the decision to ban the export of logs and also to add on the protection of the environment as an extra responsibility of the Ministry of Lands, Survey and the Environment. Since logging for export was a very popular business venture for many of our supporters, the opposition was intensely against the government. Some, such as those who had Chinese loggers on their land, started to turn against us. When we stopped the logging we had more enemies.

Since Tofilau and I were seen as always being close in all these matters, automatically some of our enemies within our own party began working in the background to remove the two of us. The thing I liked about Tofilau was that he was a fighter. He was a strategist himself. After years of being an MP and a Minister in Mata'afa's Cabinet, he had enormous political experience. His understanding of business principles was also very good, as he had owned stores and run a shop. Moreover, he studied at one time to become a pastor and had a great depth of knowledge about the Bible. Many years ago when he lost an election, he went to Malua Theological College as a mature student but failed his theology exams. This was a point that Tupua used to embarrass Tofi. In the debates he used to say that Tofilau was a poor English speaker and that he failed his examinations at the theological college.

One day, Tupua said in Parliament, 'Tofilau, you are weak. You don't speak English properly.'

Tofilau responded in the heat of the debate, 'You are right. I taught myself English under the breadfruit trees while picking cocoa pods. But didn't your eloquence bankrupt the country?'

On another occasion Tupua charged, 'You failed your exams to become a pastor.'

Tofilau responded, 'Your father sent you overseas for your education. There is one thing I remember: when I asked Professor Aikman what he knew about our Samoan students at Victoria University and how they were doing, Professor Aikman said to me, "Tofi, all the students are doing quite well, exceptionally well, except this kid Efi Nelson."' And there was laughter in the House.

Tofilau said to me later, with a grin on his face, 'Oh, it slipped my mind. I should have corrected Efi. I did not fail my exams once, I failed them three times!'

*

When I came back from China, Tofilau was still convalescing. I found that the campaign for succession in anticipation of Tofilau's death had heated up. One MP had even gone to New Zealand to see the surgeon who had treated Tofilau and ask if his patient was dying so that arrangements for his succession could be put in place. Wisely, the doctor threw him out of his office.

Meanwhile, on my way back from China I went to Singapore and linked up with Mose Sua and Vaʻai Kolone, the Financial Secretary, and flew to Austria to meet with Organization of Petroleum Exporting Countries (OPEC) on our proposed loan for a major electric power project. It was after we completed our negotiations that I spoke to my sister in New Zealand and she told me that my mother had died in New Zealand. Mose and Vaʻai travelled on to Paris to complete our negotiations, while I travelled to Auckland to prepare for my mother's funeral before I returned to Samoa. Tofilau was still convalescing in Auckland.

On the day that I arrived back in Samoa, I went to my office and tried to catch up with my mail when I got a call to say that the HRPP caucus was meeting and that I was summoned immediately to appear before the caucus to answer to some allegations.

As soon as I arrived at the meeting I saw that Patū Afa Hunter was in the chair. He was Acting Prime Minister, as Tofilau and I had been out of Samoa. Patū Afa is closely related to Tuaopepe, Professor Felix Wendt, who was party secretary. I soon worked out that both of them were eyeing the leadership of the party if Tofilau died, and considered themselves more than qualified. They also knew that they had to deal with the Minister of Finance. That is the reason they were now going to try to haul me before the caucus.

When I arrived, Afa Patū said, 'It's good that you are here. I will ask Tuaopepe Wendt to read out the minutes for your information.'

There were no written minutes but Tuaopepe said, 'We have discussed two issues. One, why certain Ministers are absent and do not attend our caucus; and, two, why should Cabinet listen to you when it comes to economic affairs? We believe our country has suffered because you did not appreciate our currency. If you had appreciated our money long ago, our debts would probably have been written off with the higher value of our Tala, and the cost of living would have come down. You have single-handedly driven the economy down. That is what the caucus has been discussing.'

Then Patū ordered me, 'Now, Mr Minister of Finance, respond immediately.'

I said, 'Patū, you are the Acting Prime Minister. The first point you raised, in the so-called minutes, asking why certain Ministers did not attend caucus, needs no answer. For your information, Mr Acting Prime Minister, one of the reasons you are Acting Prime Minister is because the Prime Minister is undergoing surgery and I hope he will get better soon. In case our caucus does not understand. Second, you will remember that the Cabinet approved my absence so that I could attend OPEC meetings in Europe. Thirdly, no Minister can depart without a Cabinet decision. It strikes me, Patū, that you, as Acting Prime Minister, don't seem to remember these things.'

My voice was rising, and rising and rising.

'And now I must address you, Professor Wendt. Professor, do you understand what minutes are? Minutes are recorded discussions of a meeting. Recorded. You said you gave the minutes. You never gave any minutes. You talk about what is in your mind. Is that the way a secretary delivers minutes? These are not minutes. Minutes are written on paper and should be presented to, and passed by, a meeting. And now I come to the main point. Acting Prime Minister, in matters of educational policies you are the Minister of Education. All public servants can deliver their thoughts and recommendations through you to Cabinet. That is also what I do. I recommend policy matters to Cabinet with the help of my advisers. No one can present any finance or economic management issues to Cabinet except through me as Minister of Finance. Do you understand, Professor Wendt? We have each been charged by law with these responsibilities.'

Apparently all this time, Wendt had been visiting everyone in caucus and promoting himself as the successor of Tofilau. Most of our people seemed to have been carried away by his arguments. And he had been running me down without my knowledge. But now I faced up to Professor Wendt.

Professor Wendt said to me, 'Minister of Finance. You listen too much to the Financial Secretary. You should listen to us. It is from us that you will get direction. Listen to the caucus.'

'Professor Wendt,' I said, 'have you forgotten that before I was Minister of Finance I was adviser to previous Ministers of Finance and previous Prime Ministers? Have you forgotten that? I listen to advice, even when the CEO is less qualified than me. I have to listen to different advisers. That's the difference between you and me. I listen to advisers before I make up my mind which advice to accept. Besides, Professor, and I will speak directly to you now, there is a big difference between us. You were a Professor of Agriculture Science, for instance, with knowledge about planting coconuts.' (I tried to simplify it for our caucus.) 'For advice on planting bananas the proper person we go to is you. Like impregnating a cow in a different way, different from what God created, we come to you, because you are a professor of those agricultural systems. You are the authority. But when it comes to finance, you come and listen to me. You are an absolute fool when it comes to matters of finance. I have never come across such an idle-minded professor as you. Do not tell me that I listen too much to my advisers.'

I was absolutely furious. My voice was right up there.

At that point some of the older MPs intervened, in the usual style, to reconcile us. Professor Wendt was absolutely dumbfounded. He did not know what to say. After the reconciliation, I shook his hand and said, 'Let's forgive each other.'

I left the caucus meeting, jumped into my car, came over to my office and worked on my Budget, which I was due to present to Parliament in a few days. I was there for something like half an hour, when Fiamē Matā'afa turned up. She sat in front of me and openly wept.

She said, 'You do not know that our party has been near collapse. Last week, when you were overseas, I was invited twice to meetings, once to a party held by To'i and another held by Professor Wendt. At these parties these guys were bragging on, "When Tofilau dies, I have seven Members in my pocket", or "I have fourteen". They all believed that Tofilau would die.'

That was the turning point. When Fiamē saw me, she said, 'You have saved the day. I think we were on the point of breaking up and your toughness has helped to bring the party together again.'

Later, Tanuvasa turned up and said to me, 'I think that you saved the day. You know, many of these old people really believed what Professor Wendt was telling them. But they were fascinated when you said that you had never met a more "idle-minded professor" and called him an idiot, because they had always treated him with respect. They expected him to respond, but he never did.'

Three days later Tofilau rang me up from New Zealand at about 11 at night.

He said, 'How are things, Tui?'

'Everything is alright,' I replied.

Knowing his condition, I did not want to tell him what had transpired.

Then he said, 'Thank you. I shall come home next week. I shall have to patch things over. I will have to talk to Patū.'

The following week Tofilau came back. None of the plotters came out to the airport to welcome him home. None of the Public Accounts Committee was present to welcome their leader.

Over the next two months Tofilau, in his own way, brought these guys back one by one, as if there had never been a rupture.

*

Tofilau was always interested in cultivating a greater and closer relationship with Washington. When the forest fires occurred in Savai'i in 1983, Tofilau's first reaction was to request help from the United States. Later that year, when Samoa hosted the 1983 Pacific Games, his first thoughts were to approach the United States Agency for International Development for help. And when the New Zealand Prime Minister David Lange banned United States nuclear warships from berthing in New Zealand ports, Tofilau welcomed the opportunity for Samoa to host United States ships to berth at Apia.

The opening of a Samoan Embassy in Washington was an extension of Tofilau's policy of building greater rapport with Washington. The New York office deals with the world at large, with a focus on the United Nations. The Washington office is more focussed on cultivating a much closer relationship with the legislative, executive and judicial branches of the United States government. Our Embassy staff would also be able to liaise more closely with the Office of the Representative of the American Samoan Government in Congress. Together, both offices could serve the interests of the two Samoas. Once the idea was accepted by Cabinet, the question arose as to who would start up the office.

Tuaopepe Felix Wendt became the logical choice for the post of Ambassador to the United States based in Washington.

What about his position as an MP? There was no legal barrier against his holding both posts at the same time. Tuaopepe and his family subsequently moved to Washington, and when necessary, he flew back to Apia to attend parliamentary meetings. The great expectations that led to the establishment of the Washington office did not materialise and, when Tuaopepe was defeated by Le Mamea in the 1991 general election, the office was closed down.

Reforms
Because of what had happened when we were both out of the country, Tofilau decided that he must formally appoint a deputy leader of the party to succeed the leader and deputise in his absence. The deputy leader position had lapsed when Tofilau became leader in 1982. This was one of a number of reforms that we put in place.

A small committee was appointed in 1990 to study the role of deputy leader and to make recommendations to the party. I chaired the committee. Our report was made to caucus late in 1990 prior to the 1991 general election. We recommended appointing the deputy leader of the party on the following conditions: every member of the caucus was to be eligible, the deputy leader was to be chosen by secret ballot, after each ballot the lowest polling candidate would be eliminated until the winner emerged, the deputy leader would automatically become a Cabinet Minister and the deputy would not automatically become leader. The reason why we recommended this was to ensure that the caucus should have the right to appoint another, worthier candidate if the deputy leader proved to be a mistake.

The proposal was deferred until after the general election. When the vote came I was appointed deputy leader.

There were many reforms introduced during this period. Financial reforms continued to be implemented by Tuila'epa and changes were made to the Electoral Act and how executive government was structured and operated. It was in this period that the number of Cabinet Ministers was extended from eight to twelve, and the role of parliamentary Under-Secretaries, later Associate Ministers, was introduced.

During 1988 and 1989 we were still reeling from the experience of the breakup, when Va'ai Kolone and other founders of the HRPP left. We decided to do something about it. A number of key reforms were set in place.

We set up and passed a law in 1989 to provide for the appointment of parliamentary Under-Secretaries. We thought that it would help to bind us together, spread the workload and provide some succession planning. Up to that time there were only eight Ministers. The Parliamentary Under-Secretaries Act provided for a post between a Minister and an ordinary MP, which was designed to help the Minister. The Under-Secretary would have an office, a car, a telephone and a slightly higher salary. But they would take their orders from the Minister. We had to be careful about the potential abuse of power. The Under-Secretary is under instructions from the Minister and he reports back to the Minister. The parliamentary Under-Secretary does not have any other mandate.

We had to be cautious as power corrupts and absolute power corrupts absolutely! You give power to a person and he is likely to abuse it, so there have to be checks and balances. The check and balance is that the Under-Secretary only moves when the Minister says so. He must report back to the Minister and must not give any orders to any person. He listens to the Minister only. It was very limited authority.

In 1990 we decided to do something about *matai pālota* and *matai* suffrage. Up to that time, only *matai* voted and there had been a great increase in the number of *matai* titles that had been created to help particular *matai* candidates to win in general elections. Furthermore, some constituencies that resisted the practice of creating multiple *matai* titles for these purposes had a very small number of voters. For example, Faleata Sasa'e had only about 40 voters. There were only 114 voters in my constituency of Lepā, and it was far easier to meet with the smaller number of voters than before the change.

When Samoa's Constitution was written in 1960 it aimed to balance Samoan custom and Western democracy. Thirty years on it was getting out of balance.

Our voting system needed urgent reform, and our Electoral Act needed to be rewritten. The only way to cut out the *matai pālota* and achieve universal suffrage was to have a referendum. Two questions were to be put. First, whether to extend the vote to women, non-*matai* and pastors; and second, to decide whether Samoa should have two Houses of Parliament, an Upper and a Lower House. That question came from the Head of State. He was very concerned that the *tama-a-'āiga* should be separated and only they and their *'āiga* should go to the Upper House, with the rest going to the Lower House. Those two issues were included in the referendum.

Another reform we wanted was the extension of the parliamentary term to five years. The Attorney-General ruled that that matter was separate and did not have to go to a referendum and could be handled by a vote in Parliament.

To amend the Constitution and extend the parliamentary term we needed to have a two-thirds majority. We needed one more person to achieve the two-thirds majority and we got Leota Itu'au 'Ale, an opposition MP who was the former deputy head of the HRPP to Va'ai. He came across, offered his support, and voted with the government to raise our parliamentary term to five years.

The people supported universal suffrage but they did not support a bi-cameral Parliament. Our people knew the expense of having one House of Parliament and could not see the value in a second House.

To cap off the changes, Tofilau moved a formal motion for the leader of the opposition, Tui Ātua Tupua Tamasese, to be moved upwards to the Council of Deputies. He rejected it, outright! His rejection was based on the assumption that Tofilau wanted him out and he didn't want to leave the Parliament. He also argued that he should have been consulted before the motion was put. Why? He genuinely thought that he could make it back to lead the government.

There is another change that we introduced. We changed the financial year from the calendar year to July to June, to coincide with the financial years of New Zealand and other donor countries. So our budgeting periods fall in the same time. It also made it easier for us to allocate funds. On top of that, I felt that the long Budget meetings at the end of the year only caused a lot of ill-feeling when we were supposed to move towards Christmas. When you argue about finance in Parliament, it leads to a lot of name-calling. That is not in the Christmas spirit.

Cyclone 'Ofa and Cyclone Val

Severe tropical Cyclone 'Ofa struck Samoa on 1 February 1990, reaching peak intensity on 4 February with heavy rain, huge waves, sea spray, storm surges and wind gusts exceeding 150 kilometres per hour. Seven people were killed, many were injured and hundreds evacuated, while the entire population was left in a state of shock. Extreme damage to crops, trees, general infrastructure, roads, bridges, wharves, seawalls and many buildings was also recorded. Samoa had made good progress on the slow road to recovery from Cyclone 'Ofa when a second severe weather event, Cyclone Val, struck Samoa in December 1991, destroying much of the recently repaired infrastructure and creating further damage. Cyclone Val lasted for five days, moving back and forth across both Samoas, generating winds of over 240 kilometres per hour and 15-metre waves. Seventeen people were killed. Damage in Western Samoa was estimated at over US$200 million.

Samoa is situated in a climate zone that is vulnerable to tropical cyclones. However, it had not experienced an extreme weather event since 1889. That was to change dramatically with two 'once-in-a-hundred-year' storms hitting Samoa within one year. Tuila'epa was in the eye of these storms and played a major role in organising disaster relief and rebuilding Samoa's crippled infrastructure.

Tuila'epa sets the scene.

In January 1990 the Commonwealth Games were held in New Zealand and the Head of State attended. He was coming back on the night of 31 January, the day our party caucus held a meeting at Matautu. We cut the meeting short at 3.30 p.m. because the winds were increasing. No one in our caucus knew of the impending damaging storm because Radio 2AP kept talking about 'cross-winds', very strong currents of 'cross-winds', interpreted literally into Samoan as *Taula'iga matagi*. All that was necessary was for the announcer to mention one word, *afā*, and everybody would know. No Samoan knew that this was a big storm, a cyclone.

When I was going around by the town clock I turned on the radio to listen to the weather forecast. It said, 'Expect strong cross-winds.' Later I thought of the importance of using our own language, of never interpreting the words literally from English to Samoan. You only had to mention *afā* and everyone here would have known to prepare. So I never prepared and my family never prepared. We were all caught unaware.

At the time Tofilau was unwell, he had just returned from heart surgery and several months' recuperation. He asked me to go, as Deputy Prime Minister, to meet the Head of State at Faleolo Airport. I waited for the plane to arrive at about 11 o'clock at night. What struck me as I was driving to the airport were the many pebbles and rocks that had been forced by the waves onto the road. I had to weave my way around them.

At 11 o'clock the plane arrived and I went to open the car door to go out and meet Malietoa. I could not open the door. At that time I realised we had a major storm and the Head of State was arriving in the middle of it. I had to tell the driver to go directly to the gangway and pick up the Head of State and drive him straight home. I followed.

When I reached Tuanaimato, there it was. Power lines were down, TV poles were down, trees were down. It was strange. It was midnight when I decided to turn in at Lepea and head up towards home on the road through the sports complex at Vaitele. I cut through a track in a plantation. Trees started falling in front of me and behind me. I was caught in between. So I manoeuvred myself and threaded my way through the cocoa trees to try and get to my home. Another tree fell in front of me. Luckily I was not hit. It was still in the middle of the night as I manoeuvred myself through the trees and it took me three hours to get home. It was 4 in the morning when I arrived.

In the morning not one of us moved from the house. All the electric wires were down. For three days you could hear this screeching sound right throughout the night, right throughout the day. It reached 125 miles per hour. I got all my children to stay inside so they would not be electrocuted.

At the end of the third day the sun came up. I went out to see the old man, the Prime Minister. We could still hear the radio communicating and the announcer, Joe Brown, said, 'It's great to see the sun. The real sun has come out.' The sun shone for two hours and everyone started to move around and clear things up. Everyone thought that this was the end. But the worst was to come.

The Cabinet all came to see the Prime Minister and we had our meeting at his place. Suddenly we heard terrible screeching, screeching sounds of an iron roofing flying, then another and another. We heard the wind changing direction, it was moving to the south. We all quickly rushed home. The worst happened that afternoon and evening. Altogether it went on for four days. Then finally it was finished.

We met, and Tofilau asked me to be the chairman of the National Disaster Council. I called in all the members of all the key organisations, as well as members of the Diplomatic Corps, the UNDP, all the heads of international agencies in Samoa and all the CEOs of government departments. We met and made decisions. The first was to issue a Declaration of Emergency. Under the Constitution that is very necessary because, for any relief action we undertake, nobody is allowed to take action for compensation against the government. The declaration gave us the necessary powers. All the powers in any other legislation are set aside as an emergency measure to enable the government's National Disaster Council to do what is necessary to provide immediate relief to the injured, deal with the dead and take any action to stop further damage. We moved very fast.

Before Cyclone 'Ofa, in February 1989, the heaviest rainfall ever fell on the mountains, which resulted in the destruction of the Vaimoso Bridge. The current bridge replaced the one destroyed in 1989. The reason why this was important was that we bury our dead outside our homes in Samoa. Some of those buried were not secure and got washed away. A lot of caskets were seen floating in the sea with the bodies inside. That was the worst rainfall that we had. We didn't know then but I suppose that this was the beginning of climate change. A lot of roads were destroyed. All this happened at the beginning of 1989 and led to our approaching the ADB to give us a programme loan for infrastructure. The Vaimoso Bridge was part of the destruction that we had to rehabilitate. Help was also given to us by Australia and New Zealand.

The way that the disaster of 1989 was handled by the Director of Public Works was a disappointment. We asked the Director of Public Works to prepare an engineering report to give an account of the damage to our donors. When the report came out it was not done by an engineering firm, but by an architectural firm that belonged to the Director of Public Works. The outcome of that was his dismissal, which caused quite a furore amongst our party because that fellow was a close friend of some senior MPs. I was abused and blamed for his removal, because it was a Treasury report that recorded the incident and Treasury was under me. My people were just doing what was honest and I was abused for it.

That was in the lead-up to 'Ofa. The experience of handling that disaster was to give me a good understanding of how to handle the next one. The destruction during 'Ofa was the worst in living memory. It was particularly bad in Fagaloa Bay and also the western tip of Savai'i where most of the houses were lost.

We had done our homework and had all these figures, enumerating the number of people affected in each village from the census. So we knew the numbers of people and could calculate very quickly what food was required. For example, with rice, we counted out so many ounces per person and we added this together to determine how many bags of rice would go to each village. Within days, everything was sent out. There are two principles that would dictate how we'd organise our help: one, the relief must reach the needy within the shortest possible time; two, it must be fair, and cover everybody affected.

A United Nations delegation arrived from Indonesia. The head said that he had arranged a shipment of rice to arrive in three months and he wanted to give it to just two villages. That is when I intervened. I said, 'No. The villages that you referred to had the most damage in terms of houses lost. In Samoa we can build a traditional house in less than 24 hours. Nevertheless, we should allocate the tents, with the majority of tents going to those two villages. But when it comes to other items, such as water containers and food, we must cover the whole country because every farm was destroyed, every crop was destroyed, and you only have to go outside of this room and look across at the mountain. What do you see? Bare earth. Most of the branches are bare. You can see the soil. Every tree has been stripped of its fruit. A lot of *taro* plantations have been uprooted. Everyone is affected.'

Then the local organisations spoke up, supporting what I had said, and the rice was subsequently distributed according to the two principles we had agreed on.

At the end of the emergency period, I did not hear any complaints about misappropriation of goods. That is an indication of how quickly we moved. We laid the foundation for managing the other disasters that were to follow. Because of the problems we had with our telecommunications, which were totally destroyed, New Zealand, Australia and Japan came in and helped us out. When Cyclone Valerie hit us we were able to send out signals and messages from Samoa. This had been the problem we faced with 'Ofa. For the first few hours all our communications were dead, and New Zealand, Australia and all the other donor countries did not know what was happening to Samoa. That was resolved before Val hit us.

When Val hit, less than one year later, it was worse than 'Ofa. It hit us on 7 December. The reason I can remember the date well is because it was the same day we were going to open our new church at Siusega. We were all gathered to celebrate when this thing hit. The gusts reached 175 miles per hour. It had far greater intensity than 'Ofa.

*

There had not been a cyclone of this magnitude since the 'Great Cyclone' of March 1889. In the nineteenth century there was a struggle between the 'Great Powers' for trade and colonial possessions in Asia, Africa, the Americas and the Pacific. Small European nations were seeking colonies to provide natural resources to fuel their industrial growth such as minerals, commodities and food. The Pacific Islands were targeted for copra, cocoa, cotton and phosphate. German traders had built up a large trade centred on Samoa, and Samoa was also important to the British and the Americans.

There had been various attempts to mediate a settlement between the competing colonial powers, and the Washington Conference of 1887 had been adjourned. However, each of the Great Powers was siding with different Samoan warlords and stirring up civil war.

The confrontation between the United States, Imperial Germany and Great Britain from 1887 to 1889 had escalated into a standoff in early 1889 involving three American warships, USS *Vandalia*, USS *Trenton* and USS *Nipsic*; and three German warships, SMS *Adler*, SMS *Olga* and SMS *Eber*, which were keeping each other at bay over several months in Apia harbour. They were monitored by the British warship, HMS *Calliope*.

The standoff ended dramatically on 15 and 16 of March when a massive cyclone wrecked all six warships in the harbour. The *Calliope* was able to escape the harbour and survived the storm. Subsequently there were protests in Washington, London and Paris from the relatives of the many young sailors and soldiers who had died. Herbert von Bismarck, son of the German Chancellor, invited delegations from the United States and Great Britain to Berlin in April to sort out territorial conflicts in the Pacific. The Treaty of Berlin was negotiated, concluded and signed on 14 June 1889.

The Treaty of Berlin divided up the Pacific amongst the Great Powers, recognising German control of 'Western Samoa', a large part of New Guinea and other territories; the United States control of 'Eastern Samoa'; and the British control of Fiji, the Solomon Islands and various other territories. The French were not present in Berlin but had already secured control over a number of island territories.

The great cyclone of 1889 was a significant event at the beginning of the colonial division of the Samoan Islands, leading to the German governance of 'German Samoa', later known as 'Western Samoa', and now Samoa.

Tuila'epa takes up the story.

In early 1989 Tofilau said to me that we should commemorate the one-hundredth anniversary of the 1889 cyclone and invite the Germans, Americans and British to come, at the same time touching them for some aid project to commemorate the occasion. They gave us a small amount of money to repair the Nelson Public Library. We had a laugh about it. Well, it was worth the effort. The commemoration was held in September 1989.

We always prided ourselves that, before these two cyclones, Samoa was in a cyclone-free zone. Then when the cyclones struck we said, 'It was bad luck to celebrate the 1889 cyclone.' We'd celebrated a cyclone a hundred years ago, not realising another cyclone would hit us a few weeks later. The cyclone in 1889 had lifted some boats out of the water and deposited them on the reef without any damage to their hulls. That is what happened a hundred years later to our big passenger vessel, the *Queen Salamasina*. In 1990 she was lifted straight out of the water and was deposited on reclaimed land. We had to wait for a spring tide to dig a hole around her and tow the boat out safely, with hardly any damage. That is why that hole is over there . . . You can see it from my office window.

We had two one-hundred-year cyclones in one year! We had all felt after Cyclone 'Ofa that this was the last one for another hundred years so when we were hit again, hardly eleven months later, we thought how wrong we were. We did what we did before. We broadcast to all the *pulenu'u*, the village mayors, saying, 'Get all the young people from the villages and organise everyone to help. Clean up. Use your free labour.' Within less than eight hours you could drive around. This is the value of having your own traditional institutions to fall back on.

Now, with any cyclone the first task is to be on the air, to use the radio to talk to the village representatives to activate our system. The young men go out and clean things up as their contribution to the national effort. We have been doing that for some time now. It was the same when the tsunami hit. The National Disaster Council moved in and immediately applied the help provided by the government through our own monies before looking to see what assistance was needed from other countries. We have always been very fortunate to have friendly governments who are ready to come and help us in our time of need. New Zealand is always the first to come to our aid. Followed by Australia, China, Japan and the United States.

Samoa has a very good record with its post-disaster performance and the use of donor funds, observing the principles of accountability and transparency. Because we have high marks there, the donors have granted to us assistance through budgetary support and other additional incentives and related concessions. With the onslaught of a sudden cyclone, it immediately reduces our revenue sources from agriculture, Customs duties and tourism. That is why we value the budgetary support provided by New Zealand and Australia. Budgetary support is an instrument that is hardly ever used by donors, because of the ease with which it can be misused, especially in countries with dictatorships. So budgetary support is rare. But Samoa has been watched very carefully and we have been using the funds properly so the door is open to us. Over the years we have developed greater self-sufficiency and reduced our dependence on donors.

January 1991 to December 1995 – Tofilau 'Eti Alesana's Fourth Administration

The first election conducted under universal suffrage gave the HRPP a comfortable win, 27 seats to Tupua Tamasese's SNDP's fifteen seats.

In the 1991 general election, Tupua Tamasese was defeated by Moananu Salale, an ordinary *matai* from Falefa district with the support of the HRPP. An agreement had been made between the two coalition leaders. Va'ai had led from 1986 to 1988; Tupua would now lead. That all changed when Tupua was defeated. Tupua reached a pact with Vaʻai to hold the post temporarily as the head of the coalition.

Tupua later took an action to court, which he won, and Moananu's appointment was annulled. Tupua was able to make it back to Parliament in mid-1992. On 17 August 1992 Vaʻai relinquished leadership and Tupua took over as opposition leader.

Tuilaʻepa takes up the story again.

Misa Telefoni was not impressed and he decided to leave the coalition. He argued that Vaʻai and Tupua should never have decided the leadership between the two of them. He felt that it was a matter for the caucus to decide and said that the moment Tupua fell he had no right to come back as leader even if he had been re-elected. Misa said that the caucus should decide who should be the new leader and that he [Misa] would have the right to challenge for the leadership. As this was a 'trick', Misa decided to leave. He said that he could not serve Vaʻai under the circumstances. He preferred to serve under the HRPP and so he went and saw Tofilau.

Tofilau, in turn, raised Misa's request to join the HRPP with our Cabinet. Many of our Cabinet Ministers had reservations as this man was known to be very ambitious. His departure from the coalition had received a lot of publicity. They argued that he would bring disruption to the party and cause disharmony, saying, 'This fellow has lots of money, so he will be able to buy members of the party and lead the party. We do not need this kind of leader.' This came from those who aspired to lead. They saw their own chances shrinking away because of Misa's decision to turn to us.

Tofilau asked for my opinion. I said, 'I am still angry with the way our government was rolled by the plotting of those two: Vaʻai and Tupua. [Vaʻai] stabbed our party in the back, and this is a golden opportunity for payback. My recommendation is that we accept Misa back in our midst. He is Tupua's cousin. Accepting Misa will be a sword in the heart of Tupua!'

I continued, 'The argument about money and ambition is also unfounded. Have we forgotten our belief that all callings come from God? Jeremiah said, "The Lord gave me this message: I knew you before I formed you in your mother's womb. Before you were born I set you apart and appointed you as my prophet to the nations." If those words are to be believed we do not have to fear.'

With regards to Misa's money, he could never be a leader of the party if that was not God's wish. On the other hand, if God chose him to be our leader, then, under the same principle, we would have to serve Misa as Prime

Malielegaoi Veni and Leasunia Lupesoli'ai, Tuila'epa's parents.

Form 1A, 1958, Marist Brothers' Primary School. Tuila'epa is sixth from left, second row, not looking at the camera.

Lepā Village.

St Paul's College Second Fifteen, 1964. Tuila'epa on right end of front row.

St Paul's College 6A, 1964. Tuila'epa, on left end of second row; Sioutu Okesene, the only other Samoan, is in the back row.

Newman Hall boarders at the 1965 Students' Ball. Tuila'epa lived in Newman Hall for four years while attending the University of Auckland.

Forestry gang after a day's work pruning pine trees near Putaruru, Tuila'epa in front.

Graduation from the University of Auckland, Master's in Commerce, 1969.

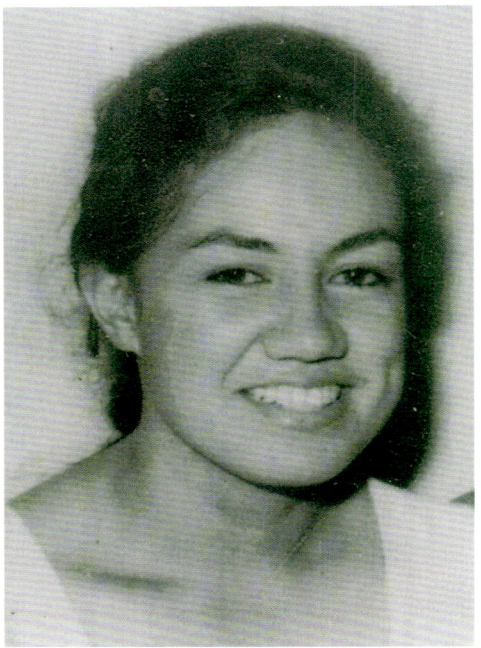
Gillian Meredith at her 21st birthday.

Tuila'epa and family in Brussels, June 1979.

'A balanced family, four girls and four boys.'

Tuila'epa and Gillian with their eight children, their spouses, and twelve grandchildren.

As Minister of Finance, Tuila'epa was required to inspect the status of the fuel pipeline that lies at the bottom of the harbour entrance.

Tuila'epa practising archery for the South Pacific Games, 2007.

Tuila'epa receiving his silver medal for archery, South Pacific Games, 2007.

Tuila'epa practising shooting for the South Pacific Games, 2007.

Tuila'epa still playing cricket. Fifty years and over team, 2016.

Palemene O Samoa, 1979–1981, Tuila'epa's first Parliament.

Palemene O Samoa, 1982–1984.

Cabinet 1988. A decade of political stability begins. Sitting from left: Polotaivao Fosi, Prime Minister Tofilau 'Eti Alesana, Pule Lameko. Standing, from left: Tanuvasa Livi, Tuila'epa Sa'ilele, Leiatua Vaiao, Patū Afa Hunter, Jack Netzler, Sefuiva Sione.

Cabinet 2011–2016. A new dress code suitable for the tropical climate.

Cabinet, 2016–2021.

'In Samoa the burden of history is personal, real and very close.' Tuila'epa at the Cabinet table watched over by his predecessors.

Tuilaʻepa, first official portrait as Prime Minister, 1998.

Tuila'epa attending the ACP Council of Ministers with Pule Lameko MP and African and Caribbean colleagues, 1980.

Meeting of the Tokyo Trade Fair, 1985.

Ministers of Finance of the Commonwealth, Jamaica, 1989.

Meeting the Chancellor of Germany, Gerhard Schroder, December 2003.

Prime Minister Tuila'epa addressing the United Nations General Assembly, New York, 2016.

Meeting the Secretary-General of the United Nations, Ban Ki-moon, New York.

Tuila'epa addressing the ACP Summit.

Meeting President Xi Jinping of China, Fiji, 2014.

Meeting Prime Minister Junichiro Koizumi of Japan.

Palm 7 Meeting of Pacific Islands Forum Leaders with PM Shinzō Abe of Japan, 2015.

Tuila'epa arriving at the ACP Leaders Meeting in Port Moresby.

Meeting Prime Minister Modi of India, New Delhi, 2015.

Meeting Pope Francis, December 2015.

Tuila'epa delivering the Plenary Address to the United Nations Conference on Small Islands Developing States, September 2014, Samoa.

Saofa'i for Ban Ki-moon, Secretary-General of the United Nations, now titled 'Tupua of Saleapāga-Lepā', to be formally addressed as 'Your Highness Tupua Ban Ki-moon'.

Inaugural Meeting of Polynesian Leaders Group, November 2011, Apia.

Tuila'epa recognised as Grand Chief of PNG with Acting Governor-General Hon. Theodore Zurenoc and Kiribati President Anote Tong.

President Obama and Prime Minister Tuila'epa and their First Ladies Michelle and Gillian.

Pacific Islands Forum Meeting, 2015, Papua New Guinea.

Prime Minister John Key and Tuila'epa watching Manu Samoa play the All Blacks, Apia Park, 8 July 2014.

Inspecting the Samoan Rugby High Performance Unit with the Chinese Ambassador, Vincent Fepulea'i, and Matafeo George Latu.

'Switch sides' protesters outside Parliament buildings.

Facing the 'switch sides' protesters with a smile and a laugh as they sing Happy Birthday to Tuila'epa, 14 April 2009.

Facing the 'switch sides' protesters.

Protest leader Toleafoa shakes hands with Tuila'epa.

Forum for India–Pacific Islands Cooperation, Fiji, 19 November 2014.

Tuila'epa.

Fiame Mataʻafa Faumauina Mulinuʻu II Building, Apia. The Cabinet room is in the rooftop *fale*.

Faleolo International Airport terminal.

Lalomanu following the tsunami.

Tuila'epa participating in a public discussion on cancer prevention.

Tuila'epa and Gillian on his maiden visit to Tokelau. The police patrol boat was donated by Australia to patrol Samoa's economic zone.

A Royal Samoan 'Ava Ceremony to welcome cast and crew of Survivor. Two series were filmed in Samoa.

Tuila'epa with Miss Pacific 2016 contestants.

Tuila'epa receiving the flag at the funeral of Leota Ituau Ale.

Tuila'epa with Joseph Parker, WBO Heavy Weight Boxing Champion.

Honorary doctorate, Victoria University of Wellington, 2015.

Prime Minister Tuila'epa Sa'ilele Malielegaoi of Samoa.

Minister with all our devotion and with all our strength. 'If we don't, we are dishonouring God,' I said. 'That is a sin of disobedience, the sin that drove Adam and Eve from the Garden of Eden.' That speech seemed to settle the opposition. Several days later the caucus met to welcome Misa. I was on my way to Fiji for a meeting. When I came back I found that our party had lost several members who had resigned out of opposition to Misa.

After the 1991 general election, four of our Ministers were not re-elected to Cabinet. They never showed up for the next six months. They were already discussing leaving us and joining the opposition. Tofilau sent for them, and they all came back to our party.

The VAGST, Taro Leaf Blight and Polynesian Airlines
Three issues galvanised the opposition to the HRPP government in 1993. First, Taro Leaf Blight[11] had quickly spread throughout Samoa and devastated most of the domestic *taro* crop. As *taro* was the main food item for Samoans, its absence from the table, and the loss of earning from exports, unsettled the population. Second, the passing of a Value Added Goods and Services Tax[12] (VAGST) added to uncertainty and provided the opposition with an issue on which to focus their criticism of the government. Third, the bankruptcy of Polynesian Airlines was a disaster for the country that the opposition relished, until the HRPP government restored the airline's financial health.

Tuila'epa gives us the inside story.

The most explosive issue was the passing of the VAGST in Parliament in June 1993, for implementation in January 1994. The opposition argued that our people would suffer. They proposed to have it deferred indefinitely. By soliciting the support of *Tumua* and *Pule*, the traditional powerbrokers who had provoked civil wars in the past, Tupua was openly inciting the

---

11 Taro Leaf Blight (*Phytophthora colocasiae*) is a highly infectious fungal plant disease that leads to large brown marks on the leaves of infected *taro* plants. An epidemic of Taro Leaf Blight struck Samoa in 1993–94. *Taro* exports made up 58 percent of Samoa's economy and brought in US$3.5 million annually, prior to the epidemic in 1993. In 1994, *taro* exports brought in only US$60,000, a 99.98 percent drop in profit in just one year.
12 It is Tuila'epa's view that the Value Added Tax is the most equitable form of tax payable by every citizen of a country for goods and services. Many nations have introduced VAT or GST to improve their revenue collection. A VAGST was first introduced in Samoa by the coalition government in 1986 when Hon. Fa'aSo'otauloa Sam Saili was Minister of Finance but it was charged on services only. Hon. Saili announced in his Budget speech of 1987 that the government intended to extend the VAGST to include goods as well. Despite that undertaking, the coalition fought to scrap the tax amendment proposed by the HRPP government in 1993 to incorporate goods.

people to revolt against Parliament's supreme authority and sovereignty. The Catholic Cardinal Pio Taofinu'u staged a March for Peace, *Savali o le Filemu,* of his own, hoping to defuse any violence that might occur in the planned *Tumua* and *Pule* protest march to take place later. Although he did not want to be involved in a political protest, under pressure Cardinal Pio was hoodwinked into leading the *Tumua* and *Pule* protest march by walking for just a few feet – 'for peace'. But when the TV news came out with the Cardinal in front, the 'few feet' became miles on the TV screen. This was what Tupua and his opposition had wanted. Any means justified the end.

The opposition kept up the pressure with protest marches and written petitions to the Head of State to oust Prime Minister Tofilau and our government from office.

Government procedures require that any petition of this nature is referred to the Prime Minister for consideration with his Cabinet, and then advice is forwarded to the Head of State. There was one petition that came with records of signatures of over 200,000 Samoans organised by the opposition. It became the subject of a Commission of Enquiry. The findings of the enquiry revealed that only eleven of the signatures could be verified.

The challenges of Taro Leaf Blight and the protests against VAGST provided valuable lessons for the HRPP leadership. Tofilau summoned an urgent meeting of our party caucus to find a peaceful way forward as we faced the first protest march in 1994. The meeting took place in the Prime Minister's conference room at the Fiamē Mata'afa Faumuinā Mulinu'u II Building whilst the opposition MPs and their supporters were outside conducting their noisy protests, of songs and dances, provoking our supporters. Police in civilian clothing were mingling with the crowd.

We were all still reeling from a very powerful speech made by Tupua in front of the government building the day before. Tupua questioned the wisdom of building the multi-storey office buildings and accused us of wasting public funds when people were going hungry. He said the same about expenditure on airlines. 'Our people are hungry. What's the use of these buildings? Our people cannot eat your buildings and your aeroplanes!' Tupua was encouraged by the bursts of laughter from the protesters surrounding him and cheering him on.

The police had been alerted that there were several bus-loads of young men from the constituency of one of the proponents of tougher actions, who were about to leave for Apia with weapons to physically remove all the protesters camping in front of the government building. The police arrived in the nick of time and successfully prevented a confrontation that could have erupted into bloodshed.

Tofilau led us in prayer in our closed caucus meeting. He appealed to God, upon whom Samoa is founded. He quoted the words of the psalmist, 'Unless the Lord builds the House, in vain shall we labour; unless God watches over the city, shall the guards watch in vain.' I could sense how tense our Members all were. Tofilau 'Eti Alesana was in great need of comfort. He too was stressed.

The first two speakers were senior Members of the caucus. They urged that we fight fire with fire. They recommended a direct confrontation. 'Let us issue a call to our constituencies for our own chiefs and young men to come forward and show to the nation their support. And if necessary to come with arms.' This was dangerous; it was a call to civil strife.

I decided to speak. 'Tofilau, if we go along with the recommendations of the first two speakers, it will be recipe for disaster. Your name must not be associated with rash judgement. The HRPP is a voice for peace. To settle our differences through talking out our differences, you have made your mark up to now. You have been a decisive leader and courageous in the face of disaster. Just take a minute and think about all those colleagues of ours in the opposition now. We can disregard Tupua and his fifteen MPs. Think hard about the twelve who deserted us. Did we ever on any occasion seek their counsel in similar circumstances to what we are facing at this very moment? No! I do not remember a single time when we heard any wise counsel from them. On many problems we faced in the past, did any one of them come out with a solution? No. In short, do not lose hope. Wisdom is in our midst. Is it not written in the Bible that if the Lord is with us, who shall dare to attack us?'

We stood strong. The rule of law held, in spite of the provocation and protests. Tofilau and the government remained calm. The opposition-led protesters finally dispersed after two weeks when they realised that government leaders would never accede to their demands. We knew in our minds that the government must lead from the front and with decisiveness. We must never bend an inch to emotional arguments.

We had reminded the country of the importance of sacrifices and that the HRPP was voted in to right the wrongs of the previous government which had led to bankruptcy. Our policy was to cultivate unused customary lands, build access roads to plantations, and bring power and water to new residences on the plantations, which would generate more productivity and give us a plentiful supply of food.

Since the HRPP government took over, Samoa had not experienced any drastic food shortages, even during the long period of the *taro* blight, while our scientists were working full time to test new varieties that were disease resistant and our people were adjusting their eating habits to alternative substitutes to replace *taro* roots. This work continued until we found the best *taro* variety for the export markets in New Zealand and Australia. Today, Samoa is the major supplier of *taro* to the New Zealand market, which is a direct result of the work of research scientists at Nu'u Agriculture Research and the Scientific Research Organisation of Samoa (SROS) at Nafanua.

Not all opposition Members supported Tupua's political protest marches, which spluttered on intermittently for some years. The final political march organised by the opposition was in 1998 on a morning Parliament met. Tupua did not attend the session when it began because he was leading the march. I recall that the first MP to ask for the floor was the Honourable Mataia Visesio, first cousin to Tupua Efi and one of the senior Members of the opposition party. He started his speech by apologising to Tofilau for 'these senseless protests'. He told Parliament that Tupua was educated overseas, listened to no one, and his behaviour was such that he, Mataia, has lost count of how many times he performed *ifoga*, the traditional rite of apology seeking forgiveness, to the families who had been wronged by the *tama-a-'aiga*. Referring to the marches, Mataia pointed out that Tupua, Tofilau and Mataia were all holders of related *matai* titles and, by implication, the protest marches reflected very bad judgement.

At about this point, Tupua entered Parliament and walked straight to his seat. Quite obviously he must have heard his cousin's speech as he was driving to Tiafau. Realising that Tupua had walked towards his seat, Mataia abruptly declared to Parliament that he was resigning from the opposition party. Tupua did not even sit down. He remained standing until Mataia sat down and then said, 'I'm terribly saddened that private matters pertaining to our family have been made public by the Honourable Mataia. These are internal matters that are best handled by members of the family.'

Then Tofilau spoke: 'Our Standing Orders stipulate only political parties with nine Members in Parliament are recognised as the formal opposition. Since the Honourable Mataia Visesio has resigned, the membership of the opposition has fallen to eight. I move that the limit be reduced to eight.'

Tofilau concluded, 'Tupua, you aspired to rule the people of Samoa. How can you achieve that objective if you cannot even convince nine people to support you?'

In 1994 Tofilau had put into effect the amendments of the Constitution to increase Cabinet numbers from eight to twelve and Misa was appointed, along with another guy from Savai'i and two of those who were disenchanted with the decision about Misa.

Tofilau had created political stability but Samoa still faced difficult times economically. The rebuilding of infrastructure after two extreme weather events was very expensive, and then a major financial crisis hit Samoa: the bankruptcy of Polynesian Airlines, the national flag carrier.

Tuila'epa was Minister of Finance and Tofilau directed him to sort out the problem. He remembers the crisis.

This was one of the most difficult periods we faced. Polynesian Airlines lost 137 million Tala through mismanagement. I had forewarned the Prime Minister in April 1994 when I found out that the airline had lost 49 million Tala. At a meeting the same day Jack Netzler, the Minister in Charge of Polynesian Air, had declared they were not losing money. Boeing flights according to Jack Netzler were consistently full from Los Angeles. Unwarranted route promotion led to passengers paying only US$200 to fly from America to Samoa. We were losing money on every flight – at least US$2,000 per seat! Tofilau had trusted Jack and ignored my advice.

At the last minute, before the creditors took action, Prime Minister Tofilau was apprised of the real financial situaton of our airline. Tofilau was sick in Auckland and, from Auckland, dismissed the board, and then directed that I take over the chairmanship of the new board and put into action a plan for its restructuring. The options available were either to declare the company bankrupt or for government to take over the debts repayment. We took the difficult option – to restructure the national airline.

Overnight I took on the leadership of the rehabilitation of the airline and the protection of the country from the massive debt that resulted. We negotiated with all the creditors to agree on a plan for the payment over time of all the debts of Polynesian Airline. We rationalised a new route structure in order to cut losses and we organised the injection of new capital finance to fund Polynesian's operations. This was achieved through a 10 percent cut across the board for all government expenditure for the remainder of the year. Finally, we engaged a competent management team to drive the reforms.

During this period from 1994, when we had to make budgetary provisions to meet Polynesian Airline's debt repayments, the opposition was relentless in its attacks. But attacks became less effective as the airline began making annual profits.[13]

13   The financial viability of airlines has changed dramatically since 1994. The 11 September 2001

150 PĀLEMIA

January 1996 to November 1998 – Tofilau 'Eti Alesana's Fifth Administration

The HRPP won 25 seats, the SNDP twelve and the Samoa Labour Party one. Twelve independent candidates were also elected, of whom ten supported Tofilau's election as Prime Minister.

Not long after his re-election, Tofilau's health became a major concern. Tuila'epa was worried that the Head of State might unilaterally appoint a successor if Tofilau died in office, as he had done on three occasions previously. As Tofilau's health deteriorated, Deputy Prime Minister Tuila'epa took on most of the Prime Minister's workload and leadership responsibilities. Tuila'epa was close to Tofilau and worked to make his final years in office comfortable and stressfree.

Tuila'epa recalls his relationship with Tofilau and the challenges and uncertainties of the leadership transition.

In 1996 we had our general election. Tofilau won the election but he was tired and unwell. In early 1996 Tofilau briefly went away for a liver operation for advanced cancer. He was sent to Australia for treatment and was given a clean bill of health. When he came back from Australia he started talking to me about my taking over and him stepping aside. He was feeling that he could not continue any more. I kept encouraging him to continue on.

Tuila'epa was Deputy Prime Minister and had been named deputy leader of the HRPP in 1992. Clearly he was in the position to be Tofilau's successor. They had been through a lot together and their relationship had not always been easy. In the early years, Tuila'epa was a young man in a hurry, not afraid to speak his mind to the elders and the leaders of the HRPP. But he always maintained respect for Tofilau because of his vast experience of Samoan culture and traditions, his deep faith, his good understanding of economics, and his strong performance as a debater in the House and fronting of public issues in the community.

Tuila'epa recalls his relationship with Tofilau.

We had a rough time early on. I had a terrible dispute with him, a very vocal one in 1982. But I think he began to trust me when I spoke in his favour

---

terrorist attacks in the United States forced many world airlines into insolvency, driving their governments to inject huge capital inputs to save their national carriers. As a small player in a global market, Samoa's Polynesian Airlines was not exempt and was eventually put up for tender, leading to a joint venture with Virgin Airlines.

at the time when Vaʻai and most of the seniors would not back him up for leadership of the party. I was the only one to stand up for him. I saw the man himself. He was a man of courage. He saw that I was not afraid to speak my mind. Such as after the final confrontation meeting of caucus before Vaʻai Kolone resigned in early 1985 when I said, 'Vaʻai, we can all do dirty tricks. One of the special gifts for us politicians when another trickster tries to play a trick on you is that you can see from miles away where it is going to go and you can see from miles away the end result. I am telling you, don't you play tricks on us. We know exactly your dirty tricks. When you continue to play those dirty tricks on us, we lose all our respect for you older people who led this party to failure.'

Some time after, referring to this exchange and the good times we had, Tofilau said, 'Those comments you made were heard by much older people. They said to me "these words should have never been spoken by young people like you". They looked at you with eyes full of hate and considered you brash and cheeky. But alas, if you hadn't said those words, no one would have said anything because they were crooks. They were sitting on the fence. No one but you had the guts to come out and say what you had to say. It was unfortunate, but it was unavoidable. You had to say those words to put right that old man [Vaʻai] and the way he created havoc in the HRPP.'

After Tofilau underwent the operation in which most of his liver was removed, they told him that he might have only three years of active life. He came back in 1996. But he was never completely the same again, and he did mention to me then that he felt like resigning and that I should take over. At that time, I did not think the environment was right, for the simple reason that we had so many people in our party who were aspiring for the post. In fact, a few of them kept asking me what my intentions were and whether I should challenge for the leadership. I said, 'No, all I am interested in is serving the old man.'

Several times Tofilau asked me about the leadership. I kept telling him, 'It doesn't really matter, do what you can do. Delegate the rest to me.' In fact I was doing much of the Prime Minister's work after he came back from that operation in 1996.

From 1996 to 1998 Tofilau was virtually confined to his wheelchair. Unbeknown to many of our caucus Members; he was working from home much of the time. A lot of the work was signed over to me. It was a kind of secret between Tofilau and me, and I was happy because I kept on working for the old man. I was quite happy with this arrangement, and in fact I thought the transition would be smooth at the end when he would transfer power.

The critical moment came in August 1998 when I went to his home to let him know that I would be leaving the following day for the meetings of the World Bank.

He said, 'Where are you heading?'

'I am going first to Brussels to attend the renegotiation of the Lomé Convention. From there I will proceed to Washington for the meeting of the World Bank IMF, and after that meeting I'll fly directly to Suva for the meetings of the Pacific Island Ministers of Finance to talk about the finances of the University of the South Pacific.'

Then he said, 'How long will you be away?'

'A good two weeks and a half.'

Then he said to me, 'When you have finished, come back quickly.'

I said, 'OK, I will come back as soon as I finish.'

I did not know at the time that he was really suffering.

Three days later I was in Brussels. When I finished our two-day meeting I was dining at the ambassador's house when I got a call from Fiamē. She said to me, 'I wanted to inform you, as Acting Prime Minister, that I have spoken to Dr Lolofie, CEO of Health, and he has expressed an opinion that Tofilau is in such a stage of health that if we send him overseas for treatment he may not come home alive.'

This was the first time that I knew for sure that he was in a very critical condition, now that a doctor had confirmed it. And then she said something that caught me. 'You better come back, some of the members of our party are getting very, very excited.' It was her way of saying that there was lots of campaigning for possible succession.

Then I said to her, 'Have you spoken to the Prime Minister?'

'Yes. I could see he is weak.'

'Listen very carefully, Fiamē. Go and see him, tell him that you have spoken to me and let him know that I am coming home directly. I should be back within 24 hours.'

I quickly rearranged my ticket and I flew directly to Samoa. At about 11 o'clock the following night I arrived in Apia. I went straight to his home and when I came he was sleeping but with a very high fever. For the first time I became aware that he was deaf. He was now using a hearing aid. I tried to wake him up. I said to his wife, 'Has he been like this for long?'

'He has been like that for some time now.'

He had a high fever and I could hear that sound of a person who is suffering a lot.

'What are some of the signs you've seen?'

And she said, 'He was weeping last night and was saying that he wanted to go overseas for treatment and if the government does not send him I will have to get my family to send him for treatment in Hawai'i.'

He did not need to say that, he was the boss. But it conveyed to me that he was out of touch, no longer in charge of his faculties.

I sent my son to get a hot-water bottle because I could see he was shivering. I was there with Gillian. My son Oscar quickly drove home and came back with a hot-water bottle which we filled and put under his blanket.

I said that I would come back the following morning.

I left, came home and slept.

At 6 a.m. in the morning my daughter woke me up. 'It's a phone call from the Prime Minister.'

I took the call and I was shocked, he sounded perfectly normal.

'How are you, Tui? I heard that you came last night. Come and have breakfast with me.'

The voice was the voice of a man who had no problems with his health. So I jumped into my car and drove to his place, laughing all the way. When I arrived, he was sitting in his wheelchair with a table already set. And what a huge breakfast! He was so jovial, so normal.

It was 6.15 a.m. I said to him, 'I want you to go overseas for treatment. There is a plane that will leave at 9 o'clock, and you will be accompanied by the head of the Prime Minister's Office, your wife and your daughter. I will ask for the seats to be reserved for you and your family. In the next 20 minutes I will see the Head of State for your travel warrant. Don't worry about the government, I will be acting in your capacity.'

He said, 'Thank you very much, thank you very much.'

I was at the airport at 9 o'clock to see him off. Everything was organised.

It was towards the end of September 1998 when Tofilau went to New Zealand. Exactly five days later I got a call from the head of the Prime Minister's Office and he said to me, 'The doctor has just informed me that Tofilau has only about six weeks to live. He is suffering from cancer of the liver and he is beyond cure. And that means he will have to come back.'

I enquired, 'Have you told Tofi and his wife?'

'No.'

'Tell the doctor to let Tofilau know, and when you have finished ring me back.'

Within an hour the news was delivered and then I rang up and said that I wanted to speak to the old man.

'Tofi, it's me.'

'Tui, I am fine. I am coming back this Saturday. Listen very carefully. I am all right. When I come back this time, I may have to spend more of my time in Savai'i. Please make preparations.'

I said, 'Sir, it shall be done.'

This was Thursday. I called the caucus and I told them that I had got a call from Tofilau and he said that he would be coming back on Saturday. I said it would be nice for all of us to welcome our leader back and that he sent his best wishes. Everyone in the caucus thought everything was OK. I never mentioned anything about his illness being terminal.

We were all out there waiting when the plane arrived at about 9 p.m. on Saturday. We waited and waited but he did not come down the steps. He was brought down in his wheelchair by the lift. He just sat there with his eyes closed. For the first time all of us knew that the man was dying. We took him to his government residence.

I knew then that it was unavoidable. We had to have a caucus meeting and select Tofilau's successor in case he died suddenly. If we did not make a selection now, what had happened previously could happen again, regardless of the fact that we had the overwhelming majority. The Head of State could easily turn around and reappoint the leader of the opposition to the role of Prime Minister.

I called an urgent caucus meeting. Prior to the meeting we had a Cabinet meeting. The senior Minister, Leniu Tafoaeono Avamagalo, spoke up. He said, 'When we go to caucus we must choose someone we have confidence in and I recommend that you, Tuila'epa, succeed Tofilau.' Then one by one all the other Ministers spoke supporting me.

Our Cabinet meeting continued until 5 o'clock in the evening. No one had the opportunity to get out and campaign. All the potential leaders were at the Cabinet meeting. Because of that, everyone who spoke at the caucus meeting would be speaking directly from their hearts.

The caucus met at 5 o'clock. I said, 'The time has come when we must decide. According to tradition and practice, everyone must speak and state their preference for who the next Prime Minister will be.' You could also put up your own name. The person with the largest number of supporters would automatically become the next leader. That is the HRPP practice.

Again, Leniu put up his hand and said, 'This is an opportunity that God has given us. Luckily Tofilau is in a coma and has not died. Without beating about the bush, I give my support to you, Tuila'epa, to be our next Prime Minister.'

Immediately another senior Member, Polotaivao, raised his hand. 'I also support you, Tuila'epa, to be the Prime Minister.'

Then four or five others raised their hands.

I said, 'Hold on, everyone must speak. Therefore we will follow some order. Politaivao was the last one who spoke. So the person next to him will speak next and then we will follow one by one in that order anti-clockwise.'

The next speaker was none other than Misa.

Up until then two speakers had spoken and they had both mentioned me. That put Misa in an awkward position. So Misa was obliged to say, 'I also support you, Tuila'epa.'

We had about 32 MPs. By the time we came to the last speaker, no other name but mine was being put forward. At the end Misa said that it would be his recommendation for me to name the Cabinet.

I said, 'I think that you have forgotten one thing. We are not electing a new Prime Minister or Cabinet. Tofilau is still alive. Tofilau is still our Prime Minister. I will not disclose or publicise the result of our decision. This is secret. There will be no publicity. It is only a decision to fall back on should Tofilau die suddenly. I want you all to take note of that. Our meeting is now concluded.'

This was now 9 o'clock in the evening. At 11 o'clock I decided it was time to go and visit Tofilau. He was still in a coma. A lot of people were praying and singing hymns, his relatives were all there. I walked straight into his bedroom where he was surrounded by his wife and daughters.

I said, 'How is Tofi?'

'He is still in a coma. It's been like this since last Saturday.'

I said, 'Can you put in his hearing aids?'

He was given his hearing aids.

This is what I said: 'Tofi. This is Tuila'epa. I wanted to let you know that the things we talked about often have materialised. I summoned a meeting of caucus and put the question of succession to the vote. It was a hundred percent to allow me to succeed you, should you not recover. I want you to know that the things you wanted to achieve have already been done very smoothly. Aside from that, we are praying for your early recovery. Everything is proceeding smoothly, nothing is a problem with government. Everything is in good hands. I pray for your early recovery. I have to leave you now. Good night.'

I asked that his hearing aids be taken away. He was still breathing. So I left.

The following day was Arbor Day, when we have ceremonies talking about the benefit of saving our forests. I came back home at about 10 o'clock. I had just arrived and was sitting down to have a cup of coffee when I got a ring from Malietoa's secretary who said to me, 'We have just heard that Tofilau is dead and the Head of State wants to know the details of the programme.'

I was shocked.

I said, 'Let the Head of State know that I will be there very shortly.'

I left my coffee untouched, jumped into the car and dashed up to Tofilau's house. When I arrived all his relatives were talking and laughing. This was not an environment that suggested that Tofilau was dead. I came in silently and listened to their jokes and laughter.

I quietly asked, 'How is the old man?'

'He's fine, fine. Immediately after you left last night, he woke up and started ordering us around. He wanted a cup of *koko Samoa* [hot chocolate] and a pancake. So we quickly fried pancakes for him. This was at 4 o'clock in the morning so all we had to give him was his pancakes and he talked with us. At about 9 o'clock he went back to sleep.'

'Is it OK if I go in and talk to him?'

'Yes, go in.'

I went in and had a good look at him and saw he was sleeping. I went closer and he was breathing.

I came out and said, 'Thank you very much.'

I jumped into my car and drove off to Malietoa's house to talk to the Head of State. He said, 'Have you got news for me?'

'Yes. Tofilau sends his best regards.'

'What!'

'He sends his best regards. I have just been to him and he is eating pancakes and drinking his *koko Samoa* and asking me to pass on his regards. You know he is fit and he may even bury you and me.'

And he laughed. 'Terrible, terrible. These people bring me false news.'

'Thank you very much. Don't worry about Tofilau. He is quite all right now. But I am beginning to be worried about your health. You need to get ready to go to New Zealand for another medical check up.'

'Thank you very much. Thank you very much.'

I came back home.

Several days later I went back to see Tofilau and he was perfect.

He said, 'Tui, I have made up my mind. I am going to resign from the post. But I want to remain as a backbencher. Perhaps later, if I am still OK, I will ask to be made Speaker of the House. I want you to go and talk to the Head of State to summon the House to give my resignation.'

I said to him, 'Look, we have already agreed that we summon the House on the 18th of December. We still have little over one month. Is it possible for you to delay your resignation?'

'No, I will not. This is the moment. I have made up my mind. I must resign while I still have my strength. Thank you very much.'

Now I faced a big problem because it is not easy just to summon Parliament so that the Prime Minister can give his resignation and a successor can be elected. This was now my worry, even though I had already been declared his successor by my party. In the situation, we had to follow the law and there was no guarantee what the outcome would be. It has been done before, *tama-a-'āiga* appointing another *tama-a-'āiga* or someone related to the *tama-a-'āiga* family. So I saw the danger.

I deferred the matter for several days. Then I went to the Head of State and broke the news to him. I only mentioned the second part.

I said to him, 'The Prime Minister wants to summon Parliament.'

'What for?'

'The Prime Minister has been in power for a long time and he wants to summon Parliament so he has the opportunity for him and his family to pay their usual respects, Samoan style. That means he wants to make a special presentation of fine mats to the Head of State and to all the MPs for the honour of making him Prime Minister for nearly thirteen years.'

I left out the bit about resignation.

The Head of State said, 'Pity. Pity, I really feel for the man.'

'I recommend that we meet on the 23rd.'

He said, 'OK. Proceed and attend to everything.'

So I arranged for Parliament to meet on Monday the 23rd of November 1998.

On the Friday I got the formal resignation letter drafted by the Attorney-General and I got the Clerk of the House to set out the full procedures and ceremony. I then went and saw Tofilau.

I said, 'I have brought your resignation and I will read it out. This is where you must sign. But before you sign, can I make one last appeal and ask you once more to postpone your resignation until the 18th of December, when Parliament meets to consider the supplementary estimates?'

'Tui, I have made up my mind. Let me sign.'

Then I got up and kissed him and said that I must go and see the Head of State.

I went and saw him and I said to him, 'Malietoa, I am sorry I have news for you. I told you before to summon Parliament because Tofilau wanted to pay tribute through a traditional presentation. Now he has told me to let you know that he will also take this opportunity to resign.'

'What?'

'That is what he said to me, that he will resign as Prime Minister but he will continue to be an ordinary MP. So I have brought this formal notice for your information. I also want to let you know that this resignation takes effect on Monday. So he could change his mind today, tomorrow or Sunday. I want to let you know all this.'

'Oh. I see.'

I told him, 'Because you ought to know the full details of what will take place: Monday the 23rd, Parliament meets and gets the resignation then Parliament proceeds to elect the next Prime Minister. Then on Tuesday afternoon at 2 p.m. will be the ceremony of swearing the oath by the new Prime Minister and his Cabinet. Then on Thursday you can go to New Zealand for your medical check up.'

'Bravo. Bravo.'

'At 3 p.m. I will send the Attorney-General and Clerk of the House to come and brief you on the legal side and what is to be expected.'

'Thank you very much.'

I left.

At 4 p.m. the Attorney-General and Clerk of the House came to report to me. When they went to see the Head of State he asked, 'Who is to be the next Prime Minister? Will it be the time for Fiamē?'

'No, Sir.'

'What about Misa?'

'No, Sir.'

'Then who is it going to be? Tupua?'

'No.'

'Who?'

'Tuila'epa, the Deputy Prime Minister.'

'Oh, but what about the others?'

At that point the Attorney-General said, 'We have brought with us the signatures of more than two-thirds of the MPs of the HRPP and they have all agreed that Tuila'epa should be the next Prime Minister.'

'Oh. But what if I find somebody else?'

'You cannot do that.'

'Why?'

'You see, you could be taken to court by the HRPP. It would be illegal and unconstitutional. We do not want to see another crisis.'

That was exactly what happened.

On Saturday evening I went to see Tofilau. But I could not talk to him immediately. There were so many people bringing fine mats because after the resignation it was inevitable that there would be a traditional presentation of fine mats.

I managed to see him at about 1 in the morning when everyone was finished. I said, 'I have come to give you your final speech.'

He looked quickly through it, but did not read it properly.

He said to me, 'It is good. Thank you very much.'

'Tofilau, I will stand ready if your health does not permit it, and I can take over and read your farewell speech.'

'Very good. Very good.'

Then I left him.

I was just about to drive off when there was a tap on my car window. It was Auseuga K. Poloma, the Secretary to Cabinet.

He said to me, 'There is a small problem.'

'What is the problem?'

'You know that I accompany the Head of State when he travels. I checked up the details this morning and I discovered that the Head of State and his travel party have changed their booking. They prefer to leave on Monday evening, instead of Wednesday morning.'

'What? Are you sure? What about the ceremony for the swearing in of the new Prime Minister on Tuesday?' The Head of State was planning to ruin our evening.

'That I do not know.'

'Thank you for letting me know.'

I came home. I thought about it and decided what to do.

I slept for short time then got up at 5 a.m. I went to the marketplace and bought some fish. At 7 o'clock I was up at the Head of State's residence. He was still sleeping out on the veranda. When I arrived there were some ladies already busy preparing the breakfast for the Head of State.

I said, 'I have brought some fish and some *'ulu* for the Head of State's *to'ona'i.*'

I walked straight in and he was still snoring.

I said, 'Wake up. Wake up.'

He woke up and laughed. 'It's you?'

'It's me.'

He called out to the ladies, 'Prepare a cup of coffee for me and the Prime Minister elect.'

I laughed. He laughed too!

'Why did you come so early?'

'I brought some fish for your *toʻonaʻi*. You know why I have come so damn early. I am worried about you. We are just about to attend to Tofilau's problem. His health is OK but I am worried about your health.'

'I am OK.'

'You are not OK until I send you to New Zealand. Are you ready?'

'Yes. Thursday we leave.'

'I want you to leave for New Zealand tomorrow evening.'

'No. No. No.'

'You leave tomorrow evening. The quicker you go, the better.'

Then I changed the subject. We talked on.

Then I said, 'I had better go, it's near Mass time.'

'All right. All right.'

I took two steps, stopped. I backtracked and said, 'Excuse me, everything that was aimed for Tuesday will be shifted forward to Monday. Have a good Sunday.'

As soon as I arrived home I called the Clerk of the House. 'Are all the invitations ready?'

'Yes.'

'OK. What time will you distribute them?'

'As soon as you clear it.'

'Distribute them at exactly 7 p.m. tonight. Don't do it before then. At 7 p.m. tonight distribute the invitations to everybody, including the MPs, telling them that there is a ceremony tomorrow.' I got into my car and went to see my pastor, the Reverend Suafai Patū from Lepā.

I said, 'You will conduct the prayer service tomorrow.'

'Who is to be the Prime Minister?'

'I do not even know. Really, I do not know. But when you listen to the House proceedings you will know. It is now shifted forwards to 2 o'clock tomorrow. We meet at 9. I anticipate we break at 10 for everyone to go home and have lunch and we start again at 2 p.m.'

Then I went home and had a good sleep, hoping that nothing would happen overnight.

At 5 to 9 the next morning everyone was seated and Tofilau was brought in, in his wheelchair. The meeting opened.

The Speaker said, 'I have summoned this House for one special purpose and that will be revealed to you by none other than the Prime Minister, who asked for this special session of Parliament.'

Member of Parliament for Lepā

On 23 November 1998 Tofilau 'Eti Alesana made his final statement in the House of Parliament.[14] Tofilau firstly acknowledged 'Our Heavenly Father', then the Head of State, the members of the Council of Deputies, the Chief Justice, the Judiciary and the Cabinet. Then the Hansard record notes: 'Hon. Tofilau 'Eti Alesana could not continue with his statement so it was read out by Hon Tuila'epa Sa'ilele.'

At the conclusion of Tofilau's statement, the leader of the opposition, Tupua Tamasese, briefly replied. Then Hon. Fiamē Nāomi Matā'afa, on behalf of the Human Rights Protection Party, formally moved that 'the Legislative Assembly recommends that the Head of State do forthwith appoint Susuga Hon. Tuila'epa Sailele to the Office of Prime Minister in accordance with the Constitution'.

The motion was seconded, and 'put and approved without a dissenting voice'.

---

14   See Alesana, 1998, for a full text of the speech.

CHAPTER 5

Pālemia
– Prime Minister of Samoa

On 23 November 1998 the motion to appoint Tuila'epa Sa'ilele Malielegaoi Prime Minister of Samoa was approved 'without a dissenting voice'. Later in the day, Tuila'epa was sworn in as Prime Minister. The long apprenticeship was over, the struggle to consolidate his leadership had just begun.

The first year would prove to be the toughest. Dissidents within the HRPP, unhappy with Tuila'epa's promotion, still harboured their own political ambitions and secretly plotted his demise. Their plots led to a political assassination (recounted in Chapter One) and put Tuila'epa's life at risk. Opposition leader Tui Ātua Tupua Tamasese's political ambitions were also still alive and his lengthy rivalry with Tofilau 'Eti Alesana was switched to focus, with renewed intensity, on the young, new Prime Minister Tuila'epa, who did not yet command the same respect as Tofilau.

Natural disasters – cyclones, tsunami and floods – continued to punctuate the progress made by Tuila'epa during his premiership in building Samoa's infrastructure, strengthening the economy and reforming the political system. Tuila'epa set in place a number of major reforms and innovations. He also hosted significant regional and international events, raising Samoa's international profile and visitor numbers, and reshaping cultural life in Samoa.

In this chapter Tuila'epa recalls and recounts some of the key events of his premiership, providing insights into the concerns that he has faced as Prime Minister, the thinking behind his decision-making, the personalities and crises he has had to manage, and his unique leadership style. The first part of the chapter covers his first two administrations from November 1998 to March 2006, when he consolidated his leadership and started to initiate reforms. The second part covers the next two administrations from April 2006 to March 2016, during which many reforms were implemented, important events were hosted in Samoa and Tuila'epa focussed on foreign affairs including Fiji. The final section covers the start of Tuila'epa's fifth administration and discusses his thoughts on leadership, succession and the future.

Prime Minister of Samoa

Part 1. Consolidation 1998–2006

November 1998 to March 2001

This was Tuila'epa Sa'ilele Malielegaoi's first administration, following his appointment as Prime Minister on the resignation of Tofilau 'Eti Alesana due to failing health.

Tofilau 'Eti Alesana's resignation, nearly three years into a five-year term, had not triggered a general election. Tuila'epa's appointment was made by Parliament and he had just over two years to consolidate his leadership of the HRPP and the government before the next general election, scheduled for March 2001. He remembered that when he started his new job as Prime Minister, it was an uncertain time as he faced dissent from within his own party and snubs from the opposition.

Tuila'epa recalls:

I was never sure that I would take over until I finally delivered my acceptance speech on 23 November 1998. Three times the Head of State had not waited for Parliament to select the leader who commanded the majority and the confidence of the House before he appointed a prime minister. That was why we had to move very carefully to ensure that the Head of State was clear about his role and that democratic processes would be followed.

My appointment as Prime Minister was not accepted in some quarters. Tupua Tamasese did not turn up to my swearing-in ceremony in 1998, and Tuimaleali'ifano, the sole member of the Council of Deputies at the time, was absent from Samoa. So the two of them did not attend my swearing-in as Prime Minister. They snubbed me again in 2001.

When I took over I re-appointed the Cabinet that Tofilau had in place to ensure some continuity, and I also appointed Tofilau as Minister of State without Portfolio. So Tofilau was still there in Cabinet for a short time until his passing on 19 March 1999.

Despite the fact that there was consensus in the HRPP on my appointment, I increasingly detected a lack of trust from some quarters within the party. I was just trying to get my foothold, to gain the complete trust of my party in me as the new leader. Leadership challenges were quick to come. I soon learnt that two particular characters, To'i Aukuso and Leafa Vitale, were plotting against me, stirring up bad feelings to split the party.

This knowledge led me to convene a special caucus meeting in April 1999 during which I called for the dismissal of Leafa and To'i from our caucus. But the senior Members of the party cautioned me against this course of action and asked me to give them another chance. I reluctantly gave them the chance to mend their ways. They did not. It turned out that they were behind the plot to shoot and kill Minister Luagalau. I later realised that if I had proceeded with their dismissal I would have been the target.

The assassination was a major trauma for Samoa. Political debate had always been robust, but political violence was something else altogether. I think that Samoa lost its political innocence the night Luagalau was shot.

As expected, the opposition tried hard to make political gains out of the crisis during the next session of Parliament. Allegations were made that this incident would never have happened in a Cabinet that had a more mature leader. I countered by reminding the House that Adam and Eve once lived in a perfect Paradise. And they chose evil. I also said that it is written that 'the wheat and darnel must grow together'. It is our fate that 'where there is good, there is also evil'.

The assassination and its aftermath ended dissent within the HRPP. Public support for the government under Tuila'epa's leadership, following the murder and trials, built up, unified the party and put paid to dissenters. The government was able to get back to the business of governing Samoa, starting to put much needed reforms in place and healing the trauma.

The run up to the 2001 general election came very quickly. It would be my first election campaign as leader. Tupua campaigned very hard, and I think he honestly believed, with Tofilau dead, that it was now his turn and that he would win.

It was at this election that another previously unknown political candidate emerged: Tuimaleali'ifano, a *tama-a-'āiga*. Tuimaleali'ifano had been a member of the Council of Deputies for quite some time and by right was now senior and in line to become the next Head of State. But he had to resign from the council to contest the election. Appointees to these posts cannot be involved in day-to-day politics.

Tuimaleali'ifano comes from Falelatai and his aim was to defeat Misa Telefoni Retzlaff, who was Deputy Prime Minister. Misa did not have roots in Falelatai village. He did not have the blood ties but was bestowed with his title for legal services he had provided *pro bono* to Falelatai. Tuimaleali'ifano thought that he, as the son of Falelatai and a *tama-a-'āiga*, could beat Misa and jump up to party leadership. But Misa had been the local MP a number of times and he had the wealth, charisma and a campaign strategy to back it up. Misa was not a pushover.

Tuimaleali'ifano did not take my advice not to run.

In 2001 Tupua really thought he would be the next Prime Minister. Misa also had leadership ambitions. Complicating the race, Tuimaleali'ifano was running as an independent. Others in the HRPP also had the idea of going independent to team up with him against the HRPP. It was becoming a crowded field and there was some 'dirty' politics going on behind the scenes.

A dramatic incident that had the potential to upset the election happened a few weeks before the 2001 general election. I got wind of it when an old man, Tapusalaia, a high chief of Siumu who is also an orator in my family of Fatialofa in Lepā, came to visit me one day to talk about family matters. One of the things he said to me was, 'This morning I went to see Tapusalaia Faletoese, the woman *matai* from my village who bears the same title as me, to talk about village issues. When I arrived she was deep in conversation with Tupua in a locked room. It appeared that they were talking about very important issues because their heads were only inches apart.'

I talked with the old man about our family matters in Lepā and then he left. I did not think too much about our conversation at the time, but later I made an important connection.

On the evening of the same day it was reported to me that the whole of Siumu village had decided to set up a roadblock and occupy land along the Cross-Island Road from Vailima up and down towards Siumu. The young men had occupied the whole area by force and were armed with guns because they believed that a thousand acres of land along the Cross-Island Road claimed by the government had a more complicated history.

During Mata'afa's days, the government had sold this piece of land to the 'A'iono family in exchange for another parcel of freehold land at Lauli'i owned by the 'A'iono family. As a consequence the Lauli'i people agitated that they would take the land by force and Mata'afa settled the land dispute by transferring to the 'A'iono family ownership of a thousand acres of government land at Siumu in exchange for the Lauli'i property, which was subsequently transferred back by government to Lauli'i village.

In 1997 Tofilau had met on the 'A'iono land issue with the Siumu people, including Tapusalaia and her husband Tu'u'u Faletoese, who was related to Tofilau. Tofilau had apparently told them that he would direct me, as Minister responsible for the Samoa Land Corporation (SLC), to arrange for the transfer of the 'A'iono land title to Siumu village and for the government to relocate the 'A'iono family on government lands elsewhere. I was subsequently informed by Tofilau of his decision, which required time on my part to sort out the likely consequences. I envisaged trouble whilst I was grappling with this potentially explosive challenge.

Tofilau had now passed on and I was Prime Minister. Days before the blockade, people from Siumu came to see me saying that Tofilau told them that I would action the land transfer.

I said, 'I confirm that it was the case that Tofilau spoke to me about your claim. But I will not do it.'

They asked, 'Why?'

'It will create more problems. First, where would I shift the 'A'iono people to? Which thousand acres will I shift them to? The moment we shift them to any government land, from here to the airport, the village people who owned these lands before they were alienated will come in strength and with weapons and will probably kill anybody who settles there. I will not do it. I will never allow it.'

The Siumu chiefs were not very happy with me and so they departed.

Their response was to forcefully occupy the lands and blockade the road.

That same evening, when the news came to me of the blockade, I suddenly remembered my meeting earlier with old Tapusalaia, who had informed me of the private and very strange head-to-head conference between Tupua Tamasese, leader of the opposition SNDP, and Mrs Tapusalaia T. Faletoese. I suspected then that Tupua was behind the blockade. He was provoking a crisis, only days before a general election.

I wondered why this old man had come, out of the blue, and landed up in my office. I sat there and I thought about it. God must have guided him to me. I thought this fellow did not come here for nothing. It was God's way of alerting me to be vigilant.

The next day I summoned Asi Blakelock, the Police Commissioner, to discuss the situation.

Asi said to me, 'I am going to move tomorrow with as many police as possible and force the people out. There must be over a hundred young men. They are armed. The police will be armed for self-protection.'

I thought to myself: it means a shootout, two or three weeks before the elections. Then I knew Tupua needed an incident. He urgently needed something dramatic. If a shootout and bloodshed took place it would be easy to blame the new Prime Minister for incompetence and immaturity, so the country should rightfully give the leadership back to Tupua, a *tama-a-'āiga*.

Just at that point, as I was talking with Asi, I heard thunder, strong wind and squalls of heavy rain.

I said to Asi, 'Asi. Stop. Don't do anything. Politics is behind this blockade. Tupua is asking for trouble and he wants an excuse to initiate it. There will be a confrontation and bloodshed if you go. He badly needs an incident as the election is not far away. But we are going to deny Tupua that luxury.'

'What should the police do?'

'Don't make any move until I clear it with you. Let the rain do the rest. Keep in communication with me.'

The Police Commissioner reported back to me two days later.

I asked, 'What is the feedback?'

'There is much dissension amongst the young men who are wet, cold and suffering from mosquito bites. We have a couple of young policemen who are also from the village who are amongst the blockaders at the camp. They are keeping us informed.'

The following day there was more rain, more thunder, more lightning and the mosquitos were still biting.

I met up with the Police Commissioner again.

'What is happening?'

'There is dissension in the camp. The reports are that the sons of the chiefs are complaining that Tu'u'u and Tapusalaia's children, who are working in town, and the children of the other chiefs who are instrumental in the whole thing, are not participating in the blockade. Instead they're sleeping in comfort at their homes whilst the rest of the sons of Siumu are working like slaves in the bush to carry out the chiefs' directions.'

I said, 'This is our time. I will write a letter to all the families and get the police to deliver it to every household directly.'

So I wrote out a letter and it went like this:

'To the Parents.

'I want to let you know that I am finding it very hard to hold back the police from doing their duty. I am asking you to please understand that when the police come, they will come in numbers and with weapons. Your sons will be hurt and probably some killed. Some policemen may be hurt too. Some of your sons will be jailed for inciting armed resistance to the Rule of Law. I am asking you to please think about the safety of your own sons, to think about your sons carefully. Remember the police can come at any time. I will find it difficult to restrain the police from taking action because they have a duty to maintain peace and sworn an oath to do so.'

We did not distribute the letters through the *pulenu'u*. They would not do it as they were under the direction of Tu'u'u. I wanted the police to distribute the letters to each of the *matai*, the heads of every family. I did not want any of the Siumu people to be missed.

As soon as these letters were delivered, many of the *matai* from the village council went to the leaders of the blockade and said, 'Let us meet now and talk about this whole affair.'

In that meeting they made the decision that they would seek a peaceful resolution.

A few days later, I was in my office when the Attorney-General came and in and said, 'The whole village of Siumu is outside there in the foyer.'

'What?'

'All the village chiefs, the young men and women are all there with their pastors.'

When I came out I was surprised to see so many of them squeezed into the limited space.

As soon as I sat down Tu'u'u said to me, 'Mr Prime Minister, we have come today to reconcile our differences with the government. Before we talk further, let us conduct a thanksgiving service to God.'

They started with a hymn followed by a long service by a Methodist minister. The main theme of this service was the doctrine of the love of Jesus Christ.

'The first commandment is to love your God, the second to love your neighbours as you would love yourself.'

The pastor, who is a distant relative of mine, and a likeable rogue, hoped that I would give priority to this doctrine. Then at the end the pastor said, 'We must now leave you to your discussion.'

I said, 'Pastor, no, stop.'

I rose and continued, 'The reason why I asked you to stop is that it is better that you witness what I have to say today to you all. In your sermon you preached the doctrine of love.'

I continued, 'Several weeks ago I attended a prayer service at the court to bless the judges and the difficult task they perform. The preacher that day was quite direct when he said: "Judges of Samoa, when you sit in your seats of judgment, always remember this. Never, ever succumb to the urgings of your heart. Never, ever guide your decisions of justice by your feelings of love. Always guide your judgment through the urgings of the mind, your intellect and your conscience to achieve justice. Justice and love do not mix." Therefore, pastor, that is what guides me in our relationship, and in our decision-making today. It is justice delivered straight from the mind, the conscience, not out of love that comes from the heart because that is the cause of wrong judgements.'

I then directed my comments to the villagers.

'Now to all of you from the village, it was wrong for you to do what you did. It was against the law. You were lawbreakers. What you must always do is subject your concerns to the rule of law. I promise you this: if your allegations are correct that the land at issue was taken by force by the Germans and passed on to the government, I promise to return it to you. But let your lawyer discuss your concerns with our lawyer. My lawyer, the Attorney-General, is a woman, Brenda Heather; your lawyer, Olinda Woodroffe, is a woman. Let our lawyers discuss it. Why don't we agree to that? Give them twelve months and, if your allegation is correct, I will return all the lands taken from you. Should we agree?'

Tu'u'u said, 'That will please us greatly. Let us now conduct a prayer of thanksgiving for this excellent outcome to our dispute.'

That was the end of the dispute.

The blockade was taken down, the crisis was over, Tupua had nothing to blame on the new Prime Minister. The elections went ahead without any big problems.

There is a postscript to the Siumu incident. Twelve months later the two lawyers reported to us. Tu'u'u, the leader of Siumu, was there and the report was presented. The outcome was that the two lawyers disagreed.

I said to Tu'u'u, 'You were the Speaker of the House. You understand government policies. My Cabinet and I listen to one legal adviser only, the Attorney-General. Therefore, our dispute has come to an end. The lawyers agree to disagree but I am not irresponsible. I will give you an opportunity to go and sue the government. Take it to court. If you win, the land is yours. And, I tell you this, the government will pay for all the court costs apart from the legal costs of your lawyer. That is your responsibility.'

Several months later we met again. Tu'u'u came to my office and asked for an appointment for himself.

He said, 'Can I bring some others?'

'OK.'

Two pastors came in and Tu'u'u said to me, 'We have some women outside.'

I said, 'OK.'

Twenty women came in.

Then he said, 'We have a few children to witness the occasion.'

'OK.'

About 25 came in and my office was crowded.

Tu'u'u asked, 'Can we conduct a church service?'

'OK.'

We had singing and another sermon from the same pastor who asked me to look at the young people and reflect on their future and their need for land. I thought about the large amount of uncultivated customary land in the hinterland of Siumu village.

Finally Tu'u'u spoke. He said 'You asked us to take the matter to the court. Olinda, our lawyer, has something to say.'

Olinda said, 'Tuila'epa, I have talked with Falefatu, the Chief Justice. He said that he will not accept the case. Therefore, I have come to ask whether you will agree for the matter be decided by a tribunal similar to the Waitangi Tribunal in New Zealand?'

I said, 'Olinda, no Samoan lawyer has ever thought of touching the issue of the Reparation Estates that were passed over from New Zealand to the government of Samoa. No Samoan lawyer except you. Remember, I told you, if you could prove that these lands were taken illegally by the Germans, you could always take the matter to the court? And what did you tell me just now? You spoke to Justice Falefatu and he disagreed. I would have thought that you would have put down your arguments on paper, advancing all the reasons why this thing should be reopened. Even with the law, if there is such a thing called justice, I am sure there is room for review if a transaction is done by mistake.'

Olinda countered, 'You are not a lawyer. You can't understand these things.'

I said to Tu'u'u, 'You were the Speaker of the House when I first entered Parliament. I think you will agree with me, you being a lawmaker and I being a lawmaker, that our knowledge of the law is sufficient.'

Tu'u'u replied, 'Yes, we made the laws of this country. We know the law.'

I said to Olinda, 'There you are, Olinda, you should have prepared a proper submission. I did not envision you just going to have a yarn with the Chief Justice. You should state your arguments clearly on paper. Therefore our meeting is now at an end. I can never, never agree to a tribunal. You know why? The land you referred to in New Zealand was subject to a treaty signed with the leaders of the Māori people. The land in dispute in Samoa was the subject of over a thousand court cases heard by the High Court in Germany and Samoa. Many land transactions were invalidated, and many others were considered legal and approved, including the land at Siumu. All the lands passed to the New Zealand government and then passed to Samoa at independence were therefore validated by the High Court of Germany. Now, Siumu, our meeting has come to an end.'

The armed blockade by the people of Siumu reminded me that land is a very sensitive issue and that land conflicts can quickly escalate, particularly if stirred up for political ends, and they can get out of hand if calm and strong leadership does not prevail.[1]

With the Siumu situation settled, we now had the general election.

April 2001 to March 2006

This was the period of Tuila'epa Sa'ilele Malielegaoi's second administration. The HRPP won 25 seats, the SNDP ten, independents thirteen and the Samoa All People's Party (SAPP) one. Later, two independents joined the HRPP, and three HRPP candidates won by-elections following electoral petitions.

After the election there was confusion amongst the opposition about who was to lead.

When the results came out I was indirectly informed that there would be a coalition between Tupua Tamasese and his few MPs, and Dr Asiata Sāle'imoa, who had the numbers to negotiate. The result for Tuimaleali'ifano was not good. He lost to Misa and he could therefore not become part of any coalition arrangement.

Tupua wanted to form a coalition with himself as the leader. Asiata wanted to be the leader of the coalition. At the same time within Tupua's party many Members wanted Le Mamea Ropati to be leader. They had lost six general elections over nineteen years under Tupua's leadership and their confidence had shifted to Le Mamea. With all this divisiveness in the two camps, the efforts to form a coalition were bound to fail.

It was reported to me that my deputy, Misa, was considering leaving the HRPP and taking some of the independents from us to join forces with the opposition and lead a coalition. Therefore there would have to be a tussle between four people for leadership.

Faced with these rumours, I had to move fast. I summoned our party caucus three days after the general election to hold a vote for the leader and deputy leader of the HRPP. I won the leadership. The tussle for deputy was

1   This was not the first, nor the last, land dispute Tuila'epa had to deal with. A decade before, another contested land claim at Tuanaimato, also with Tupua in the background, had hit the headlines. Later, he was confronted by another armed blockade over disputed land at Faleolo Airport. Each of these incidents involved an armed blockade and required strong leadership to resolve.

between Fiamē and Misa. Misa won.

So with Misa back as deputy leader the possible fragmentation of our party was prevented. The potential coalition numbers were now depleted, so the others would be unable to form a coalition.

We had put through the necessary legal requirements for appointing a prime minister during the last term so that we did not have to wait for Parliament to sit to elect a new prime minister. We followed the practice in New Zealand and Australia that, once the majority is confirmed, the party leader is automatically elected prime minister. In fact, I had just been confirmed leader of my party on Tuesday, four days after the elections, when I got my appointment letter from the Head of State proclaiming that I was the new Prime Minister because I commanded the majority in the House.

When I arrived home that evening I got a call from Radio New Zealand International and the reporter said, 'I have just spoken to Dr Asiata Sāle'imoa and he expects to be the new Prime Minister when the Parliament meets on Thursday. Can I have some confirmation from you?'

I said, 'I don't really know what to say. I have a confirmation letter in my hand from the Head of State that says I am now appointed Prime Minister as I am the leader of the party with the majority in Parliament.'

Then I quipped, 'I think it was only in Fiji that there were ever two prime ministers at one time. Here in Samoa we only have one. Never two at any one time.'

I heard this fellow laughing. So I knew then that Asiata had no idea of the new Standing Orders relating to the appointment of the prime minister.

When we gathered in the House on Thursday I delivered my victory speech. The list of Cabinet Ministers was read out and we were all sworn in. There was to be a response from the leader of the opposition and I was expecting Tupua to fulfil that task. But it was Asiata who responded to me, and it was a weird response. I expected high oratory. What he said to me was, 'Tuila'epa, now that you are Prime Minister, I want to warn you to play the ball, not the man, thank you very much.' And he sat down.

This was the most stupid speech of Samoan oratory ever delivered at the first meeting of a new Parliament in Samoa.

Several days later Tupua left for Australia. In a speech he made at his village of Lufilufi, following his return, Tupua confirmed he had needed urgent medical treatment in Australia. What emerged from the opposition was that Tupua's most trusted supporters in the caucus, Fuimaono Mimio and Masoe F. Kruse, had recommended that Tupua step down in favour of

Mamea Ropati. With six consecutive general election defeats over nineteen years of leadership, Tupua Tamasese Efi was the only one in the opposition camp who did not accept that he was an 'overstayer'. The shock of the realisation that he was no longer needed was very stressful and his health had suffered. The matter of leadership of the opposition party was now between Mamea and Asiata. Mamea Ropati, the veteran politician, got the upper hand and emerged the undisputed leader.

Tupua's district asked him to resign from Parliament and move upwards to become a member of the Council of Deputies. Lufilufi said it was unbecoming for the Tui Ātua to be under the direction of a Mamea. Tupua rejected this outright. He said, 'Lufilufi, I don't want to become a member of the Council of Deputies, anybody who accepts that position is an *'ai āfu* (sweat eater).'[2]

A delegation from Tupua's village led by Faamatuainu Tala Mailei later came to petition for their MP Tupua Tamasese to be directly appointed to the Council of Deputies. I told them to go and talk first with Tupua. I never heard from them again.

The Apology
There was a CHOGM in 1999 in Southern Africa. On the way back I travelled with New Zealand's Prime Minister, Helen Clark. We stopped at Perth and she asked for a brief meeting with me. She said that she wanted to come to Samoa to apologise on behalf of the New Zealand government for unfortunate incidents that had happened under New Zealand's administration of Samoa: namely, the police shooting of Tupua Tamasese Lealofi III in 1929, and the administration's negligence in relation to the influenza epidemic of 1919 that resulted in many deaths. She asked me what I thought. She also said she had been strongly advised to come and apologise. I think that she had also apologised to the Māori and Chinese in New Zealand over historical incidents. She wanted to do the same thing here and asked my opinion.

I said, 'I don't recommend that you come and apologise.'

She asked, 'Why?'

'There is so much politics in Samoa that you are not aware of. My recommendation is that you do not come.'

She came, nevertheless, despite my advice.

Helen Clark came for the occasion of our 40 years of independence in 2002. And she was determined to make an apology.

I thought, since she came, I would have to meet her and make a speech.

2   A common Samoan term for someone who gets something for nothing.

But I would have to deal with her very subtly. There was a lot of history and politics around the time of the Mau. There are different sides to the story that still have political echoes today.[3] Tui Ātua Tupua Tamasese, my long-time political rival, was directly related to two key figures of the time: Tupua Tamasese Lealofi III, of the Mau, and the businessman Taisi Olaf Nelson.

Politics in Samoa during the colonial period was very complex. Our traditional cultural connections run deep. The Malietoa clan supported New Zealand; the Tupua clan opposed New Zealand. Falealili district also supported New Zealand. The salutation of the Tofilau title, held by my predecessor Tofilau 'Eti Alesana, is: 'Welcome Tofilau, the ninth family of the Malietoa.' The formal address of the Tuila'epa title is, *'Le alo o Malietoa'* – literally, the son of Malietoa.

The formal address of my title Lolofietele is: *'Le alo ole Tui Ātua'*, the son of Tui Ātua. Through my titles Fatialofa and 'Auelua I am the talking chief of the Tui Ātua. Through my title Neioti I am of the Safenunuvao family whose son is Tui Ātua. My other titles, Lupesoli'ai of the Salevalasi family and 'Ai'ono of the Satuala family, are of Tui Ātua origin. All my chiefly titles are of Tui Ātua origin except Tuila'epa, which is Malietoa related. And remember, in 1999 Malietoa Tanumafili II was Head of State, I, Tuila'epa the son of Malietoa, was the Prime Minister, and Tui Ātua Tupua Tamasese was leader of the opposition. These are some of the complex issues of chiefly relationships that have political implications.

So, imagine the Tupua clan is on this side, and the Malietoa clan on this other side. There is a lot of cultural history to the alignment of the government and the opposition in Samoa. It goes back to well before the New Zealand colonial administration. Helen Clark was walking into a situation about which she had a very limited understanding.

I had said to Helen Clark, 'I do not recommend you come. There is a lot of politics.' But instead of explaining to her the really complex cultural issues, I told her a very brief version of the Christian belief, 'We forgave you.' The longer version is that we Samoans are deep in the Christian faith, and in the Old Testament it is decreed by the Lord Himself that if somebody does wrong to you, you must never, ever, continue to bear that in your heart after sundown. You must forgive the wrongdoer before sundown. This is an often-quoted saying from the Bible that Samoan chiefs like to utter in their speeches, especially on occasions that require forgiveness.

I was trying to tell Helen Clark that an apology was unnecessary.

3   For a range of views on these events, see Davidson, 1967; Field, 1984 and 2006; and Meleisea, 1987.

'Whatever you did we forgave before the sundown of that very day.'

But she came. She succumbed to the pressure of Tupua's supporters in New Zealand, who were in constant contact with Helen Clark. Helen Clark was misadvised.

After she gave her speech during the official government luncheon in her honour, I responded as follows:[4]

'I rise on behalf of the Head of State, the government and people of Samoa, to warmly thank the Prime Minister of New Zealand, the Right Honourable Helen Clark, for her address and for the very kind sentiments she has expressed about Samoa on the occasion of our fortieth independence celebrations.

'I would like to acknowledge the formal apology the Prime Minister has most graciously offered on behalf of the government and people of New Zealand to the people of Samoa for the injustices that occurred in earlier years of New Zealand's administration of this country.

'Prime Minister, we say in Samoa, *A iai ni lape poʻo faʻaletonu, ia faʻatafea ia i nuʻu lē ainā*. Which means that whatever wrongs and transgressions took place, let these be consigned to uninhabited lands.

'I would also recall the words of the eighteenth-century English poet Alexander Pope, which, given the long shadow that his country cast over New Zealand and Samoa in the period in question, seem to me to be prophetically appropriate to this occasion, when he wrote, "To err is human, to forgive divine."

'Indeed, we have long ago forgiven and moved on. We have certainly not allowed the past to encumber the development of the excellent relations that Samoa and New Zealand now enjoy.

'Our nation's Constitution required Samoa to be an independent state based on Christian principles and Samoan customs and traditions. The importance of forgiveness runs through our customs and traditions and it is a key cornerstone of the Christian faith that we have embraced.

'His Highness the Head of State is among the very last surviving founding fathers of our Constitution. He continues to remind us to always remember that on the day Samoa's National Flag was first raised on Independence Day, all remaining wrongs were forgiven. The seal of the government adopted in parallel with the National Flag very appropriately also displays prominently the Cross of Redemption surrounded by olive branches signifying everlasting peace in and beyond Samoa.

'Prime Minister, the Treaty of Friendship between Samoa and New

---

4   See Malielegaoi, 2002, for the full texts of Tuilaʻepa's speech in English and Samoan.

Zealand signed in 1962 expressed the warmth of the relationship that Samoa and New Zealand had attained by the time of independence. In a real sense the treaty demonstrated the desire of both countries to put to rest the past and to concentrate on the future and ways in which New Zealand could assist with Samoa's nation building . . .

'Finally, I would also like to use this opportunity to express our gratitude for everything too numerous to recount separately that New Zealand has done for Samoa in the long association between our two countries. It goes without saying that we look forward to the continuation of the excellent bilateral relationship between Samoa and New Zealand as well as the close working relationship we have at regional and international fora.

'If you would excuse me, Prime Minister, I would now like to turn to our language and give in Samoan the extended version of what I just said briefly in English.'

At 7 a.m. the following morning I got a call from Radio New Zealand. The reporter said, 'Mr Tuila'epa, we have been reading and reading, and replaying your speech. Nowhere in your speech did you accept the apology. Was it useful?'

'Yes, it was very useful.'

'Yes?'

'Yes. Very useful to New Zealand Samoans and the New Zealand public in general.'

'Why?'

'Because we know our own history. So its use is for the New Zealand public and for the New Zealand-born Samoan who don't understand our history.'

'Thank you very much, thank you very much,' the reporter said.

I did not think that the reporter caught the subtlety of my words. My words conveyed the message that it was useless for Helen Clark to come to Samoa. She should have given her apology in New Zealand to the New Zealand public and for the benefit of Samoans in New Zealand. It is virtually unnecessary here. We know our own history.

Appointments

I had decided to leave the remaining positions on the Council of Deputies vacant for a time. Later on we appointed a non-*tama-a-'āiga*, the Honourable Faumuinā Anapapa, to fill one vacancy. Two vacancies remained until twelve months before the 2006 general election. Before we could fill them, I had to speak to Tui Ātua Tupua Tamasese and Tuimaleali'ifano to gauge their interest.

I talked first to Tupua. I said to him, 'It is known that you are opposed to being on the Council of Deputies. You objected to us when we made that motion way back in 1990 to appoint you to the Council of Deputies and you rejected it outright, alleging that we wanted to kick you out of the House. You also delivered a speech to your constituency in 2001 saying that anybody who accepts a post on the Council of Deputies is an *'ai āfu*. I am going to announce the two new appointees in the House tomorrow, but before I do so I want to give you two *tama-a-'āiga* the opportunity to reconsider. What do you think?'

He smiled his smile and said, 'You know, Tui, I said that as a joke, a war of humour between me and Tofilau. It was only a joke. I want to be a member of the Council of Deputies. Please.'

'Decision made.'

I then met with Tuimaleali'ifano. He too wanted to come back and expressed regret for not listening to me when he resigned his post as a member of the Council of Deputies to run for Parliament.

I said, 'By that decision you made, you are no longer the senior member to accede to the post of Head of State when it is vacant.'

So that is why when Malietoa Tanumafili II died, Tupua Tamasese had to be appointed as Head of State, ahead of Tuimaleali'ifano.

After I had the confirmations from Tuimaleali'ifano and Tupua, Parliament proceeded with the appointment of the two *tama-a-'āiga* to the Council of Deputies.

Salary Reviews and Strikes

There was a major disruption at this time. The shadow of the 1981 public service strike was always on my mind. I knew the cause of the strike. There was no uniform method to put our government employees' salary scales on a proper footing. Public servants' salaries were set by the Public Service Commission. The other employees, not under the Public Service Commission, like the police, the Judiciary, and the Legislative Assembly, including MPs, had their salaries reviewed and determined on an *ad hoc* basis.

In the case of Parliament, whenever Tofilau proposed reviewing MPs' salaries, Tupua, the leader of the opposition, would be the first to stand up in the House making emotional appeals to the country, saying: 'You hear that we, the servants of the people, want to raise our salaries, but you the people are poor.'

Salary reviews were always a hot political issue and Prime Minister

Tofilau consistently refrained from reviewing salaries. I knew well that Tupua's government had failed the greatest challenge of his administration over the public servants' demand for a salary increase. I was determined to find a solution.

The remedy was to set up a Salaries Tribunal that would be responsible for determining a unified scale of salaries for the whole of government services, including the corporations, the Judiciary and parliamentarians. It would also continuously monitor the growth of the economy and the rise in the cost of living, and recommend to government appropriate adjustments taking into account the necessary balance in the relativity of salaries structure between the government and the private sector. The government, therefore, would be proactive in matters of salary adjustments in relation to the rise in the cost of living.

The first report from the tribunal reflected what the government wanted. Because salary scales were so low, they recommended a 42 percent increase right across the board. Because we did not have enough money in the budget to meet the outgoings in one year, we decided to implement the salary adjustments over three years. The first year would be 20 percent, then 11 percent and another 11 percent in the final year.

That action raised the level of salaries for all public servants. But the private sector complained that the relativity favoured the public sector. That was a minor twist that could be straightened out over time.

When we announced the rise in salaries in 2005, the young doctors decided to go on strike. They wrongly assumed that with the elections coming in 2006, we would buckle under. They felt their salaries should be above everybody else in the government service because as doctors they dealt with the survival of our people.

The young doctors announced the date of their proposed strike. They asked for support from the Doctors' Association, who voted overwhelmingly in favour of the strike. What the young doctors did not fully understand was that their association was dominated by doctors who were in private practice. The doctors in private practice knew that when the young doctors in the hospital went on strike, their private practices would benefit.

Cabinet decided to set up a Commission of Enquiry to look into the doctors' concerns, and its recommendations pointed to the need to review the salaries of some of the doctors who genuinely had missed out on annual increments. The doctors' request for another raise, above the unified scale set by the Salaries Tribunal, was not supported.

The striking doctors sought support from the Public Service Association, but the PSA declined as they agreed with the tribunal's recommendations and they remembered that the doctors had not supported the 1981 PSA strike.

They all believed that I would give in. On the day they started their strike, I addressed the nation on television and radio. I informed our people that the government hospitals would continue to provide healthcare by the doctors who were not on strike, assisted by the nurses. I told them that all the doctors in private practice were also available to ease the pressure and deal with emergencies, and there was no need to panic.

I said, 'As for all those 30 doctors who have voluntarily withheld their services, the government has decided to accept their decision to withdraw from government service and, as from 4.30 p.m., all their posts have been declared vacant. Those who might wish to be re-engaged should reapply. Meanwhile, those who live in government houses must immediately vacate the government premises for use by new recruits. Those who still have outstanding debts with government must settle their accounts before they can travel overseas again.'

The following day I left for the meeting of the CHOGM in Malta.

Several days later the strikers went back to the hospital and begged to be readmitted. That was a big victory for the government and a crisis was averted before the next general election came around.

There was a little-known incident that happened when I was out of the country at the CHOGM in Malta. In my absence Tupua Tamasese, who was now a member of the Council of Deputies, had tried to convene a meeting of the Executive Council to deliberate on the doctors' strike. He had Tuimaleali'ifano on his side, but the Head of State and the third member of the Council of Deputies, Faumuinā, would not go along with him so the attempted 'coup' was stalled. On my return to Samoa, the Attorney-General raised with me the possibility of a charge of treason being laid. I ruled against it.

PĀLEMIA

Part 2. Nation Building 2006–2016

April 2006 to March 2011

This was Tuila'epa Sa'ilele Malielegaoi's third administration. The HRPP won 30 seats to the Samoa Democratic United Party's ten and nine independents. Subsequent defections and by-elections increased the HRPP seats to 37.

The South Pacific Games in Samoa during 2007 was the first of a number of regional and international events that Tuila'epa's government hosted. The games had significant economic benefits, increased inbound tourist numbers, and raised Samoa's prestige in the Pacific region and beyond. A number of other events followed over the next decade. The largest was the United Nations Small Islands Developing States (SIDS) Conference in September 2014. The Commonwealth Youth Games and the first rugby test match in Samoa between Manu Samoa and the All Blacks were two other high-profile events in 2015. The facilities necessary to host these events were established during Tuila'epa's premiership, but the acquisition of land for these facilities was the outcome of a conflict over land that had its origins in the German colonial period.

Over 80 percent of Samoa's land remains in traditional ownership under the stewardship of *matai*, while 12 percent of the land is held in freehold title. The government controls around 8 percent of the land, much of which had been former German plantations taken over by the New Zealand administration that became government assets at independence. Known as the 'Reparation Estates', this land was placed under government administration through the Samoa Trust Estates Corporation. From time to time disputes have arisen when claims have been made over the ownership of this land.

Four hundred acres of land at Tuanaimato, Vaitele, just outside Apia, had been subject to a dispute for some years. In the late 1990s a group of armed young men occupied the land, set up camp and defied a court ruling that this was government land. Securing the land and establishing a sports complex was a task in which Tuila'epa was deeply involved over a number of years. He takes up the story.

The decision to turn the 400 acres at Tuanaimato into a sports complex was one of the best decisions we made. It was in the face of threats, protests and gunshots that we went ahead and made that decision.

In the midst of these threats, Tofilau had called me and said, 'I am worried about your safety. Subdivide the land for settlement.'

This was because there were photos in the newspapers of armed protesters wearing masks and making threats.

Some of them said, 'The Minister lives not far away, we will go and shoot him.'

We had 400 yards of new fence put up at Tuanaimato and they just pulled it down. But when they put up roadblocks and took up weapons, that was the beginning of the end.

I summoned Asi Blakelock, the Police Commissioner.

I said, 'By 4.30 today, when people go home from work, I want that roadblock cleared.'

'Yes. Yes, Sir.'

Thirty minutes later he called me: 'Minister, is it OK for you to give us permission to carry firearms?'

'Carry firearms. And remove all those roadblocks by 4.30. It is an embarrassment to the government. It is as if we have no law and order.'

So I gave Asi the written authority for the police to carry firearms.

The whole area was a cocoa plantation, with trees and young coconuts just starting to bear fruit. We had to clear the land to deprive the occupiers of shelter where they were hiding.

I gave the order, 'Hire all the earthmoving equipment from Rudy Otts and clear the area right through so we can look across. But before we can clear the area, we have to move the hooligans out.'

Lapi[5] told me what happened. 'The police came from both sides, advancing on the occupiers from the north and the south.'

Tuila'epa draws a map.

We were here. This is the lay of the land. All of these rascals were here, concentrating on this road from the north. Because it was very difficult to come through the thick bush and forest, the police started approaching from here and moved towards the south.

The squatters were squeezed in between the advancing police.

Lapi told me that these guys had their 12-gauge shot guns, primed with birdshot. The police were coming with .308s. These were real guns. The occupiers ran blindly backwards from the north with their guns. Suddenly they turned around and there, confronting them, were all of the police with their .308 automatic rifles pointing at them. The occupiers went white with

---

5   Lt. Vaovasamanaia L. Filo (Lapi), who was involved in the operation, is now attached to the PM's Office as a Special Security Officer.

fright and threw their guns down. Thirty of them were arrested and charged.

Earlier, in about 1990, Tofilau had asked me to subdivide and sell off the whole 400 acres for settlement. I formed a committee and developed a quick plan to turn the land into a sporting complex. I took the plan to Cabinet and laid out the vision we had for the future. Tofilau and the Cabinet approved the plan.

In order to speed up the process we created the Samoa Land Corporation to take up all the lands that were previously under the STEC[6] to be utilised for economic, sporting and recreational purposes. We directed the SLC to subdivide a hundred quarter-acre sections of government land in the neighbourhood. The sale of the sections aimed to raise 3.2 million Tala to assist funding the development of the sports complex.

At the time, I thought 400 acres was too much. However, we quickly handed out one large part of the land for a horseracing track, a second area for an eighteen-hole golf course and a third area we turned into the cricket field with five pitches suitable for hosting international cricket tournaments. This still left a large area where we built the swimming pool complex, an international soccer pitch, three gymnasia and other sports facilities for the 2007 South Pacific Games.

After the games we continued to host international events at Tuanaimato. The United Nations SIDS meeting was the big one. Because of the way we constructed the gyms, it made them so easy to handle and adapt to a number of uses. They turned out to be the best ever conference facilities for a meeting of the United Nations, compared to all the other host nations where they have to juggle distances from one meeting place to another place. But here everything is concentrated in one location. So the beauty was immediately recognised when the United Nations made the decision to host the SIDS meeting in Samoa.

The 2007 South Pacific Games

The South Pacific Games came at an opportune time for us to improve our sports facilities. This involved quite a lot of money, over US$50 million. We solicited overseas help and the Chinese agreed to build an Olympic-size swimming pool with separate pools for warming up and diving, along with facilities for spectators and competitors. The pool was the major item demanded by participating countries.

The 2007 Games required a lot of resources from us, and they coincided with the Global Financial Crisis. I remember one of the bank managers

---

6   Except for 6000 acres at Mulifanua that STEC would continue to develop.

told me that the cash reserves in the banking system had come down considerably because of this major project undertaken by the government. I had faith that the investment would pay off in the long run.

I believed that the Games were an excellent opportunity for our people to showcase their talents. To encourage local sportspeople to participate, I talked a lot through the media and urged our youth to take up a sport and try to win a medal for the country. Because Samoa was hosting the Games, it was cheaper for us to have a bigger contingent than we'd ever had before.

To back my public comments, I decided to take up a sport and lead by example. I took up shooting. I also took up archery and concentrated on archery to win a medal. We had an archery compound established for practice and it became the venue for the competition. I went out of my way to encourage as many people as possible to participate in the sport. It seemed as if I was never taken seriously. People thought I was joking when I said that I was taking archery. I joked that one of the reasons for taking up archery was that, if the opposition needed to be calmed down in the House, I would be able to shoot their legs with my arrows! It was all done in great fun. I used to make that joke and laugh. Because I was joking all along, nobody took me seriously until they saw me competing at the Games. I won a silver medal in archery. I was told that I was the only sitting leader of a country to compete in an international sporting competition, and the only one to win a silver medal.

Samoa came second in the South Pacific Games: we earned the most medals ever. We had never reached second place before. The Games were a great success and showed to us, and the region, that Samoa has the capacity to successfully host international events.

Switching Sides

In late 2007 I announced that we would change the road code so that we could drive on the left-hand side of the road and thus many lower income families would have access to owning a vehicle. Immediately the opposition erupted. Even in my own Cabinet. As Prime Minister I had many requests to allow right-hand-drive vehicles into the country. At that time there were only two motor vehicle dealers of substance controlling the market: Nissan and Toyota. There were several second-hand dealers who imported from the United States. The cost of vehicles was very high. By changing the code we could access the cheapest second-hand market in the world, Japan, and access vehicles directly through the internet. We would also now have the chance to get vehicles from our relatives who had migrated to New Zealand

and Australia. There was a lot of opposition, including the formation of an organisation called PASS, People Against Side Switch, to oppose the policy. The organisers succeeded in putting together a huge protest march on Parliament while the House was in session. We had to break our meeting and go into recess to formally receive the protesters' petition.

I did not waver. I kept educating the public with my frequent talks in the media about the benefits of a switch. Several of my Ministers objected without doing it in the open; instead, they encouraged their wives and children to distribute 'Down with Right-Hand-Drive Vehicles' posters and stickers. Even members of my own caucus were trying to sabotage our project by holding secret seminars. Some of the opposition was ridiculous: PASS predicted that up to seven hundred children would be killed daily by traffic accidents.

Treasury released a study that condemned the policy as being harmful to the economy, and forecast a run-down on Samoa's foreign exchange reserves. I maintained there would be major benefits to our country and boosts to our exports.

A major boost to our confidence level came from an unexpected source when a senior official from Toyota spoke to the Honourable Tuisugaletaua Sōfara, the Minister in charge of the switch, and told him that Toyota would accommodate the proposed switch in their production plans.

Two things stood out. Of those who protested most already owned or worked for companies that dealt with left-hand-drive cars. They were mostly wealthy or middle-class and were a vocal minority. The silent majority did not own cars but could have right-hand-drive vehicles supplied from their families in New Zealand and Australia if the policy changed.

We set up a Technical Committee to look at how best to effect the change and manage all the potential challenges. Our roads are not very complex: single-ring roads with very little criss-crossing and few traffic lights. The most difficult part was where there were traffic lights and the need to change them. We did not have many traffic lights at that time. It was a transition that we were able to carry out with the minimal costs. Good signage, reducing the speed limit and plenty of publicity were important common-sense factors in a smooth transition.

Eventually the great day came. We had a brief ceremony on Beach Road on 7 September 2009 at 6 a.m. that was televised. The street-lights were all on, casting beautiful reflections on the sea, presenting an extraordinary image early in the morning. Lines of cars on each side of the road with their lights on were ready and waiting.

After a thanksgiving prayer by the Reverend Oka Fauolo, I said, 'Now I declare this project officially open.'

The sirens sounded together with the horns from the cars. The cars lining up on the seaward side of the road turned inward to the left, whilst the cars lining up on the left turned simultaneously to the seaward side of the road. The change that took place was visible and beautiful in the early hours of the morning. It was all done in style to the sounds of the horns and clapping. The protests had fizzled out. There were crowds all along Beach Road watching the change take place and people throughout Samoa watched the change on TV.

Not one traffic accident occurred on the day of the switch. Arrows painted on the roads, to remind drivers of the correct side to drive on, and a reduction of the speed limit were most effective in promoting road safety.

We had a very successful launch. When I called up the same bank manager I had spoken to several weeks earlier, I said to him, 'How are the bank's cash reserves?'

He said to me, 'You know, things were very bad with our balances but as soon as you announced the new policy, immediately our balances went up and up. I was beginning to wonder if the switch was a measure that you deliberately put in to improve our balance.'

The real reason was that merchants were scared to import vehicles in case the government's proposed measure failed. But of course it was a great success. The response was electric. Six months later many people in the country suddenly owned beautiful vehicles sent by their families in New Zealand and Australia.

Salelologa Township
The chiefs of Sakalafai village in Savai'i boycotted the road switch in September 2009 to gain publicity about a land dispute that went back to Tofilau's time as Prime Minister.

Tofilau 'Eti Alesana had long promoted the grand vision of building a modern port and township at Salelologa that would be a gateway for the development of Savai'i. As holder of the Luamanuvae title of Salelologa, Tofilau had a strong commitment to seeing this project completed. However, a scoping study by a potential donor estimated the cost of the project at US$600 million. The high cost put the project on hold.

As Minister of Finance, I suggested that the project could proceed in stages. The first stage could be the construction of a township on some rocky, uncultivated customary land adjacent to the proposed port facilities. Over time the government could provide the funds from the Budget. Tofilau accepted the staged plan and, through his Luamanuvae title, obtained the agreement of his village council for the use of 2872 acres of land for the project. Compensation was to be negotiated later when the formal legal process for the takeover of customary land for public purposes was completed. Meanwhile, advances of the compensation monies in lots of several hundreds of dollars at a time were made to Salelologa by the Minister of Lands, Survey and Environment, the Honourable Tuala Sale Kerslake.

The 2872 acres of land were surveyed and the Minister of Public Works, Luagalau Levaula Kamu, was directed to build a ring road around the whole area.

This was a large project involving customary lands and was potentially fraught with difficulties. However, the benefits of a new township, the potential of new employment opportunities and the improved access to education, health and other government services to be located at Salelologa, along with the sponsorship of the Prime Minister silenced any doubters. Furthermore, the immediate distribution of advances of compensation was seen as manna from Heaven. The whole Salelologa district was behind the project.

In early 1999 Luamanuvae Tofilau 'Eti Alesana died. Negotiations with the Minister of Lands, Survey and the Environment dragged on, with the Salelologa chiefs demanding 300 million Tala compensation. Tuala informed me that he was getting nowhere and was unable to continue the negotiations.

Samoa's Constitution states that customary land cannot be sold, and thus there is no market value placed on customary land. When the government takes customary land for public purposes, it pays compensation on the basis of a special valuation fixed by the Ministry of Lands and the Environment. The value of the 2872 acres of land at Salelologa was fixed at 3.2 million Tala.

When Tuala told me of the impasse I ordered him to arrange a final negotiation meeting with the Salelologa district. I led the delegation, comprised of the Honourable Tuala Kerslake, the Honourable Ulu Kini Leva'a MP and the Attorney-General, Brenda Heather. Our meeting with the chiefs and orators of the Salelologa, with many of the local women and children in attendance, started with an *'ava* ceremony.

In accordance with custom the *'ava* roots were presented to my delegation and Leva'a delivered a long-winded oration that brought laughter to the *matai* and lightened up the serious atmosphere that had greeted our arrival.

When the formalities were completed I spoke: 'Salelologa, we have come to conclude our negotiation of the final compensation for your lands taken for the township. We should all be thankful that we had a man of vision in your own brother Chief Luamanuvae, Prime Minister of Samoa, who thought to create this township for the development of your district and the whole of Samoa. Thousands of years from today, your great-great-grandchildren will sing songs of praise and thanksgiving for the decision that you have taken to build this township on your lands. We could have easily reclaimed some of the sea for the township but we followed the direction of your great leader, Luamanuvae, to use your wasteland of rocks and turn it into a township that you will be proud of.

'Is there any other single district in Samoa that has received the kind of monies that you have received for a similar project? None.

'The value of this customary land has been determined as 3.2 million Samoan Tala. We are not going to give you fractions of the whole. We will give you compensation of 4 million Tala. If you accept 4 million, the project will continue. If you decline this offer, the project will be stopped as from today. If I turn and go back to Apia without an answer, the project is as good as dead.'

Matamua, the chief spokesman for Salelologa, wiped his sweating forehead several times with a towel before he finally said, 'Let it be done, we accept 4 million Tala.'

The final *'ava* chant, *'Ava Taumavae*, was issued to signal the successful conclusion of the day's deliberations, and the first cup was presented to Chief Matamua, who blessed his *'ava* with the comment, 'Mr Prime Minister, let the 4 million begin with this part-payment received today. Whatever was received before does not count.' He downed his *'ava* rapidly with one quick tip of his palm.

The second cup was for me. Before I drank it, I responded to Matamua. 'Let us not complicate Luamanuvae's trip to Heaven by side-tracking him to Purgatory because of your evil conditions. The 4 million includes every cent paid to you while Luamanuvae was still alive. Cheers.' And I downed my cup.

Several days before White Sunday in October I received a delegation from Salelologa requesting a 1 million cash advance, on the 4 million compensation we had agreed to, for their White Sunday preparations. They readily understood my refusal when I reminded them of my story about spending time in Purgatory, and happily accepted 500 Tala from me for their bus fare back to Salelologa.

The dispute on the compensation did not end there. The people of Sakalafai village decided to take a 300 million compensation claim to court. The decision of the Land and Titles Court is yet to be delivered and this was the reason the Sakalafai chiefs tried to boycott the road switch in September 2009. Meanwhile, Cabinet decided to retain only 440 acres for the township and returned 2432 acres to Salelologa village. When the court delivers its judgement, government will then be in a position to claim a refund of payment in cash or in kind.

Tsunami
After the traffic changes were made I took off to New York for the United Nations General Assembly. When we finished I flew back to New Zealand, heading for Samoa. We arrived on the morning of the 29th of September. The plan was to spend a week in New Zealand for medical checks and drive to Hamilton to support David Tua in his fight against Shane Cameron.

I had just checked into a hotel in Māngere, sat down and turned on the TV. The first item was the breaking news that a tsunami had hit Samoa. A few minutes later I got a call from my daughter in Samoa telling me of the seriousness of the disaster. I said to Mose Sua, the Secretary of Foreign Affairs who was accompanying me, 'We have a change of plan. I want to fly back to Samoa as soon as possible.'

My wife, Gillian, interjected, 'What about the medical checks and the boxing?'

'When you are Prime Minister all those things are secondary. We have to be in Samoa now.'

Mose tried to book seats and was told that it was a small Boeing 737 and there were no places. I asked him book me on the next flight out, which would be 24 hours later. In the meantime the news media were pressuring Air New Zealand because they wanted to fly to Samoa to be on the spot. The media practically forced Air New Zealand to fly a larger Boeing 777. They made the decision to upgrade the plane and called us. The scheduled departure time was 2 p.m. I was on that plane with my delegation.

The media people did not know that I was on that plane until we were just about to land and they begged me for an interview.

I said, 'I haven't seen the damage yet.'

'It doesn't matter.'

'All right. Give me five minutes after arrival.'

I was briefed by the Acting Prime Minister, the Honourable Tu'u'u Anisii. Then I gave the media an interview with a full knowledge of the events. That interview was beamed right across the world to CNN and soon it was flashed around the world on the major networks.

It was when I arrived at home, at about 8 p.m., that I learnt that a funeral service for Mrs Tui Annandale, who died in the tsunami, would be held that evening at 9 o'clock at her residence at Tanumapua, five minutes' drive from my home at Ululoloa. I attended that funeral.

Immediately after the funeral I issued a call, via television and radio, asking the National Disaster Council members to assemble in front of the government building at 6 the following morning for our first inspection visit. I had learnt from previous disasters that it was important to see for myself the damage rather than relying entirely on second-hand reports. Fortunately, bulldozers and other earthmoving equipment were already on their way to clear the debris and we were able to get into the affected areas and witness the impact of the disaster. It was at Saleapāga village when we were talking to people that we heard people crying who had just discovered family members under the debris. And there was that thick smell hanging in the air of decayed vegetation killed by the salt water. Many of those we spoke to were in shock.

We moved pretty fast from Siumu through Lepā to Aleipata, the worst-affected areas. This is the region of Samoa that directly faces the Tonga Trench, the source of many earthquakes that hit Samoa.

Lepā was hit very badly. We had 49 dead from my district alone, and many from Saleapāga village towards the east. My sister told me that she was in our house in Lepā when she heard people yelling about the oncoming waves. She dashed outside to look as the waves hit the walls of our meeting house and in a second she was swept off her feet by the waves and carried inland through the gorge where the river flows. Fortunately, there was extensive flat land where the seawater kept pushing with such powerful force until the flows weakened. She was able to grab on to a tree branch and was saved. At Saleapāga village towards the east, the steep hillside was very close to the houses and when the water hit the steep rock wall it piled up and up and up and got very deep as the incoming waves kept coming and coming. The current it created was so strong that many people, especially the young and the old, could not escape and drowned. Trees, boulders, torn roofing iron and other debris were all brought in by the waves and battered people who had no way to get to safety.

The September 2009 tsunami was the worst disaster in living memory. We had thoroughly enjoyed launching the change to right-hand-drive at the beginning of the month and then we had a big disaster at the end of the month. Between Samoa and American Samoa, 189 people died and three thousand people lost their homes. The tsunami was estimated to have done 400 million Tala in damage.

We moved very quickly to provide relief from our own resources for immediate needs, and we were very grateful to New Zealand and Australia for the rapid help they provided.

In Saleapāga, one and a half years before the tsunami hit, a new primary school funded by Japanese aid was opened. In my dedication speech I said to the chiefs, 'You will recall I asked you not to build in the village so close to the shoreline for fear of tsunami and I asked you to move the school to higher land in the hinterland and you laughed. I said, if a disaster occurs and destroys this school building, the chiefs of Lepā will say, "What else can we expect from Saleapāga village?"'

Sadly, the new school was destroyed. Luckily not all the children were killed because some of them had seen the televised government disaster warning programmes and as soon as they felt the powerful earthquake hit, they took off immediately to higher ground. Others refused to move and tragically they died.

When we arrived at Saleapāga one of the chiefs wept as he addressed me and the National Disaster Council members.

He said, 'Prime Minister, we can still remember your warning. We never listened to you. I can tell you we are now all moving inland to higher ground.'

Saleapāga was the first village that relocated inland.

Shifting the International Dateline and Introducing Daylight Saving
The change in the International Dateline was inspired by the need to help our people fulfil their cultural obligations and to make business easier with New Zealand and Australia. Over 99 percent of our people who emigrate go to New Zealand or Australia. The disadvantage of the old time zone for Samoa was that if the death of a loved one took place on a New Zealand Saturday, it was our Friday. Usually we would get notification after office hours. We could do nothing until Monday. If the burial was to be on a Tuesday, you could hardly be there in time. Banks open on Monday and you would have to run around to get the money and fine mats to take. By the time you finished your preparations, it would be impossible to go. The burial would already have taken place.

The preference was for Samoans in New Zealand and Samoa to be in the same time zone, which would give us time to prepare for our cultural obligations. Not only that, on the business side we only had four working days in common. We could only work between Monday and Thursday in the old time zone.

When I summoned my officials and said that I wanted to shift the

International Dateline, no one knew how to go about it. They got in touch with the authorities in London, who regulate Greenwich Mean Time, to seek their consent. They advised us that all we were required to do was inform our neighbours of our decision and they would redraw the International Dateline. We gave them our preference that the line should pass between Samoa and American Samoa.

We would have liked American Samoa to be on this side, but they are under the United States of America. In the process of changing our time zone, we discovered that what we wanted was in fact what it had been before it was changed in 1872, when Samoa was put in the same zone as American Samoa. At that time the main direction of trade and shipping was from the United States. Today the direction of trade and shipping is reversed. This revelation reminds me of King Solomon's wisdom conveyed in his words, 'there is nothing new under the sun.'

The change has worked out extremely well with little push back.

Another interesting point is that, on the eve of the new millennium, we received huge numbers of visitors who came to be in the last country in the world to see the millennium disappearing, to witness the last sunset and the first sunrise. With the change, Samoa shifts to being the first country in the world where the sun rises and the first country to receive the news in the 24-hour day. This is something that is an excellent gimmick to promote the two Samoas. I say, 'We are the only people where the sun rises in the west (Western Samoa) and sets in the east (Eastern Samoa).' This is the irony. Eastern Samoa is east when you consider us as one people. But when you consider the whole world, Western Samoa becomes east! And Eastern Samoa becomes west! American Samoa is the last country in the world to see the setting sun, which is a blow to their ego as they love to be first in anything we both do.

Daylight saving was another item on Tuila'epa's reform agenda.

I raised this issue about the year 2000 but the Attorney-General discouraged me from taking it any further. Somehow in my mind it was something that we had do. Then early in 2005 I attended a meeting of the CHOGM. I got up early to go for a walk. It was 8 o'clock and the sun was high and very hot. I found absolutely no people or cars on the road. When I asked about this, I was told they were still sleeping. They don't start work until 9 o'clock. This gave me the idea of how to artificially stretch the hours of the day so that people can use their time more productively.

When I came back to Samoa I felt strongly that I should always look for areas to save money. So I put a paper through to Cabinet to change the working hours and it was approved. From then onwards we would begin our government and school working hours at 9 o'clock. It received a lot of support, particularly from parents and schools. That went on for about two years and then we decided to introduce daylight saving. It now made more sense because we had shifted the working hours and the advance of one hour would not impact so much on school children because we had already prepared ourselves by changing the time of business hours.

There are still questions asked about the benefits of daylight saving. I explain that for six months from October every year when we shift our watches forward by one hour, until April when we shift them back, you can save 184 hours of electricity if you consistently sleep and turn off your lights at 11 p.m. every night. Farmers gain 23 days at eight hours of work a day on the plantation. But for a loafer, the daylight saving policy is absolutely useless. Daylight saving is now the law but we had to do it in phases: first, change the working hours for government ministries and schools, and, second, introduce daylight saving.

Fine Mats, Canned Fish and Island Shirts
Tuila'epa had introduced daylight saving, changed Samoa's time zone and the side of the road cars drove on. In each of these reforms he had faced opposition but, in the end, he won the dissenters over. He also turned his mind to aspects of Samoa's cultural traditions that had bothered him and led another crusade for change. Again Tuila'epa was criticised.

Since 1996, Samoan Women in Business (Women in Business Development Incorporated, WIBDI) were trying to revive fine mat making (*'ie Samoa 'ie toga*). To revive this art they also needed the cooperation of the Ministry of Women, Community and Social Development and the Ministry of Agriculture and Fisheries. So they asked these two ministries for help. They did not get much help. In fact they were 'told off' for engaging in these things, which the ministries saw as their responsibility. The women tried many times and got frustrated. Finally, WIBDI wrote to me for assistance.

I read their letter and I was fascinated. Essentially, the women asked for government's support for their efforts to revive the art of fine mat-making as it used to be traditionally. They argued that this would strengthen the community of women's weavers at the village level and encourage the cultivation of pandanus to provide a better supply of weaving materials.[7]

I had just returned from the funeral of the Governor of American Samoa. The funeral service was delayed by three hours by a massive presentation of fine mats. There were six bus-loads of fine mats presented by the family of the First Lady – six thousand fine mats, I heard. To present these fine mats, a long line of young men was formed across the field and they passed each bundle from one person to the next, and the next. It took ages. There was not any 'fineness' in the mats that were produced for that occasion. We called them *fa'alavelave* mats, *lalaga*. They were ugly, they cost US$10 or $20 each but they were rubbish. They just bundled them up into rolls of ten for presentation. Quantity was more important than quality.

The awareness of what happened in Pago, and the letter from WIBDI, provided the motivation to do something about this deplorable degradation of our cultural practices. The office and status of the Prime Minister is such that any project would receive a major boost if I got involved. I took the matter to Cabinet and secured the approval for a Fine Mats Committee that I would chair. The Minister of Agriculture, the Minister of Women and their chief executives would also be in attendance along with WIBDI.

Public criticisms were immediate. 'Now Tuila'epa is even interfering in our cultural practices and traditions, the *Fa'asamoa*.'

But I went on the radio and had articles in the papers explaining what we were trying to achieve.

In March 2003 the *Samoa Observer* reported: 'The Prime Minister, Tuila'epa Sailele Malielegaoi, yesterday called for a return to the authentic traditional Samoan fine mat, *'ie Samoa*, to be used in cultural ceremonies. "I urge the mothers of Samoa today to return to weaving the traditional *'ie o le Malo* (Mat of State). I also call on the traditional authorities to outlaw the use of the *lalaga*, which has blemished the honour of Samoa." In reference to the American Samoan influence, he remarked, "hundreds to thousands of *lalaga* costing lots of money . . . have led to unnecessary financial burdens on families. This practice of flaunting wealth is not truly Samoan." Tuila'epa pointed out that in the past one or two *'ie Samoa* or *'ie o le Malo* of high quality were exchanged. "The exchange was thus dignified and very honourable in a cultural sense. I ask you to return to that practice."'

No cultural presentation in Samoa is complete without the exchange of fine mats. The extended families involved are categorised into male and female, and culture has prescribed that women should make their presentation in the form of fine mats, reflecting the duty to weave, whereas

---

7   And also popularise the use of the names, *'ie Malo* and *'ie Samoa*, at customary events.

the men's contribution is in the form of cash. Convenience, the cash economy and limited time available these days result in more and more families opting to present cash instead of following the traditional means of exchange.

Traditional weavers will tell you that the *'ie Samoa* is intimately integrated into the *Fa'asamoa*. In the old days, when a girl was born, her mother started weaving her a mat for her dowry presentation to her bridegroom's family on the day of her wedding. That mat would take years to complete and become her personal treasure and a family heirloom. The wife of a paramount chief would keep her treasured mat for many years, and in the event of her husband's passing, it would be presented to his family as their parting gift, *'ie o le mavaega*.

The project has received great support. We set up an inspection committee and got support from the villages by forming weaving committees. To give a major boost to their morale, we decided to have demonstrations and exhibitions of the women's artwork every year. We also secured an amount of 200,000 Tala to give out as special prizes to the women. That has been ongoing ever since and that is the reason that we now have beautiful fine mats at our *fa'alavelave*.

Maintaining the high quality of weaving requires regular inspection by members of the committee. Annual parades in the city of Apia to demonstrate the art of fine mat weaving are occasions for celebrations. Prizes are awarded to those weavers' committees that have woven the finest mats. Since fine mats presented at all our cultural ceremonies remain the most important item of exchange in our traditions, government's participation and leadership will continue and the necessary Budget allocation for the programme is expected to grow.

With government support, WIBDI continues to work out in the villages with women to provide them with opportunities to earn an income through weaving fine mats, harvesting virgin coconut oil and other sustainable development programmes. Adi Tafuna'i says that, 'Sustainable development cannot happen without due consideration to culture, tradition and context, and so our programmes very much reflect the cultural context in which they were developed.'

The fine mat project got me thinking about the high cost of other parts of our cultural customs. The custom of making presentations of pigs and cattle had become a headache for the Ministry of Agriculture and Fisheries, undermining their promotion of piggeries and cattle farming for import substitution. Cartons of canned fish became a popular substitute but they came in cartons of 48 cans and they were expensive. I thought that there must be a way of cutting this cost so that the price of 100 Tala a carton could be reduced to 40 or 50. If you make a presentation of ten cartons, the cost would be lowered from a thousand to 450 Tala. So I had a chat with the head of the Customs Department.

'How can we do this?'

'Simple. By issuing a Customs Directive that we will no longer accept for sale cartons of 48, and we only accept cartons of 24.'

The next move was to talk with the major importers and I asked them to cooperate in making the cost of living cheaper for our people. I told them that I wanted to cut the cartons from 48 to 24 cans. In a few weeks all the 48-can cartons disappeared.

As usual, members of the opposition were full of criticism in the House. They asked, 'Why do you want to control what our people give for their presentations when they aim for the sky?'

I replied, 'It is always a personal choice. You can always pack up a hundred cartons, bind them together and use a forklift to make your presentation!'

Within a few months, the popularity of the smaller cartons was assured. No one wanted to pay more money than was necessary.

One day I attended the funeral service of one of the most senior MPs. It was very hot and the service took about three hours. There were fourteen eulogies. When it came to the concluding eulogy, delivered by the presiding reverend, I remember him saying, 'This fellow worked very hard. If I had the *mana* I would have asked God to save this fellow and that he let me die in his place because he is more useful than me.'

Of course it was given as a joke, a throwaway line. He did not realise it was prophetic.

When it came to the burial I had to present a flag to the family, an appropriate honour for a long-serving MP. A final feast followed. We sat at the head table. I asked the reverend to please conduct the thanksgiving prayer, as I was hungry.

He said, 'I have to slip away. I am wet right through because of this heavy formal suit jacket I am wearing and I want to change. I am feeling feverish.'

He asked another minister of religion to say the grace as he stood up to leave.

As usual, we all closed our eyes in prayer. One minute later I opened my eyes and saw people rushing over to one corner, about 15 yards from me.

'What's the commotion about?' I asked.

'It is the minister who was sitting beside you. The poor fellow has collapsed and died from heat exhaustion.'

At the following meeting of Cabinet I directed one of my Ministers, Joe Keil, Minister of Tourism, to work on creating a national dress, a national clothing style that is light, fits our tropical climate and can be used by men on formal occasions. This would be an alternative to the heavy formal suit and tie that we adopted after the missionaries from London introduced their cold-climate dress code to Samoa in the nineteenth century.

Six months later Joe Keil submitted fourteen different samples of very colourful styles and materials to Cabinet. We rejected them all.

Then, on my way home that day, Sgt. Lapi casually asked, 'What happened to the proposed national wear?'

I said, 'We rejected the lot.'

Lapi said, 'Why don't we use the *'elei* material which is our own creation?'

I said, 'What a great idea. We are going to take it on.'

When I arrived home I said to Gillian, 'Please can you get me a shirt of *'elei* material.'

At the following meeting of Cabinet I turned up with my *'elei* shirt with the national flower, *Teuila*,[8] and the word 'Samoa' embroidered on it. And Cabinet formalised it as our national dress code. So now we have a national style. At all formal occasions you either wear the *'elei* shirt and *'ie lāvalava*, or the entire European suit and tie.

Of course, the opposition complained that we were treating our parliamentarians like school kids and making them wear uniforms. But they all soon turned up to government occasions wearing *'elei* shirts and *'ie lāvalava*.

The End of an Era

In 2007, we had another big matter to resolve. The Head of State, Malietoa Tanumafili II, died. Malietoa had been Head of State since independence in 1962. The question of succession became an immediate challenge.

An envoy from the Malietoa family sought clarification on the government process for his funeral. I advised that all the cultural traditions proper for the Malietoa title must be performed at his residence. That's the extent of their responsibilities. The government would organise a State Funeral.

---

8   The national flower of Samoa, *Teuila* (*Alpinia sp.*), was named by Fanny Osbourne, the wife of Robert Louis Stevenson. She decorated their house at Vailima with bouquets of red ginger flowers because they shone in the morning sun (*teu*, bouquet, *iila*, to shine). Tuila'epa attended the Fiji Hibiscus Festival in 1991, which gave him the idea of establishing a similar event in Samoa. The Teuila Tourism Festival is held in the first week of August, when many overseas Samoans come to Samoa for a holiday at the cooler time of the year. It includes cultural events and entertainment and goes hand-in-hand with the village beautification programme throughout Samoa.

We conducted the State Funeral service at Mulinu'u and it ran very smoothly.

Article 17 of the Constitution provided for the position of Head of State to be held jointly for life by two *tama-a-'āiga*. Malietoa Tanumafili II and Tupua Tamasese Mea'ole took up the roles. Tupua Tamasese Mea'ole died in April 1963. For 45 years Malietoa had reigned continuously as Head of State of Samoa. Under the requirements of the Constitution (Article 18), successors would be elected by Parliament for terms of five years. Members of Parliament could nominate candidates for the Head of State, which must be seconded by another MP. The nominee must have the same qualifications for eligibility to run for Parliament. These provisions written in 1962, before the birth of the party system, were outmoded. If the Constitution's provisions were to be literally adhered to, we could end up with 49 nominees, which would be most untidy and undignified.

When our party caucus met, prior to Parliament convening for the election of the Head of State, I recommended that we should take a secret ballot on how many candidates we should put up as a party before we proceeded to vote on particular candidates. This process was accepted.

We decided to put up only one candidate and started the process of voting. The three candidates who emerged on the first vote were Tupua, Fiamē and Tuimaleali'ifano. So we voted gain. Fiamē dropped out. We voted again and Tuimaleali'ifano dropped out. Thus, by a process of elimination, Tupua Tamasese Efi had won.

The following day I took the HRPP nomination to Parliament. I was informed that three opposition Members had each put in a single nomination, all for the same candidate. So when we met in Parliament, Tupua was elected by consensus.

I delivered a speech of congratulations when Parliament met.

I said, 'It was envisaged by our forebears that we should take a secret vote to elect the Head of State. And we did take a secret vote in our own party and out of that three names emerged. We voted again until we were left with one, and that was Tupua. We note that the opposition Members put in three nominations but for the same candidate. The fact that Tupua was the single nominee we believe was a divine decision, and on behalf of this Parliament I congratulate the Head of State on his election.'

Tupua was very, very happy. In his speech on the day that he took his Oath of Office he said, 'I will take on this appointment with much trepidation. There is a saying in Samoa: *"O le avega ma le fafa"*, meaning that I will carry the heavy burden of this office upon my shoulders, but over and above this load there are additional weights to make it heavier. Because, when you look around, there stand many, many projects that I had objected to when I was leader of the opposition. I must thank the HRPP leadership for basing their decision not on political considerations but on what they felt was the right thing to do.'[9]

That was the beginning of a new era. When Tupua Tamasese, the Tui Ātua, became the Head of State, it ended the long political contest between us.

Changing the Rules
Stability of government remained a major political challenge for the party in power and we made important changes to ensure stability. We could never forget the incident of party-hopping in June 1985 when the HRPP government, which enjoyed a two-thirds majority after the general election in March, became a minority government only three months later. In June, Vaʻai Kolone and fourteen other members of our party left and joined up with Tupua Tamasese Efi and eleven members of his party to form a coalition. As a consequence of party-hopping, we were forced to surrender government and became the opposition.

Clearly the solution to stop party-hopping lay in amending our laws. The law allowed an elected MP to stay in their party for the whole term of Parliament. It was my view that, should an elected MP change their party, their seat should be declared vacant and they must seek a fresh mandate from their constituency in a by-election. For independent Members, they should either stay an independent throughout their term or join a political party of choice before taking the Oath of Office. That is fair for both the politician and the voters.

It soon became evident that it was not enough just to amend the electoral laws. The Constitution, which protects the right of freedom of choice of MPs, would also need to be amended. This requires a two-thirds majority support in Parliament.

Independent advice by a constitutional lawyer suggested that the electoral law, as amended, would be sufficient if the presiding judge in a court case accepts the argument for stability. If he does not, the safest course would be to amend the Constitution.

The Head of State, Tupua Tamasese Efi, was concerned that the HRPP government was being overly tough on the opposition. He said, 'Every time I listen in to your parliamentary debates, and an opposition MP expresses a point of view, you get up and hit him square on the head. It is my wish, Tui, that you do not proceed with the amendment.'

9 See Samoa Parliamentary Hansard, 16 June 2007.

I reminded the Head of State of the coalition spectacle of 1985, when party-hopping destroyed our government, and that he was the main player.

The point I stressed is that the proposed Constitutional Amendment is aimed at protecting the stability of government now and in to the future. Of all the laws we have passed since independence, this amendment is the most powerful and will guarantee the stability of a government at any time. Whilst our neighbours in the region will continue to have unstable governments, Samoa will be sufficiently cushioned against such instabilities in the future.

The Constitutional Amendment was passed.

Balancing the Books
During this five-year parliamentary term, the 2007–8 Global Financial Crisis struck. The subsequent recession badly affected the global economy, heavily impacting on Samoa's foreign exchange income. The careful management of the government's financial resources kept Samoa's finances relatively stable. The economy performed well with good overall growth. The GDP reached 1.5 billion Tala at the end of the period, up from 1.1 billion Tala at the start of the five-year period. The GDP per capita had risen to 8,000 Tala. Samoa was ready to graduate from the United Nations Least Developed Country (LDC) status at the end of 2010, but this was postponed to 2014 because of the costs related to the devastation suffered by the disastrous tsunami in September 2009.

At the 2011 general election Tuila'epa campaigned on the government's major achievements in recent years: the election of the Head of State; the development of infrastructure; economic growth, and the development of businesses and the private sector; a well-managed Budget; the hosting of the 2007 Pacific Games; switching to right-hand driving; and the government's response to the 2009 tsunami. Tuila'epa promised to focus on health, education, agriculture, infrastructural development and the development of renewable energy, and pledged to 'turn Samoa into the sports hub of the Pacific'.[10]

The newly formed Tautua Samoa Party (TSP) campaigned on lowering the cost of living, raising salaries, abolishing the VAGST, raising pensions for the elderly, improving health services and developing agriculture. When asked how this would be funded, deputy leader Palusalue Fa'apo II stated that 'God will provide for us', and that the party would seek additional international aid. He added that the HRPP government had 'wasted millions on unnecessary developments such as the new buildings towering over everything in Apia', and that under a TSP government all public spending would be transparent and accountable.

10   See HRPP, 2016a, for the text of the 2011 HRPP Election Manifesto.

March 2011 to March 2016

This was Tuila'epa Sa'ilele Malielegaoi's fourth administration. On election night the HRPP had won 29 seats, the TSP thirteen and independents seven. Subsequently, the independents joined the government, giving the HRPP 36 seats.

During his previous term, Tuila'epa had set in place many of his planned reforms and Samoa's economic recovery had progressed well. At the start of his fourth administration, Tuila'epa continued his reform agenda and strengthened his focus on foreign affairs, particularly on the situation in Fiji, which was having a negative impact on the Pacific region and the way Pacific leaders had traditionally worked together.

Foreign Affairs

While the very public exchanges between Tuila'epa and Commodore Josaia Voreqe 'Frank' Bainimarama have dominated the headlines, Tuila'epa has always taken a considered, pragmatic approach to foreign affairs, preferring to use the 'Pacific Way' to deal with conflict and negotiate positive outcomes. His early experiences working at the ACP in Brussels, and later as Minister of Finance negotiating with the World Bank, the IMF and the ADB, provided Tuila'epa with a wide range of international and regional contacts and a full suite of diplomatic skills when he took up the role of Prime Minister. A decade and a half later he is now the senior Pacific Islands Prime Minister and a veteran statesman.

Tuila'epa reflects on his approach to foreign affairs.

In the context of Samoa, our foreign affairs policies focus on ensuring that we give priority to our national interests. Our approach and decision-making at the United Nations is based on that principle and also includes the interests of our development partners: Australia, New Zealand, Japan, China, the United States and the European Union. Where an apparent clash of policies emerges between Samoa and our partners, this is where we have to exercise great caution and look for compromises so that we don't keep one and alienate the other. We try very hard to maintain an independent foreign policy.

When we became independent in 1962 there was only one regional organisation in the Pacific, the South Pacific Commission, which was dominated by the colonial powers of Australia, New Zealand, France, Great Britain and the United States, who had colonies and interests in the Pacific.

The relationship came into focus when we became independent.

We then sat alone, an independent country alongside the colonial powers. That was new for them and strained our relationships. With much of our international policies we deferred to New Zealand and they took care of our policies overseas, following on from the Treaty of Friendship. Under this treaty, New Zealand would represent us in all major overseas organisations, and where we did not have an office, New Zealand High Commissions represented us and would give to Samoans the same treatment as they would New Zealanders.

The same happened when we arrived at international ports. The New Zealand High Commission staff would turn up to meet us. This was gradually phased out as we began to establish our own foreign missions. Today, Samoa has overseas diplomatic missions in Wellington; Brussels, with accreditation to the United Kingdom, selected European countries and the European Commission; New York, with accreditation to the United States, Canada and the United Nations; Canberra, with accreditation to Thailand, Malaysia and Singapore; Beijing; and Tokyo; and Consulates General in Auckland, Pago Pago and Sydney. The Consul-Generals provide consular services, particular passport renewal to our own people who may need urgent assistance, and help with residential problems due to a lack of understanding of immigration laws. Honorary Consuls are located in strategic locations around the world including Argentina, Austria, Australia, Denmark, Germany, Hong Kong, Singapore and Cyprus.

The countries that donate generously to our development only require from us, by way of reciprocity, some consideration when one of their nationals applies for a big job at the United Nations or a policy matter arises there, for example, when Helen Clark sought the Secretary-General's job, or where the country requires the support of votes on resolutions at the Security Council or the International Whaling Commission.

In the Security Council there are the five permanent seats held by United States, China, France, the United Kingdom and Russia. They are the 'big boys' with the power to veto. They are also responsible for the mess in many parts of the world because of their rivalries and one of them vetoing a decision that they should have done collectively. There have been some times they acted collectively, but very few. The very fact that the United Nations Security Council still works and protects us from going to war proves that the United Nations has its uses in ensuring peace and facilitating the continuous development of countries in a condition of peace.

Let's return to the Pacific region. In 1970 Fiji became independent, then

Tonga. Along with Samoa, they formed the big three who decided to establish the Pacific Islands Forum. Initially it was to be the big three with no other countries; Australia and New Zealand were to be excluded. Of course, in the end, reality set in. It was OK for the three to work together on good ideas, but to implement ideas takes money, and we didn't have the money. The countries that have the money are Australia and New Zealand. They had to be brought in, so the five kicked off the PIF.[11]

The forum was established because of a big problem with the South Pacific Commission. Every time the commission met, the independent countries found that it was ineffective. The three independent countries can say 'yes' to implementing a decision, but the other small territories of the big boys cannot say 'yes'; instead, they have to refer back to the capitals and their colonial masters. This drove the South Pacific Commission into a becoming a useless organisation. The big three wanted an organisation that could deal with major issues but instead the commission focussed on smaller technical matters and stayed away from anything 'political', like regional development matters. This is where the limitations of the organisation became obvious.

The decision was made to establish the forum, and more and more countries decided to come in as they became independent. Papua New Guinea (PNG), Vanuatu, the Solomon Islands, Tuvalu, Kiribati . . . Then there was a need to have small organisations dealing with specific areas of development. We now have the CROP agencies (Council for Regional Organisations in the Pacific), which include the Pacific Islands Forum Secretariat, the Secretariat of the Pacific Community (SPC, formerly the South Pacific Commission), the Pacific Islands Forum Fisheries Agency, the Secretariat of the Pacific Regional Environment Programme (SPREP), the South Pacific Tourism Organisation, the University of the South Pacific, the Pacific Islands Development Programme, and the Pacific Power Association (PPA). Before their integration into the SPC in 2010 and 2011, the South Pacific Applied Geoscience Commission and the South Pacific Board for Educational Assessment had been individual members. The Fiji School of Medicine was a member before its merger with Fiji National University in 2010.

Money was still the problem as more and more countries became independent. Then there was a great desire to develop and develop fast. The problem is that the reality of the small island nations is that they are not only short of resources, but they are also short of everything, including capacity. There are not enough people to do the work and this problem has continued

---

11 Nauru and the Cook Islands were also invited to attend the first forum meeting, taking the total to seven founding Pacific Island nations.

on right up to today. These problems perpetually confront the forum and other CROP agencies. Fortunately, other donor countries and international organisations, like the European Union, have become interested and assist the Pacific Island nations.

About twenty years ago a new development started with bilateral meetings between Pacific leaders and major donors with interests in the Pacific. The Japanese wanted to have a meeting between the Japanese leader and leaders of the Pacific Islands Forum to discuss Japanese–Pacific relationships, map out their regional aid programme for the North and South Pacific, and strengthen relationships between Japan and Pacific Island nations. The first PALM (Pacific Island Leaders' Meeting) was held in 1997. We are now onto PALM 8 and I am the only Pacific leader to have attended all these meetings. One result is the Okinawa Partnership, established in 2006, in which Japan has agreed to increase its commitment to the development of Pacific Forum nations.

Then we had the Chinese coming in, pouring in funds. We had the first meeting of Chinese leaders with the PIF in 2006. Then of course the French came in too, to meet the forum leaders. We had two meetings with President Mitterrand, first in Tahiti then in Paris the following year. Last year we had a meeting in Tahiti, to map out our stance on climate change, and we met with President Hollande in Paris prior to the 2015 United Nations Climate Change Conference in France. The French have come to realise the importance of having bilateral meetings with all the leaders of the Pacific. The United States has recalibrated its diplomatic approach to the Pacific. We have had meetings with the Secretary of State several times, and meetings with the President on the margins of the United Nations General Assembly.

The whole world's interest in the Pacific is increasing. In November 2014 we met in Fiji with the President of China, and later on with Prime Minister Modi of India. Both were in Australia for the meeting of APEC, Asia–Pacific Economic Cooperation, then they flew to Fiji to meet with all the PIF leaders. It was in Fiji that the Chinese revealed to us US$2 billion of soft loans for the eight countries that have a special relationship with China, and 2 billion more in grants for the same eight countries.

There is great interest zeroing in on the Pacific. Of course, this has been causing some worry in New Zealand, Australia and also the United States because of the great interest the Chinese are showing in our region. I have been often questioned about this in my meetings with the leaders of New Zealand and Australia, especially when Samoa was seen to have received considerable assistance from China.

I was asked, 'What will the Chinese get from you in return?'

This is a normal question to be expected.

I said, 'Well, it is the same, exactly the same request that you make of us, nothing different: our vote in the United Nations and our support for policies that benefit the national interests of New Zealand and Australia in the United Nations. In this case it is also in relation to job opportunities that the Chinese and Japanese are vying for at a very high level at the United Nations agencies.'

On one occasion in 1999 I was visiting Japan to talk to the Japanese about our Matautu Wharf Project. We planned an extension of the wharf. Before I went, the job of head of the United Nations Educational, Scientific and Cultural Organization (UNESCO) was up for grabs and Gareth Evans, the former Australian Minister of Foreign Affairs, was a candidate for that post. We were on the board of UNESCO. The vote of the Asia-Pacific group was held by Samoa. This is very important because whoever Samoa recommended would certainly get the post.

Before I went to Japan I was aware that the Japanese had put their candidate up to head UNESCO way ahead of everybody. There was only one candidate for a long time and then right before the end, suddenly out of the blue, Australia put up its candidate, Gareth Evans. I felt it was very bad judgement on the part of Australia. They should have conceded that prospect in advance. When Australia's candidacy came in, our Foreign Affairs people informed Canberra that they had come too late and we were already committed to support the Japanese candidate. Therefore, first come first served; that is our policy. If the one we give our vote to on the first ballot misses, then we are free to switch.

We informed the Australians about our decision well before I went to Japan to meet the Japanese Prime Minister, Keizō Obuchi. I think we had only five minutes allocated for our meeting time. Of the five minutes, four minutes were spent on my counterpart's request for his candidate.

He said, 'I know that Samoa has very close relations with Australia and probably we have lost your vote, but please consider us.'

I said, 'No, you have not lost. Australia's candidacy was too late. Therefore we have already informed Australia that our vote goes to your candidate.'

In the last minute we discussed the Matautu Wharf Project. That was the reason for my trip.

He asked me, 'How much?'

'About US$60 million.'

'Done. Deal done. We will give you a grant.'

And that was it. The national interests of Japan were important to them in the same way that the national interests of Samoa and the construction of our port facilities were important to us.

There was potential for a major rift between Samoa, Japan and China in late 2006 when debate about reforms of the permanent seats on the United Nations Security Council came up. That was when the Prime Minister of Japan, Junichiro Koizumi, had visited the Yasukuni Shrine, a memorial to the Japanese war dead. This angered the Chinese. With the debate looming at the United Nations, and with Germany and Japan strongly campaigning for the two permanent seats, the issue of who would hold the permanent seats came to a head and led to a rift between China and Japan. We were caught in the middle.

The difficulty for Samoa was that I had already spoken at the United Nations, several times encouraging reform of the Security Council, and I strongly mooted the membership of Germany and Japan for the simple reason that these two countries were contributing the most money to the United Nations. When our two friends began to fight against each other, Samoa was one of the countries that was drawn in because we were not an insignificant friend of Japan and China. We were subjected to a number of pressures coming from all angles and this was serious because the Chinese were actually progressing in the building of an Olympic swimming pool at that time, a project we needed to continue for our own South Pacific Games.

Faced with this dilemma, I had to try and find some compromise. I was under great pressure. In the end I had to remind both Japan and China, firstly, that they had to respect the integrity and sovereignty of Samoa; and, secondly, that our word is our honour and we cannot appear to say one thing and not follow it up. I said that we were already on record at the United Nations supporting permanent membership for the Japanese, and also for Germany, and that we could not renege on that policy. I also said that I hoped China would remember that Samoa had supported it and the 'One China' policy since 1975. In the end the two recognised that we could not be shifted. We kept talking and we held fast to our principles. We did not appear to be compromising on these issues. Eventually the solution came as we expected. The United Nations decided to agree to disagree and therefore postpone the issue permanently. We were saved by that decision and the friendships between our countries has continued.

This example is typical of the way that we have conducted our foreign affairs.

Fiji

Since the Fijian military coup in December 2006, led by Commodore Bainimarama, there had been political tensions in the region. These tensions eventually led to Fiji losing its membership of the PIF and the Commonwealth as a consequence of its failure to comply with the membership criteria of these organisations (that is, free democratic elections, maintenance of the rule of law, etc.). Tuila'epa was one of the few Pacific Island leaders who spoke out publicly about Bainimarama's actions. Their exchanges were picked up and reported with great glee by the Pacific media.

Scoop reported in April 2010:

'Samoa's Prime Minister Tuila'epa Sa'ilele Malielegaoi believes it is best that Fiji dictator Commodore Frank Bainimarama keeps quiet and learn from the valuable lessons he is imparting "free of charge".

'The Commodore this week lashed out at his "Samoan counterpart" as "desperate" to have the Pacific Islands Forum Secretariat relocated from Suva to Apia.

'"My counterpart?" said a bemused Prime Minister Tuila'epa. "You know, calling the Commodore a Prime Minister is like calling a skinny dog a vicious lion, a scrawny chicken a soaring eagle."

'Of the Forum Secretariat, the Prime Minister said, "Best he (Bainimarama) sticks to planting cassava and leave Forum issues to bonafide elected leaders."

'"He has neither say nor business with either the Forum nor its Secretariat."

'Fiji, three years after Commodore Frank Bainimarama usurped its elected government, was suspended by the Pacific Islands Forum in February last year.

'And what becomes of the Forum Secretariat will be the result of a collective decision by the Pacific Islands Forum leaders, Prime Minister Tuila'epa said.

'"Whether it gets relocated to Samoa, Papua New Guinea, Tonga, Vanuatu or even Bikini Atoll is neither Bani's nor those working at the Secretariat's decision to make.

'"And if it (the Forum Secretariat) does relocate, well Bani only has himself to blame for it. He is the root cause of all these problems."

'Tuila'epa maintains that the Secretariat cannot operate "under the thumb" of an unelected military regime. "Especially a regime that has done away with the rule of law, democratic government, an independent Judiciary and suppression of the media and freedom of speech. It's against the exact fundamental principles the Forum was founded on."

'How the Commodore connected any possible relocation of the Forum Secretariat headquarters with Samoa bewilders the Prime Minister.

'"It appears that he is scared that it'll be relocated to Samoa? Well, thank you very much Mr Bainimarama for your vote of confidence in us. But, frankly, we don't need your endorsement."'

Five years later, the public spat between Bainimarama and Tuila'epa was still going strong. Radio New Zealand International reported in April 2015:

'Tuila'epa said Mr Bainimarama was new to governance and with his military background, he could only "play the drums and train".

'The Fijian Prime Minister has responded, telling the website *Fiji Village* Tuila'epa was a lapdog and his yapping is nothing new.

'"You know he's the only prime minister that attacks everyone, left, right and centre. He attacks his dog, he attacks his rugby team, he attacks everything he can get his hands on. But we've heard this yapping from the Samoan lapdog before, for a long time, day in day out and it really means nothing. He's talking about me playing drums. At least I can play an instrument. All he can do is bark and dance to tunes until they feed him again."

'Tuila'epa says he was not insulted by the words but he would not say the same to another respected government leader.

'"I consider Baini as fresh, young, because the words he mentioned of another leader are not the words of a mature leader. They are the words of a young and rough, still to develop into maturity, so I give him that benefit, and I forgive him."'

Underneath the public conversations, Tuila'epa had long been concerned about the instability in the region following the series of coups and the failure of democracy in Fiji. He reflects on Fiji and the demise of the 'Pacific Way' of solving regional problems.

In the situation with Bainimarama we took the decision of the forum. The forum is an organisation of independent countries: other countries can become members but only as observers. Only independent countries are full members and all these countries practice democracy, the ideals of the rule of law and general elections that are conducted fairly. Now we were suddenly confronted with a situation in which Fiji broke all the conditions of membership, so we had to deal with the problem and suspend Fiji.

During that time Bainimarama was always condemning the PIF as a forum that is monopolised and influenced by New Zealand and Australia and he was insisting on that view for quite some time. To me, this was deplorable, because we were not there just as statues, 'lapdogs' in Bainimarama's words. We also have a Pacific Way of doing things. The Pacific Way is that we solve our problems by talking. Bainimarama solved his problems through the gun. If one Pacific leader does a terrible thing, the proper thing, in the Pacific Way, is to shut up and not do anything. We remained quiet, and that's what we did. New Zealand and Australia did all the talking. Bainimarama continued to 'shoot at' the forum as an organisation led by New Zealand and Australia. I think to a certain extent he was led to that belief by our adoption of the Pacific Way.

In order to try and find a solution, we set up a Ministerial Action Group, comprising forum Foreign Ministers, to go and talk some sense to Bainimarama and his cabinet of dictators. At the first meeting there were three on his side: Bainimarama; Ratu Epeli, who was a former general and is now the Minister of Foreign Affairs; and his Attorney-General, the Indian Aiyaz Sayed-Khaiyum. On our side were all of the forum Foreign Ministers.

Bainimarama told us that there was so much corruption he had to stamp out, and 'only after stamping it out, we will go back to the barracks'.

What we were interested in was for Fiji to have democratic elections in 2010. He said that they would be held, which of course later on did not come to fruition.

The Australian Minister of Foreign Affairs said, 'Bainimarama, if you are going to wipe out corruption, and then you go back to the barracks, it means that you will be here for eternity.'

Everybody laughed.

Bainimarama said, 'Oh. The chiefs of Fiji are a pack of crooks, the same thing with the leaders of religion. They are telling people not to vote for me. That's it, all the Ratus are crooks.'

We all looked at Ratu Epeli.

Then Bani looked at us all looking at Ratu Epeli sitting next to him and he realised what he had said.

Then he said, 'Except for Ratu Epeli.'

That was the situation we faced. When I came away from that meeting, I knew that Bani would not take the forum seriously. Of course, the rest is history.

The reason he singled me out was that I could not carry on in silence so I had to break the code of the Pacific Way. I had to speak up and tell Bainimarama that we were not all fools and what he was saying was stupid. That resulted in many, many exchanges between us. Some people suggested that I go and talk to him.

I said, 'Of course I am talking to him. Through the media.'

I can still remember the embarrassment felt by the chairman of the forum, the Prime Minister of Tonga, Feleti Sevele, who had gone with the most senior Prime Minister of the Pacific, Sir Michael Somare of PNG, to talk to Bainimarama in secret, in the hope that they could reach some compromise. The moment they left Fiji, Bainimarama summoned the media and revealed to the world that he had just had a meeting with the two leaders and that they had agreed with him that what he was doing was right and the forum was wrong. He said that the two of them would try to talk sense into the forum.

I realised then that when you are talking to Bainimarama, you are talking to a person who does not value the importance of behind-the-scenes negotiation to reach a compromise. When this news came out, I spoke to Somare. Somare, point blank, said, 'I never said such things.'

Faced with that, I thought the most effective way to communicate, where you don't compromise your views and where you are not reported erroneously, is to talk through the press.

One of the issues I raised in the forum meeting in Tonga, when Bainimarama appeared and assured us that he would go ahead with the general elections in 2010, was whether, if Laisenia Qarase [former Prime Minister and Bainimarama's opposition] won the proposed election, would he [Bainimarama] go back to the barracks? He made that assurance in Tonga. Bainimarama did not turn up the following meeting in Niue, and from that time onwards the decision was made that he was not welcome anymore.

It was at the Tonga meeting that I put forward a paper about the fragmentation of the forum. I questioned the existence of the Melanesian Spearhead Group (MSG) and the Association of Small Island States (AOSIS). I was questioning the wisdom of allowing these different groupings to be created as it was a sure way of weakening the forum. The Kingdom of Tonga, Samoa, the Federated States of Micronesia, New Zealand and Australia were not in any grouping at that time.

In the discussion that followed the views of the MSG were voiced by Sir Michael Somare. He said that ever since the MSG was formed, it had focussed more on Melanesian problems and in that spirit it had been very successful; rather than fragmenting the forum, it had strengthened the organisation.

Then Sir Michael said to me, 'You should form a Polynesian group.'

In our conversation, I said to Sir Michael, 'Well, if we form a Polynesian group then we will have to take Helen Clark, and you can have Mr Howard in the Melanesian Spearhead Group.' And we all laughed amongst ourselves.

But the conversation did set in motion the foundation of the Polynesian

Leaders Group (PLG). I started to talk with the Tongan Prime Minister, Feleti Sevele, and then later talked to Tuvalu, the Tokelauans and others. I got our Attorney-General to prepare a draft constitution and circulate it amongst the Polynesian countries and we had our first meeting in Samoa. Eight of us attended. When we came together, on 17 November 2011, I was elected the first chairman. When the PLG insisted that I stand again, I said we must abide by our constitution that we rotate the chair every year. That is the situation now. The members are Tokelau, American Samoa, Samoa, Nauru, Tonga, Niue, French Polynesia and the Cook Islands. In our constitution we allow for Polynesian minorities in independent states who may like to participate. We have already had meetings with New Zealand Māori, the Hawai'ians, Wallis and Futuna, and Rapa Nui (from Easter Island) and other Polynesian outliers.

We have maintained the position that we should start small on identified issues of cooperation and gradually build up as our confidence deepens. For example, with American Samoa we can cooperate on air services. With the Cook Islands we have several of their businesses set up here in Samoa and ours in the Cook Islands. We started discussing a joint venture in air services between French Polynesia and Samoa with Tahiti Nui. We have already established shipments of agricultural products between Samoa and Tonga, focussing on intra-Pacific trade. Fisheries have been on the agenda of the last three PLG meetings. There have also been times when we have communicated about support on regional matters. We have met every year.

The highest priority of the PLG is to preserve and promote Polynesian cultures. That has been the main objective we addressed at our early meetings.

I did not want the formation of the PLG to cause unnecessary alarm in the wider Pacific region. When I was chairman, I was often asked by the media to comment, and they frequently tried to find some conflict.

One interviewer asked, 'Now you have established the PLG, you are a very powerful group in terms of numbers and your governments are very stable. Would you pose a challenge to the Pacific Islands Forum?'

I replied, 'No. We are a new organisation and we are trying to copy from the masters who started it all, the Melanesian Spearhead Group. We are learning from them!'

I think my comments disappointed some of the media who expected fireworks.

I said, 'No. No. You are all wrong. We are more interested in promoting our Polynesian culture, which is fast dying out. Yet we are supposed to spread far and wide. There are historians who say that there should only be two groups in the Pacific: the Melanesians and the Polynesians because Micronesians and Polynesians have many similar features.'

They laughed.

I like taking the fire out of issues by introducing humour.

'We start small. We do not want to come in with a fanfare and say we are going to do this and that. We start with some small things. Build up as we gain experience. Small is beautiful.'

The Pacific Way
What does it mean when we talk about the Pacific Way of doing things? *Talanoa*, talking together, that is what I mean by the Pacific Way. *Talanoa* has the same spelling, the same pronunciation and the same meaning in Samoan and Fijian.

When Bainimarama was angry and threatening out loud about Tonga violating Fiji's territorial waters when a Tongan naval vessel came and picked up Ratu Mara's son, there was nervousness in the region. There was the possibility of an all-out war of canoes between these two great nations, in this most peaceful part of the vast Pacific Ocean.

So, when an interviewer came up and asked me, 'What do you think of the territorial excursions by the Tongans?', I said, 'I think that there is a big misunderstanding of the issues involving Tonga and Fiji. The Tongans are saying their patrol boat was out patrolling the Tonga Trench when suddenly, out of the blue, General Ratu Mara, who is part Fijian, part Tongan and part Samoan, was sighted struggling in the water, being swept towards the Trench. So they picked him up and took him to Tonga. To me it was a very simple rescue operation. This boat was patrolling the deep Tonga Trench, which extends from Tonga to the southern tip of Upolu in Samoa. The current is so strong that it draws boats, lost swimmers and anything else into the Trench. Tongans are deeply religious so, of course, they helped this man in distress. What Bainimarama should also do is to go for a swim. All he needs to do is to swim out of the lagoon and he will be captured by the same current and be drawn into the Tonga Trench where the Tongans' one patrol boat will be conscientiously patrolling the Trench. Then they'd pick up Bainimarama and take him to Tonga and he could have a good breakfast of fresh paw-paw with General Ratu Mara. Then through *talanoa*, in the Pacific Way, they could settle their differences. The whole thing was only a small storm in a coconut *kava* cup. But it came close to becoming a mother of all cyclones because the media was ignorant of our ancient history.

'A thousand years ago the Fijians, the Samoans and Tongans all used the power of the same current. The Fijian boys would go bird-watching in Tonga. The Tongans came and did the same in Samoa, and the Samoans paddled over in their canoes and looked for birds in Fiji. That was the origin of our *talanoa*, the Pacific Way. But the Samoans found out that the Fijians and Tongans always managed to end up with most of the girls. That is why the Samoans coined the word *togafiti* as our word for trickery.'

I said all this using Pacific humour to deflate the situation.

The New Zealanders and Australians had learnt a lot from this territorial water incident. Their 'strictly business' approach is not the way to handle problems in the Pacific. It is better to *talanoa*, to use the Pacific Way. Meaning, even if it takes two, three or four years of talking, let us talk our problems out, especially where our customs and traditions are impacted.

Pacific Island people understand the metaphorical nature of our words. We have a saying in Samoa: '*Moe le Toa*'. What it means is, 'If we cannot arrive at an agreement today, let the warriors sleep. When they wake up again they'll have fresh ideas that can solve the problem.'

That is why the words *tōfā* and *moe* emerged. *Moe* is a word that is given to an orator's thoughts, his ideas. The simple meaning of *moe* is to sleep. *Tōfā* is related to the deep thoughts expressed by a prominent chief, a *tama aliʻi*. *Tōfā* also means the sleep of the *tama aliʻi*. *Moe* means the sleep of the *tulafale*. So when you refer to the *tulafale* sleeping, you say '*moe*'. And when you talk of the *tama aliʻi* sleeping, you say '*tōfā*'. When you respond to a speech by a *tama aliʻi*, you say 'The thoughts you have expressed are so deep and so convincing to me that we will take your arguments and agree with your proposition: it makes sense.' You say *tōfā*. If a *tulafale* expresses his thoughts, you say *moe, faʻamālō le moe*. 'Why don't we agree to the suggestions and agree to end our discussions on that note?'

When the village *matai* meet on a difficult issue and they do not arrive at a consensus, older *matai* end the meeting with the words '*Moe le Toa*. Let the warriors sleep. We will meet again tomorrow.' This is the same as the European saying 'Let us sleep on it.' It is interesting that Samoans have come to their own understanding of this phenomenon that modern psychologists refer to as the workings of the subconscious mind; it is a process that assists us in working out a solution when we are asleep or not even thinking specifically about the issue.

Partnerships

When Prime Minister John Key came on one of his visits to meet with me, Fiji's preparations for its elections seemed to be going smoothly. After our brief meeting in my office, just before our media conference, Mr Key informed me that he was easing his stance on Fiji and New Zealand would provide Fiji with assistance for their elections.

The first question that was put to me by the media was, 'Tuila'epa, you have been the only one who has consistently been telling Bainimarama that what he is doing is wrong. What do you think now that New Zealand and Australia have suddenly decided to give assistance to Bainimarama without consulting you?'

I had only just learnt that New Zealand and Australia had changed their tune. The question by the media had a nasty implication. I seemed to be the only one of the sixteen forum leaders who took a hard stance. While everybody else seemed quite moderate, I had become the bad guy. And yet I was the only one backing the decision of the forum that, in effect, was upholding the rule of law in Fiji. I was caught. I had to think fast and be diplomatic to preserve good relations.

'So what do you think?' they asked.

I said, 'Samoa has also been offering Fiji help, especially early on in the crisis when we hosted officials from Fiji to look at our computerised voting system which they thought they might want to adopt. They were interested in how it operated. Several visits took place so they could talk to our people who were responsible for inventing our system. I had also sent a delegation to Fiji to help out. I am happy that New Zealand and Australia give assistance. You see, we have to be seen to be helping Bainimarama to realise the objective of Fiji holding general elections. So it is good to give them the benefit of the doubt and continue to provide help and not to be negative all the time. I congratulate New Zealand and Australia for their decisions.'[12]

I had to get myself out of this bind that had suddenly occurred. That was a very tricky situation for me. Not only were our own people watching, but the critics in New Zealand were looking for an opportunity to hit their government. I did not want to be used as a springboard to launch that kind of attack, which is very much below the belt. When it comes to national

---

12 The relationship between Samoa and Fiji continues to evolve. At the 71st General Assembly of the United Nations, in September 2016, Samoa supported Fiji's bid for their Ambassador, Peter Thomson, to become the first Pacific Ambassador to chair a General Assembly. The *Samoa Observer*, of 26 September 2016, carried a front-page photograph of a smiling Tuila'epa congratulating Fijian Prime Minister Bainimarama, who thanked him for his support.

interests, a country often goes ahead and does its own thing and forgets about the other guys. I was getting tired of the way that New Zealand and Australia treated us. We are their 'partners' in the Pacific. Consultation and discussion, before significant policy changes, would strengthen our partnership in the PIF and beyond.

The SIDS conference

The Third International Conference on Small Islands Developing States (SIDS) was a very special occasion for Samoa. It was held from 1–4 September 2014 in Apia, preceded by activities related to the conference from 28–30 August 2014, also in Apia. The conference aimed to focus the world's attention on a group of countries that remain a special case for sustainable development in view of their unique and particular vulnerabilities. The overarching theme of the conference was 'the sustainable development of small island developing States through genuine and durable partnerships.'[13]

The SIDS conference was to become the largest international event hosted by a small island nation. Tuila'epa made sure that Samoa would be the host of this prestigious event, as he recalls.

I was casually asked whether I was interested in hosting the conference by our man in New York, Ambassador Ali'ioaiga Feturi Elisaia. This was three years before the SIDS conference. It has always been my hobby to encourage all our ambassadors, all our diplomats and all of our officials to grab any opportunity that comes up for hosting an international event in Samoa. There are two reasons: firstly, because we are promoting tourism and I am interested in creating business for Samoa, and, secondly, the prestige of leadership. Our forebears provided the leadership that led to Samoa becoming the first independent Pacific Island country. We should never lose sight of that image of Samoa, and the leadership role that puts us where we are today.

I have always encouraged our public servants to be vigilant. Let us worry about the costs and the logistics later. So when our Ambassador in New York raised the issue of Samoa hosting the SIDS conference with me, I asked, 'How many will be coming?' I was thinking immediately of the visitor room capacity.

He said to me, 'Eight to twelve hundred.'

I said, 'Proceed. We must take it on.'

'OK. I can put it across to the United Nations agencies that they send only

---

13 See SIDS, 2014, for documentation on the SIDS conference.

the most important people. I would also urge that most of the negotiations be completed in New York so when they come to Samoa they only have the resolutions to complete.'

I said, 'Proceed now.'

Several weeks later the phone rang on a Saturday as I was driving to Lepā and it was my Ambassador. It was unusual for him to call at 10 on a Saturday morning so I knew it must be important.

He said, 'Tui, I am ringing to notify you that Fiji is launching a very strong campaign. Do you think we should still push ahead?'

As soon as he mentioned Fiji, I became furious.

'Make sure that we get it, not Fiji.'

That was enough encouragement for him.

The next issue was to get the support of the PIF that we should be ahead of Fiji. The occasion was the forum meeting in the Cook Islands. We met on a boat and during the meeting the President of Nauru, who was currently chair of the Association of Small Island States, raised the issue of the SIDS meeting. Apparently the United Nations delegate in Fiji had said that Samoa was unsuitable to host the meeting because of a lack of accommodation. They were therefore recommending that Fiji should host. At that time Fiji was still outside of the forum and was not represented at the meeting.

Immediately I put up my hand and said, 'I have to tell you something by way of background. Back in 1999, I was Minister of Foreign Affairs and co-spokesman for the ACP group renegotiating the ACP–EU Convention. We were discussing the investment agenda in the financial chapter of the convention. We had agreed to all of the items except one. We had campaigned very strongly to have the new Lomé Convention signed in the Pacific and we proposed Fiji. This would be the first ACP–EU Convention with the name of a Pacific Island capital in its title, and we proposed Suva, Fiji. We pushed hard and we finally managed to convince the ACP Council of Ministers at 1 a.m. At 3 a.m. we met with the Council of the European Union at their headquarters in Brussels to agree on the last item of the convention, the venue. As the Pacific spokesman I gave a brief address to both councils at the headquarters of the European Council of Ministers.'

I continued, 'We, the Council of Ministers of the ACP group, have now agreed that the signing ceremony will be in Suva, Fiji, and it will be known as the Suva Convention. We ask for your support.

'They all applauded. They all wanted to come to the Pacific for the signing ceremony. This was at the end of 1999 and we would sign in September 2000.

Everybody was looking forward to the great day when the Pacific would finally feature as the venue for the ACP–EU Convention.

'In May 2000 Speight launched his coup in Fiji and that put an end to the Pacific signing, so the present convention has a different name.'[14]

This was the background. I told the forum leaders, 'You will also recall that the timing of the SIDS meeting in 2014 coincides with the proposed general election in Fiji. To me it could be used as an excuse not to hold the elections and I for one would recommend that we do not give Bainimarama another excuse to defer the timing of the elections. Furthermore, we faced this embarrassment before in 2000, and we do not want to host a big meeting of the United Nations where members of 197 nations will attend and we end up with a similar experience to that of 2000.'

Samoa got the support of the forum, which would now go forwards to the AOSIS meeting. Nauru was the president at the time. It was a great moment for me when AOSIS agreed to have the meeting in Samoa.

In Rio in 2012, at the United Nations Conference on Sustainable Development, we hoped to finalise the SIDS conference venue. All the countries had agreed that the meeting should be in the Pacific and that Fiji and Samoa should talk. While we were considering possible options for our consultations, I learned that Bainimarama had gone ahead already and invited all the countries to come to Fiji, saying that they would host the meeting. I decided that in my conference speech I would also issue an invitation for everyone to come to Samoa and we would deal with the issue of the venue right there in front of the conference.

I said to the conference, 'I would like to invite you to come to Samoa. As you all know, Samoa has now graduated from Least Developed Country status to a new status of Middle Income Country. This is due to the help we get from our donor countries. So inviting you to come to Samoa, I have a story to tell. It is an opportunity for all the developed countries to come and witness for themselves the results of their investment in small LDCs, in the hope that the example put forward by Samoa will encourage all the developed partners to give generously and developing countries to raise their standard of living and to know that their efforts have been put to good use.'

The next speaker was United States Secretary of State, Hillary Clinton. I had earlier in my speech made reference to Clinton's initiative for women, saying that the head of Women in Business in Samoa, Adi Tafuna'i, was a recipient of Clinton's award. I congratulated Clinton on the benefits that

---

14 The Cotonou Agreement was signed in Benin in June 2000.

her award had given the women of the developing world, including Samoa.

When I stepped down from the podium, Hillary Clinton was waiting to give her speech.

She called out, 'President Sa'ilele, President Sa'ilele. Please.'

I turned around and, in front of everybody, she came and hugged and kissed me and thanked me for mentioning her initiative. There was clapping and clapping. And I thought that was the 'thumbs up' for the decision for the SIDS conference to come to Samoa, and it was given right there in front of the World Assembly.

My next visit was to the head of UNDP, who was none other than the former Prime Minister of New Zealand, Helen Clark.

When we met she said, 'Congratulations, Tui. In the interests of Samoa we will help you. It will be a great meeting.'

I said, 'Helen, tell me.' I was so worried about the accommodation. 'Tell me, in your honest opinion, how many delegates will be coming? One thousand?'

'You've got to be kidding. Everybody wants to come. It will be not less than three thousand.'

'What?'

'Not less than three thousand.'

Then, for the first time, I became worried. We already had made the commitment in front of the World Assembly.

We had gone too far, we had reached the point of no return. What should we do? We had appeared firm and eager in public, but behind the scenes I was hoping that the other guys would beat us so that we could bow out gracefully with honour, without anybody knowing our major weakness that we couldn't host a meeting for that many people. We went on preaching the benefits of the meeting in Samoa while quietly praying for a miracle.

Then out of the blue, Victoria University of Wellington decided to confer on me a Doctorate of Laws *honoris causa*, and Luamanuvao invited me to come to Wellington for the ceremony. That gave me the opportunity to meet up with the Minister of Foreign Affairs for New Zealand, Murray McCully.

We had just started our meeting when Minister McCully said, 'We are going to contribute a cruise ship to provide accommodation for those attending the SIDS conference.'

I was so relieved. McCully had saved the day! I had not even asked. But out of the blue McCully made the offer. Suddenly everything seemed to fall into place. My problem was solved. Later on, when New Zealand came calling for support for their bid for a seat on the United Nations Security Council, I understood McCully's generosity. Every member of the United Nations family would be in Samoa and the SIDS conference would also provide the occasion for New Zealand to lobby support for its Security Council bid.

Meantime, we arrived at a compromise with Fiji. The conference would be in Samoa, and Fiji would host the regional meeting of the Pacific region SIDS prior to the conference. At the United Nations General Assembly in New York in September 2013, we celebrated the occasion by drinking *kava* at the Embassy of Fiji with Fijian Minister of Foreign Affairs, Inoke Kubuabola; the President of Nauru, Baron Waqa; the President of Kiribati, Anote Tong; myself; and others. It was significant that we, from the Pacific, could sit around our *kava* bowl and take the *kava* cup for a sip of peace.

The hosting of the SIDS conference was a great success and we had over four thousand registered delegates. There was no problem with the accommodation. Many of the United Nations delegates came to me later saying that the conference had proceeded without a hitch.

Credit must go to the energy of our Ambassador at the United Nations, Ali'ioaiga Feturi Elisaia, for securing the SIDS conference for Samoa, to our Conference Coordinator, Fa'alavaau Perina, who kept the preparations on target, the Ministers chairing each committee and the Secretary-General of the conference. We set up a special unit to plan the SIDS meeting and committees to plan travel, provide transport, prepare venues, cater and train local chefs, and train police, security and all the other necessary preparations.

The United Nations Secretary-General Ban Ki-moon[15] addressed the conference saying, 'We are here to seek a renewed commitment to small island developing states by focussing on practical actions and durable partnerships.' The outcomes of the conference, referred to as the SIDS Accelerated Modalities of Action (SAMOA) Pathway, provided the inputs for the seventeen Sustainable Development Goals approved by the United Nations in New York in September 2015. They will guide developments till 2030. Goal number thirteen is on climate change, the subject of the Paris Agreement, and sets out what member countries must do to save our planet. Samoa has signed both agreements. The added importance of the SIDS conference in Samoa is in the SAMOA Pathway, so that whenever a world leader addresses issues of sustainable development and climate change, the mention of the SAMOA Pathway is surely a cost-free commercial for Samoa's tourism and a recognition of Samoa's leadership.

---

15 During his visit to Samoa, Ban Ki-moon was bestowed with the princely *matai* title Tupua. He is now addressed by Samoans as Afioga Tupua Ban Ki-moon.

Economic Development

The successful hosting of the South Pacific Games in 2007, the SIDS conference in 2014 and the Commonwealth Youth Games in 2015 were a direct consequence of the one major decision made in 1991: to develop the 400 acres at Tuanaimato and build facilities for sports and conventions. It has proven to be an asset for the nation, with significant economic benefits for the future flowing from this decision.

Samoa has a relatively small economy that is vulnerable to external factors. Tuila'epa has maintained a close watch and intervened from time to time to ensure that the economy remains on an even keel. The government of Samoa purchased the Pacific Forum Line (PFL) in 2012. The regional shipping line was in financial difficulties but was seen as critical for Samoa's trade with the outside world, and the loss of the PFL to a private operator could have restricted or endangered Samoa's trade. The decision to buy it was made following a submission by Fonotoe Meredith, Deputy Prime Minister and Minister in Charge of Shipping. By 2015 the PFL was starting to operate profitably and the ships also provide jobs for locally trained seamen.

In December 2012, Cyclone Evan struck, causing significant damage to Samoa's infrastructure and the loss of fourteen lives. An 'inland tsunami' raged down the Vaisigano River valley, destroying roads, bridges, tourist facilities and personal property. The Tanugamanono power plant was heavily damaged, power and water supplies disrupted, and airport facilities at Faleolo wrecked. Substantial losses to key economic infrastructure were estimated at 470 million Tala. As a consequence, GDP growth fell to less than 1 percent in 2011–12, followed by a negative 2 percent in 2012–13. Recovery, fuelled by cyclone recovery work, rebounded in 2013–14 to 1.2 percent.

In January 2014 Samoa celebrated its graduation from the United Nations Least Developed Country status to Middle Income Country status, a clear recognition of Samoa's progressive development and Tuila'epa's prudent fiscal management over nearly three decades.

Manu Samoa v the All Blacks

Samoa is a rugby-mad nation. On 6 October 1991, in the days before satellite television became ubiquitous, thousands of Samoans sat out in the early hours of the morning at Apia Park to watch, on a large, specially erected TV screen, Samoa play Wales at Cardiff Arms Park. Samoa won sixteen to thirteen. Apia Park erupted. The small island nation had shocked the rugby world by defeating a top-level international team at the premium tournament, the Rugby Union World Cup. Samoa had arrived on the international stage. Samoan and other Pacific Island rugby players, imported or locally born, can now be found playing in most international teams, including the New Zealand All Blacks.

In the decades since that historic win, Manu Samoa have taken on, and sometimes beaten, many top teams. But there was one piece of unfinished business that had become a matter of concern for foreign relations between Samoa and New Zealand. The New Zealand All Blacks Rugby team had never travelled to Samoa for a test match against Manu Samoa on their home soil. For some years this was a source of irritation. A media campaign in New Zealand started to scratch the itch and a spirited public debate ensued. Behind the scenes Tuila'epa, as the chairman of the Samoan Rugby Union, quietly turned up the diplomatic heat in meetings with New Zealand Prime Minister John Key, Minister of Sport and Recreation Murray McCully and others. The irritation was becoming an embarrassment with the potential to develop into a running sore.

Enter All Blacks Coach, Steve Hansen, who was planning his 2015 Rugby World Cup campaign and saw the opportunity for an early test match as part of the All Blacks' buildup towards the finals in the UK in September–October. Hansen consulted senior All Blacks players of Samoan origin, including Keven Mealamu, Jerome Kaino and Ma'a Nonu, and identified a window of opportunity for a match in early July. The question was, could Samoa host a test match at the standards now required for international rugby in time? The answer was yes. Samoa pulled out all the stops and the New Zealand Rugby Union responded.

The All Blacks team arrived at Faleolo Airport and stepped off their plane dressed in *'ēlei* shirts, *'ie faitaga* and *'ulafala*. The villages on the road from the airport were decorated with flowers, coloured lights, coconuts painted in the team colours, signs supporting both teams and thousands of cheering fans. A parade through Apia mobbed both teams and drew the largest crowd ever.

Prime Minister John Key and a large entourage flew in from New Zealand for the day. He sat beside Tuila'epa in the recently refurbished Apia Park's grandstand. On 8 July 2015 Sky Television coverage of the game was broadcast to 141 countries. The television presenters all wore *'ēlei* shirts, *'ie faitaga* and *'ulafala*, and the pre-match buildup beamed world-wide included scenes of Samoa targeted at the global audience. Lead commentator Fauono Ken Laban said, 'It is an historic moment to see both Prime Ministers sitting side by side watching Manu Samoa play the All Blacks in a home test match. In the highly competitive world of international sport, there would be no Manu Samoa without Prime Minister Tuila'epa's personal support and his government's financial backing.'

In most previous encounters in New Zealand, the All Blacks had put 50 points on Samoa. The last match in 2008 resulted in a 101 to 14 points thrashing. Would a 'home game' be any different? At half time Manu Samoa were still in touch, but down three points to twelve. In the 66th minute Samoa's hopes were raised and the Apia Park crowd erupted when Alafoti Fa'osiliva crashed over for a try following two storming runs up the middle of the park. At 22 to 16 the All Blacks were under pressure as Samoa had outscored them in the second half, but New Zealand kicked a late penalty goal and managed a scratchy 25 to 16 win.

Early the following morning All Black Coach Steve Hansen was bestowed the chiefly title Tupuivao by the high chief Patū Ativalu of the village of Vaiala in recognition of the part Hansen had played in bringing the All Blacks to Samoa and his long history of nurturing Samoan rugby players in New Zealand. At the end of the *saofa'i*, the titling ceremony, Chief Patū Ativalu looked directly at Steve Hansen and said, 'Tupuivao Steve, when you are finally axed by the All Blacks you will come back here and coach our village team.'

Tuila'epa reflected that relations between Samoa and New Zealand were at an all-time high point when the two rugby-mad nations played the test match in Samoa.

Joseph Parker, World Boxing Champion

Tuila'epa is a keen fan of boxing and supported Joseph Parker's successful challenge for the World Boxing Organisation's heavyweight championship title in Auckland on 11 December 2016.[16]

When the New Zealand government and the Auckland City Council declined to contribute funding for the fight, Tuila'epa saw an opportunity, stepped in and put up US$100,000 from Invest Samoa to help sponsor the event. Television coverage of the fight went out to over a hundred countries and attracted an estimated 100 million viewers.

The *Otago Daily Times* saw that Samoa was set for a tourism boost from the Joseph Parker fight and reported:

---

16 Joseph Parker is the latest in a long line of Samoan boxers who have fought at the highest level. Maselino Masoe won the world middleweight boxing championship title in 2004. David Tua won a bronze medal at the 1992 Olympics before he turned professional and challenged Lennox Lewis for the world heavyweight championship title in 2000. Jimmy (Thunder) Peau won the World Boxing Foundation and the International Boxing Organisation heavyweight titles, in 1993 and 1995, two minor versions of the world heavyweight championship. Earlier, in 1964, Tuna Scanlan won the British Empire Middleweight title. Samoans have also reached the highest levels in martial arts with stars including kick-boxer Ray Sefo, Sumo wrestler Konishika (Saleva'a Fuauli Atisano'e) and professional wrestler Dwayne 'The Rock' Johnson.

'The Samoan Government's decision to contribute about NZ$137,000 into the fight is widely considered a smart move by Prime Minister Tuilaepa Sailele Malielegaoi. As a result, Prime Minister Tuilaepa will be given time in the ring to make an introductory speech. Samoa Tourism will also get a number of television advertisement spots throughout the live tele-cast, as well as promotional banners ring-side.

'Samoa Tourism New Zealand spokesman Sonny Rivers said the prospect of reaching a global audience for such a mammoth event was a marketing dream. "Obviously, broadcasts like these ones – which go all around the globe – it's a really good channel for us to present ourselves out there as an emerging destination."'

After winning the fight, Joseph Parker said that he couldn't have done it without Samoa's support, and commented, 'What a great feeling to represent Samoa and New Zealand', before embarking on a victory tour of Samoa to celebrate and personally thank Samoa.

Part 3. Leadership and Succession 2016 . . .

March 2016 to Present Day

This was Tuila'epa Sa'ilele Malielegaoi's fifth administration. The HRPP won 47 seats, four women were elected directly and a fifth was added to make up the new 10 percent quota of women MPs, totalling 47 MPs in government and three independents opposing.

The 2016 general election resulted in a virtual whitewash, with the HRPP holding 94 percent of the seats in Parliament. The main opposition party, the Tautua Samoa Party, was wiped out with only one Member elected, forming a depleted 'opposition' along with two independents.

Given this result, involving the historical shift away from *tama-a-'āiga* hegemony and personality-based consensus politics to adversarial political parties and a dominant party, it is timely to reflect on the history and future of politics in Samoa.

At the time of Samoa's independence the early governments, led by Fiamē Mata'afa, relied on a general agreement that the interests of Samoa were paramount, a firm view that 'party politics' was not for Samoa and the acceptance that *tama-a-'āiga* were the 'natural' leaders, born to rule. The HRPP was established in 1979, in part as a response to the nepotism and cronyism of the *tama-a-'āiga* leaders, and a need to reform politics and to strengthen the democratic spirit of the Constitution. The HRPP is Samoa's first and longest surviving political party. Other political parties have risen to seek to become an adversary to the HRPP but quickly fallen, in most cases centred on a single political personality. Tupua Tamasese led coalition governments and later various political parties (CDP, SNDP) but none in government.[17]

Three Prime Ministers, Vaʻai Kolone, Tofilau ʻEti Alesana and Tuilaʻepa Saʻilele Malielegaoi, have led the HRPP in government, and Tofilau was a particularly effective opposition leader.

The HRPP has aimed to shift Samoa's political discourse away from personality politics and to develop a political debate based on policies rather than personalities. To that end the HRPP has regularly published an election manifesto that sets out its policies[18] and monitors progress against the policies. It has also made a number of constitutional amendments and electoral reforms that have woven democratic processes and cultural practices into the constitutional arrangements, in a uniquely Samoan manner, so that Samoa now has a 'Parliament of Chiefs'.

The success of the HRPP, and the results of the 2016 general election, presented Tuilaʻepa with a unique set of problems of political management: how to manage a Parliament with effectively no opposition; how to distribute ministerial portfolios and associate ministerial positions fairly; how to manage a large backbench of MPs; and how to maintain the credibility and accountability of the government against the accusations that Samoa is now a 'one-party state' – in short, how to turn the overwhelming electoral success into an effective working government.

Entering his fifth term as Prime Minister, Tuilaʻepa is also faced with questions about his future and leadership succession. In the days following the 2016 election Tuilaʻepa reflected on these issues, made a series of presentations to government MPs[19] and issued media statements to outline his vision for the future.

I think it is important at this time to anticipate the tight watch on the policies and performance of the government and ensure that we have checks and balances in place. With a large government team in Parliament, we will have one Minister and one Associate Minister for each portfolio, with the other MPs forming the bulk of the 'opposition'. It is now an 'internal opposition',

---

17 See Soʻo (2008: 97–129) for an extensive discussion of the development of political parties in Samoa.
18 See HRPP, 2016b, for the 2016–2021 HRPP Manifesto.
19 See Malielegaoi, 2016a, 2016b, 2016c, 2016d.

acting as an internal check against the government from steering off course. The *HRPP Manifesto 2016–2021* provides the direction and backbenchers have to keep an eye on that as part of the checks and balances. This is some adjustment from our previous way of working.

It is another model, an addition to the continuing checks and balances that the government has installed for self-audit. For example, we have greatly strengthened the Audit Office by increasing the number of auditors. There used to be four or five, and now there are over twenty auditors. They work across all government departments and agencies. We have also established the Ombudsman's Office and greatly strengthened its role with the incorporation of the Office for Human Rights. That office has responsibility directly to Parliament, not to the government.

We still have the power to create Commissions of Enquiry to run investigations into the government itself. We have done that many times. The latest one resulted in the exposure of corruption within the police, with the result that we exited both the Police Commissioner and the Head of the Prison Service and replaced them. The Samoan Police have been strengthened by separating the pure police work from the custodial function of the Prison Service. We have separated Corrections from the Police. So we have a Commissioner for Police and a Commissioner for Prisons.

While the HRPP won an overwhelming victory, there was a significant change of personnel. Several of our 'independent' HRPP candidates ousted sitting MPs, including several Ministers, which resulted in a refreshed Parliament and a renewed Cabinet.

I was happy in the sense that five of the Ministers were unseated and two retired. So that gave me seven who brought new blood to Cabinet. But I had to make it eight by dropping my former Deputy Prime Minister Fonotoe Pierre, giving him another good opportunity to understudy the art of leadership from a different perspective – that of a backbencher.

We have been gradually working towards creating a Parliament of Chiefs. Firstly, in 2006–11, we brought about the requirement that everybody must be a *matai*. We had two Individual Voters' seats that were established at independence for non-*matai*. In the election of 2011 Joe Keil resigned. He did not want to come back because he refused to take on a *matai* title. But, although complete, the fact remained that the two Individual Voters' seats still existed in the Constitution. So we had to go further and formally eliminate those two seats and we replaced them with two 'Urban' seats. To eliminate these two seats required an amendment to the Constitution. That's what we did in November 2015.

That is why in one of my public speeches I mentioned that this new Parliament is historical for a number of reasons. Firstly, the Parliament of Samoa is now comprised only of Samoan *matai*. That reflects the true nature of a Samoa *fono* where only *matai* exchange ideas and make decisions on the future of the village, and now on the future of this country. Secondly, we have achieved what we aimed to do with changes to the Constitution to ensure that more women come into Parliament. Now we have the greatest number of women ever, including two Ministers. In achieving that, we had to activate the new law and increase the number of MPs. For the first time we have 50 MPs. Four women were elected to seats and the other came in as the highest polling woman to make up the required minimum of 10 percent of women MPs. The final historical event was that for the first time we have a political party taking almost all the seats in the House. Ninety-four percent was quite an achievement.

Tuila'epa reflected on the problem of the political management of a large backbench.

We create monsters along the way. We could never forget the breakup in 1985. That breakup was essentially over the leadership of the party. When the leadership went to Tofilau rather than Va'ai Kolone, it created a major rift that eventually broke up our party. Tofilau was over-confident about our two-thirds majority and did not take into account the balance he needed to have in his Cabinet formation. I am now dealing with that same sort of challenge.

We have a large number of new MPs. I have to make them understand how I elect my Cabinet. I mentioned that due consideration should be given to a balance that must exist between Savai'i and Upolu, between *Tumua* and *Pule*, and between the districts themselves. There has to be a balance between the two sexes, and I also have to be careful and draw some balance between the new Members, the old Members and those in between. Lastly, the capabilities of the Members and the fact that some constituencies that have not had a ministerial post for a long time need to be considered. These multi-faceted issues make the job difficult. Nevertheless I proceeded in the hope that what I said would be understood. What I said to the MPs in Samoan sounds different in English. This is roughly what I said.

'Firstly, I need to remind people that I am from the Ātua district. The Head of State comes from the Ātua district. The Chief Justice comes from Ātua. One of the members of the Council of Deputies comes from the Ātua district. The Deputy Prime Minister comes from the Ātua district. Therefore, I would remind the Ātua MPs, let us give priority to the other districts and be good distributors. You know, in the *Fa'asamoa*, when you are in charge of distribution the best and most ideal distributor is the one who distributes the goodies fairly to everybody and he goes without.'

With those comments I proceeded to announce the new Cabinet. I axed one of my relatives, a *matai*, who stood from my Falevao district. He went nuts afterwards. I had to axe the other Tui Ātua, Tafua, who later shouted verbal abuse at my wife who was sitting not far from him in Parliament that day. But the heaviest axe was to fall on my previous Deputy Prime Minister, who is also from Ātua. If he had been reappointed by the caucus as deputy leader, he would have been spared.

Before I announced the Ministers in the new Cabinet, I summoned our caucus, the old and the new Members, and I said to them, 'You have seen that many people are watching us and how we behave because the checks and balances between the three branches of government are now impacted by the election result. With an overwhelming majority we cannot maintain our previous policy of picking the thirteen Members of Cabinet and appointing the rest as Associate Ministers. That cannot be sustained now. It was OK last time when we had fewer MPs. Now we have 47. If we proceed with the old policy we will be accused of corrupt practices. This is not on. My recommendation is that we should now reform our policies. If we have one Associate Minister per Minister, and add on the Speaker and Deputy Speaker, that makes 28 with nineteen backbenchers. With the three independents that allows 22 MPs to form an informal opposition to government. Today we are the darlings of the voters. Forty-seven seats in the House is great. If we abuse the power handed to us by the people, what will they say five years from today? Good riddance! Always remember, power corrupts and absolute power corrupts absolutely.'

A small working committee was appointed to consider the suggested reforms. The committee reported back strongly supporting my recommendations and also asking to review the entitlements of the Committees of Parliament where the backbenchers are expected to be fully engaged.

The HRPP caucus now owns the reforms completely.

Electoral Reforms
Tuila'epa has a further electoral reform in mind.

The size of the electorates has never been reviewed since independence and more and more MPs were asking for additional seats. Electoral boundary reform is long overdue. I have already discussed this with the High Commissioner of New Zealand. New Zealand has reviewed its boundaries many times and they are experts in boundary reviews and changes. What I want to do is to get some New Zealand experts to study and report on our electoral boundaries.

Their report will then be analysed with a view to implementing those recommendations that are appropriate for Samoa today. This will be a very controversial matter. Issues that need to be addressed include the fairness of representation in Parliament and the cultural and geographical spread of some of the constituencies. Culture has dictated the determination of our electoral boundaries in the past when we had *matai* suffrage. Some electorates are now very small, others quite large. And there is the effect of urbanisation in Apia to consider. There are anomalies that must be eliminated to simplify the election process and make it fairer.

We may need to establish an Electoral Boundaries Commission and get them to work out a solution. A wish for a more equal distribution of voters in electorates has been expressed so that there is some kind of parity in the numbers. There will need to be a determination to fix up the traditional boundaries on the basis of our Samoan culture. There are many issues to consider.

Because the government has a large majority it provides an opportunity to put in place the reforms now. There may never be another time for us to make these electoral boundary changes.

Leadership and Succession
Perhaps I can say something about leadership and succession from another angle?

Tofilau was a very sick man from 1989 onwards, and a number of times after his bypass operation he raised with me the issue of succession. At that time I knew that any succession after Tofilau would not be plain sailing because in our own party there were quite a few MPs who would go all out campaigning for the honour. And outside our party many still held the traditional belief that the *tama-a-'āiga* were the natural leaders of Samoa. That meant that the posts of Head of State, Prime Minister and Council of Deputies would go to a *tama-a-'āiga*, despite the fact that the Constitution declares these roles are open to all.

The break in that tradition was made by Tupuola Efi in 1976 when he was elected, at age 38, the youngest Prime Minister, not as a bearer of a *tama-a-'āiga* title but as an ordinary *tulafale* from Leulumoega. At the time, Tupuola was viewed as a man of change, a young leader with education and fresh ideas. Young Tupuola became an immediate idol of the educated youth of Samoa who had returned with degrees from overseas universities. He was the manifestation of modern and Western ideas, and indeed, the hope of the future. He would take over from the old guard and their very slow way of doing things.

From 1976–79 great changes were therefore expected to take place. There was great joy. The new leader had vision and charisma. He had a plan for rural development from the bottom up. It turned out to be a total failure.

Tupuola Efi was an elegant Samoan orator. He often joked that finance and economics were boring issues. He believed that his oratory would raise the necessary funds required by his government. Tupuola Efi had some successes, including taking Samoa into the United Nations in 1976 and establishing diplomatic offices in New York, Wellington and Canberra, but his dismissal of a large number of senior officials, the poor handling of the PSA strike and his failure to take the people with him to the bright future he had promised contributed to his demise. He did manage to scrape through in the 1979 election but this was the period when big problems began to emerge. Tupuola's individualistic approach to politics meant that he did not attract a loyal following or build a lasting political party to support his leadership ambitions.

I was acutely aware of this history during the years of Tofilau's decline and so I thought I was not ready for leadership. Yet there were many in our party who would talk to me on the quiet about what I should do to prepare myself to take over. Remembering that nothing is secret in Samoa, and to preserve my own position, I could never confide in anybody. I was approached several times by members of the party saying things like, 'You should prepare yourself.'

I said, 'I'm not interested, I am just doing my job.'

I concentrated on performing as Minister of Finance. I gave Tofilau my committed support. In Parliament I would always stand up to defend the party and Tofilau.

The first time I got up to defend our leader was an initial debate on the Budget. Tupuola had attacked the Prime Minister for ordering the government's heavy moving equipment to prepare the ground for a new school that was to be built in his village. When Tupuola made the allegations, Tofilau just sat still. Tupuola kept attacking and attacking. I knew the policies, so I got up on a Point of Order and said, 'This is an old policy of government to help the villages. If a village undertakes a major project such as building a school or a village hall, the government has usually provided the heavy equipment to help with the moving of the soil, the most difficult part of the construction. But that work has to be done after hours. When the road-making machinery finishes working on the roads at 4.30, then the village, the village can requisition the help of the government equipment.'

Then I said, 'Perhaps the ex-Prime Minister has forgotten that this has been government policy since 1962?'

That was the end of the allegations on that occasion.

I had been making these sorts of interventions to protect the Prime Minister and to protect the government, and I had been pushing the Cabinet to respond in terms of policy not personalities. I have always believed that when we respond in terms of policy we will safeguard the HRPP government. I had been doing that all the time. I was very vocal in our defence and initiated a new tactic in Parliament. The tactic was to strike the opposition as soon as a false allegation was made.

I would rise on a Point of Order and have the matter corrected. I became a nuisance during the debates because I was up all the time making Points of Order against the opposition. That way we gained a reputation that we were thoughtless and did not give the opposition time to respond. But what can you do when the opposition is making false allegations all the time? We could not just sit tight, and our defence comes from the famous edict that the easiest way to straighten a bent iron bar is when it is red hot.

Up to that time, Budget debates would take two weeks and the custom was that no Minister would break into the debate. They would wait until all the MPs had spoken and then they would respond. Written responses were prepared by ministry technicians so that all a Minister had to do was read out the written response. The difference I established was that when questions were posed I gave the answers right away. There was no need to refer to technicians or advisers.

That was how we were able to make our way through the first term when Tofilau 'Eti Alesana faced a seasoned politician in Tupuola Efi and the young educated politicians supporting him. Some of them were engineers, lawyers and other professionals, but I knew my stuff because I had been a senior Treasury official and had been dealing with the Budget all the time.

We shifted the debate to policy and facts rather than personal opinions and personalities. It was from that time onwards I realised that when the time came for me to face Tupuola as a leader, I would know exactly what I had to do. I would focus on detail and technical issues all the time and that would give him much trouble because Tupuola was an expert in generalities.

In one of our early exchanges in 1983 Tupuola said, 'I would like to strongly recommend that this young Member from Lepā take all his figures to his constituency, bake them and feed them to his chiefs and orators.'

That kind of comment could have destroyed me if I wasn't able to respond properly.

I got up and asked the Speaker for the floor.

The Speaker asked me why I wanted to take the floor.

I said, 'Point of correction. I want to let Tupuola know that the people of my district eat well from the products of their own labour and from food from the sea. They are well fed and are very healthy. I have never believed, up until now, that statistics are edible. I had always wondered why every time Tupuola asked for figures from Treasury and I supplied the figures, tons and tons of paper had to be produced to provide the statistics to confirm the government's stance. I wondered why, but I can now see why he was asking for these figures to be provided on the floor of the House. I now find that he is eating the statistics. Tupuola, if you find the statistics edible, feed them to your mother and your brother and sisters and all the chiefs of your constituency.'

I asked the Speaker for Tupuola's insulting words about me to be removed from the Parliamentary record and sat down.

The Speaker agreed.

Tupuola did not respond to me straight away.

Then, a young fellow went to Tupuola and asked him to take a phone call.

Later, Tupuola came back and said, 'Mr Speaker, I raise a Point of Order.'

'What is it?'

'You ruled that my words be removed from the records. You have not removed Tuila'epa's words against my family and my district. I want to move too that Tuila'epa's words remain in the records forever.'

The Speaker said, 'No. My direction covered you both. Your intervention was unnecessary.'

Someone had rung up to remind Tupuola that the parliamentary debate was broadcast live on radio throughout the country and he did not want a record of my riposte preserved in the Hansard.

Our debates had created enormous interest throughout the country. Politics became a contest of ideas not just personalities.

When Tofilau began to raise his health concerns with me, I did not think I was ready to take over. I was not sure whether Tofilau was really sick or just testing me. So to be on the safe side of my relationship with my boss, I kept telling him, 'No. You keep on and I will provide the support that you need.'

That was from 1989. After he came back from the heart bypass operation, he was never the same again. Seven years later he went back for another major operation on his liver and when he returned he was even more insistent that the change should be made but I kept on saying, 'Don't worry. I will take care of most of your responsibilities while you take it easy. If you need to go home, go home and work from there.'

I was counting on the fact that if there was a leadership change to be made it would take place at the general election in 2001. But then things moved very fast from September 1998, when Tofilau had to be taken to New Zealand and then came back in a coma. In our discussion with him on succession he laid out his plan to resign with a ceremony during which he would make presentations of fine mats to our party. At that time he would appeal to the party to take me as his successor. This was his plan.

I had reservations about his plan. I did not believe it was the way it should be done. Leadership should not be passed down from one leader to the next. I wanted to leave it as it was and, when the time came, to go through the normal process of letting the caucus decide on the next leader. I believed that my way to the leadership was by faithfully doing my own work and doing it properly and by being watchful. But I must also admit, members of the public would appear in my office and, when I asked them what they wanted, they would say, 'Just a little time to talk to you, Tui. We would love to see you as successor to Tofilau.'

Tofilau's illness was well known. People were worried. They would say to me, 'We have some recommendations.'

'What are your recommendations?'

'You have got to spruce up the way you talk. You talk too straight to the point. You have to show some kind of subtlety, more respect for the leader of the opposition.'

I would smile. My normal response was, 'Sorry, I am not in a beauty contest, you know. I am me. If I change my style I am no longer me. I am sorry I cannot be another person. My preference is to speak my mind. I am sorry but I will use whatever words come to me to express what I think. My preference is to use the language of conversations. That way, I am better understood.'

I was often reminded that my way of speaking was too direct and seemed disrespectful to the opposition.

I said, 'I have no time, absolutely no time, to polish my language. I always use simple and direct language.'

I found that a complex economic or monetary policy speech, if delivered in everyday language, could easily be understood by the people in the streets. Which, incidentally, made me friends with many people because they could understand what I was talking about.

Many people in the party did not like my direct style or the way I was very rigid in my control of the government's finances, as Minister of Finance. Some were blunt in Cabinet and said that I over-controlled the finances and that I should remember it was not my money, it was the people's money.

Many people think in terms of grooming leaders. A king can groom his son or daughter to be his successor. But in a democratic state, where the caucus makes the decision, a prime minister does not appoint the next prime minister. That is the duty of the members of the caucus of the party in power.

We must remember that every MP has an ambition to become prime minister, and those who are more senior will have a greater aspiration. The moment you start grooming somebody, everybody will know, particularly in a small country where family connections are extensive. You cannot hide these things in Samoa. I was never groomed for leadership by Tofilau. I was fortunate in the sense that when I entered Parliament there were three very senior leaders – Tofilau 'Eti Alesana, Va'ai Kolone and Tupuola Efi – who were constantly demonstrating their political skills. They were all mentors for me.

What does that mean? I watched them perform. When a motion was proposed in Parliament, I listened and I tried to understand why that motion was put forward. I listened to the words that were used. When I did not understand a term, as my vocabulary was limited then, I wrote it down on a sheet of paper in front of me. At the end of every meeting the sheet was filled with my writings: the words that I heard and the things that I saw, the rulings by the Speaker, even simple things like attendance at the beginning of the meeting and the need for a quorum before a meeting could proceed. I faithfully attended the sessions of Parliament and watched and listened. I hardly ever left that chamber, compared to my many colleagues. Right now that is happening. Where are they? Out there drinking *kava* and plotting in the backyard, where they miss a lot of the wisdom that is expressed on the floor of the House. You miss a lot of new words. You miss the reason why things are accepted. You have to be there. You have to understand how Parliament works and know how to make things happen.

Now I will tell you of one instance. In 2016 we had an important amendment to the Constitution planned. When we have an amendment to the Constitution we must have a two-thirds majority or it will not pass. The practice of this party is that on the morning of the vote we all breakfast together. After the breakfast, at 9 o'clock, we all go to the House and we count the numbers to ensure that we have the numbers for the vote. On this occasion we were short by one member, a Minister, who should have known better and had gone out to open meetings thinking that she would be back in time. We had her called up to return urgently to the House.

As soon as we arrived in the House, the Speaker moved very quickly through the agenda items and we soon came to the vote. It was then that I realised my Minister of Health was not sitting there, and I could see the giggling of the opposition MPs. They knew that we were short by one and they would vote out the amendment to the Constitution. The Speaker proceeded to call for the vote.

I intervened, 'Mr Speaker.'

'Yes, Prime Minister.'

'I want to speak on a technical point.'

I demanded the right to deliver a Ministerial Statement. When a Minister delivers a Ministerial Statement no one can intervene.

The Speaker asked, 'Why?'

I said, 'We finished the second reading six months ago. It is a requirement of the Act that we must have six months' lapse before we move to the final vote. This is to ensure that if the government wishes to change its mind it can do so.'

Meanwhile I had already alerted our Chief Whip to find out where this Minister was and to tell her to get back here quickly. I quietly said to him, 'I shall keep on talking until she arrives.'

I turned to the Speaker and said, 'You must know that the whole country is tuning in to hear about this amendment to the Constitution and I want to talk to explain the essence of the constitutional amendment before we pass it.'

The Speaker said, 'OK. This sounds relevant. Proceed.'

I proceeded with my speech, going through the history of the amendment, the pros and cons, and why we urgently needed to pass this amendment.

I paused and saw our Chief Whip behind me and turned around. 'How is our Member doing?'

'She is on her way. She will be here in five minutes.'
'Mr Speaker . . .'
And I went on and on and on . . .
It was a great relief when I saw the missing Minister walking in.

I concluded, 'Mr Speaker, I hope I have explained myself sufficiently so that the public is well informed and that Members can vote with a complete knowledge of the importance of this amendment.'

I sat down. We now had the numbers.

The question was put and there was a division. We had to stand up and be counted. There was no dissension. The opposition saw that it was useless to oppose the vote as we had the numbers. Rather than embarrassing themselves by being on the defeated side, they all got up and voted with us.

So much for grooming future leaders!

If you want to be a successful MP you have got to understand the Standing Orders. You have got to understand why certain strategies are put forth. You must also understand your culture. You should physically attend the meetings of your village *fono* so that you can participate in debates and the exchange of views in the village. If there is dissension on substantive issues on that level, watch very carefully how the old chiefs settle these issues peacefully through a process of 'give and take'. In the same manner, you must also understand your Bible, because that book has all the ingredients on how to be a good leader. These are the things you should be aware of and knowledgeable about.

That is exactly what I said to my new MPs. These are the principles I learnt from Tofilau 'Eti Alesana.

During the election campaign I was asked, 'Who are you grooming to be the next leader?'

I replied by providing a biblical answer.

'In our own beliefs as Christians there are numerous examples in the Bible about the selection for leadership. Abraham, Moses, King David, King Solomon. The selection of David himself is a beautiful story where David was the divine choice ahead of his older brothers.'

We too have numerous ways to prepare ourselves for leadership. I was never groomed by anybody for leadership but I watched the other guys perform and I kept a mental picture, a record of what they were doing and why they were doing it, and that is how I got myself into this position. Leaders of this country are taught through their active involvement in politics and you do not need to have any special person to teach you how to become a leader of a country or government. The things that you ought to know to be leader are all there in front of your eyes. You just have to observe, listen, reason, ask questions and you are there. Our system is democratic and leaders come out of that system rather than through inheritance, succession planning or grooming. This is what I have tried to explain to my caucus in various critical meetings. The moment you groom someone in party politics, that person becomes a target.

When the caucus was getting into different factions, some senior Ministers against other senior Ministers, I openly said to them, 'Perhaps I was at fault when I mentioned to you that every one of you must think about the issue of succession. Remember that I will not be with you all the time. Who knows? This could be my last term. If that is the case, somebody must be ready to take over.' I think it was misinterpreted because after that meeting I began to hear words coming back: 'This is his last term.' It got so widely circulated so that in one debate in the House the leader of the opposition got up and said, 'Mr Prime Minister, you are telling us that we should not be unnecessarily worried about the status of the economy and the level of debt, and you reminded us you were responsible as Minister of Finance in 1982 for putting in place an economic package that stabilised the economy. That's OK if you are going to be there at the next general election, but you've indicated that this is your last term and that you will resign or retire.'

After that people were asking me, 'Are you going to retire?'

They had been listening to the debate.

Two days later I responded, 'Now I come to the point where the leader of the opposition has asked me if I will retire at the end of this term. I have been saying explicitly over the radio and on television that when it comes to the matter of a calling, it is not our business. That is the Lord's business. Ask him!'

Later, during a radio interview, one of the journalists put a very dubious question to me. He asked, 'This proposed constitutional amendment, in which you are saying that the governing party nominates the Head of State, means that the government of the day names the person so Parliament can make the appointment. This means the opposition is a mere onlooker and has no say. And they are saying that you have deliberately done this in order to become the Head of State. What do you say?'

This interview was broadcast live. I suspected that this question had a political motivation. I quickly saw the danger of the question. I had to state my answer in a Samoan context, so that our people out in the villages would understand.

I answered, 'You know, I hold the post of Prime Minister. The Head of State is a figurehead. The Prime Minister's position is where you eat *pisupo* [corned beef], *luʻau* and *palusami* every day. As the Head of State, all you eat is a can of fish. It would be stupid for a Prime Minister to surrender his job in order to eat nothing but canned fish.'

Immediately, our people out in the villages understood.

CHAPTER 6

Tuila'epa's Premiership

Tuila'epa is Samoa's longest-serving Prime Minister. His premiership has been marked by political and economic crises, natural disasters, regional tensions and local challenges. Tuila'epa's political career started during turbulent times but has resulted in an unprecedented period of political stability in Samoa.

Shortly after becoming Prime Minister, Tuila'epa Sa'ilele Malielegaoi had to deal with the aftermath of the assassination of his Cabinet Minister and colleague Luagalau Levaula Kamu. Tsunami, cyclones and the vagaries of global climate change have regularly punctuated his premiership, as have economic crises. The Asian economic crisis in 1997, the Global Financial Crisis in 2007–08 and regular fluctuations in commodity prices have buffeted Samoa's fragile economy. Political unrest has also disturbed the Pacific region: coups in Fiji, instability in Vanuatu, West Papua's uncertain status, civil war in the Solomon Islands, and crises in Pacific regional agencies have tested Tuila'epa's diplomacy and leadership. Critics and political opponents have also had their say, accusing Tuila'epa of corruption, nepotism and a range of other alleged failings.

The British historian Arnold Toynbee is said to have written, 'History is just one damned thing after another.' At times, Tuila'epa might have felt that his premiership had been spent responding to events, one damned thing after another.

His time in office has been buffeted and shaped, in part, by a series of events that he has had to respond to. However, this narrative has shown us that Tuila'epa's premiership has not just been reactive. He has had a clear sense of direction and a reliable compass: he has steered a steady course. Tuila'epa has always had his own policy and political goals for Samoa that he has consistently worked towards achieving over many years, and has taken a hard-headed, pragmatic approach to decision-making. We can see that the political stability, economic growth and social development of Samoa during his time in power have been systematic, clearly planned and well coordinated.

As we look back over his premiership, spread over two decades, we can see the key events, challenges, issues, goals, policies, successes and failures, planned and reactive, that have defined Tuila'epa's time as Prime Minister of Samoa. Are there some patterns and themes that emerge?

Six themes, amongst many, stand out: the stability of Samoa's governance; the modernisation of Samoa's economy; the management and mitigation of natural disasters; the leadership of regional and international relationships; Tuila'epa's dealings with critics and naysayers; and the way that he has taken the people of Samoa with him on his political journey.

These themes are not exclusive. While each is distinct, they overlap, interact with and contribute to each other. Tuila'epa's pragmatic political leadership is the strong common factor linking the six themes we will now consider.

Stable Government

Tuila'epa Sa'ilele Malielegaoi entered Parliament in May 1981. Over the next seven years there were seven governments and four different prime ministers of Samoa. This was the least stable period in Samoa's political history since independence. The young MP from Lepā observed the instability with great concern, and Tuila'epa's political experience as a new MP laid the foundation for his long-term aim to establish and maintain stable governance in Samoa. It took the good part of a decade before Tuila'epa was established as a senior member of a government with significant portfolios and could start working towards achieving that aim.

When Tofilau 'Eti Alesana's third administration was elected in April 1988, a decade of political stability commenced. Tuila'epa, as Minister of Finance, played a key role in building policies, processes and relationships to establish and maintain stable government. After Tofilau's health gave out, Tuila'epa became Prime Minister and the maintenance of political stability became a central theme of his subsequent premiership.

Tuila'epa's drive for political stability has led some critics[1] to complain that Samoa has become a 'one-party state' or a 'dictatorship' ruled by the HRPP, first under Tofilau's then Tuila'epa's leadership. The evidence would suggest otherwise. Tuila'epa has regularly put his leadership of the party to the vote and the HRPP has won substantial majorities in successive general elections. Samoa has become increasingly democratic, with the introduction of universal suffrage and reforms to increase women's representation.

Stability does not mean stagnation. Tuila'epa has led a wide range of constitutional and other electoral reforms. The Constitution has been updated to ensure that its 'spirit' and the vision of the founding fathers have been

---

1 See Field, 2010; Iati Iati, 2013; Toleafoa, 2013.

maintained whilst unintended problems have been eliminated. A balance between preserving traditional values whilst preserving human rights has had to be achieved. Universal suffrage has been introduced and the participation of women in the political realm strengthened. The role of the Head of State in government formation has been clarified. The Electoral Act has been revised to modernise electoral processes. The Samoan public service has been reviewed, reformed and restructured to meet modern best-practice standards and requirements, and to improve service delivery. 'Permanent Secretaries' have been replaced by contracted CEOs. Performance management processes have been introduced at all levels, and educational standards have been raised for appointment to senior positions. Audit requirements have increased and levels of transparency accountability made explicit. Similar reforms have been applied to state agencies and corporations.

Perhaps Tuila'epa's most important public service reforms have been in economic development, market reforms, financial planning and fiscal management. Some of these reforms required new legislation, but others needed deregulation and the freeing up of markets. New agencies like the Scientific Research Organisation of Samoa have been established to add value to agricultural products, improve manufacturing and quality standards, and develop marketing strategies. Building intellectual property and strengthening human resource capacity are essential for Samoa to compete in global markets, and the National University of Samoa is playing an important role in that regard. For example, scholarships for postgraduate and doctoral study overseas for NUS and SROS staff, staff exchanges, and research partnerships with Victoria University of Wellington and other universities in New Zealand and Australia have been established to strengthen Samoa's human resource capacity.[2] These reforms have laid the foundations for Samoa's successful economic and social development.

Other reforms of Tuila'epa's have focussed on improving the quality of life in Samoa, including moving the International Dateline, introducing daylight saving, switching the side of the road cars are driven on, improving the quality of fine mats, reducing the cost of cultural presentations, introducing a national dress style, and establishing an open marketplace to attract a wide range of goods and services whilst protecting consumer rights and the environment.

A visitor to Samoa in 1998 returning in 2016 would see many significant

---

2   As a result of these initiatives three Samoan scholarship students completed their doctoral studies at Victoria University of Wellington in December 2016: Dr Seeseei Molimau-Samasoni, PhD in Cell and Molecular Bioscience; Dr Potoae Roberts Aiafi, PhD in Public Policy; and Dr Fuapepe Rimoni, PhD in Education.

changes to the landscape of infrastructure and facilities: a new airport on arrival, improved roads and bridges, high-rise buildings in Apia, a new market, shops with a wide range of products, many new government buildings, more and better-quality vehicles, international-standard sports facilities, a new hospital with better services, upgraded schools, improved telecommunications, and plenty more taxis and tourists. Samoa's modernisation is clearly visible to the casual observer.

Tuila'epa is aware that when a political party has been in power for a long time it may become 'an obstacle for democratic consolidation'. In May 2016 he made a series of presentations[3] to the incoming HRPP caucus to discuss this issue and ensure that checks and balances were in place to manage political dominance. His presentation of 29 May was entitled *HRPP Longevity: Political, Economic and Social Implications*. Tuila'epa outlined the 'Dominant Party System' theory 'in which, despite the multi-party situation, only one party is so dominant that it directs the political system and is firmly in control of state power over a fairly long duration of time, [so] that even opposition parties make little if any dent on the political hegemony of a dominant ruling party'. This political theory, particularly notable in South Africa, proposes 'that a dominant-party system can ignite political instability in a nation'. He cites the examples of Tonga (anti-monarchy riots), Fiji (a series of military coups) and dictatorships in some African countries but argues that the situation in Samoa is different as the 'HRPP's dominance has been for the most part a success story' and has achieved 'political stability, economic development and social development' through democratic means.

In his presentations to newly elected MPs, Tuila'epa outlined Samoa's history of democratic development, the development of the HRPP and its commitment to human rights (freedom of expression, universal access to education and healthcare, the protection of law and freedom to practise religious beliefs, etc.), and addressed accusations against the ruling party. He discussed criticisms by Iati Iati (2013), who argues that there is a 'price to pay' for political stability, critiques the government's changes to the role of the Auditor-General, the independence of the Judiciary and the role of opposition political parties, and makes accusations of corruption. In response, Tuila'epa set out the benefits that have accrued from political stability (citing So'o, 2006): 'the absence of drastic social and political upheavals' or 'public disorder and lawlessness' (peace and tranquillity, in other words); economic development and modernisation; and social development through improving education and health and poverty reduction.

---

3   See Malielegaoi, 2016a, 2016b, 2016c, 2016d.

Tuila'epa concluded his presentation to his caucus by answering his own question: 'What makes Samoa stable as an immovable rock in politics? The party's strategy is quite simple really; it ensures that the executive holds sufficient power of control. This strategy may be opposed by democratic advocates who immediately label it a form of authoritarianism; however, from [my] perspective, it is not. The practice adopted by the party is a strategy to ensure that all institutions will work together in achieving their goal, that is, to develop Samoa. It also aims to ensure that all democratic institutions, whose original roles and responsibilities are to keep government accountable, can exercise those roles but with limitations attached. Finally, the HRPP strategy reflects the Samoan culture where authority and power to make laws, the power to make decisions, is vested in the high chiefs of each village. This may not be completely ideal in the context of what a real democracy is and should be, but it has certainly worked for Samoa.'

Tuila'epa is modest about his achievements and gives much of the credit to his Cabinet, caucus colleagues and the public servants of Samoa. In his eyes, their collective loyalty, competence and service have contributed to Samoa's success. Political continuity, along with Tuila'epa's political pragmatism, have been key factors contributing to political stability and Samoa's journey towards becoming the leading independent democratic nation in the Pacific Islands region.

Modernisation of the Economy

Samoa is a small island nation with limited natural resources. The village-based subsistence economy is supported by remittances from overseas-based family members and supplemented by a developing market economy based on agriculture, tourism and manufacturing.[4] Government expenditure is funded by taxation, including a value-added goods and services tax, and infrastructure development is supported by overseas development assistance (ODA) and loans.

Samoa's economy was in the hands of German administrators from 1898–1914 and New Zealand administrators from 1914–62. Many Samoans were economically active during the colonial period, but the Samoan economy was essentially run by outsiders – Europeans with their own particular interests, goals and priorities. Independence in 1962 provided the opportunity for Samoans to take responsibility for their economic, as well as political, future.

Samoa's first government adopted a planned approach for national

4   See Lockwood, 1971; Va'a et al., 2012.

economic development. The first five-year development plan (1966–70) focussed on investment in infrastructure development projects and agriculture, and the primary sector, financed by 'soft' loans by aid donors. The second and subsequent plans continued and expanded this project-by-project approach. Roads; wharves; airports; bridges; water and electricity supplies; postal, communications and telephone services; and educational and health facilities and other infrastructure were all built. Export markets for agricultural products were explored during the 1960s and 1970s. Bananas, cocoa, pineapples, *taro* and coconut products were the main export crops.

Samoa's economy slowly grew but was hampered by dependence on aid donors and fluctuating commodity prices. Tropical agricultural products are perishable, vulnerable to pests, and need to be transported quickly and carefully to markets. Biosecurity and phytosanitary requirements become increasingly onerous and expensive; competition from other developing economies in Asia, Africa and South America, and high transport costs due to distance from markets, tend to reduce profit margins. Continuity of supply has been an ongoing problem. Furthermore, the impact of irregular but frequent natural disasters has led to heavy borrowing to finance repairs to infrastructure.

Samoa's early economic development was slow, stuttering and faced many crises. Inflation rose to 25–30 percent in the early 1980s, companies would not accept government credit, oil tankers refused to unload fuel until they were paid in cash, foreign exchange earnings were held to pay the fuel bill, consumer goods were in very limited supply, public servants had little to do as the government's coffers were empty and then the Public Service Association went on strike.

The early promise of independence had faded and Samoa was facing severe economic and political crises.

In their analysis of Samoa's weakening economic development, Va'a et al. (2012) concluded: 'By the 1990s the belief that Samoa's economy could be built on agricultural exports had all but disappeared.' They noted 'the reasons for retreat from agricultural export markets is not easy, because there have been many factors at work. But chief among them must be the unfavourable macroeconomic environment in which export industries have operated.'

The realisation that the approach the Samoan government had taken to economic development in the first two decades following independence was failing led to the conclusion that a new approach, new thinking and new leadership were required.

Tuila'epa Sa'ilele Malielegaoi was to become that leader. His academic grounding in Commerce and Politics; his early experience in Samoa's Treasury and later at the ACP Secretariat in Brussels; his years in Parliament; and then his role as Minister of Finance uniquely fitted Tuila'epa to become the leader of the modernisation of Samoa's economy.

Tuila'epa was appointed Minister of Finance following a Cabinet reshuffle in early 1984, during Tofilau 'Eti Alesana's first administration. This was a period of political instability. However, modernising the economy was a top priority for Tuila'epa. The Central Bank of Samoa was established to regulate monetary policies and the transactions of banking institutions in order to protect the economy of Samoa. In April 1985 Tofilau's first administration ended. His second short administration ran from April to December 1985, and Va'ai Kolone's coalition with Tupuola Efi from January 1986 to April 1988. Tuila'epa's modernisation plans were put on hold.

Tofilau became Prime Minister again in April 1988 and remained in office until November 1998. This was the stable period that gave the government time to address systematically the economic problems facing Samoa. Tuila'epa continued as Minister of Finance throughout this decade and was thus well placed to lead Samoa's transition from a state-led, project-based, donor-funded, planned economy to a strategic approach for economic development with 'a policy environment that aims to release the energy of the private sector', supported by deregulation and trade liberalisation.

In parallel with the restructuring of Samoa's economy, there was a need to rework the policies and processes for overseas development assistance. The earlier five-year development plans were replaced by a *Strategy for the Development of Samoa*, which is refreshed every four years.[5] Two mechanisms were put in place to implement the plans and to provide overall responsibility for the direction and coordination of overseas development assistance: the Cabinet Development Committee and the Aid Coordination Committee. These committees replaced the Economic Aid Division of the Ministry of Foreign Affairs and were relocated to the Ministry of Finance. As Minister of Finance, Tuila'epa chaired both these committees and has continued to chair them as Prime Minister.

In 1971 Samoa had been categorised by the United Nations as a 'Least Developed Country'.[6] This status entitled Samoa to take advantage of

5   The current plan is *Strategy for the Development of Samoa 2016/17–2019/20*.
6   The Least Developed Countries is a United Nations list of the countries that have the lowest socioeconomic development measured through the Human Development Index (HDI) of all the countries in the world. The idea of the LDC started in the late 1960s and was the subject of a United Nations resolution in 1971. A country is classified as an LDC if it meets three criteria related to poverty, human resource weakness and economic vulnerability. Only four countries have ever graduated from LDC to 'Developing Country' status: Botswana (1994),

grants and soft-term loans from friendly governments and multilateral donor institutions such as the UNDP and the Asian Development Bank. In accepting 'soft' loans from donors, many LDCs found themselves 'aid dependent' and suffering from a loss of sovereignty as a consequence. This has not been the case in Samoa.

A recent study[7] has identified a series of 'markers of development sovereignty' that demonstrate how the government of Samoa asserts its sovereignty when dealing with donor agencies. These markers show that Samoa has 'educated, well-informed officials, with lengthy experience, confident in themselves, and unafraid to speak their minds; clear governmental development policies and processes; and effective and trusted leadership'. The 'strong leadership of Prime Minister Tuila'epa, and the team of officials he developed and led' are also identified as key factors in Samoa's successful management of overseas development assistance whilst maintaining its sovereignty.

An informant in the study noted: 'People put their faith in leadership. Samoans are strong minded [and] they therefore need someone with a thick skin. The Prime Minister is bright, intelligent and has a lot of international exposure. He has a finance background, [as] Minister of Finance, and has strong leadership skills.' In addition, 'Tuila'epa isn't fussed on protocol, but he has a good understanding of finance that puts him in a good position to run the country.'

The success of Tuila'epa's economic development and financial management policies over two decades has led to Samoa's graduation in 2014 from LDC status to Middle Income Country status, and a steady improvement in measures of Samoa's human development.[8]

Cape Verde (2007), the Maldives (2011) and Samoa (2014). LDC status gives countries access to 'soft' loans from international financial institutions with a ten-year grace period, repayment periods of up to 30 years and interest as low as half a percent. Such loans assisted Samoa's development significantly. As Samoa's economic development improved, graduation from LDC status was targeted by the United Nations for 2010, but when Samoa was struck by the tsunami in September 2009 the commencement date was put back to January 2014. Graduation from LDC status was a major point that led to Samoa winning its bid to host the United Nations SIDS conference in Samoa during 2014. Middle Income Country status now means that Samoa no longer has access to 'soft' loans, which adds another challenge for funding future economic development programmes.

7   See Ulu, 2013, for a discussion on aid sovereignty and the quotations from informants cited.

8   When it comes to measuring a country's socioeconomic progress, it is often hard to separate political rhetoric from hard data. One way of getting a clear view of the progress made by any nation is to look at objective data that have been gathered over a long period of time by a well-respected and independent organisation. The UNDP's annual *Human Development Report* is one such publication that meets these criteria. The HDI is 'a composite index measuring average achievement in three basic dimensions of human development: a long and healthy

Management and Mitigation of Natural Disasters

Samoa's location in the tropical cyclone belt and on the Pacific 'rim of fire' makes it vulnerable to earthquakes, tsunami, cyclones and related natural disasters. Tuila'epa's premiership has been punctuated by an irregular series of natural disasters, and his management of these crises and mitigation of their consequences have been hallmarks of his premiership.

Tuila'epa was Minister of Finance and Deputy Prime Minister in Tofilau 'Eti Alesana's government when the severe tropical Cyclone 'Ofa struck Samoa on 1 February 1990. Cyclone Val struck on 7 December 1991. Val was the second 'once-in-a-hundred-year cyclone' in two years and did not dissipate until 17 December.

Cyclone 'Ofa was destructive, but Cyclone Val was more so, destroying over 65 percent of the residential homes on American Samoa and up to 80 percent on the Samoan islands of Upolu and Savai'i. Cyclone Val cut communications and power lines on the islands. It devastated fire stations, hospitals, government buildings, schools and churches, particularly wooden buildings. Cyclone Val destroyed over 80 percent of agricultural crops. Parts of Savai'i were described as looking as if an atomic bomb had hit. A local remarked that 'there was no green, no buildings standing, no shelter, just total and complete devastation'. Cyclone Val was reported to have killed seventeen people and left four thousand people homeless in American Samoa alone. It was also assessed to have had an impact that was 50 percent worse than Cyclone 'Ofa. On top of infrastructure destroyed, food production was halted, forests were damaged, and animals and birds were lost. The impact on flying foxes, or fruit bats, was severe. Many were caught on the ground as they searched for food. The forest loss was severe: 45 percent of Savai'i's timber logs were ruined. People had no

---

life, knowledge, and a decent standard of living'. The HDI gathers standard data on life expectancy, years in school and gross national income per capita and calculates an index based on this data. Other data on employment, gender inequality, labour conditions, housing, access to potable water and access to health services etc. are also gathered. Nations can be ranked and compared, and the progress, or lack of progress, each has made can be measured objectively. In 2016 Samoa was ranked number 105 of 188 nations by the HDI, in the UNDP Human Development Report, as a 'High Human Development' nation. By way of contrast, Indonesia, Micronesia (FSM), South Africa, Timor-Leste, Vanuatu and Kiribati are ranked below Samoa in the 'Medium Human Development' category, and the Solomon Islands and Papua New Guinea ranked in the 'Low Human Development' category.

Over the years 1990–2014 Samoa's HDI has steadily trended upwards from 0.621 (1990), 0.649 (2000), 0.696 (2010), to 0.702 (2015). The average annual HDI growth from 1990–2014 was 0.51. These years roughly coincide with Tuila'epa's premiership and provide objective evidence to support the view that Samoa has made steady progress on social and economic development during his successive administrations.

electricity for weeks, and food and water supply for many days depended on emergency aid.

New Zealand and Australia provided considerable emergency assistance and helped with the post-cyclone reconstruction and recovery of infrastructure and facilities. Samoans in the United States, Australia and New Zealand also helped finance the recovery by way of remittances to their relatives who suffered in the islands.

Two decades later, on 29 September 2009, a devastating tsunami struck the south-west coast of Samoa, and on 12 December 2012 Cyclone Evan precipitated an 'inland tsunami' that roared down the Vaisigano River valley, destroying homes and bridges and damaging the historic Aggie Grey's Hotel.

Once more, Tuila'epa provided the day-to-day, hands-on leadership of disaster management and relief efforts. This time the government of Samoa did not actively seek out funding and support from international donor nations. Tuila'epa stated that Samoa now had the capacity to manage the impact of the national disaster itself and promptly went about doing just that. This was a reflection of the growing confidence of Samoa to manage its own affairs.

Officials who observed Tuila'epa in action following Cyclone Evan provide 'eye witness'[9] accounts of his leadership of the relief efforts and Samoa's growing self-confidence, and capacity, to manage the aftermath of natural disasters:

'Following the 2009 tsunami I was fortunate to accompany the government of Samoa on an inspection of the devastated areas. Following the inspection, a meeting was called at the National University of Samoa lecture theatre, and all government ministers; public, private and civil society organisations; church leaders; and the donor community were invited along. It was the first time I had seen Tuila'epa in action. It was obviously a stressful time for Samoa, but Tuila'epa was assertive and confident in his address. As the area that was affected was only on the south coast of the main island of Upolu, Tuila'epa assured his people they could work together to fix the situation. Tuila'epa turned and asked each government department CEO to provide an update on the status of their work. After each update he gave them instructions on what to do from there, creating sub-committees to support their work. Tuila'epa also activated the Disaster Advisory Committee.

'It was so impressive to watch him take control of the situation and nothing fazed him, he was confident and didn't allow emotions to get in the way. He was remarkable and I felt so proud to be Samoan that day.'

9   See Ulu, 2013, for comments on post-tsunami recovery reports and Tuila'epa's role in the distribution and accounting of donor funds.

During natural disasters, donors usually appear to provide assistance, but there are varying motivations for their support. Our informant talked about a particular donor who had only recently arrived in Samoa and was not aware of the strength of the Samoan people. The donor tried to stand up to announce their contribution to the disaster but Tuila'epa closed down the announcement by directing the donor to a relevant committee. 'This wasn't about donors shining and wanting their assistance heard by the media, the focus was on Samoa and its people. We were so happy Tuila'epa did this; the donors would be acknowledged at another time.'

Following the relief efforts, Tuila'epa came under fire from the New Zealand news media. The narrative continues.

In 2009 TV3 presenter John Campbell aired a story accusing Tuila'epa of misappropriating donor funds for disaster relief efforts. An informant was keen to defend Tuila'epa, expressing loyalty and trust in his leadership. He said that all the funds for the tsunami were received, accounted for and disseminated through the government of Samoa's financial systems: 'Tuila'epa didn't touch it. He was never involved in the distribution of any money. Roads were operational the day after the tsunami with power line poles going up. Even relocation roads to the hills were starting to be cut out, it's an ongoing programme that is where the money was spent.'

Tuila'epa asked officials to prepare two reports: one shortly after the tsunami and another post-disaster relief action report. Both reports outline how 48 million Tala was spent.

Informants spoke with great respect of Tuila'epa and also felt he was unfairly accused by John Campbell. Following Campbell's story, donors who contributed money to the disaster relief effort returned to survey how their money was spent. They left feeling pleased with what they saw and did not question Tuila'epa or the government of Samoa on Campbell's accusations:
'With a strong Prime Minister, who is not intimidated by anyone, the government of Samoa officials who were interviewed held similar characteristics when working with donors. There is a level of patriotism attributed to Tuila'epa, and public servants were very protective of the Prime Minister and looked to him as a role model.'

Following Cyclones Val and 'Ofa, Samoa relied for many years on international aid donors and overseas disaster relief management experts for funding and guidance. In the two decades between Cyclones Val and 'Ofa and the tsunami and Cyclone Evan, the government and people of Samoa have developed the capacity, strategies and resilience to deal with the consequences and to mitigate the impact of natural disasters.

Over the last decades of the twentieth century and the first decade of the twenty-first, there appeared to be a marked increase in severe weather-related events impacting on Pacific Island nations. Research indicated an emerging pattern of increases in the frequency and intensity of cyclones and 'king' tides, increased coastal erosion and other related phenomena. Was this part of the normal range of natural events? Or was there an underlying cause or pattern?

During the early 1990s, climate scientists were slowly building research data that pointed towards increasing global warming and consequent climate change, including a rise in sea levels, precipitated by a range of 'man-made' (anthropogenic) factors. There appeared to be two main contributing causes: first, increased carbon dioxide, methane and other gas emissions from the burning of fossil fuels (coal, oil, diesel, etc.), the clearing of forests for agriculture, and agricultural emissions from large numbers of livestock creating a 'greenhouse' effect and heating the Earth's atmosphere; and second, the release of CFCs (chloro-flouro-carbons) from spray-cans and refrigerants leading to an enlarging hole in the ozone layer that protects the Earth's atmosphere.

The small island states of the Pacific, particularly coral atoll communities, were especially vulnerable to sea-level rise. In 1990 the Prime Minister of Tuvalu, Bikenibeu Paeniu, identified the impacts on his home island communities and was an early advocate for the reduction of the consumption of fossil fuels by large industrialised nations. The PIF soon became the focus for campaigns demanding political action on rising sea levels.

For some years the science of climate change was disputed, the producers of fossil fuels and the oil industry strongly resisted regulation, and there was very little political will from the USA to reduce emissions, who was producing over 25 percent of global carbon dioxide emissions. In contrast to carbon dioxide emissions, the emissions of CFCs and refrigerants were quickly regulated and bans enforced. Alternative technologies were developed and the hole in the ozone layer is now shrinking. Clearly, some aspects of man-made climate problems can be controlled through global action, but the larger problem of putting a halt to and reversing carbon dioxide emissions has proved to be more difficult.

Twenty-five years after the first Pacific Island leaders raised their concerns about climate change, the issue has become 'the world's most urgent problem and the greatest moral challenge of our time', said Prime Minister Tuila'epa in his address at the General Debate of the 69th Session of the United Nations General Assembly in New York on 26 September 2014.[10]

10   See Malielegaoi, 2014b.

Earlier that week Tuila'epa had addressed a United Nations 'Climate Change Summit',[11] reminding global leaders that 'Our Pacific countries had advocated, and continue to make the case that climate change has significant security implications . . . Climate change has political, social and economic implications for peace and security. It impacts on every country, more extensively on some, like small island states, than others because their capacity to respond quickly and effectively is constrained by their realities.' Tuila'epa warned that 'The time for waiting is over. Today, we are here to be part of the solution in our fight against the causes of climate change.' He went on to outline what Samoa was doing to achieve 20 percent carbon neutrality by 2030, achieve 100 percent renewable energy in power generation by 2017 and work towards energy-efficient transport. He concluded by saying that 'Samoa's approach is rooted in our conviction that the pathway to an energy-secure future is through a "Many-partners-one-goal approach".'

In late 2015 the issue of climate change moved from a marginal matter of interest for a few remote small island states to a major global concern, culminating in a series of international leaders' conferences and an agreement for action from all nations.

In December 2015, leaders from 196 nations participated in the United Nations Climate Change Conference, held in Paris. Negotiations were long and hard. The outcome was the conclusion of the Paris Agreement, an ambitious global accord on the reduction of climate change. The agreement sets a goal of limiting global warming to less than 2°C, compared to pre-industrial levels, and calls for zero net anthropogenic greenhouse gas emissions to be reached during the second half of the twenty-first century. The parties to the Agreement will also 'pursue efforts' to limit the temperature increase to 1.5°C. The 1.5°C goal will require zero emissions some time between 2030 and 2050.

The conclusion of the Paris Agreement was a triumph for Pacific Island leaders of vulnerable small island states, including Samoa. The intense diplomatic and moral campaign, based on scientific evidence and carried out over more than two decades, was successful. Tuila'epa's leadership within the Pacific region, and his international reputation, played an important part in this achievement.

Samoa will continue to experience severe weather events in the years to come. However, there is some comfort in knowing that Samoa is playing a key role in the international fight to mitigate and reduce the effects of anthropogenic global climate change.

11 See Malielegaoi, 2014a.

Regional Leadership and International Relations

Tuila'epa is now one of the Pacific's most senior statesmen and has also built considerable political influence outside the Pacific Islands region. Because of his early work at the ACP Secretariat in Brussels, Tuila'epa has long held an international perspective. His influence and relationships with global leaders has grown over the years. On first becoming Prime Minister, relations with New Zealand, Australia and the PIF nations were the priority. Now, regional and bilateral meetings with Chinese, Japanese, European and American leaders have become more significant. Wider relationships were particularly important during negotiations at the 2015 United Nations Climate Change Conference, leading to the Paris Agreement.

It is often said that all politics is local. Tuila'epa's grounding in political leadership started in the village *fono* of Lepā. To this day he is a regular participant as a local *matai* in village *fono*. This connection to the grassroots is important to Tuila'epa and is the basis of his confidence to participate in and speak at national, regional and international meetings. Successful leaders in any village *fono* must listen to their constituents, mediate conflicts, achieve compromises, make decisions and take action. Most importantly, good village leaders must build enduring relationships and work with people with whom they may disagree. The village *fono* is a great proving ground for gaining the skills of relationship-building, leadership and political savvy.

During his time as Prime Minister of Samoa, Tuila'epa's skills have been tested time and again in the regional and international arenas. Tuila'epa has regularly employed the 'Pacific Way' of *talanoa* in regional meetings and to manage regional problems through quiet conversations in private with other leaders. At annual PIF leaders' meetings, there is always a 'leaders' retreat' where leaders meet, without officials present, and where much of the talking takes place, problems are solved and key decisions are made. This strategy fits well with Pacific Island leaders who, like Tuila'epa, come from village communities where collective, consensus decision-making is customary.

The Pacific Way has been largely successful when leaders respect each other and each nation's sovereignty. However, in the case of Fiji, where the Fijian leader has been reluctant to sit and talk with his peers, the Pacific Way has not worked and Tuila'epa has had to employ other strategies.

Tuila'epa's international leadership was acknowledged recently when he was invited to address the United Nations Security Council, the first Pacific Island leader to be accorded this rare honour. The invitation came during New Zealand's term as a non-permanent member and chair of the Security Council.

Australia and New Zealand do not always acknowledge the role Tuila'epa and other Pacific leaders play in the Pacific Islands region and beyond. Although they are founding and senior members of the PIF, Australia and New Zealand do not instinctively view their own interests as closely linked to other smaller Pacific Island nations. This is perhaps a hangover from their colonial past and a denial of their Pacific future.

Dealing with Critics

Samoa has a lively and robust public discourse on matters of the day. In earlier times, debates were restricted to village *fono* where cultural protocols had to be observed and only certain people could speak and participate. Today, village *fono* remain a place where local and wider issues are discussed and cultural protocols continue to be observed, but discussions are also conducted through local newspapers, television, radio stations and social media, and anyone can, and does, participate.

Samoa is a small country and the public media debate can become very heated, personal and pointed. Critics can make comments that verge on slander and defamation, and from time to time legal actions are threatened and taken. This is the nature of the modern political discourse in Samoa.

Prime Minister Tuila'epa is often the focus of these public discussions and he participates in many of the debates by setting out and defending government policies and decisions. Indeed, there are times when he provokes discussion through his forthright public comments. However, Tuila'epa recognises that the office of the Prime Minister, and the government, need to maintain a certain level of dignity and at times to stand above the public fray.

Tuila'epa has his share of critics to whom he responds mostly with patience and humour and with the understanding that there is an aspect of media attention that is an entertaining game played in the public arena, with winners and losers. Maintaining the dignity of the office of Prime Minister, keeping a sense of proportion and having a sense of humour are important to Tuila'epa. Dignity, proportion and humour in the public domain are not easily achieved when commentators use the banners of 'freedom of speech' and 'freedom of the media' as vehicles to make unsubstantiated allegations of corruption, favouritism and wrongdoing.

The *Samoa Observer* newspaper is the major forum for public debate in Samoa. Most weeks, a casual reader will find a controversial headline, editorial or article about a current issue. Comments from local people, interviewed in the streets, are often published. And there are many Letters to the Editor expressing a wide range of opinions. For example, following Manu Samoa's poor showing in the 2015 Rugby World Cup, the *Samoa Observer* headline shouted: 'SHAMEFUL'. Team selections, performance, strategies, management, coaching and all aspects of the Rugby World Cup campaign, including the Prime Minister's role as president of the Samoan Rugby Union, were up for comment, debate and criticism. Sport, along with politics, excites passionate opinions from many Samoans.

The *Samoa Observer* is proud of its media freedom awards[12] and has been a long-standing advocate for public debate through a free press. Often leading the charge is executive editor Savea Sano Malifa who has been an open critic of successive prime ministers and other public figures over the years. Prime Minister Tuila'epa has been a frequent target. Malifa's editorial, entitled 'Justice versus corruption!' (*Sunday Samoan*, 12 July 2015), is just one example of his attacks on the Prime Minister and his government.

The timing of this editorial was interesting. The previous week had seen Samoa host a hugely successful event: New Zealand's All Blacks playing Samoa's Manu Samoa at Apia Park. Villages from Faleolo Airport to Apia were decked out in flags and flowers to welcome the All Blacks team. John Key, the New Zealand Prime Minister, led a large delegation to watch the game. A close result ensued and Samoa was in party mode for a week.

The *Sunday Samoan* editorial, four days after the rugby game, pricked and deflated the party balloons. Malifa's editorial began: 'Now that the mesmerising euphoria, sparked by the All Black's visit last week, is truly out of the way, perhaps it's time to return to our everyday life and confront those nagging, unfinished businesses that are continuing to stare at us defiantly in the face. One of which features Prime Minister Tuila'epa Sa'ilele Malielegaoi on one side, and on the other side is the Associate Minister of Public Enterprises Papali'i Niko Lee Hang. [This e]merged three months ago when it was dealt with publicly for the first time, somehow it was aborted and since then it had not been heard of again.'

Malifa then went on to rehearse the details of a matter of alleged corruption, including quotations from documents that had been 'leaked' to the *Sunday Samoan*. The Prime Minister's attempts to set the record straight were turned back on him. When Tuila'epa is quoted as saying, 'As MPs and the legislators of the country, we have to look at what is best for Samoa. That is our overall goal,' Malifa sarcastically responds, 'Fine speech. The only little snag is that from what's been gathered from his speech it looks as if Tuila'epa's brain is the

---

12 They won the 2000 'World Press Freedom Hero' Award from the International Press Institute, and the 2001 PINA/PNG Media Council Press Freedom Award.

one that needs to be checked: and then instead of just at 10 am, it should be ten times ten every day.'

After this very personal insult, the editorial comes very close to calling the Prime Minister corrupt and a liar. Malifa continued, 'as the prime minister of this country for the last fifteen years – he should know what the word honesty means. And if for some unknown reason he'd still not known by then, then obviously that explains why this country has become so immune to corruption so that it might as well be scuttled, and let's say goodbye to life.'

A number of further *Observer* articles reported 'rumours' that a new political party was to be set up, 'speculation' about Papali'i Niko Lee Hang's political ambitions and a leadership challenge. These were finally laid to rest in an article headlined 'Papali'i Niko remains loyal', and the matter quietly faded away.

This is but one example of the criticism Tuila'epa regularly faces in the media.

When asked how he deals with the constant public criticism, Tuila'epa said: 'There is a wise saying in Samoa, "Leave the birds to sing their songs to their death." Sano deliberately over-sensationalises for money, to sell his newspapers. I have a way now to get at Sano. He knows that I know what he is doing, so I play the game. At the same time Sano remembers that I saved him from going to prison from a court case put in by Tofilau.[13] What he does not know is that I was behind that court case. I had been pressuring Tofilau to take the case because the defamation was enormous on the old man and he [Sano] was heading towards prison until I intervened. So he knew I saved him. It's all part of the game.'

The *Samoa Observer* appears to have a 'love–hate' relationship with Tuila'epa. On 3 January 2012 the Prime Minister was named the Person of the Decade by the newspaper.

In profiling Tuila'epa as Person of the Decade, the editor of the *Samoa Observer* wrote 'one has to understand that he believes he's always right, never wrong'. While Tuila'epa has many detractors and critics, he still receives overwhelming support from his district and fellow MPs. It was noted that Tuila'epa has been Prime Minister of Samoa for thirteen years and an MP for his constituency of Lepā for 30 years.

'As far as he is concerned,' according to the *Observer*, 'anyone who questions him is either insanely wrong or an unforgivable idiot. His uncompromising controversial views are usually the heart of many heated political arguments

---

13 See Bisson, 1998, for the Judgement in Alesana v Samoa Observer Co. and Savea Sano Malifa.

among Samoans locally and overseas.' The newspaper claimed that Tuila'epa feels that way because 'he believes he is chosen to do anything he thinks is right to move Samoa forward economically, never mind what anyone else thinks'. The *Samoa Observer*'s sardonic Person of the Decade headline read: 'Tuila'epa Sa'ilele Malielegaoi — The Chosen One.'

Tuila'epa subsequently wrote to the editor declining the award and setting out in detail why he did not meet the three criteria for the award (that he was anointed by God, that he is right all the time, and that he talks to God person to person). Tuila'epa said that he failed on all three counts. Savea declined to take the award back and replied, 'Whether you like it not, I am going to give you the award.'

It is a fact that sensational stories and controversies sell newspapers. This is true in Samoa as it is elsewhere. Samoa is a small country and public figures know each other well. Often they went to school together, live nearby, and are related to each other through cultural and family connections. The public utterances of the editor-in-chief of the *Samoa Observer* and the Prime Minister need to be viewed in this context. Despite earlier critical editorials and cutting remarks, the front page of the *Samoa Observer* of 1 April 2016 sported a large photograph of Savea Sano Malifa and Tuila'epa Sa'ilele Malielegaoi standing side by side as the Prime Minister launched *Our Heritage, the Ocean*, a book of Pacific writing edited by Savea Sano Malifa.

Tuila'epa says that he worked out that one way of 'playing the media game' and avoiding having his words distorted or flung back at him was to get on the front foot by communicating his message to the public through other means. Radio is very popular in Samoa and has proven to be a useful vehicle for Tuila'epa.

Way back in 2011, a week before the election, 2AP (Samoa's main radio station) management came and asked if they could interview me. The purpose was really to provide information leading up to the general election. Of course, the additional purpose was to make their news popular. So I told them to shoot. And as usual I gave them exactly what I thought.

I remember one of the typical questions was whether I would ever consider opening up absentee votes from overseas. I said, 'I am the sixth Prime Minister and since PMs one, two, three, four and five saw the wisdom of keeping the status quo, I will never allow it to change. If you want to vote for your country, come on a plane and vote here.' We have only about 200,000 people here in Samoa. There are many more Samoans overseas and, if we give them the green light, there will be a time when decisions on leadership will be made by Samoans living overseas who do not know the needs of Samoa. Worse still, it could lead to a Parliament of Samoans, all living in South Auckland, convening their parliament in a pub in Māngere! So I will never allow it so long as I am Prime Minister.

Ever since then, 2AP have been coming to me. They do an interview every Thursday and call it *The PM and 2AP*. Now, I have had that programme for six years and it's still going. They throw me any kind of question. That's dangerous if you don't have the answers. But I have always managed to turn that [to my advantage]. Many people are listening into that programme each Thursday and I use the occasion to also explain government policies related to anything they put to me that has a public interest so that these are better understood. I think about the political angle I am using on this programme. By educating our people we are getting more mileage in preparation for the next general elections.

*

Samoa is a conservative society where social change is often slow. The role of women in Samoan society is a sensitive issue that has sparked much debate and discussion. A report on political representation and women's empowerment authored by Leasiolagi Dr Malama Meleisea, Director of Samoan Studies at the National University of Samoa, based on his research in many village communities, sparked controversy and debate.

Tuila'epa claimed parts of the report were 'nonsense', and Meleisea's rejection of the Prime Minister's comments were headlined 'Academic rejects P.M.'s claims' in the *Sunday Samoan* (12 July 2015).

Tuila'epa's argument that part of the report was inaccurate was quickly misrepresented as him calling the whole report 'nonsense'. As he explained, 'I think Meleisea is feeling the brunt of my words. It was a debate in Parliament about the shortage of women in Parliament, in which somebody mentioned that there was a report written by Dr Meleisea of the National University of Samoa. I said I had read that report and was disappointed with the views expressed which talk of the "village" of the young men, the "village" of the women and the "village" of the *matai*. That's all rubbish, there is only one village – the village under the direction of the council of *matai*.'

Tuila'epa explains his position.

Flowing from the chiefs are the orders to be executed by everybody. Executed by the *taule'ale'a*, the young men. Executed by the women. Since the women have also taken on *matai* titles, that council is all inclusive. Therefore, all this rubbish about a separate village of *matai*, a separate village of young men and a separate village of women can only come from people who do not spend enough time in the village to understand the complex role of the *fono matai*. There is only one authority and that is the authority that flows in from the decisions of the *matai* of the village. Everybody must listen to them and abide by their rulings.

I think he [Meleisea] took it badly. The reason why? There are people who like to go around [saying things] which sound original and nice without really looking at where the power comes from. And the power emanates from the *matai*. That's the core issue. The *taule'ale'a* don't have any power. They do what the *matai* tell them to do.

Referring to the parliamentary debate, Tuila'epa said:

I spoke at length emphasising the need for the chiefs and the councils of the villages to give those alleged to have committed a crime a chance to answer for themselves before any sanctions are imposed. That's all you need to do. If they do that, the likelihood is that, if the village is sued in court, the very question raised would be, 'Did you give them an opportunity to defend themselves?' Then if the answer is yes, the court sides with the village. It comes back to the question of fairness – fairness to people who you rule. You must recognise the dignity of the people that you rule. Due process must be followed.

When he is talking about social and moral issues, as he frequently does in Parliament, Tuila'epa frequently uses Samoan custom or biblical references for exemplars.

I told them of two instances. One, the first court case that God presided over as judge was when He gave judgment to Adam and Eve. They disobeyed an order. As we all know, a judge gives the accused the opportunity to defend themselves before he makes a decision. In the case of Adam and Eve the judge [God] knows every everything, but he nevertheless gave the opportunity to Adam and Eve to say their bit before judgment was given. And why did he do that? It was a precedent that the Lord set for us to follow.

The second question is related to the famous biblical edict of the Persian

Empire that a law enacted should remain effective for eternity and that inflexibility could only lead to its demise. The clear lesson is for *matai* to be pragmatic. The council of the *matai* must take into consideration the reality of our times and the kinds of matters they are dealing with. That is what I said. And Meleisea must have listened.

This exchange with Meleisea in the media could be interpreted as Tuila'epa taking a reluctant, conservative approach towards the advancement of women in Samoan society. His record of leading steady, gradual change, in tune with the mores of Samoan society, challenges that view. For example, in an address to a Global Leaders' Meeting on Gender Equality and Women's Empowerment delivered in New York in October 2015, Tuila'epa set out his government's policies and achievements on promoting equal access to education and employment opportunities, strengthening women's participation in the private and government sectors, and increasing the representation of women in leadership roles.

Tuila'epa readily admitted that improvement is still needed and stated, 'Samoa recognises that gender equality and women's empowerment and the full realisation of human rights for women and girls have a transformative and multiplier effect on sustainable development.' He continued, 'Women can be powerful agents of change.' The outcome of his commitment to women's leadership was illustrated in a ceremony on 5 February 2016 when thirteen CEOs of government were sworn in. Seven of the new appointees were women. This fact was not commented upon or talked up in the media; Tuila'epa was happy to let the facts speak for themselves.

Political Leadership

When it comes to social change, Tuila'epa is a gradualist and pragmatist, rather than a revolutionary or a conservative. He appears to be able to sense the mood of the Samoan general public and tailors his legislative programme, political policies and public comments to reflect that mood and move at their pace. In this way, he takes the people with him.

All successful political leaders must find a way of 'taking the people with them'. Particular challenges in Samoa are the underlying tensions between central government and village government.

Writing about Samoan politics in a 1983 book, Meleisea quoted the Samoan proverb '*O lē i'a vai a Malo*' (governmental power is like a slippery fish), and noted that 'Samoan political action, authority and power, has its roots in the extended family (*'āiga*) and from these roots, political authority is legitimated at village, district and national levels. At least, for Samoans, this is the way things should be and the way things are remembered to have been.'[14]

More recently, So'o (2008) stated, 'Centralised state power under the leadership of the government of the day is a modern phenomenon that conflicts with the existing indigenous political system, whose most visible expression in modern Samoa is village governments. Village governments have always detested central government interference with their traditionally established authority. Accordingly, succeeding central governments have found it wise and practical to cooperate with them rather than trying to impose their constitutional powers.'

How has Tuila'epa managed to catch the slippery fish?

The stories and evidence presented in this book lead us to the conclusion that Tuila'epa has successfully managed to net the slippery fish of Samoan politics by maintaining his role in the *Fa'asamoa* as a *matai* and keeping a close connection between central government and village governance, thereby taking the people of Samoa with him on his political journey.

As a boy in Lepā, Tuila'epa was schooled in the ways of the *Fa'asamoa*, and later as a *matai* he was engaged in *fa'amatai* in the village *fono*. Throughout his life, in spite of working overseas and his responsibilities in Apia, this thread connecting Tuila'epa to village life remains unbroken. He has always maintained his *monotaga*. There is much in Tuila'epa's political 'style' (telling stories and jokes, teasing critics, citing biblical stories) that is part of the banter popular amongst village *matai*, which all Samoans can relate to. Pompous leaders who take themselves too seriously often become the butt of jokes in the village and around the *'ava* bowls. Tuila'epa has the 'common touch'.

Complementing his role in *fa'amatai* in the village *fono*, Tuila'epa has long demonstrated his competence in the *palagi* world through his political management, administration of the economy, financial acumen, and governance skills in national, regional and international settings. Tuila'epa has been referred to as 'Samoa's most outstanding contemporary politician and leader'.[15]

Political leadership is the defining theme of Tuila'epa's career, and it has been his ability to combine the *Fa'asamoa* and the *fa'apalagi* that has enabled him to 'take the people with him' and maintain a long and successful political career.

Tuila'epa's political career has been linked closely with the development

---

14 See Crocombe and Ali, 1983.
15 See Victoria University of Wellington, 2012.

of political parties in Samoa and growth of the HRPP. He entered Parliament during the time of the consolidation of the HRPP, refused overtures to join other political groupings and has led the HRPP for five terms. The core principles and guiding slogans of the HRPP bear the stamp of Tuila'epa's political leadership philosophy:

'[The] HRPP's core principle is that physical works speak louder than words. It is our vision to raise the standard of life for all people throughout Samoa. Hence our guiding slogan:
  "*O le mea e lelei i Apia, e lelei foi i nu'u i tua.*
  O le mea e lelei i Apia, e lelei foi mo Savaii.
  What's good in town is also good in the rural villages.
  What is good for Apia is also good for Savaii."'[16]

Political slogans can be inspiring or just cheap rhetoric. To become meaningful they must be backed up by action and results.

Samoan society is intimate. In a country of less than 200,000 people, where identity is tied to family and village, politics remains personal and reputations rise and fall according to how you live your life. It is said that Samoa is a village. And like all villages, gossip is the currency of exchange in Samoa.

Tuila'epa's daily life is as much that of a village *matai* as it is a Prime Minister. He often drives himself in an unmarked car, he shops at the local village store, plays golf with his old friends, lives in an unguarded household with his extended family, and lacks the ever-present security detail, minders and communications advisers that other prime ministers see as necessities. Each Sunday he goes to church, sings in the choir and presides over his church's fund-raising committee. After church, he enjoys *to'ona'i* alongside the other village *matai* at Lepā. Tuila'epa's deep Catholic faith, his wife Gillian and his large extended family are his anchors.

Throughout Samoa, village people convey their problems and concerns to their *matai* for advice, help and resolution. Tuila'epa's many *matai* titles bind him to a string of village communities and the day-to-day concerns which they frequently bring to him. Delegations from village *matai*, church leaders and other organisations often turn up at his office or home to seek an audience. These meetings frequently involve long speeches and can be very time-consuming. In many other countries officials of the Prime Minister's Office would deal with most issues and shield their prime minister from all but the most urgent and important matters. This is not the Samoan way, and Tuila'epa

---

16 See HRPP, 2016c.

accepts this reality and maintains his availability. Relationships in his view are important and are best transacted face-to-face.

Working and living this way ensures that Tuila'epa maintains a close finger on the pulse of life in Samoa and is able to take the people with him.

Epilogue: The Future

Prime Minister Tuila'epa Sa'ilele Malielegaoi sits at the head of the large table in the Cabinet Room. He can see the photographs of his five predecessors looking down on him. They have been his constant companions through his seventeen-year political apprenticeship and now his longer premiership. Some have been his mentors; others his rivals. All have influenced him.

Fiamē Mata'afa Faumuinā Mulinu'u II, who steered Samoa through the process of gaining independence and the first decade of the new parliamentary democracy, showed Tuila'epa the need to keep the *Fa'asamoa* constantly in mind. As *tama-a-'āiga* he symbolised continuity with the past and stability as Samoa moved into an unknowable future. Mata'afa's preference for consensus politics, his gravitas, wisdom and chiefly presence, deeply grounded in *fa'amatai* and the *Fa'asamoa*, shaped the unique style of Samoa's governance and political development and made a deep impression on the young Tuila'epa.

Consensus politics went into decline when Tupua Tamasese Lealofi IV, Samoa's second Prime Minister and another *tama-a-'āiga*, was elected following intense negotiations between traditional factions supporting candidates for ministerial positions. So'o argues that Tamasese's 'government's liberal economic policies, accelerated development programmes, and departure from consensus politics cost it the 1973 general election'. Tuila'epa learned that a prime minister must take the people with him or his tenure will be brief.

Mata'afa returned for another term, rebuilding consensus politics, but passed away in office to be replaced by Tamasese Lealofi IV as 'custom overrode the Constitution' when the Head of State appointed the former Prime Minister. This 'extra-constitutional' intervention by Mālietoa Tanumafili II was to be repeated on two more occasions and led to Tuila'epa developing a suspicion that *tama-a-'āiga* would always look after *tama-a-'āiga,* ahead of adhering to the Constitution, and deepened his mistrust in the motives of the individuals involved.

Tupuola Tufuga Taisi Efi was the first non-*tama-a-'āiga* elected Prime

Minister. He was the leader of a new generation, keen to push aside the conservative post-independence politics of the older generation and who moved to modernise Samoa from the bottom up. Tuila'epa, a young government technocrat at that time, was initially an enthusiastic supporter, but his experience of working closely with Tupuola Efi quickly led to disenchantment with and resentment of Efi's high-handed approach to governance and his autocratic tendencies. This was young Tuila'epa's first experience of the harsh realities of Samoan politics. He learnt fast and toughened up. Tuila'epa considered Tupuola Efi a leader who surrounded himself with 'yes' people, that he was not open to contrary views, did not value constructive arguments and succumbed to hubris. Tuila'epa subsequently headed overseas to Europe for better career opportunities. Tupuola Efi, later as Tui Ātua Tupua Tamasese, would become Tuila'epa's greatest political rival.

Meanwhile, in 1976, Va'ai Kolone began his bid for leadership in a close contest against Tupuola Efi and was successful in 1979, heralding the birth of political parties with the establishment of the HRPP. This was the beginning of a period of intense political instability with several quick changes of prime minister. Returning from Europe, Tuila'epa entered Parliament in 1981 at a time when Tupuola Efi had regained the premiership. Va'ai, Tofilau 'Eti Alesana and Va'ai again had short terms as prime minister. The political instability during his early years in Parliament, and the advantages of political parties, left a deep impression on Tuila'epa.

Tuila'epa first sat at the Cabinet table during Tofilau 'Eti Alesana's first administration. He had some early confrontations and conflicts with Tofilau but developed a very close relationship with him over time. Tuila'epa stood up for Tofilau against Va'ai in 1985, when Va'ai split and left the HRPP. Tuila'epa admired Tofilau's integrity when he stood down as leader rather than create a constitutional crisis. And Tuila'epa turned down offers by Va'ai, for CEO of the Samoa Trust Estates Corporation in April 1982, and by Tupuola Efi, for the Finance portfolio in October 1982. Tuila'epa's loyalty to Tofilau was absolute.

During Tofilau's decade as Prime Minister, Tuila'epa was at his side, learning from the successes and failures and deepening his understanding of what it meant to be a leader in Samoa and in the wider world. As Tofilau's health failed, Tuila'epa, like a dutiful son, took on much of the ailing Prime Minister's workload, responsibilities and duties. When his time came, Tuila'epa had developed the knowledge, experience and political skills to manage a smooth succession.

As he looks back, Tuila'epa observes that he has learnt much from each of his predecessors, reflects on those who have supported his political career, and remembers the saying that his father gave him for guidance: *E le taua le*

Epilogue

tofi, ae taua le fa'amaoni (it is not the status or the position that is important, it is your ability to work hard, do good and serve others).

Now, as he looks to the future, Tuila'epa wonders who will be his successor. Tuila'epa believes that callings are divinely determined and, like Abraham, has the faith that at the right time a lamb will be chosen for the sacrifice. Is the next Prime Minister of Samoa already sitting at the Cabinet table looking at the six leaders' photographs and wondering if they will be next? Or is the next leader outside, waiting for their chance to enter? These are questions for the future.

In the meantime, Tuila'epa Sa'ilele Malielegaoi continues his lifelong commitment to serve Samoa, the country he loves.

Samoa Observer, 2016

Appendix: Tuila'epa Sa'ilele Malielegaoi's Parliamentary Career and Matai Titles

May 1981 to November 1981
Tupuola Tufuga Taisi Efi's second administration

Member of Parliament for Lepā

April 1982 to August 1982
Va'ai Kolone's first administration

Member of Parliament for Lepā

August 1982 to December 1982
Tupuola Tufuga Taisi Efi's third administration

Member of Parliament for Lepā

December 1982 to April 1985
Tofilau Eti Alesana's first administration

Member of Parliament for Lepā
Minister of Economic Affairs
Minister of Transport and Civil Aviation
Associate Minister of Finance
Minister of Finance (after Cabinet reshuffle in 1984)

April 1985 to December 1985
Tofilau 'Eti Alesana's second administration

Member of Parliament for Lepā

Minister of Economic Affairs
Minister of Finance

January 1986 to April 1988
Va'ai Kolone's Coalition administration

Member of Parliament for Lepā
HRPP (Opposition) Finance Spokesman

April 1988 to December 1990
Tofilau 'Eti Alesana's third administration

Member of Parliament for Lepā
Minister of Finance
Minister of Tourism
Minister of Trade, Commerce and Industry

January 1991 to December 1995
Tofilau 'Eti Alesana's fourth administration

Member of Parliament for Lepā
Minister of Finance
Minister of Tourism
Minister of Trade, Commerce and Industry

January 1996 to November 1998
Tofilau 'Eti Alesana's fifth administration

Member of Parliament for Lepā
Deputy Prime Minister and Minister in charge of:
Ministry of Finance
Ministry of Tourism
Ministry of Trade, Commerce and Industry

November 1998 to March 2001
Tuila'epa Sa'ilele Malielegaoi's first administration

Member of Parliament for Lepā
Prime Minister and Minister in charge of:

Appendix

Ministry of Finance
Ministry of Police
Ministry of Foreign Affairs
Ministry of Legislative Assembly
Ministry of Telecommunications

April 2001 to March 2006
Tuila'epa Sa'ilele Malielegaoi's second administration

Member of Parliament for Lepā
Prime Minister and Minister in charge of:
Ministry of Foreign Affairs and Trade
Ministry of Police
Minister of Telecommunications

April 2006 to March 2011
Tuila'epa Sa'ilele Malielegaoi's third administration

Member of Parliament for Lepā
Prime Minister and Minister in charge of:
Ministry of the Prime Minister and Cabinet and Immigration
Ministry of Foreign Affairs and Trade
Office of the Attorney-General

March 2011 to February 2016
Tuila'epa Sa'ilele Malielegaoi's fourth administration

Member of Parliament for Lepā
Prime Minister and Minister in charge of:
Ministry of the Prime Minister and Cabinet and Immigration
Ministry of Foreign Affairs and Trade
Office of the Attorney-General
Samoa Tourism Authority
Samoa Land Corporation
Public Service Commission

March 2016 to Present
Tuila'epa Sa'ilele Malielegaoi's fifth administration

Member of Parliament for Lepā
Prime Minister and Minister in charge of:
Ministry of the Prime Minister and Cabinet [inclusive of Cabinet Affairs and Immigration]
Ministry of Foreign Affairs and Trade
Office of the Attorney General
Public Service Commission

Matai Titles

Samoan chiefly titles *matai* are conferred on men and women who have the requisite genealogy *gafa* and have served their families, villages and communities. Each title is linked to a specific location.

Tuila'epa is the bearer of seven other *matai* titles: Fatialofa, 'Auelua, Lupesoli'ai, Neioti, 'A'iono, Galumalemana, Lolofietele, and also the title 'Grand Chief of Papua New Guinea'.

Lepā village is divided into three main villages: Lepā Central, Salepāga and 'A'ufaga. Lepā Central, the seat of power, includes Lealetele and Vaigalu. Salepāga has two sub-villages. 'A'ufaga has two sub-villages.

Tuila'epa lists his titles and their locations:

In 1975 I became **Tuila'epa**, which is a high chief's title at Lealetele.
In 1977 my mother said to me one day, 'Let us go to my village, 'A'ufaga, we will grant you the title in my family **Lupesoli'ai**.'
In 1996 I was conferred the title of **Neioti** from Falevao.
In 2003 my grandfather's village, Fasito'o, conferred on me the **'A'iono** title
In 2010 I was conferred the **Fatialofa** title in Lepā. This is the highest of all my titles throughout the district.
In 2015 I was conferred the **'Auelua** title from the Lepā village.
'Auelua and Fatialofa are the top orators of our village and the top orators of our district which goes all the way from Aleipata to Lufilufi.
In 2015 September I was conferred the **Galumalemana** at Vaitele from my wife's family.
In January 2016 I was conferred the **Lolofie** title from Lealetele.

Through my titles I am a representative of four significant families:

Malietoa Family, Sa Fenunuivao family, Sa Tuala Family, Sa Levalasi family. Tuila'epa is a title within the Malietoa family. A long time ago a Tuila'epa held the title Malietoa. Neioti is of the Sa Fenunuivao family that controls Tui Ātua, Tupua Tamasese's title. Tui Ātua is the royal son. But the families control the title. I hold the Sa Fenunuivao title, Neioti. The 'A'iono title is from Fasito'o. The Sa Tuala family that also has a say in the control of the Tupua title. Lupesoli'ai is of the Sa Levalasi family.

As a Galumalemana, they call me Alo Ali'i.

Glossary of Samoan Terms

Notes: The Samoan language contains many terms that have ordinary/common versions and polite/respectful versions. Context is important in determining word choice. Formal language is used when addressing chiefs or in formal settings and often has metaphorical meanings, e.g., sleep, *tōfā (polite form)* or *moe* (common). Colloquial, casual speech often utilises the 'k' style and formal speech the 't' style (e.g., *kalofa, talofa; kava, 'ava*).

Samoan language has five vowels and thirteen consonants, plus the glottal stop, an additional speech sound represented by a reversed apostrophe ('). It occurs before or between vowels in many Samoan words and is treated as a consonant. Glottal stops and macrons (e.g., ā, ō, ū) must be carefully observed to ensure correct meaning (e.g., *ava*, reef passage; *'ava*, cup of *kava*).

See Hunkin (2009), Milner (1966) or Pratt (1977) for further explanation of Samoan grammar and the terms listed in this glossary.

afā	cyclone, storm
'ai āfu	person who lives off other's work, *lit.* sweat eater
'āiga	family
'āiga potopoto	extended family
aisakulimi	ice cream
aitu	traditional household gods, ghosts, spirits
ala	road, way or path
ali'i	high chief, sitting chief
alo	child, son or daughter
Ātua	God
aualuma	the daughters of the village
'aumāga	the sons of the village
'ava	kava, beverage made from the root of *Piper*

	methysticum used in Samoan ceremonies; it also refers to the ceremony itself. This is the more chiefly expression, *kava* is more common.
'ēlei	dyed material made by rubbing on pattern-board, traditionally on *siapo* or *tapa* cloth, now on cotton
fa'aatuaatua	talk about spirits, ghosts
Fa'afetai tele lava	thank you very much
fa'alavelave	special event: funeral, wedding, church opening etc., often requiring contributions of food, mats and money
fa'alupega	traditional honorific address referring to the order of precedence at village, district and national levels
fa'apalagi	the European or Western (*palagi*) way
fa'amatai	the customary political system
Fa'asamoa, fa'a Samoa	Samoan custom and way of life
fa'avae	foundation
faife'au	church minister, pastor
failoto	pastor
faipule	Member of Parliament; electoral area
fale	house or building
fale sa	large church building
faletua	the wife of an *ali'i*
faletua ma tausi	the wives of *ali'i* (*faletua*) and *tulafale* (*tausi*)
fatauliga matagi	cross-winds
fautasi	long boat
feagaiga	sacred covenant between a woman and her brother or two kin groups
fiafia	happiness, celebration or entertainment
fono	council or meeting
fono matai	village council of chiefs
gafa	genealogy

gagana Samoa	Samoan language
i'a	fish
'ie faitaga	formal, tailored *lāvalava* for men
'ie toga, 'ie Samoa,	fine mats made from pandanus leaves bleached white and finely woven to a silky texture, also referred to as: *'ie sina, 'ie Malo, moe I le aufuefue, pepeve'a, pipii I le eleele*
ifoga	traditional rite of apology seeking forgiveness
igāve'a	hide and seek
itūmālō	district
kava	see *'ava*
kilikiti, kirikiti	Samoan cricket
koko alaisa	cocoa rice
koko Samoa	hot drink made from grated cocoa
komiti faletua ma tausi	village women's committee
kopai	a sweetened soup of round flour balls
lalaga	mats of lesser quality, also *fa'alavelave* mats
lauga	speech or oratory
lāvalava	clothes, man's kilt
lu'au	*palusami*, see below
Mafutaga a Tina	Church Women's Fellowship
mālō	government, legislative assembly, power
mālō!	well done
malosi	strength
maota	house for high-ranking chief
matai	chief
matai pālota	*matai* title created for electoral purposes
moa	centre
moe	sleep (common form)
monotaga	traditional chiefly service to one's village
nonu	fruit of the Nonu tree

Glossary

niu	coconut palm, juice from coconuts
Niu Sila	New Zealand
nu'u	village
O le Ao o le Malo	Head of State
'ofu lu'au	the person who prepares lu'au
palagi, papalagi	foreigner, *lit.* cloud burster
Pālemia	Prime Minister
palusami, lu'au	dish made with young *taro* leaves and coconut cream baked in an *umu*, a delicacy
pāpā	high title, with *au pāpā* being the most prominent title
patele	priest
pisupo	corned beef
povi māsima	salt beef, usually beef bones in a barrel (*paelo*, today in a white plastic bucket) of salty water
Pule	a political group of paramount orator chiefs representing districts on Savai'i
pule	leadership, authority
pulenu'u	village mayor
sa	sacred
saofa'i	ceremony for the conferral of chiefly titles
Savali o le Filemu	March for Peace
siapo	bark-cloth made from paper mulberry; see also *tapa*
sua	formal presentation
Sui O Le Fono a Sui Tofia	Council of Deputies
tagāti'a	stick flyer game
talanoa	the Pacific Way; talking together
tama	boy
tama ali'i	chief
tama-a-'āiga	the holder of one of the four paramount titles of Samoa

tamaʻitaʻi	untitled women of the village, young women
tapa	bark-cloth made from paper mulberry; see also *siapo*
taro, talo	taro, *Colocasia sp.*
tauleʻaleʻa	untitled men of the village, youth
taupou	title of village maiden, usually the daughter of *aliʻi*
tautua	service to one's *matai*
teine	girl
teuila	red ginger shrub, *Alpinia sp.*, Samoa's national flower
toa	warrior, brave, hero
tōfā	sleep (polite form)
tōfā soifua!	good-bye, farewell
togafiti	trickery
togi-a-gogu	*nonu* fruit throwing game at night
toʻonaʻi	Sunday lunch
toʻotoʻo	staff held by an orator speaking on a formal occasion
tuafafine	sister
tuagane	brother of a woman
tulafale	orator chief
Tumua	a political group of paramount orator chiefs representing districts on Upolu and Safotu on Savaiʻi
ʻula	garland of flowers, necklace
ʻulafala	necklace of seeds, often painted red
ʻulu	breadfruit, *Artocarpus sp.*
umu	stone oven
va fealoaʻi	respect
velovelo	spear-throwing game

Abbreviations

ACP	African, Caribbean and Pacific
ADB	Asian Development Bank
AOG	Assemblies of God
AOSIS	Association of Small Island States
APEC	Asia–Pacific Economic Cooperation
CDP	Christian Democratic Party
CFCs	chloro-flouro-carbons
CHOGM	Commonwealth Heads of Government Meeting
CROP	Council for Regional Organisations in the Pacific
EFKS	Ekalesia Faapotopototoga Kerisiano Samoa (Congregational Christian Church of Samoa)
EPC	Electrical Power Corporation
FSM	Federated States of Micronesia
HDI	Human Development Index
HRPP	Human Rights Protection Party
ICT	Information and Communications Technology
IMF	International Monetary Fund
LDC	Least Developed Countries
LMS	London Missionary Society
MSG	Melanesian Spearhead Group [of the Pacific Islands Forum]
NUS	National University of Samoa

ODA	overseas development assistance
OPEC	Organization of Petroleum Exporting Countries
PALM	Pacific Island Leaders' Meeting
PASS	People Against Side Switch
PFL	Pacific Forum Line
PIF	Pacific Islands Forum
PLG	Polynesian Leaders Group [of the Pacific Islands Forum]
PNG	Papua New Guinea
PPA	Pacific Power Association
PRC	People's Republic of China
PSA	Public Service Association
SAMOA Pathway	SIDS Accelerated Modalities of Action Pathway
SAPP	Samoa All People's Party
SIDS	Small Islands Developing States
SLC	Samoa Land Corporation
SNDP	Samoa National Development Party
SPC	Secretariat of the Pacific Community, previously known as the South Pacific Commission
SPREP	Secretariat of the Regional Environment Programme
SROS	Scientific Research Organisation of Samoa
STEC	Samoa Trust Estates Corporation
TSP	Tautua Samoa Party
UE	University Entrance (New Zealand)
UNDP	United Nations Development Programme
UNESCO	United Nations Educational, Scientific and Cultural Organization
USAID	United States Agency for International Development
USP	University of the South Pacific
VAGST	Value Added Goods and Services Tax
VUW	Victoria University of Wellington
WIBDI	Women in Business Development Incorporated

References

Note: A substantial part of *Pālemia: Prime Minister Tuila'epa of Samoa – A Memoir* is based on the recordings of Tuila'epa's conversations with Peter Swain. After publication, digital copies of the recordings and the transcripts will be deposited in the J.C. Beaglehole Room in the Library at Victoria University of Wellington and will be available for academic research.

Alesana, T., 1983. *Budget Statement by the Prime Minister and the Minister of Finance, Hon Tofilau 'Eti Alesana*, Western Samoa Parliamentary Hansard, 8 February 1983, pp 4–13.

Alesana, T., 1998. *Statement by Hon Tofilau 'Eti Alesana*, Samoa Parliamentary Hansard, 23 November 1998, pp 970–75.

Bisson, Sir G., 1998. *Judgement in the Supreme Court of Western Samoa, WSSC 1; C.P. 042/1997, between Tofilau 'Eti Alesana, Plaintiff, and Samoa Observer Company Limited, First Defendant and Savea Sano Malifa, Second Defendant*, delivered 6 July 1998.

Campbell, I., 1992. *A History of the Pacific Islands*, Christchurch: University of Canterbury Press.

Crocombe, R. and A. Ali, 1983. *Politics in Polynesia*, Suva: University of the South Pacific.

Davidson, J., 1967. *Samoa Mo Samoa: The Emergence of the Independent State of Western Samoa*, Melbourne: Oxford University Press.

Field, M., 1984. *Mau: Samoa's Struggle Against New Zealand Oppression*, Wellington: A.H. & A.W. Reed Ltd.

Field, M., 2006. *Black Sunday: New Zealand's Tragic Blunders in Samoa*, Wellington: Reed Books.

Field, M., 2010. *Swimming with Sharks – Tales from the Pacific Frontline*, Auckland: Penguin Books.

Firth, S. (ed.), 2006. *Globalisation and Governance in the Pacific Islands*,

Canberra: ANU E Press.

Gilson, R., 1970. *Samoa 1830 to 1900: The Politics of a Multi-Cultural Community*, Melbourne: Oxford University Press.

Government of Samoa, 2016. *Strategy for the Development of Samoa 2016/17–2019/20*, Apia: Ministry of Finance.

Hancock, K., 2003. *Men of Mana – Portraits of Three Pacific Leaders*, Wellington: Steele Roberts.

HRPP, 2016a. *Human Rights Protection Party Manifesto for the 2011 General Election*, http://hrpp.org.ws/about-hrpp/manifesto

HRPP, 2016b. *Human Rights Protection Party Manifesto 2016–2021*, http://www.savalinews.com/2016/04/06/human-rights-protection-party-manifesto-2016-2021/

HRPP, 2016c. *HRPP Vision and Values*, http://hrpp.org.ws/about-hrpp/vision-and-values

Hunkin, G., 2009. *Gagana Samoa, A Samoan Language Coursebook*, rev. edn, Honolulu: University of Hawai'i Press.

Iati Iati, 2013. 'Samoa's Price for 25 Years of Political Stability', *Journal of Pacific History*, 48 (4), pp 443–63.

Johnstone, I. and M. Powles (eds), 2012. *New Flags Flying – Pacific Leadership*, Wellington: Huia.

Kramer, A., 1994a. *The Samoa Islands Volume I*, trans. T. Verhaaren, Auckland: Polynesian Press.

Kramer, A., 1994b. *The Samoa Islands Volume II*, trans. T. Verhaaren, Auckland: Polynesian Press.

Levine, S. (ed.), 2016. *Pacific Ways – Government and Politics in the Pacific Islands*, 2nd edn, Wellington: Victoria University Press.

Lockwood, B., 1971. *Samoan Village Economy*, Melbourne: Oxford University Press.

London Missionary Society, 1958. *O le Tusi Faalupega o Samoa*, Malua: LMS Press.

Mahon, J., 1985. *Judgement in the Supreme Court of Western Samoa, WSSC 1, between Vermeulen W.J. and The Attorney-General et al.*, delivered 2 May 1985.

Malielegaoi, T., 1981. *Maiden Speech*, Western Samoa Parliamentary Hansard, 3 September 1981, pp 91–97.

Malielegaoi, T., 1998. *Motion for Appointment of Prime Minister*, Samoa Parliamentary Hansard, 23 November 1998, pp 979–80.

Malielegaoi, T., 2002. *Prime Minister's Vote of Thanks to the Prime Minister of New Zealand on the Occasion of Samoa's 40th Independence Celebrations, Saunoaga a le Palemia, I le Palemia o Niu Sila ma Lana Faatoesega*, Speech Notes in Samoan and English, 3 June 2002.

Malielegaoi, T., 2014a. *Remarks at Climate Change Summit*, http://www.samoagovt.ws/2014/09/pms-remarks-at-climate-change-summit-2014-in-new-york-23-sept-2014/

Malielegaoi, T., 2014b. *Statement by the Prime Minister at the 69th Session of the UN General Assembly*, http://www.samoagovt.ws/2014/09/statement-by-the-prime-minister-at-the-69th-session-of-the-un-general-assembly-26-september-2014/

Malielegaoi, T., 2016a. Saunoaga a le Afioga a le Pālemia. Tatalaina Polokalame Faamasani mo Sui Usufono o le Palemene Lona XVI, 15 March 2016.

Malielegaoi, T., 2016b. *Presentation 1. System of Government: The Samoan Arrangement*, Folasaga 1. Afioga i le Pālemia, Faataatiaga o le Faiga-Malo a Samoa, 29 March 2016.

Malielegaoi, T., 2016c. *Presentation 2 HRPP Longevity: Political, Economic and Social Implications*, Saunoaga a le Afioga i le Pālemia. Fonotaga Faale-Aoaoga mo Sui Usufono o le Palemene Lona XVI, 29 March 2016.

Malielegaoi, T., 2016d. *Parliamentarians: Varied Expectations and Leadership Qualities*, Saunoaga a le Afioga i le Pālemia, Fonotaga Faale-Aoaoga mo Sui Usufono o le Palemene Lona XVI, 30 March 2016.

Malo O Samoa, 1960. *Lipoti Faamaonia O Felafolafoaiga O Le Fono Faavae A Samoa, Tusi I, II, III, [I Le Gagana Samoa]*, Ofisa O Le Failautusi, Fono Aoao Faitulafono. Mulinuu: Samoa.

Mara, K., 1997. *The Pacific Way: A Memoir*, Honolulu: University of Hawai'i Press.

Meleisea, M., 1987. *The Making of Modern Samoa*, Suva: Institute of Pacific Studies, University of the South Pacific.

Meleisea, M., 1992. *Change and Adaptions in Western Samoa*, Christchurch: Macmillan Brown Centre for Pacific Studies.

Meleisea, M., 1995. '"To whom the gods and men crowned": Chieftainship and Hierarchy in Ancient Samoa', in J. Huntsman (ed.), *Tonga and Samoa: Images* of Gender and Polity, Christchurch: Macmillan Brown Centre for Pacific Studies.

Meleisea, M., E. Meleisea and P. Schoeffel (eds.), 2012. *Samoa's Journey 1962–2012, Aspects of History*, Wellington: Victoria University Press.

Meleisea, M. and P. Schoeffel, 1983. 'Western Samoa: Like a Slippery Fish', in R. Crocombe and A. Ali (eds.), *Politics in Polynesia*, Suva: University of the South Pacific.

Meleisea, M. and P. Schoeffel (eds.), 1987. *Lagaga: A Short History of Western Samoa*, Suva: University of the South Pacific.

Milner, G., 1976. *Samoan Dictionary*, London: Oxford University Press.

Powles, M. (ed.), 2016. *China and the Pacific – The View from Oceania*, Wellington, Victoria University Press.

Pratt, G., 1977. *Pratt's Grammar and Dictionary of the Samoan Language*, Apia: Malua Printing Press.

Rich, R. (ed.), (2006). *Political Parties in the Pacific Islands*, Research School of Pacific and Asian Studies, Australian National University, Canberra: Pandanus Press.

Saipele, Nuʻualiʻi Mulipolo Ma'ilo, 1995. *Proverbs of Samoa*, Apia: Australian High Commission for Western Samoa.

Schultz, E., 1980. *Samoan Proverbial Expressions (Alagaʻupu faʻa Samoa)*, Suva: Polynesian Press.

SIDS, 2014. *The Third International Conference on Small Island Developing States*, https://sustainabledevelopment.un.org/sids2014

Snell, R., 1992. 'Western Samoan Trade Unionism: The 1981 Public Service Strike', *New Zealand Journal of Industrial Relations*, 17, pp 69–84.

Soʻo, A., 2006. 'More than 20 Years of Political Stability in Samoa Under the Human Rights Protection Party', in S. Firth (ed.), *Globalisation and Governance in the Pacific Islands,* Canberra: ANU E Press, 2006, pp 350–51.

Soʻo, A. (ed.), 2007. *Changes in the Matai System – O Suiga i le Faʻamatai*, Apia: Centre for Samoan Studies, National University of Samoa.

Soʻo, A., 2008. *Democracy and Custom in Samoa: An Uneasy Alliance*, Suva: Institute of Pacific Studies Publications, University of the South Pacific.

Soʻo, A., 2009. 'Samoa', in S. Levine (ed.), *Pacific Ways, Government and Politics in the Pacific Islands*, Wellington: Victoria University Press.

References

So'o, A., 2012. 'Political Development: Samoa's Parliamentary Journey from 1962 to 2012', in M. Meleisea et al. (eds), *Samoa's Journey 1962–2012, Aspects of History*, Wellington: Victoria University Press.

So'o, A. et al. (eds.), 2006. *Samoa National Human Development Report, Sustainable Livelihoods in a Changing Samoa*, Apia: Centre for Samoan Studies, National University of Samoa.

Stevenson, R.L., 1892. *A Footnote to History: Eight Years of Trouble in Samoa*, London: Dawsons (reprinted 1967).

Swain, P., 1999. 'Civil Society and Development: Pacific Island Case Studies', PhD dissertation, Massey University.

Swain, P., 2014. 'Fitting into the Pacific', in J. Schultz and L. Jones (eds.), *Griffith Review 43, Pacific Highways*, Brisbane: Griffith University.

Toleafoa, A., 2013. 'One Party State: The Samoan Experience', in D. Hegarty and D. Tryon (eds.), *Politics, Development and Security in Oceania*, Canberra: ANU-E Press.

Ulu, A.J., (2013). 'Pule: Development Policy Sovereignty in Samoa', Masters in Development Studies thesis, Victoria University of Wellington.

United Nations Development Programme, 2015. *UNDP Human Development Report 2015: Work for Human Development*, Table 2: Trends in the Human Development Index, 1990–2014, and Samoa Country Profile.

United Nations, 2016. Least Developed Countries, http://unohrlls.org/about-ldcs/criteria-for-ldcs/, https://en.wikipedia.org/wiki/Least_Developed_Countries

Va'a, F.P.S., T.U. Va'a, F.L. Fuata'i, M.I. Chan Mow and D. Amosa, 2012. 'Aspects of Economic Development', in M. Meleisea et al. (eds.), *Samoa's Journey 1962–2012, Aspects of History*, Wellington: Victoria University Press.

Vaiao, L. and F. Alailima, 1994. 'Restructuring Samoa's Chiefdom', in W. von Busch, M. Crocombe, R. Crocombe, L. Crowl, T. Deklin, P. Larmour and E. Williams (eds.), *New Politics in the South Pacific*, Suva: Institute of Pacific Studies, University of the South Pacific.

Victoria University of Wellington, 2012. *Citation for the Degree of Doctor of Laws, honoris causa, Hon Tuila'epa Malielegaoi*, Victoria University of Wellington, June 2012.

Whitehead, A. N., (1927). *Symbolism, Its Meaning and Effect,* Barbour-Page Lectures, University of Virginia Press.

Index

Note: Professor Asofou So'o's *Democracy and Custom in Samoa* (2008) outlines how to present Samoan names and *matai* titles in relation to name order. So'o uses the *matai* title by which a person is primarily known for the alphabetical listing, and that is the convention that is used here. Otherwise, standard names are presented in the usual reverse order for indexing.

Ā'ana Ālofi No. 2 constituency, 117, 118
absentee voting, 254–55
accountability, of government, 129, 143, 223, 239, 241; *see also* public service, accountability of
Adams, Sister T., 50
Aeau Peni, 121
Afoa Kolone Va'ai, 66, 90, 98
African, Caribbean and Pacific (ACP) General Secretariat, Brussels, 25, 62–64, 65, 78, 98–99, 108, 200, 243, 250; ACP–EU Convention, 215–16; *see also* Tuila'epa Sa'ilele Malielegaoi, **Employment and Negotiations: Overseas**, and African, Caribbean and Pacific General Secretariat, Brussels
Aggie Grey's Hotel, 246*f*
agricultural production and exports: and climate change, 248; as revenue source, 143, 241–42; decline in, 20; devastation of, 245; development and improvement of, 82, 95, 114, 199, 210, 239, 242; *see also* Avele Agricultural College; Suspensory Loan Scheme for Agriculture; University of the South Pacific, at Alafua
agriculture, subsistence, 37, 40, 241
aid, 25, 142, 190, 199, 203, 242; and development, 201, 243–44; and disaster relief, 142, 143, 246, 247–48; dependence on, 242–44; *see also* Australia, and aid from; development partners; development and development experts; Economic Aid Division; Japan: and aid from; loans, overseas; National Disaster Council; New Zealand, and aid from; overseas development assistance; People's Republic of China: and aid from; sovereignty, and aid; Tuila'epa Sa'ilele Malielegaoi, **Political Life and Experience**, and disaster relief; United States Agency for International Development; United States of America: and aid from
Aid Coordination Committee, 243
'āiga (extended family), 29, 33, 34, 75, 136, 258
Aikman, Professor Colin, 131
'Ai'ono family, 74, 165–66
'Ai'ono Fanaafi, 106, 115
'Ai'ono *matai* title, 32, 70, 74, 174
'Ai'ono Mose Sua Pouvi, 98, 131, 188
Air Tahiti Nui, 210
airline disaster, first in Samoa, 54
airports, building of, 242; *see also* Faleolo Airport
Alafoti Fa'osiliva, 221
Alafua, , 56, 128
Aleipata village, 82, 189
ali'i (sitting chiefs), 33, 34, 74, 212
Aliimalemanu Sasa Tevita, 91
Ali'ioaiga Feturi Elisaia, 214–15, 218
Alipia, Chief, 122
All Blacks, 180, 220–21, 252
Alliance of Small Island States (AOSIS), 215, 216
American Constitution, 53
American Samoa, 50, 75, 191, 193; and Cyclones Val and 'Ofa, 245; and Polynesian Leaders Group, 210; and tsunami, 189; *see also* Pago Pago; United States of America: and American Samoa
Annandale, Tui, 188–89
Ānoāma'a East constituency, 115
Ānoāma'a Sasa'e, 117
Apia, 9, 32, 36, 40, 41–43, 46–48, 54, 55, 56, 59, 65, 68, 70, 72, 74–75, 78, 90, 107,

Index

135, 146, 152, 187, 220, 252, 258, 259; as conference venue, 206, 214; buildings in, 17, 42, 128, 199, 240; harbour in, 37, 141–42; parades in, 194, 220; roads in and around, 32, 43, 46–47, 82; schools in, 44–46; urbanisation in, 227; US ships berthing at, 134; *see also* Fiamē Mataʻafa Faumuinā Mulinuʻu II Building; Saleufi; Tuanaimato, Vaitele
Apia Park, 219–21, 252
Aquino, President Benigno, 124
Arbor Day, 155
archery, 183
Argentina, Samoan Honorary Consul in, 201
Asau village, 89
Asi Blakelock, 166–67, 181
Asia–Pacific Economic Cooperation (APEC), 203
Asian Development Bank (ADB), 59, 200, 244; Board of Governors of, 124–27, 128; programme loan from, 140; *see also* Beijing: and Asian Development Bank; Japan: and Asian Development Bank; People's Republic of China: and Asian Development Bank; Tuilaʻepa Saʻilele Malielegaoi, **Employment and Negotiations**: **Overseas**, and negotiations with Asian Development Bank
Asian economic crisis 1997, 237
assassination, *see* Tuilaʻepa Saʻilele Malielegaoi, **Prime Minister**, and assassination of Luagalau Levaula Kamu
Assemblies of God, 34
Associate Ministers, 96, 135, 223–24, 226, 252
Association of Small Island States (AOSIS), 209, 215, 216
athletics, 51
Attorney-General, 96, 111, 136, 157, 158, 168–69, 179, 191, 210; *see also* Garneau, Mr; Heather, Brenda; Office of the Attorney-General
atua/Atua (gods and God), 34
Ātua district, 32, 73, 225–26
aualuma (girls and young women in village), 33–34
Auckland, 97, 149; and World Boxing Organisation's heavyweight championship in, 221–22; Samoan Consulate General in, 201; Samoans in, 255; visits to, 9, 61, 128, 131; *see also* Newman Hall; Tuilaʻepa Saʻilele Malielegaoi, **Early Life**, going to Auckland; Tuilaʻepa Saʻilele Malielegaoi, **Early Life**, schooling of; Tuilaʻepa Saʻilele Malielegaoi, **Early Life**, university qualifications of; University of Auckland; Whenuapai Airport
Auckland University Catholic Students' Association, 52
Audit Office, 224, 239
Auditor-General, 240
ʻAuelua *matai* title, 32, 70, 74, 174
ʻAuelua Tufi, 68–69
Aʻufaga village, 41, 68, 73–74
aumāga (young men in village), 33–34, 70, 120
Auseuga K. Poloma, 159
Australia, 21, 66, 150, 172, 200, 203, 209, 239; and aid from, 140, 141, 143, 190, 246; and cars from, 183–84, 185; and Fiji, 208, 213; and Pacific Islands Forum, 202, 207–8; and Pacific Way, 208, 212; and People's Republic of China, 128, 203–4; and relationship with Samoa, 213–14, 250–51; and South Pacific Commission, 200; and United Nations Educational, Scientific and Cultural Organization, 204; as development partner, 200, 203; as export market, 148; business with, 190; Samoan Honorary Consul in, 201; Samoans in, 190, 246; *see also* Canberra, Samoan diplomatic mission in; Evans, Gareth; Howard, John; Ministers of Foreign Affairs: Australian; St John, Chief Justice R.J.B.; Sydney, Samoan Consulate General in
Austria: Samoan Honorary Consul in, 201; visit to, 131
Avele Agricultural College, 39–40, 114–15

Bachelor of Commerce degree, 51, 52, 77, 98, 242
Bainimarama, Commodore Josaia Voreqe 'Frank', 200, 206–9, 211, 213, 216; *see also* Fiji; Tuilaʻepa Saʻilele Malielegaoi, **Political Life and Experience**, and political relationships, with Commodore Josaia Voreqe 'Frank' Bainimarama
Ban Ki-moon, 218
bananas, 37, 40, 48, 242
bankruptcy, of the country, 65, 88, 98, 130, 147; *see also* Polynesian Airlines
Beijing: and Asian Development Bank, 126–28; Samoan diplomatic mission in, 201
biosecurity, 242
blackbirders, 77
boxing, 188, 221–22; *see* Cameron, Shane; Parker, Joseph; Tua, David; World Boxing Organisation
breadfruit and breadfruit trees, 36, 39, 88,

130
bridges: building of, 43, 240, 242; destruction of, 137, 139–40, 219, 246; *see also* Vaimoso Bridge
Brown, Joe, 139
Brussels, 62, 63, 215; Samoan diplomatic mission in, 201; work in and visits to, 62–63, 64, 66, 78, 98, 152, 200, 215, 243, 250; *see also* African, Caribbean and Pacific General Secretariat
Budget debates, *see* debates: Budget
budgetary reforms, 64
budgetary support, 143
Budgets, 178, 185, 194, 199; 1982, 21, 91–93, 94; 1983, 92, 95–96; 1985, 106, 111; 1986, 22, 112
by-elections, 21, 22, 81, 90–92, 94, 171, 180, 198

Cabinet, 17, 23, 57–58, 62, 66, 89–90, 96, 102, 107–9, 128, 132, 134, 139, 144, 146, 154–55, 158, 159, 161, 164, 169, 178, 182, 183, 188, 192–93, 195–96, 229, 232, 241; appointments to, 22, 26, 29–30, 84, 88, 91, 94–95, 101–2, 106–7, 118, 119, 123, 135, 145, 148–49, 155, 163, 172, 223, 224, 225–26; numbers in, 23, 135, 148–49; reform of, 135; reshuffles of, 99, 243; *see also* Tofilau ʻEti Alesana, Cabinet of; Tofilau ʻEti Alesana, in Cabinet; Tuilaʻepa Saʻilele Malielegaoi, **In Cabinet**
Cabinet Development Committee, 243
Cabinet Room, 17, 261–62, 263
Cameron, Shane, 188
Campbell, John, 247
Canada, 58, 96, 201
Canberra, Samoan diplomatic mission in, 201, 204, 228
cars, *see* Australia, and cars from; Japan: and cars from; New Zealand, and cars from; Toyota cars; United States of American: and cars from
cash economy, 194
Catholic Church and faith, 34, 45, 47, 48, 49, 52, 146, 259; *see also* Maria Imakulata Cathedral, Mulivai; Moamoa Catholic church
cattle, cultural presentations of, 194
Central Bank of Samoa, 98, 99, 243
checks and balances, to government, 53, 136, 223–24, 226, 240
chess, 51
Chief Justice, 161, 225; *see also* Patu Falefatu; St John, R.J.B.
children, and village life, 33, 36–37

Children's White Sunday, 91, 187
China, *see* People's Republic of China
chloro-fluoro-carbons (CFCs), 248
Christian Democratic Coalition Party, 112
Christian Democratic Party (CDP), 100, 223
Christian denominations, 34; *see also* Assemblies of God; Catholic Church and faith; Church of the Latter Day Saints; Congregational Christian Church of Samoa; Methodist Church
Christian faith and politics, 114, 117, 120, 121, 137, 144–45, 147, 161, 168–70, 174, 175, 197, 234, 235, 256–57, 258; *see also* Tuilaʻepa Saʻilele Malielegaoi, **Personal**, beliefs, values and philosophy of, and Christian faith
church buildings, 34; destruction of, 245; *see also* Maria Imakulata Cathedral, Mulivai; Moamoa Catholic church; Nazareth church; Siusega, Catholic church at
Church of the Latter Day Saints, 34
circumcision, 37
Clark, Helen, 173–76, 201, 209, 217
Clerk of the House, 93, 157, 158, 160
climate change, and Pacific nations, 25, 139–40, 203, 218, 237, 248–49; *see also* chloro-fluoro-carbons; global warming
Clinton, Hillary, 216–17
cocoa and cocoa trees, 49, 89, 130, 141, 181, 242
coconuts and coconut products, 37, 38, 47, 48, 49, 89, 133, 181, 194, 220, 242; *see also* copra
colonisation, *see* Fiji: British control of; France: in the Pacific; Germany: and administration of Samoa; Germany, and colonisation of Samoa; Great Britain, as colonial power; New Zealand, and administration of Pacific nations; New Zealand, and administration of Samoa; Solomon Islands: British control of; United States of America, and colonisation in the Pacific
Commissioner for Prisons, 224
Commissions of Enquiry, 20, 146, 178, 224
commodity prices, fluctuations in, 20, 237, 242
Commonwealth Games 1990, 138
Commonwealth Heads of Government Meeting (CHOGM), 129, 191; in 1999, 173; in Malta, 179
Commonwealth Youth Games 2015, 180, 219
communications, improvement to, 29, 78, 141, 240, 242
competition, from other developing

Index

economies, 239, 242
Congregational Christian Church of Samoa (EFKS), 34, 35–36, 41, 44, 117
consensus politics, 19–20, 222, 261
Constitution of Samoa, 18, 71, 93, 95, 136, 139, 161, 175, 186, 197, 223, 224, 228, 258, 261; amendments to, 22–23, 136–37, 148, 198–99, 223, 224–25, 233–34, 235, 238–39; see also crises: constitutional
consumer rights, 13, 239; see also South Pacific Consumer Protection Programme
Cook Islands, 39, 56, 114, 215; and Polynesian Leaders Group, 210
Coopers and Lybrand, 78, 84
copra, 30, 37, 141
Correspondence School, Wellington, New Zealand, 50
corruption and dishonesty, allegations and instances of, 30–31, 97, 114, 224, 226, 237, 240, 251–53; see also journalists and the press, criticisms by; Tuila'epa Sa'ilele Malielegaoi, **Political Life and Experience**, and media: criticisms by
cost of living, 82, 132, 178, 195, 199
cotton, 141
Council for Regional Organisations in the Pacific (CROP), 202, 203
Council of Chiefs, 121; see also fono
Council of Deputies (Sui O Le Fono a Sui Tofia), 18, 137, 161, 163, 164, 173, 176–77, 179, 225, 227–28; see also bankruptcy, of the country; Tuimaleali'ifano Suatipatipa; Tupua Tamasese Efi, and Council of Deputies
Council of the European Union, 215
Crichton, Reverend Liki, 101–2
cricket, 38, 39, 51, 71, 182; see also kirikiti
crises: constitutional, 20, 262; economic, 14, 20–21, 80, 237, 242; financial, 149; political, 27, 31, 158, 162, 163–64, 166–71, 179, 237, 242; see also Asian economic crisis; demonstrations and protests; Global Financial Crisis; natural disasters; strikes
Cross-Island Road, 165
cultural practices and customs, 32–33, 46–47, 71, 115, 162, 174–75, 190, 192–94, 196, 212, 223, 239, 251, 254; costs of, 194–95, 239; see also cattle, cultural presentations of; fa'amatai; Fa'asamoa; fish, canned, as cultural exchange; fono; hospitality, Samoan; pigs, cultural presentations of; political power, traditional; tautua
customary lands, cultivation of, 147, 170, 185–87

Customs Department, 195
Customs duties, as revenue source, 65, 82, 143
Cyclone Evan, 219, 246, 247
cyclone of 1889, 141–42
Cyclone 'Ofa, 137–41, 142, 245, 247
Cyclone Val, 137, 141–43, 245–46, 247
cyclones, 14, 137–43, 162, 237, 245, 247–48; see also American Samoa, and Cyclones Val and 'Ofa; Lepā village, and cyclones
Cyprus, Samoan Honorary Consul in, 201

Dawn Raids (New Zealand), 61
daylight saving, 191–92, 239
debates: Budget, 92, 97, 113, 137, 228–30; parliamentary, 17, 72, 92, 99, 106, 108, 116, 123, 130–31, 150, 164, 198, 223, 230–31, 235, 255–56; public, 220, 251–52, 255–56; traditional, 71, 72, 75, 106, 234; see also Tofilau 'Eti Alesana, and parliamentary debates; Tuila'epa Sa'ilele Malielegaoi, **Entering Politics**, and parliamentary debates
defections, party political, 22, 83, 91–92, 106, 115, 123, 180, 198–99
democracy: establishment of, 18–19, 136, 222–23, 261; failure of, 207, 240; in practice, 11, 14, 78, 163, 207, 223, 232, 235, 238, 240–41; philosophy of, 110, 206, 207; see also media, democratic
demonstrations and protests, 124, 145–47, 148, 165–71, 180–82, 184–85, 187–88; see also strikes: public service
Denmark, Samoan Honorary Consul in, 201
Department of Education (New Zealand), 49
Department of Lands and Survey, 20, 88; see also Director of Lands and Survey; Ministry of Lands and Survey; Ministry of Lands, Survey and the Environment
deregulation, 13, 98, 239, 243
development and development experts, 10, 77, 199, 202–3, 219, 239–42, 243–44; see also aid; overseas development assistance; United States Agency for International Development
development partners, 98, 200, 201, 216; see also Australia, as development partner; European Union, as development partner; India, as development partner; Japan: as development partner; New Zealand, as development partner; People's Republic of China: as development partner; United States of America: as development partner
development, sustainable, 194, 214, 216, 218,

257; *see also* United Nations Conference on Sustainable Development
Diplomatic Corps, 139
diplomatic missions, Samoan, 66, 134–35, 201, 228; *see also* Argentina, Samoan Honorary Consul in; Auckland, Samoan Consulate General in; Australia, Samoan Honorary Consul in; Austria: Samoan Honorary Consul in; Beijing: Samoan diplomatic mission in; Brussels, Samoan diplomatic mission in; Canberra, Samoan diplomatic mission in; Cyprus, Samoan Honorary Consul in; Germany: Samoan Honorary Consul in; Hong Kong: Samoan Honorary Consul in; New York: Samoan diplomatic mission in; Pago Pago, Samoan Consulate General in; Singapore: Samoan Honorary Consul in; Sydney, Samoan Consulate General in; Tokyo, Samoan diplomatic mission in; Washington, Samoan embassy in; Wellington, Samoan diplomatic mission in
Director of Economic Development, 58, 98; *see also* Economic Development Department
Director of Lands and Survey, 20, 88; *see also* Department of Lands and Survey; Ministry of Lands and Survey; Ministry of Lands, Survey and the Environment; Patū Afa Hunter
Director of Public Works (and Acting Deputy Director), 11, 57–58, 140; *see also* Public Works Department; Tuila'epa Sa'ilele Malielegaoi, **Employment: Samoan Public Service**, as Deputy Director (and Acting Deputy Director) of Public Works
Disaster Advisory Committee, *see* National Disaster Council
disasters, *see* natural disasters
Doctors' Association, 178
Drake, Mr, 96
Dreaver, Mary, 52

earthquakes, 189, 190, 245
Economic Aid Division, 243
economic development, 77, 78, 219, 239, 240, 241–44
Economic Development Department, Ministry of Finance, 54, 58, 62, 98–99; *see also* Tuila'epa Sa'ilele Malielegaoi, **Employment: Samoan Public Service**, as Deputy Director of Economic Development Department
economy: liberalisation of, 25, 78; modernisation of, 13, 25, 124, 238, 240, 241–44; strengthening and stabilising of, 10, 52, 80, 81–83, 95–96, 98, 99, 124, 162, 178, 199, 200, 219, 235, 237, 241–42, 243; weaknesses in, 20–21, 25, 63, 65–66, 80, 81, 88, 107, 132; *see also* bankruptcy, of the country; crises: economic
education system: and opportunities and access to, 115, 186, 240, 257; colonial, 44–45, 49; development of, 29, 78, 82, 107, 162, 199, 239, 240, 242; *see also* schools
Electoral Act 1963, 21, 135, 136, 239
electoral reforms, 223, 227, 238–39
electorates, size of, 227
Electrical Power Corporation (EPC), 26, 29–30
electricity coverage and restoration, 22, 131, 147, 242, 245–46, 247, 249; *see also* hydro-electric power generation; Tanugamanono power plant
environmental issues and protection, 13, 130, 239; *see also* Tuila'epa Sa'ilele Malielegaoi, **Political Life and Experience**, and environmental issues
Epati, Semi, 96–97
Epeli, Ratu, 208
erosion, coastal, 248
European American Bank, New York, 65–66
European Union, 65; as development partner, 200, 203; and relationship with Samoa, 98–99, 250; *see also* African, Caribbean and Pacific General Secretariat, Brussels, ACP–EU Convention; Council of the European Union
Evans, Gareth, 204

fa'atuatua (talk about spirits; ghosts), 36
Fa'alavaau Perina, 218
fa'alavelave (special event), 70, 193, 194
fa'alavelave mats, 193; *see also lalaga* mats
fa'alupega (record of traditional salutations), 71, 73, 74, 76
fa'amatai (customary political system), 73, 76, 258, 261; *see also* political power, traditional
Fa'amatuāinu Tala Mailei, 115, 173
fa'apalagi (European or Western way), 77–78, 258; *see also* Tuila'epa Sa'ilele Malielegaoi, **Personal**, beliefs, values and philosophy of, and *fa'apalagi*
Fa'asamoa (Samoan custom and way of life): as guiding principle, 17, 18, 54, 78, 193, 258, 261; concept of, 32–33, 34–35, 70–77; practice of, 76, 111, 116, 194, 226, 258; *see also* Tuila'epa Sa'ilele Malielegaoi,

Index

Personal, beliefs, values and philosophy of, and *Faʻasamoa*
Fagaloa Bay, 114, 140
Faigaa, Tina (aunt), 48–49
Falealili village and district, 28, 32, 42, 43, 46, 74, 174
Falealupo village, 121
Faleata Sasaʻe, 136
Faleata village, 48
Falefa village and district, 32, 40, 46, 74, 75–76, 143
Falelatai village, 87, 91, 116, 117, 119, 164
Faleolo Airport, 50, 138, 219, 220, 240, 252
Falevao village and district, 40, 74–76, 226
Faolotoi Vaalele (cousin), 68–70
Fasitoo Uta, 35, 106
Father Feliseʻs school, 45, 46; *see also* Tuilaʻepa Saʻilele Malielegaoi, **Early Life**, schooling of
Fatialofa Alaifatu (cousin), 68–69
Fatialofa *matai* title, 32, 68–69, 70, 74, 165, 174
Fatialofa Momoe, 64, 70
Faumuinā Anapapa, 176, 179
Fauolo, Rev. Oka, 185
Fauono Ken Laban, 220
feasts, 35, 38–39, 47, 56, 195
Federated States of Micronesia (FSM), 209
Felise, Father, 45, 46
Fepuleaʻi Semi, 103, 115
Fiamē Mataʻafa Faumuinā Mulinuʻu II, 17, 18–19, 91, 112, 130, 165, 261
Fiamē Mataʻafa Faumuinā Mulinuʻu II Building, Apia, 17, 128, 146
Fiamē Nāomi Matāʻafa, 101, 115, 133, 152, 158, 161, 172, 197, 222
Fiji, 162, 172, 218; and elections in, 206, 207, 208, 209, 213, 216; and Pacific Islands Forum, 201–2, 203, 213, 215; and Pacific Way, 211, 250; and rivalry with Samoa, 214–18; and Tonga, 211–12; British control of, 142; civil unrest in, 25, 200, 206–9, 216, 237, 240, 250; independence of, 201; visits to, 145, 152, 203; *see also* Australia, and Fiji; Bainimarama, Commodore Josaia Voreqe 'Frank'; Epeli, Ratu; Kubuabola, Inoke; Mara, Ratu Sir Kamisese; Ministers of Foreign Affairs: Fijian; Nadi; New Zealand, and Fiji; Qarase, Laisenia; Sayed-Khaiyum, Aiyaz; Speight, George; Suva; Tonga, and Fiji; Tuilaʻepa Saʻilele Malielegaoi, **Political Life and Experience**, and Fiji
Fiji National University, 202
Fiji School of Medicine, 202

Financial Secretary (and Deputy Financial Secretary), 25, 57, 58–59, 64, 65, 66, 90, 97, 131, 133; *see also* Afoa Kolone Vaʻai; Hutchison, Alistair; Tuilaʻepa Saʻilele Malielegaoi, **Employment: Samoan Public Service**, as Financial Secretary (and Deputy Financial Secretary); Vaʻai Kolone, as Financial Secretary
financial year, 137
financial planning, 239
fires, 134
fiscal management, 219, 239
fish, canned, as cultural exchange, 122, 194–95
fishing, 33, 96, 210; and selling of fish, 48–49; reef, 41; spear, 40, 41
five-year development plans, 242, 243
floods, 162
fono (council of *matai*), 33–34, 70, 71, 225, 234, 250, 251, 255, 256, 258
Fonotoe Pierre Meredith, 219, 224
food: availability of, 37, 47–49, 65, 122–23, 140–41, 145, 147–48, 230; preparation of, 33, 38, 47; production of, 33, 141, 145, 245–46; *see also* breadfruit and breadfruit trees; cocoa and cocoa trees; coconuts and coconut products; feasts; fishing; guavas; hunger; paw-paws; pineapples; Samoan hospitality; *taro*; *umu*
foreign affairs, 124, 162, 199, 200–5, 206–11, 220; *see also* Tuilaʻepa Saʻilele Malielegaoi, **Political Life and Experience**, and foreign affairs
foreign exchange income and reserves, 98, 184, 199, 242
foreign investment and trade, 25, 82, 98
France: and South Pacific Commission, 200; and United Nations Climate Change Conference, 203; and United Nations Security Council, 201; in the Pacific, 142, 200, 203; *see also* Hollande, President François; Mitterrand, President François; Paris; Paris Agreement
French Polynesia, 210
Fruean, Matagitau, 41
Fruean, Mose, 41
Fuimaono Mimio, 172
funerals, attendance at, 64, 70, 131, 188–89, 193, 195–196

Gafa Elisaia, 26
Galumalemana *matai* title, 32, 70
games, *see* chess; *igāveʻa*; *kirikiti*; marbles; sports; *tagātiʻa*; *togi-a-gogu*; *velovelo*
Garneau QC, André, 96

Gato'aitele *pāpā* title, 18
gender, issues of, 33, 38–39
genealogy (*gafa*), 33, 70–71, 72–73, 117
General Election Manifesto 2016, 9
general elections, 9, 41, 68, 69, 83, 111, 112, 121, 129, 136, 163, 171, 173, 179, 207, 235, 238, 255; 1964, 17; 1967, 17; 1970, 19; 1973, 19, 261; 1976, 19; 1979, 20, 228; 1982, 10, 21, 81, 83, 85–86, 87, 94, 103; 1985, 22, 99, 198; 1988, 22, 115, 116, 123, 129; 1991, 22, 135, 143, 145; 1996, 23, 150; 2001, 23, 163, 164, 165, 166, 171, 231; 2006, 23, 176; 2008, 178; 2011, 23, 199, 224, 254; 2016, 9, 23, 222, 223, 235
Geneva, visits to, 98
Germany: and administration of Samoa, 241; and colonisation of Samoa, 141–42, 169, 170–71, 180; and independence celebrations, 142; and United Nations Security Council, 205; Samoan Honorary Consul in, 201
Global Financial Crisis, 182, 199, 237
Global Leaders' Meeting on Gender Equality and Women's Empowerment, New York, 2015, 257
global warming, 248, 249; *see also* climate change
Grand Chief of Papua New Guinea *matai* title, 32
Great Britain: and independence celebrations, 142; and South Pacific Commission, 200; as colonial power, 141–42, 200
guavas, 49

Hancock, Kathleen, 14
Hansen, Steve, 220, 221
Hawai'i and Hawai'ians, 153; and Polynesian Leaders Group, 210
Head of State (*O le Ao o le Malo*), 18, 59, 95, 111, 136, 146, 150, 164, 172, 177, 179, 197–98, 199, 225, 227–28, 235–36, 239, 261; *see also* Human Rights Protection Party, and Head of State; Malietoa Tanumafili II; Tuila'epa Sa'ilele Malielegaoi, **Prime Minister**, and Head of State; Tupua Tamasese Efi, as Head of State; Tupua Tamasese Mea'ole
health and sickness, 36–37, 78
healthcare and hospitals, 82, 179, 186, 199, 240, 242
Heather-Latu, Brenda (Attorney-General), 28, 169, 186
Hollande, President François, 203
Hong Kong: Samoan Honorary Consul in, 201; visits to, 127

hospitality, Samoan, 46–47
Howard, John, 209
HRPP Longevity: Political, Economic and Social Implications, 240
HRPP Manifesto 2016–2021, 224
human rights, 20, 239, 240, 257; *see also* Office for Human Rights
Human Rights Protection Party (HRPP), 9–10, 67, 68, 69, 91–92, 113; and Head of State, 90–91, 197–98; caucus of, 11, 84, 85, 106–7, 131–3, 135, 138, 146, 151, 154, 163–64, 171, 226, 232, 235, 240–41; election manifestos of, 223, 224; formation and consolidation of, 20, 21, 80, 81, 222–23, 240, 259, 262; in government, 10–11, 22–23, 88–90, 94, 100–12, 123–61, 147–48, 163–71, 171–79, 180–99, 200–22, 222–36; in opposition, 21, 90, 91–92, 113–16, 117–20; leadership of, 10, 20, 22, 25, 26, 100, 101–6, 128–30, 131–34, 135, 137, 144, 146, 147, 150–55, 158, 162, 163, 164, 171–72, 198, 225, 228–29, 238; meetings of, 86–87, 103–6, 163–64; membership of, 144–45; reforms within, 135; struggles within, 10, 22, 26, 83–88, 99, 100–6, 110–12, 129–30, 135, 144–45, 151, 162, 163, 164–65, 171–72, 198, 225, 262; vision of, 10, 147–48, 222–23, 240–41, 259; *see also HRPP Longevity: Political, Economic and Social Implications*; *HRPP Manifesto 2016–2021*; Tofilau 'Eti Alesana, and Human Rights Protection Party; Tuila'epa Sa'ilele Malielegaoi, **Entering Politics**, and party leadership issues; Tuila'epa Sa'ilele Malielegaoi, **In Cabinet**, as Deputy Leader of the Human Rights Protection Party; Tuila'epa Sa'ilele Malielegaoi, **Political Life and Experience**, and Human Rights Protection Party
hunger, 47–48, 146; *see also* food
Hutchison, Alistair, 58–59, 62, 63–64, 66, 97
hydro-electric power generation, 82

Iati Iati, 240
igāve'a (hide and seek), 37–38
independence, Samoan, 14, 17–19, 20, 35, 49, 71, 78, 115, 170, 173–76, 180, 196, 199, 201, 214, 227, 238, 241, 242, 261–62
independent MPs, 22, 68, 80, 81, 83, 84–85, 86, 103, 116–18, 150, 165, 171, 180, 198, 200, 222, 224, 226
India, as development partner, 203; *see also* Modi, Prime Minister Narendra
Individual Voters' seats, 18, 224
Indonesia, 99, 140; *see also* Jakarta

Index

inflation, 20, 242
influence and power, in traditional Samoa, 34, 256, 258
influenza epidemic 1919, 173
Information and Communications Technology (ICT), 29, 78, 240, 242; *see also* communications, improvement to
infrastructure and facilities: destruction of, 137–38, 162, 219, 242, 245–46; development of, 124, 162, 199, 239–40, 241–42; loans for, 140, 241; rebuilding of, 149, 242
instability, political, 25, 207, 237, 238, 240, 243, 262; *see also* stability, political
instability, social, 21
Inter-College Athletics Competition, 51
International Dateline, 50–51, 190–91, 239
International Monetary Fund (IMF), 59, 61, 63, 98, 108, 200; meetings of, 63, 152; relationship with, 98–99; *see also* Tuila'epa Sa'ilele Malielegaoi, **Employment and Negotiations: Overseas**, and negotiations with International Monetary Fund
International Whaling Commission, 201
Investigating Officer, Treasury Department, *see* Tuila'epa Sa'ilele Malielegaoi, **Employment: Samoan Public Service**, as Investigating Officer, Treasury Department
Iuli Sefo, 115

Jakarta, 99
Japan: and aid from, 141, 143, 190, 204–5; and Asian Development Bank, 127; and cars from, 183; and People's Republic of China, 204, 205; and relationship with Samoa, 205, 250; and United Nations Security Council, 205; as development partner, 200, 203; visits to, 109; *see also* Koizumi, Junichiro; Obuchi, Keizō; People's Republic of China: and Japan; Tokyo, Samoan diplomatic mission in; Toyota cars
Johnstone, Ian, 14
journalists and the press, criticisms by, 14, 209, 210–12, 235–36, 252–54; *see also* Campbell, John; Radio 2AP; Radio New Zealand International; *Samoa Observer*; Savea Sano Malifa; *Sunday Samoan*; Tuila'epa Sa'ilele Malielegaoi, **Political Life and Experience**, and media
Judiciary, 53, 161, 177, 178; independence of, 206, 240

Kaino, Jerome, 220
Keil, Joe, 196, 224
Key, John, 213, 220, 252
Kiribati, 218; and Pacific Islands Forum, 202; *see also* Tong, Anote
kirikiti (cricket), 37, 38, 39
Koizumi, Junichiro, 205
Komiti a Faletua ma Tausi (Women's Committee), 34
Kruse, Hans, 58
Kruse, Herman, 98
Kubuabola, Inoke, 218

Laeimau, 75
lalaga mats, 193
Land and Titles Court, 75, 115, 187
land disputes and questions of ownership, 71, 165–71, 180–82, 185–88; *see also* Samoa Land Corporation; Tuila'epa Sa'ilele Malielegaoi, **Prime Minister**, and land disputes
Lange, David, 134
Lapi, *see* Vaovasamanaia L. Filo
Lauli'i village, 121, 123, 165
Lauofo Meredith, 99
Le Mafa Pass, 32, 40
Le Mamea Ropati, 91, 114, 128–29, 135, 171, 173
leadership: and women, 48, 257; issues of, 10, 17, 20, 21, 22, 23, 80, 83, 116, 144, 164–65, 166, 171, 173, 194, 224, 227–36, 242, 244, 253, 255, 262; Pacific, 14, 214, 218, 234, 241, 250–51; traditional, 17–19, 31, 33, 48, 71–72, 104, 214; *see also* Human Rights Protection Party, leadership of; succession; Tofilau 'Eti Alesana, leadership of; Tuila'epa Sa'ilele Malielegaoi, **Political Life and Experience**, leadership of; Tupuola Efi, leadership style of
Leafa Vitale, 26, 27, 28–31, 121, 163–64
Lealetele village, 69, 74
Leamy, Father, 56
Leasiolagi Dr Malama Meleisea, 255, 256–58
Least Developed Country (LDC) status, 199, 216, 219, 243–44
Leaupepe Faimaala, 85
Lefaga and Faleaseela Constituency, 128–29
legislation, amendments to and redrafting of, 13, 82, 89, 95–97, 239
Legislative Assembly, 17, 18, 161, 177
Leniu Tafoaeono Avamagalo, 154
Leota Leulua'iali'i Itu'au 'Ale, 81, 137
Leota Lu, 121
Lepā Political District, 41, 136
Lepā village, 31, 32, 34, 38–39, 41, 43, 46, 47,

53, 64, 70, 72, 74, 136, 160, 165, 190, 215, 250, 258, 259; and cyclones, 189; MP for, 67, 68, 73–74, 79, 80–161, 230, 238, 253; number of voters in, 136; primary school at, 39, 45; road to, 47, 48, 82; *see also* Tuila'epa Sa'ilele Malielegaoi, **Early Life**, childhood and boyhood in Lepā; Tuila'epa Sa'ilele Malielegaoi, **Early Life**, schooling of
Leulumoega district, 43, 118, 121, 122, 228
Leutele (ancestor), 75–76
Li Peng, Premier, 128
loans, overseas, 65–66, 131, 140, 203, 241–42, 244; *see also* Suspensory Loan Scheme for Agriculture
Logologo Secondary School, 39
Lolofie, Chief, 68
Lolofie, Dr Eti Enosal, 152
Lolofietele *matai* title, 32, 70, 174
Lolofietele Sialavai, 39–40
Lomé Convention, 152, 215
London Missionary Society (LMS), 35, 41
Lotofaga, 82
Luagalau Levaula Kamu, 25–31, 164, 186, 237
Luamanuvae *matai* title, 185–86, 187
Luamanuvao Winnie Laban, 13, 15, 217
Lufilufi village, 115, 172–73
Lupematasila Fa'amalama, 117, 119
Lupesoli'ai *matai* title, 32, 68, 70, 74, 174
Lupesoli'ai, Leasunia (mother), 36, 41, 50, 56, 68, 73–74, 131
Luxembourg, 65
Lythe, Brian, 52

Mafutaga a Tina (Church Women's Fellowship), 34
Mahon, Justice Peter, 20
Malae-o-Matagofie, 102
Malaga *matai* title, 75–76
Malaysia, 201
Maldives, visit to, 108–10
Malielegaoi, Gillian (wife), 54, 55–57, 59, 60, 61, 63, 64, 87, 153, 188, 196, 226, 259
Malielegaoi, Manoa (brother), 42
Malielegaoi, Manue (sister), 48
Malielegaoi, Oscar (son), 153
Malielegaoi Veni (father), 35, 39–40, 41, 42, 43–44, 46–47, 48, 51, 56, 73, 74; advice from, 72–73, 262–63
Malietoa clan, 111, 174, 196
Malietoa *matai* title, 18, 111, 174
Malietoa Tanumafili II, 18, 19, 21, 22, 90–92, 94–95, 111–12, 123, 136, 138, 146, 150, 153, 154, 156–61, 163, 174, 177, 196–97, 261
Malua Theological College, 130

Manila, visit to, 124
Mano'o Lutena, 87, 91
Manu Samoa, 180, 219–21, 252
manufacturing, 239, 241
Māori, 170, 173; and Polynesian Leaders Group, 210
Maposua *matai* title, 121
Mara, Ratu Sir Kamisese, 14, 211
March for Peace, *see Savali o le Filemu*, March for Peace
Marcos, Ferdinand, 124
Maria Imakulata Cathedral, Mulivai, 48, 54–55, 56
Marist Brothers' School, Apia, 45–46, 47, 48, 49; *see also* Tuila'epa Sa'ilele Malielegaoi, **Early Life**, schooling of
market reforms, 25, 239
Masoe F. Kruse, 172
Master of Commerce degree, 25, 52, 54, 57, 67, 77, 98, 242
mat making, 33, 192–94, 239; *see also lalaga* mats; mats
matai (chief), 20, 33–34, 143, 165, 168, 186, 212, 225–26; as MPs, 18, 71, 136, 143, 224–25; qualifications and qualities of, 33, 70–73; rights of wives of, 34; roles of, 180, 255–56, 257; *see also fono*; Tuila'epa Sa'ilele Malielegaoi, **Personal**, as *matai*
matai suffrage, 18, 21, 71, 80, 136, 227
matai titles, 17, 18, 33, 70–71, 72, 74–76, 136, 148, 174, 224, 256; *see also* 'Ai'ono *matai* title; *ali'i*; 'Auelua *matai* title; Fatialofa *matai* title; Galumalemana *matai* title; Grand Chief of Papua New Guinea *matai* title; Lolofietele *matai* title; Luamanuvae *matai* title; Lupesoli'ai *matai* title; Malaga *matai* title; Malietoa *matai* title; Maposua *matai* title; Misa Telefoni Retzlaff, *matai* title of; Neioti *matai* title; *pāpā* titles; Salelologa *matai* title; *saofa'i*; Taisi *matai* title; *tama-a-'āiga, matai* titles of; Tofilau 'Eti Alesana, *matai* titles of; Tuailemafua *matai* title; Tufuga *matai* title; Tui A'ana *pāpā* title; Tui Ātua *pāpā* title; Tuila'epa *matai* title; Tuila'epa Sa'ilele Malielegaoi, **Personal**, *matai* titles of; *tulafale-ali'i* title; Tupua Tamasese Efi, *matai* titles of
Mataia Visesio, 148
Matamua, Chief, 187
Matatumua Maimoana, 20, 92
Matautu village, 138
Matautu Wharf Project, 204–5
mats: as gifts and cultural exchange, 55, 122–23, 157, 159, 190, 192–94, 231; quality of, 193, 239; *see also fa'alavelave* mats;

lalaga mats; mat making
McCully, Murray, 217, 220
McDonald, Norman, 51
Mealamu, Keven, 220
media, *see* journalists and the press, criticisms by
media, democratic, 82, 251–52
Melanesian Spearhead Group (MSG), 209–10
Meredith, Gillian, *see* Malielegaoi, Gillian
Meredith, Oscar, 55–56, 64
Meredith, Sam, 56
Methodist Church, 34, 168
Middle Income Country, 216, 219, 244
Minister in Charge of Shipping, 107–8, 219
Minister of Agriculture, 91, 193; *see also* Manoʻo Lutena; Ministry of Agriculture and Fisheries
Minister of Finance, 13, 23, 25, 56, 57, 59, 63, 66–67, 81, 85, 91, 92, 98–99, 101, 107–8, 111, 124, 131–33, 149, 185, 200, 228, 232, 235, 238, 243–44, 245, 262; *see also* Aliimalemanu Sasa Tevita; Economic Development Department; Ministry of Finance; Saili, Sam; Tuilaʻepa Saʻilele Malielegaoi, **In Cabinet**, as Minister of Finance (and Associate Minister of Finance); Vaovasamanaia Filipo
Minister of Foreign Affairs, 99, 215; *see also* Lauofo Meredith; Ministry of Foreign Affairs; Tuilaʻepa Saʻilele Malielegaoi, **In Cabinet**, as Minister of Foreign Affairs
Minister of Lands, Survey and the Environment, 26, 29, 31, 186; *see also* Ministry of Lands and Survey; Ministry of Lands, Survey and the Environment; Tuala Sale Kerslake
Minister of Public Works, 11, 26, 30, 57, 102, 186; *see also* Leafa Vitale; Luagalau Levaula Kamu; Public Works Department; Tupuola Efi
Minister of Telecommunications, 29; *see also* Ministry of Postal and Telecommunications
Minister of Tourism, 195–96; *see also* Keil, Joe
Ministers of Finance, Pacific, 152
Ministers of Foreign Affairs: Australian, 204, 208; Fijian, 208, 218; New Zealand, 217; Pacific, 208
Ministry of Agriculture and Fisheries, 192, 194; *see also* Minister of Agriculture
Ministry of Finance, 13, 56, 59, 61, 96, 98, 99, 243; *see also* Economic Development Department; Financial Secretary (and Deputy Financial Secretary); Minister of Finance; Treasury Department
Ministry of Foreign Affairs, 61, 99, 188, 204, 215, 243; *see also* Minister of Foreign Affairs
Ministry of Lands and Survey, 20, 130; *see also* Minister of Lands, Survey and the Environment
Ministry of Lands, Survey and the Environment, 130, 186; *see also* Department of Lands and Survey; Minister of Lands, Survey and the Environment
Ministry of Postal and Telecommunications, 26, 99; *see also* Minister of Telecommunications
Ministry of Trade, Commerce and Industry, 13
Ministry of Transport and Civil Aviation, 99
Ministry of Women, Community and Social Development, 26, 192; *see also* Leafa Vitale
Misa Faitala, 119–20
Misa Telefoni Retzlaff, 116–17, 119–21, 123, 144–45, 148–49, 155, 158; as Deputy Prime Minister, 164–65, 171–72; *matai* title of, 119, 164
missionaries, 35, 77, 196; *see also* London Missionary Society
Mitterrand, President François, 203
Moamoa Catholic church, Apia, 56
Moananu Salale, 143
modernisation, 25, 77, 239–40, 243, 262; *see also* economy: modernisation of; sanitation, modern, 43
Modi, Prime Minister Narendra, 203
monotaga (traditional service to village), 72, 258
Motoʻotua, Apia, 55, 120
Muldoon, Robert, 21, 89
Muliaumasealii, Rev. Toese Petaia (grandfather), 35
Mulinuʻu, 123, 197
Mulivai, 45
Muller, Mr, 65

Nadi, Fiji, 50
Nafanua, 148
Nanai, Chief, 119
National Disaster Council, 139, 143, 189, 190, 246
national dress, 195–96, 239
National Public Service Examinations, 49
National University of Samoa, 78, 114, 239, 246, 255
natural disasters, 25, 162, 238, 242; management and mitigation of, 138, 142–43, 245–50; *see also* aid, and disaster

relief; cyclones; earthquakes; fires; floods; tsunami; Tuila'epa Sa'ilele Malielegaoi, **Political Life and Experience**, and disaster relief
natural resources, 14, 141, 202, 241
Nauru, 215, 216, 218; and Polynesian Leaders Group, 210; see also Waqa, Baron
Neioti *matai* title, 32, 70, 74–76, 174
Nelson Public Library, 142
Nelson, Efi, 131; see also Tupua Tamasese Efi; Tupuola Efi
Nelson, Taisi Olaf, 174
Netzler, Jack, 101–2, 149
New Guinea, 142
New York: meeting of United Nations General Assembly in, 188, 218, 249; Samoan diplomatic mission in, 134, 201, 214–15, 228; see also American-European Bank; Global Leaders' Meeting on Gender Equality and Women's Empowerment
New Zealand, 156, 158, 209; and administration of Pacific nations, 39, 200–1; and administration of Samoa, 39, 44, 49, 170, 174, 180, 201, 241; and aid from, 39, 114, 140, 141, 143, 190, 246; and cars from, 183–84, 185; and Fiji, 213; and medical treatment in, 128, 131, 134, 153–54, 156, 158, 160, 188, 231; and nuclear policy, 134; and Pacific Islands Forum, 202, 207–8; and Pacific Way, 208, 212; and parliamentary procedures in, 172; and People's Republic of China, 128, 203–4; and relationship with Samoa, 175–76, 200–1, 213–14, 217–18, 220–1, 250–51; and rugby match with Samoa, 219–21; and South Pacific Commission, 200; apology from, 173–76; as development partner, 137, 200, 203, 213–14; as export market, 148; business with, 190; electoral boundaries in, 227; High Commissioners and Commissions of, 28, 59, 201, 227; immigrant status of Samoans in, 21, 89, 112; judges from, 21; racism in, 59–61; Samoans in, 21, 49, 51, 64, 73, 96, 131, 176, 183–84, 190, 246; universities in, 78, 239; visits to, 9, 43, 50, 54, 59–61, 62, 89, 188; see also All Blacks; Auckland; Clark, Helen; Department of Education (New Zealand); Key, John; Lange, David; Māori; McCully, Murray; Ministers of Foreign Affairs: New Zealand; Muldoon, Robert; nuclear ships; *Otago Daily Times*; Price, Mac; Privy Council; Radio New Zealand International; Rotorua; School Certificate; Treasury, New Zealand; University Entrance; Waitangi Tribunal; Wellington
Newman Hall, Auckland, 52
New Zealand Rugby Union, 220
Niue: and Avele College; 39, 114; and Polynesian Leaders Group, 210; Pacific Islands Forum meeting in, 209
Nofoali'i village, 121
Nomeneta, Pastor, 117, 120
Nonu, Ma'a, 220
Nonumalo Sōfara, 110, 113–14
nuclear ships, see New Zealand, and nuclear policy
nuclear waste, dumping of, 114
nu'u (village), 33
Nu'u Agriculture Research, 148

O le Ao o le Malo, see Head of State
O le Komiti a le Losa (women's committee), 48
Obuchi, Keizō, 204
Oceania University of Medicine, Apia, 78
Office for Human Rights, 224
Office of the Attorney-General, 96, 97
Office of the Representative of the American Samoan Government in Congress, 134
Okinawa Partnership 2006, 203
Ombudsman's Office, 224
oratory, 46–47, 72–73, 74–75, 76, 104, 113, 118, 121–22, 165, 172, 186, 212, 228, 230; see also speechmaking, caucus and parliamentary; Tofilau 'Eti Alesana, and speechmaking; Tuila'epa Sa'ilele Malielegaoi, **Political Life and Experience**, speechmaking and storytelling of; *tulafale*
Organization of Petroleum Exporting Countries (OPEC), 131, 132
Otago Daily Times, 221–22
overseas development assistance (ODA), 10, 241, 243–44, 247–48

Pacific Forum Line (PFL), 219
Pacific Games 1983, 134
Pacific Island Leaders' Meeting (PALM), 203
Pacific Islands Development Programme, 202
Pacific Islands Forum (PIF): business of, 203, 210, 213–14, 216; campaigns of, 248; criticisms of, 207; establishment of, 202; meetings of, 89, 209, 215, 250; membership of, 206, 207, 209, 215, 251; Secretariat of, 202, 206; see also Australia, and Pacific Islands Forum; Fiji, and Pacific Islands Forum; Kiribati, and Pacific Islands Forum; New Zealand, and Pacific Islands Forum; Papua New Guinea, and Pacific Islands Forum; Tonga, and

Index

Pacific Islands Forum; Tuila'epa Sa'ilele Malielegaoi, **Prime Minister**, and Pacific Islands Forum; Tuvalu, and Pacific Islands Forum; Vanuatu, and Pacific Islands Forum
Pacific Islands Forum countries, and relationship with Samoa, 250
Pacific Islands Forum Fisheries Agency, 202
Pacific Power Association (PPA), 202
Pacific regional agencies, 78, 176, 200, 237; see also Melanesian Spearhead Group; Pacific Island Leaders' Meeting; Pacific Islands Development Programme; Pacific Islands Forum; Pacific Islands Forum Fisheries Agency; Pacific Power Association; Polynesian Leaders Group; Secretariat of the Pacific Community; Secretariat of the Pacific Regional Environment Programme; South Pacific Applied Geoscience Commission; South Pacific Board for Educational Assessment; South Pacific Commission; South Pacific Consumer Protection Programme; South Pacific Tourism Organisation; Tuila'epa Sa'ilele Malielegaoi, **Political Life and Experience**, leadership of, and regional and international organisations and groups
'Pacific Way', 200, 207–8, 211–12, 250; see also Australia, and Pacific Way; Fiji, and Pacific Way; New Zealand, and Pacific Way
Paeniu, Bikenibeu, 248; see also Tuvalu
Pafelio, Brother, 46
Pago Pago, American Samoa, 50, 75; Samoan Consulate General in, 201; visits to, 112, 193
Palusalue Fa'apo II, 199
Pandit, S.A., 61–62, 108
Panoff, Professor, 58–59
pāpā titles, 18; see also Gato'aitele pāpā title; Tamasoali'i pāpā title; Tui A'ana pāpā title; Tui Ātua pāpā title
Papali'i Niko Lee Hang, 252, 253
Papua New Guinea (PNG), 35; and Pacific Islands Forum, 202, 206, 209; see also Grand Chief of Papua New Guinea matai title; New Guinea; West Papua
Paris, 131, 142, 203; see also United Nations Climate Change Conference
Paris Agreement, 218, 249, 250
Parker, Joseph, 221–22
'Parliament of Chiefs', 18, 223, 224
parliamentary reforms: seats, 9, 23; terms, 22, 23, 136–37

parliamentary system: bi-cameral, 136–37; Westminster, 18, 71, 111
Parliamentary Under Secretaries Act, 136
partnerships, 213–14, 218
party-hopping, see defections, party political
party politics, 10, 11, 20, 22, 83, 108, 116, 124, 197, 222–23, 235
patronage, traditional, 25
Patū Afa Hunter, 20, 86, 87–88, 131–32, 134
Patū Ativalu, 221
Patū Falefatu, 96, 170
Patū, Fei (Aunty Fei), 13
Patū, Rev. Suafai, 160
paw-paws, 37, 49, 211
People Against Side Switch (PASS), 184
People's Republic of China: and aid from, 128, 143, 182, 203–4, 205; and Asian Development Bank, 124–27; and Chinese workers in Samoa, 130; and Japan, 205; and relationship with Samoa, 203, 205, 250; as development partner, 200, 203–4; and United Nations Security Council, 201, 205; visits to, 127–28, 131; see also Australia, and People's Republic of China; Beijing; Japan: and People's Republic of China; Li Peng, Premier; New Zealand, and People's Republic of China; Tiananmen Square incident; Tofilau 'Eti Alesana, and state visit to People's Republic of China; United States of America: and People's Republic of China
Pereira, Tony, 92
Permanent Secretaries, 239
personality politics, 19, 108, 222, 223, 229–30
Pesega College, 48
Philippines, 124; see also Aquino, President Benigno; Manila, visit to; Marcos, Ferdinand
phosphate, 141
phytosanitary requirements, 242
Pierre, Fonotoe, see Fonotoe Pierre Meredith
pigs, cultural presentations of, 118–19, 194
pineapples, 242
plantation access roads, construction of, 57–58, 147
plantations, 28, 33, 40–41, 48–49, 89, 92, 138, 141, 180, 181; see also Vaitele village, plantation at
Points of Order, 92, 229, 230
police, 27, 28, 30, 146–47, 166–67, 173, 177, 181–82, 218, 224; see also Asi Blakelock
Police Commissioner, 28, 166–68, 181; see also Asi Blakelock; Unasa Lavea Schmidt
political power, traditional, 241, 250, 251, 256–57, 258; see also debates:

traditional; *fa'amatai*; *Fa'asamoa*; *fono*; influence and power, in traditional Samoa; leadership, traditional; Tuila'epa Sa'ilele Malielegaoi, **Political Life and Experience**, leadership of, traditional; village government
Polotaivao Fosi, 154–55
Polynesian Airlines, 62–63, 149
Polynesian Leaders Group (PLG), 209–11; *see also* American Samoa, and Polynesian Leaders Group; Cook Islands, and Polynesian Leaders Group; Hawai'i and Hawai'ians, and Polynesian Leaders Group; Māori, and Polynesian Leaders Group; Niue, and Polynesian Leaders Group; Rapa Nui, and Polynesian Leaders Group; Tonga, and Polynesian Leaders Group; Tuila'epa Sa'ilele Malielegaoi, **Prime Minister**, and Polynesian Leaders Group; Tuvalu, and Polynesian Leaders Group
port facilities, 204–5; *see also* Matautu Wharf Project; shipping
poverty, reduction of, 240
power politics, 20
Powles, Michael, 14
Powles, Sir Guy, 128
Pownall, Ross, 51
Price, Mac (New Zealand High Commissioner), 28
Prime Ministers of Samoa, *see* Fiamē Mata'afa Faumuinā Mulinu'u II; Tupua Tamasese Lealofi IV; Tupuola Efi; Va'ai Kolone; Tofilau 'Eti Alesana; Tuila'epa Sa'ilele Malielegaoi
private sector development, 10, 78, 95, 199, 243
privatisation, of public assets, 25
Privy Council, New Zealand, 21, 89, 112
Public Accounts Committee, 129, 134
Public Moneys Act, 111
public service, 10–11, 20–21, 66, 132; accountability of, 25; and salaries of, 177–78; government's relationships with, 82; reform and restructuring of, 25–26, 124, 239; *see also* strikes, public service; Tuila'epa Sa'ilele Malielegaoi, **Employment: Samoan Public Service**
Public Service Association (PSA) (trade union), 10, 20–21, 178–79, 242
Public Service Commission (government agency), 63, 66, 177
Public Works Department, 29, 58, 65, 119; *see also* Director of Public Works (and Acting Deputy Director); Tuila'epa Sa'ilele Malielegaoi, **Employment: Samoan Public Service**, as Deputy Director (and Acting Deputy Director) of Public Works
Puipaa village, 48
Pule (political group of paramount chiefs from Savai'i), 104, 145, 146, 225
Putaruru, New Zealand, 52

Qarase, Laisenia, 209
Queen Salamasina (passenger vessel), 142
quota system, for Samoans in New Zealand, 21

racism, *see* New Zealand, racism in
Radio 2AP, 82, 105, 138, 139, 254–55; *see also The PM and 2AP* radio show
Radio New Zealand International, 172, 176, 207
Rapa Nui, and Polynesian Leaders Group, 210
reconciliation, the Samoan way, 76, 89, 120, 133, 168
referenda, 18; on universal suffrage, 22, 136
reforms, government, 23, 25, 95, 98, 124, 127, 135–37, 149, 162, 164, 200, 222–23, 226, 238, 239; *see also* budgetary reforms; Cabinet, reform of; daylight saving; electoral reforms; fish, canned, as cultural exchange; Human Rights Protection Party, reforms within; International Dateline; market reforms; mat making; mats: as gifts and cultural exchange; national dress; parliamentary reforms; public service, reform and restructuring of; roads: and right-hand driving; Tuila'epa Sa'ilele Malielegaoi, **Prime Minister**, reforms brought about by
regional and international events, hosting of, *see* Tuila'epa Sa'ilele Malielegaoi, **Prime Minister**, and hosting of international events
Reid, A., 51
remittances, 51, 241, 246
Rex, Sir Robert, 14
right-hand driving, *see* roads: and right-hand driving
Rio de Janeiro, 216
Rivers, Sonny, 222
roads: and right-hand driving, 183–85, 187–88, 192, 199, 239; building of and improvements to, 22, 47–48, 82, 119, 186, 240, 242; destruction of, 137, 138, 140, 219; quality and condition of, 43, 82, 119, 184; rebuilding of, 247; *see also* Apia, roads in and around; cars; Cross-Island Road; Lepā village, roads to; plantation

Index

access roads, construction of; traffic lights
Rotorua, New Zealand, 89
rugby, 38, 51, 82, 180, 219–21, 252; see also All Blacks; Manu Samoa
Rugby Union World Cup, 219, 220, 252
Russia, and United Nations Security Council, 201

Safa'i village, 57–58
Safenunuvao family, 174
Sagapolutele Sipaia, 116, 117
Sailau, 75–76
Saili, Sam, 89, 101–3, 104
Saina village, 48–49
Sakalafai village, 185–86, 187–88
Salani village, 43
Salaries Tribunal, 178–79
salary reviews, 21, 65, 177–78
Saleapāga village, 38, 41, 68, 69, 70, 73–74, 189, 190
Saleaula, 57
Salega constituency, 21, 94
Sāle'imoa, Dr Asiata, 171, 172–73
Salelologa *matai* title, 185–86
Salelologa township, 185–88
Saleufi, Apia, 46–47, 48, 49
Salevalasi family, 174
Samatau, 91
Samoa All People's Party (SAPP), 171
Samoa College, 49
Samoa Democratic United Party, 180
Samoa Labour Party, 150
Samoa Land Corporation (SLC), 165, 182
Samoa National Development Party (SNDP), 22, 23, 143, 150, 166, 171, 223
Samoa Observer, 97, 193, 251–52, 253–54
Samoa Tourism, 222
Samoa Trust Estates Corporation (STEC), 68, 89, 180, 182, 262
Samoan Rugby Union, 220, 252
sanitation, modern, 43
saofa'i (titling ceremony), 33, 72, 221
Satuala family, 174
Savai'i, 20, 50, 57, 84–85, 104, 106, 107, 134, 140, 149, 154, 185, 225, 245; see also Salelologa township
Savali o le Filemu, March for Peace, 146
Savea Sano Malifa, 252–53, 254
Sayed-Khaiyum, Aiyaz, 208
School Certificate (New Zealand), 49
schools: building of, 229; Catholic, 45–47; church, 82; destruction of, 245; government, 36, 39, 44, 45–46; primary, 190; private, 45; upgrading of, 240; village, 39; see also Apia, schools in; education system; Father Felise's school; Lepā village, primary school at; Logologo Secondary School; Marist Brothers' School; Samoa College; St Joseph's College; St Mary's College
Scientific Research Organisation of Samoa (SROS), Nafanua, 78, 148, 239
Scoop, 206–7
Secretariat of the Pacific Community (SPC, formerly the South Pacific Commission), 202
Secretariat of the Pacific Regional Environment Programme (SPREP), 202
Sefuiva Sione, 109–10
Seoul, South Korea, 62
Seumanufagai Tupea, 84–85
Sevele, Feleti, 209, 210; see also Tonga
sex education, 36
shark-lassoing competitions, 38–39
shipping: and purchase of ships, 107–8; direction of, 191; improvements to, 82; see also Pacific Forum Line; port facilities
SIDS Accelerated Modalities of Action (SAMOA) Pathway, 218
Sila, Chief, 120
Singapore: Samoan Honorary Consul in, 201; visits to, 131
Siumu district, 117–18, 165–71, 189
Siusega, Catholic church at, 56, 141
Smith, Adam, 77
social change, 255, 257
social development, 10, 237, 239, 240
Sogimaletavai, Leo, 68
Solomon Islands: and Pacific Islands Forum, 202; British control of, 142; civil conflict in, 25, 237
Somare, Sir Michael, 209
So'o, Fui Leapai Tu'u Ilaoa Professor Asofou, 90–91, 240, 258, 261
South Pacific Applied Geoscience Commission, 202
South Pacific Board for Educational Assessment, 202
South Pacific Commission, 200–1, 202; see also Australia, and South Pacific Commission; France: and South Pacific Commission; Great Britain: and South Pacific Commission; New Zealand, and South Pacific Commission; Secretariat of the Pacific Community; Tuila'epa Sa'ilele Malielegaoi, **Prime Minister**, and South Pacific Commission; United States of America: and South Pacific Commission
South Pacific Consumer Protection

Programme, 13
South Pacific Games 2007, 180, 182–83, 199, 205, 219
South Pacific Tourism Organisation, 202
sovereignty, and aid, 205, 244
Speaker of the House, 81, 91, 92–93, 95, 121, 156, 160, 169, 170, 226, 230, 232, 233–34; *see also* Aeau Peni; Nonumalo Sōfara; Tu'u'u Faletoese
speechmaking, caucus and parliamentary, 86–87, 92, 95, 100, 102–3, 104–5, 106, 110, 112, 122, 146, 148, 161, 172, 174; *see also* debates: parliamentary; oratory; Tofilau 'Eti Alesana, and speechmaking; Tuila'epa Sa'ilele Malielegaoi, **Political Life and Experience**, speechmaking and storytelling of
Speight, George, 216
sports, 37–38, 51, 115, 147, 182, 183, 199, 220; mixed sex, 38; *see also* All Blacks; archery; athletics; boxing; cricket; games; Inter-College Athletics Competition; *kirikiti*; Manu Samoa; rugby; Rugby Union World Cup; Tuila'epa Sa'ilele Malielegaoi, **Personal**, and sports and games; World Boxing Organisation
sports facilities, 49, 138, 180, 182, 199, 219, 240; *see also* Vaitele village, sports complex at
St John, Chief Justice R.J.B., 21
St Joseph's College, Lotopā, 26, 46, 49–50, 52; *see also* Tuila'epa Sa'ilele Malielegaoi, **Early Life**, schooling of
St Mary's College, 49–50
St Paul's College, Auckland, New Zealand, 50, 51; *see also* Tuila'epa Sa'ilele Malielegaoi, **Early Life**, schooling of
STABEX funds, 65–66; *see also* Tuila'epa Sa'ilele Malielegaoi, **Employment and Negotiations: Overseas**, and negotiations with STABEX fund
stability, political, 19, 22, 23, 25, 80, 110, 149, 198–99, 237–38, 238–41, 261; *see also* instability, political
standard of living, 10, 107, 216, 259
Standing Orders, 81, 92, 148, 172, 234
Stevenson, Robert Louis, 71
Stevenson, Trevor, 96–97
Strategy for the Development of Samoa, 243
street vending, 48–49
strikes: doctors', 178–79; public service, 10, 20–21, 64, 65, 66, 67, 80, 177, 179, 228, 242
Suafa'i, Reverend, 44
subsistence economy, *see* agriculture, subsistence
succession, 17, 23, 124, 131, 136, 152, 155, 162, 196, 223, 227, 231, 235, 262
Sui O Le Fono a Sui Tofia, *see* Council of Deputies
Sunday Samoan, 252, 255
Sunday School, 35, 36, 41
Supplementary Appropriations Bill, 81, 92
Supreme Court, 20–21, 90
Suspensory Loan Scheme for Agriculture, 82
Suva, 152, 206, 215
Sydney, Samoan Consulate General in, 201

Taefu, Chief, 119–20
Tafuna'i, Adimaimalaga (Adi), 194, 216
Tagaloa (deity), 34, 77
Tagaloa Pita, 99–100, 106
Tagaloa Tuala Sale, *see* Tuala Sale Kerslake
tagāti'a (darting a light stick along the ground), 37
Tahiti, visits to, 203
Tahiti Nui, *see* Air Tahiti Nui
Taimalie, Chief, 122
Taisi *matai* title, 122
Taiwan, 124–27
talanoa, *see* 'Pacific Way'
tama-a-'āiga (holders of one of four Samoan paramount titles), 19, 91, 119, 136, 157, 177, 197, 228; as 'natural' leaders, 18–19, 222, 227–28; *matai* titles of, 20, 115–16; status of, 17, 18, 118, 164–65, 166, 222, 261;
tama'ita'i (untitled women), 33
Tamasoali'i *pāpā* title, 18
Tanugamanono power plant, 219
Tanumapua, 189
Tanuvasa Livi, 117, 118–22, 123, 133–34
Taofinu'u, Cardinal Pio, 146
Tapusalaia, Chief, 165–66, 167
Tapusalaia T. Faletoese, 165–66
taro, 37, 39, 40, 43, 47, 141, 145, 148, 242
Taro Leaf Blight, 145, 146, 148
Tasi, Semi (cousin), 41–42
Tasi, Tafale (aunt), 41–42, 46, 47–48
Taufusi village, 48
taule'ale'a (untitled men), 33, 35, 70, 256
tautua (to serve; service), 40–41, 54, 70, 71, 76; *see also monotaga*; Tuila'epa Sa'ilele Malielegaoi, **Personal**, beliefs, values and philosophy of, and *tautua*
Tautua Samoa Party (TSP), 199, 200, 222
taxation, 25, 65, 95, 96, 98, 241; *see also* Value Added Goods and Services Tax
telemedicine, 29
Thailand, 201
The PM and 2AP radio show, 255

Index

Tiafau, 148
Tiananmen Square incident, 127–28
tides: high, 43; 'king', 248; spring, 142
timber industry and forests, 68, 130, 155; clearing of, 248; destruction of, 245
Toalepai Toeolesulusulu Siueva, 20, 103
Toamua village, 48
Tofilau 'Eti Alesana, 10, 69, 119–20, 130, 174, 180, 182, 185, 253; and health of, 124, 128–29, 131, 133–34, 138, 149, 150–60, 227, 228, 231, 238, 262; and Human Rights Protection Party, 20, 22, 86–87, 102–5, 135, 225; and parliamentary debates, 113, 130–31; and Salelologa township, 185–87; and speechmaking, 104–5, 112, 121–22; and state visit to People's Republic of China, 127–28; and Tupua Tamasese Efi/Tupuola Efi, 162, 164, 177–78, 228–29; as Prime Minister, 23, 80–81, 145, 177, 186–87, 223, 225, 227, 228–29, 232, 234, 262; Cabinet of, 26, 101–2, 109, 163; in Cabinet, 89–90, 163; in opposition, 21, 92–93, 113, 114, 115, 117, 120–23, 223; leadership of, 80–81, 102, 103–4, 124, 134, 145, 147, 148–49, 150–51, 225, 238; *matai* titles of, 111, 121–22, 148, 174, 185–86; resignations of, 29, 112, 156–61, 163, 231; first administration of, 22, 94–99, 101–2, 123, 229–30, 243, 262; second administration of, 22, 100–7, 109, 111–12, 171–79, 243; third administration of, 22, 123–43, 238, 243, 245; fourth administration of, 22–23, 143–49, 182; fifth administration of, 25, 29–30, 150–61, 165–66; death of, 163, 166, 186; see also Tuila'epa Sa'ilele Malielegaoi, **Political Life and Experience**, and political relationships, with Tofilau 'Eti Alesana
Togafuafua village, 45
togi-a-gogu (*nonu* throwing at night), 37, 38
To'i Aukuso, 26, 28–29, 30–31, 91, 104, 129, 133, 163–64
Tokelau, 39, 114, 210
Tokyo, Samoan diplomatic mission in, 201
Tong, Anote, 218
Tonga, 210; and anti-monarchy riots, 240; and Fiji, 211–12; and Pacific Islands Forum, 202, 206, 209; and Polynesian Leaders Group, 210; and trade with Samoa, 210; independence of, 202; see also Fiji, and Tonga; Sevele, Feleti
Tonga Trench, 189, 211–12
to'oto'o (orator's stick), 122
tourism, 29, 43, 78, 143, 180, 214, 218, 219, 221–22, 240, 241; see also Samoa Tourism

Toyota cars, 183, 184
trade, 64, 78, 98, 141, 191, 210, 219, 243; see also foreign investment and trade
trade barriers, removal of, 25
traders, 77
traffic lights, 184
transnational corporations, 77
transport and transport costs, 40, 64, 78, 218, 242, 249
Treasury, New Zealand, 59–61, 62; see also Tuila'epa Sa'ilele Malielegaoi, **Employment: Samoan Public Service**, at the New Zealand Treasury
Treasury Department, 25, 53, 54, 57, 58–59, 61–62, 63, 64, 66, 67–68, 98, 107, 108, 109, 140, 184, 229, 230, 242; see also Ministry of Finance; Tuila'epa Sa'ilele Malielegaoi, **Employment: Samoan Public Service**, as Investigating Officer, Treasury Department; Tuila'epa Sa'ilele Malielegaoi, **Employment: Samoan Public Service**, in Treasury
Treaty of Berlin 1889, 142
Treaty of Friendship between Samoa and New Zealand 1962, 175–76, 201
tsunami, 14, 143, 162, 219, 237, 245; September 2009, 188–90, 199, 246–47; see also American Samoa, and tsunami
Tua, David, 188
Tuailemafua *matai* title, 122
Tuala Falani Chan Tung, 13
Tuala Sale Kerslake (later Tagaloa Tuala Sale Kerslake), 186
Tuanaimato, 138, 180–82, 219
Tuatagaloa, Keli, 75–76
Tufuga *matai* title, 89
Tui A'ana *pāpā* title, 18
Tui Ātua *pāpā* title, 18
Tui Ātua Tafua, 226
Tuigamala Anetipa Lam Sam, 102, 121
Tuila'epa *matai* title, 70, 74, 174

Tuila'epa Sa'ilele Malielegaoi
Early Life
birth date of, 43–44
childhood and boyhood in Lepā, 34–41, 46–48, 70, 250, 258; see also Lepā village
going to Apia, 41–43, 44–50, 70
going to Auckland, 50–53
parents of, see Lupesoli'ai, Leasunia (mother); Malielegaoi Veni (father)
schooling of, 32, 34–36, 39, 43–44, 44–46, 47, 49–50, 51; see also Father Felise's school; Lepā village, primary school at; Marist Brothers' School, Apia; St Joseph's

College, Lotopā; St Paul's College, Auckland
university qualifications of, 25, 50, 51–53, 54, 55, 57, 62, 67, 77, 98, 242–43; see also Bachelor of Commerce degree; Master of Commerce degree; University of Auckland

Personal
and music, 55, 56, 259
and sports and games, 47, 48, 51, 183, 219–21, 221–22, 252
as *matai*, 72–74, 250, 258–59
beliefs, values and philosophy of, 31, 32, 34, 51–52, 57, 70–77, 231–32, 250, 251, 258–60, 263; and Christian faith, 31, 45, 55, 56, 57, 114, 144–45, 166, 168–69, 256, 259, 263; and *fa'apalagi*, 54, 76, 77–79, 258; and *Fa'asamoa*, 54, 70–76, 77, 79, 226, 258; and *tautua*, 70–71, 76, 107
family life and marriage of, 54–56, 57, 59, 61, 64, 259; see also Malielegaoi, Gillian (wife)
matai titles of, 32, 35, 70, 72, 74–76, 77, 174, 259

Employment and Negotiations: Overseas
and African, Caribbean and Pacific General Secretariat, Brussels, 25, 62, 63–65, 68, 78, 98, 108, 200, 215–16, 243, 250, 262
and negotiations with Asian Development Bank, 124–27, 128, 200
and negotiations with International Monetary Fund, 63, 98, 152, 200
and negotiations with World Bank, 59, 63, 98, 152, 200
and STABEX fund, 65–66
and World Bank Economic Development Institute, 56, 62

Employment: Samoan Public Service
and public service, 53, 57–59, 61–62, 63, 64–66, 67, 78, 107, 109
as Deputy Director (and Acting Deputy Director) of Public Works, 11, 57–58
as Deputy Director of Economic Development Department, 54
as Financial Secretary (and Deputy Financial Secretary), 58–59, 64
as Investigating Officer, Treasury Department, 53, 54, 57, 98
at the New Zealand Treasury, 59–61, 62
in Treasury, 25, 58, 59, 63, 67, 68, 98, 107, 108, 132, 229, 242–43

Entering Politics
as Independent Member for Lepā, 22, 41, 67–70, 78–79, 80, 81, 83, 86, 103, 107, 123, 232–33, 238, 253; see also Lepā village, MP for
and maiden speech of, 81–82
and parliamentary apprenticeship, 80, 123–24, 232–33, 234–35, 243, 261–63
and parliamentary debates, 107–8, 228–31, 256
and parliamentary procedure, 92–93, 94, 102, 110–11, 113–14, 172, 232–34
and party leadership issues, 101–7; see also Human Rights Protection Party, leadership of
in opposition, 112–16, 116–18, 120–23

In Cabinet
and challenging party decisions, 107–8, 132–33
as Acting Prime Minister, 129–30
as Deputy Leader of the Human Rights Protection Party, 135
as Deputy Prime Minister, 23, 138, 150–61, 245
as Minister of Economic Affairs, 98–99
as Minister of Finance (and Associate Minister of Finance), 13, 23, 57, 95–96, 99, 107–8, 111, 124, 131–34, 149, 185–86, 200, 228–29, 232, 235, 238, 243, 244, 245
as Minister of Foreign Affairs, 215
as Minister of Trade, Commerce and Industry, 13
diplomacy of, 98, 200, 213, 237

Political Life and Experience
and disaster relief, 138–43, 162, 189–90, 246–50
and environmental issues, 248–50
and Fiji, 172, 200, 206–11, 213, 215–16, 218, 250
and foreign affairs, 162, 200–4
and Human Rights Protection Party, 68, 80, 83–88, 100–1, 101–7, 131–34, 135, 144–45, 223, 228–29
and media: criticisms by, 14, 30–31, 97, 237–38, 247, 251–57; use of, 183, 184, 188, 206–7, 209, 210–12, 213, 220, 223, 254–57
and political relationships, 259–60: international, 63, 64–65, 98, 200, 237–38, 250–51, 258; with Commodore Josaia Voreqe 'Frank' Bainimarama, 200, 206–9, 213; with Tofilau 'Eti Alesana, 89–90, 102, 130, 150–61, 228–29, 232, 234, 262; with Va'ai Kolone, 151; with Tupua Tamasese Efi/Tupuola Efi, 61–62, 63, 64, 84–86, 198, 228–30, 232, 261–62

Index

as voice of reason, 31, 146–47, 184, 235
honours bestowed on, 14, 78, 217
leadership of, 26, 27, 73, 80–81, 149, 150–51, 162, 163, 164, 171–72, 228, 231, 234–35, 242, 244, 247; and regional and international organisations and groups, 14, 214, 218, 237, 238, 249, 250–51, 258; philosophy about, 162, 259; style of, 14, 31, 54, 73, 78, 162, 163, 223, 227, 231–32, 238, 244, 246, 250, 258–59; traditional, 54, 234
speechmaking and storytelling of, 72–73, 75–76, 81–83, 100–1, 115, 144–45, 163, 172, 175–76, 186–87, 197, 225–26, 231–32;

Prime Minister
and apology from New Zealand, 173–76
and assassination of Luagalau Levaula Kamu, 25–31, 162, 164, 237
and doctors' strike, 178–79
and Head of State, 176–77
and hosting of international events, 180, 182–83, 214–18, 219; *see also* Polynesian Leaders Group; South Pacific Games; United Nations Small Islands Developing States Conference 2014
and land disputes: at Salelologa, 185–88; at Siumu, 165–71
and management of the backbench, 225–26
and Pacific Islands Forum, 202, 207–8, 209–11, 213–14, 215–16, 250
and partnerships, 213–14
and Polynesian Leaders Group, 209–11
and popular mandate, 9, 231–32, 235–36, 238, 257–60, 261
and Samoan culture, 193–95
and South Pacific Commission, 200–2
as Prime Minister, 23, 25, 29–30, 57, 80, 161, 162–236, 237–38, 253
reforms brought about by, 25–26, 95, 98, 135–37, 162, 164, 183–85, 190–99, 200, 224–25, 226, 227, 239
first administration of, 162, 163–71
second administration of, 162, 171–79
third administration of, 162, 180–99
fourth administration of, 162, 200–22
fifth administration of, 222–36

Tuilagi Vavae, 122
Tuiloma Pule Lameko, 90
Tuimaleali'ifano Suatipatipa, 18, 19, 163, 164–65, 171, 176–77, 179, 197
Tuisugaletaua Sōfara, 184
tulafale (talking chiefs or orators), 33, 71, 74–75, 212, 228

tulafale-ali'i matai title, 74
Tumua (political group of paramount chiefs representing Upolu and Safotu), 104, 145–46, 225
Tupua clan, 174
Tupua Tamasese Efi (formerly known as Tupuola Efi), 18, 22, 115–16, 174, 175, 262; and coalition administration, 22, 116, 117, 118, 119–20, 121, 122–23, 143–44, 198, 223; and Council of Deputies, 137, 173, 176–77, 179; as Head of State, 177, 197–98; in government, 177–78; in opposition, 122–23, 130–31, 137, 143–44, 145–48, 149, 158, 161, 162, 163, 164, 165–67, 171–73, 174, 177, 223; *matai* titles of, 18, 115, 117, 122, 148; *see also* Tofilau 'Eti Alesana, and Tupua Tamasese Efi/Tupuola Efi; Tuila'epa Sa'ilele Malielegaoi, **Political Life and Experience**, and political relationships, with Tupua Tamasese Efi/Tupuola Efi; Tupuola Efi
Tupua Tamasese Lealofi III, 173–74
Tupua Tamasese Lealofi IV, 11, 19–20, 58, 261
Tupua Tamasese Mea'ole, 18, 19, 197
Tupuola Efi (later known as Tupua Tamasese Efi), 10, 19, 61–62, 63, 64, 65, 67, 68, 69, 80, 81, 84–86, 89, 107, 111, 115, 223, 232, as Minister of Public Works, 57–58; as Prime Minister, 20, 21–22, 59, 61, 63, 65, 67–69, 83, 228, 261–62; in coalition administration, 111, 114–15, 198–99, 223, 243; in opposition, 22, 88, 94, 97, 100, 110, 111, 198, 223, 228–31; leadership style of, 228; first administration of, 61–62, 86; second administration of, 80, 81–88; third administration of, 21, 90–93, 94, 111; *see also* Tuila'epa Sa'ilele Malielegaoi, **Political Life and Experience**, and political relationships, with Tupua Tamasese Efi/Tupuola Efi; Tupua Tamasese Efi; Va'ai Kolone, and coalition with Tupuola Efi; Va'ai Kolone, and power struggle with Tupuola Efi
Tupuola Siaosi Hunt, 116, 117–18
Tu'u'u Anisii, 188
Tu'u'u Faletoese, 165, 167–70
Tuvalu: and climate change, 248; and Pacific Islands Forum, 202; and Polynesian Leaders Group, 210; *see also* Paeniu, Bikenibeu

Uden, John, 52
Ulu Kini Leva'a, 186
Ululoloa, 9, 28, 51, 189
umu (stone oven), 33, 39

Unasa Lavea Schmidt, 20
Under-Secretaries, role of, 22, 135–36; *see also* Associate Ministers
unemployment, reductions in, 82
United Kingdom, and United Nations Security Council, 201
United Nations, 18, 58, 134, 140, 200, 201, 204, 205, 214–15, 216, 218, 228; *see also* Ban Ki-moon; Least Developed Country status; Middle Income Country
United Nations Climate Change Conference (Paris, 2015), 203, 249, 250; *see also* France: and United Nations Climate Change Conference
United Nations Conference on Sustainable Development, 216
United Nations Development Programme (UNDP), 58, 139, 217, 244
United Nations Educational, Scientific and Cultural Organization (UNESCO), 204–5; *see also* Australia, and United Nations Educational, Scientific and Cultural Organization
United Nations General Assembly, 73, 188, 203, 218, 249; *see also* New York: meeting of United Nations General Assembly in
United Nations Security Council, 73, 201, 205, 217–18, 250–51; *see also* France: and United Nations Security Council; Germany: and United Nations Security Council; Japan: and United Nations Security Council; People's Republic of China: and United Nations Security Council; Russia, and United Nations Security Council; United Kingdom, and United Nations Security Council; United States of America: and United Nations Security Council
United Nations Small Islands Developing States (SIDS) Conference, 2014, 180, 182, 214–18, 219
United States Agency for International Development (USAID), 134
United States of America: and aid from, 134, 143; and American Samoa, 191; and cars from, 183; and climate change, 248; and colonisation in the Pacific, 141–42, 200; and flights from Samoa to, 149; and independence celebrations, 142; and People's Republic of China, 128, 203; and relationship with Samoa, 73, 134–35, 250; and the Pacific, 200, 203; and South Pacific Commission, 200; and United Nations Security Council, 201; as development partner, 200; Samoans in, 246; visits to, 56; *see also* American Constitution; American Samoa; Apia, US ships berthing at; Clinton, Hillary; Hawai'i and Hawai'ians; New York; nuclear ships; nuclear waste; Washington
universal suffrage, 18, 21, 71, 136–37, 143, 238–39; referendum on, 22, 136
University Entrance (UE) (New Zealand), 49, 50, 52
University of Auckland, 50, 51–53, 54, 55, 62, 77
University of the South Pacific (USP), 152, 202; at Alafua, 128
Upolu, 32, 104, 211, 225, 245, 246
Urban, Brother, 50

Va'ai Kolone, 14, 90, 107, 121, 232; and coalition with Tupuola Efi, 22, 110, 111, 112–16, 121, 143–44, 198, 243; and Human Rights Protection Party, 20, 83, 86–88, 101–6, 110, 135, 144, 151, 198, 262; and leadership of Human Rights Protection Party, 10, 20, 81, 137, 143–44, 150–51, 225, 262; and power struggle with Tupuola Efi, 20, 83, 262; as Financial Secretary, 131; as Prime Minister, 10, 21, 88–90, 112, 223, 262; *see also* Tuila'epa Sa'ilele Malielegaoi, **Political Life and Experience**, and political relationships, with Va'ai Kolone
Va'ai, Papu, 87, 105–6
Vaiala village, 88, 221
Vaigaga, 48
Vaigalu sub-village, 74
Vailima village, 165
Vailoa village, 48, 84–85
Vaimauga West by-election, 91, 94
Vaimea village, 117
Vaimoso Bridge, 139–40
Vaisigano River valley, 219, 246
Vaitele village, 48; plantation at, 48; sports complex at, 138, 180–82
Value Added Goods and Services Tax (VAGST), 145–46, 199, 241
Vanuatu: and Pacific Islands Forum, 202, 206; political instability in, 237
Vaovai, 28
Vaovasamanaia Filipo, 63, 65, 67, 85, 86
Vaovasamanaia L. Filo (Lapi), 181, 196
velovelo (spear throwing), 37
Vermeulen, Dr Walter, 20
Victoria University of Wellington (VUW), 14, 78, 131, 217, 239
village government, *see* political power, traditional

Index

village life, 32–35, 37–39, 40–41, 70–73, 259; *see also* Lepā village
Vitale, Eletise, 26, 27–31
von Bismarck, Herbert, 142

Waitangi Tribunal, New Zealand, 170
Wallis and Futuna, and Polynesian Leaders Group, 210
Washington, 142; Samoan embassy in, 134–35; visits to, 86, 90, 152
Washington Conference 1887, 141
water reticulation, 147, 242
Waqa, Baron, 218; *see also* Nauru
wedding practices, 55–56, 194
Wellington, 50, 59–61, 217; Samoan diplomatic mission in, 201, 228; *see also* Correspondence School; Victoria University of Wellington
Wendt, Albert, 36
Wendt, Professor Tuaopepe (Felix), 128–30, 131–33, 134–35
West Papua, 99, 237
whalers, 77
wharves, building of, 242; destruction of, 137; *see also* Matautu Wharf Project
Whenuapai Airport, Auckland, 50
Whitehead, A.N., 77
Women in Business Development Incorporated (WIBDI), 192, 193, 194, 216
women, in Parliament, 222, 225, 238, 239, 255–57
women's rights, 255–57; and the vote, 136; *see also* gender, issues of; Global Leaders' Meeting on Gender Equality and Women's Empowerment; leadership, and women; *matai*, rights of wives of; O le Komiti a le Losa
Woodroffe, Olinda, 169, 170
World Bank, 56, 59; meetings of, 63, 90, 152; *see also* Tuila'epa Sa'ilele Malielegaoi, **Employment and Negotiations: Overseas**, and negotiations with World Bank; Tuila'epa Sa'ilele Malielegaoi, **Employment and Negotiations: Overseas**, and negotiations with World Bank Economic Development Institute
World Boxing Organisation, 221
World Trade Organization, 78

Yugoslavia, 63